09864

D1338887

Also by S.K. Keogh

THE PRODIGAL
THE ALLIANCE

# THE FORTUNE

## A Novel

## By
## S.K. Keogh

The Fortune
S.K. Keogh

Copyright 2014 S.K. Keogh
Leighlin House Publishing

ISBN: 978-0-9906774-0-6 (paperback)
ISBN: 978-0-9906774-1-3 (ebook)

Connect with S.K. Keogh at

www.skkeogh.com
www.facebook.com/S.K.Keogh
www.twitter.com/JackMallory

This book is also available in e-book format at most online retailers.

Cover design by Annette Tremblay
www.midnightwhimsydesigns.com

# CHAPTER 1

Jack Mallory and six of his pirate crew sailed the *Prodigal*'s yawl across the long Atlantic swell toward their prey. The pink had struck her colors without a fight when the *Prodigal*'s ensign had billowed out at the masthead—a black flag that bore the images of a white stone gate and skeleton. Now, hove to, the coaster looked old and slow, not one to take as a consort to assist in Jack's current endeavor, but she had what he needed most—spars for his damaged brig. On the pink's deck her small crew awaited not only the yawl but the *Prodigal*'s pinnace as well, which also carried an armed boarding party and now sliced ahead of the yawl in a race to be first to board.

Sunlight off the indigo water reduced Jack's mahogany eyes to mere slits in his young, darkly tanned face. From his place in the stern-sheets, he glanced back at the *Prodigal* where she rode the swells, hove to. She had been wounded cruelly yesterday by the eighteen-pound guns of the privateer *Alliance*, her fore topmast now threatening to go by the board with the first strong puff but for the boatswain's double preventer stays. The spritsail yard had been shattered, and the gaff of the fore-and-aft main sail had been splintered as well. Then there was the sad main topgallant mast, originally fished after weather had felled her, then fished again after being toppled during the short, vicious fight with the *Alliance*. Fortunately the guns had not suffered beyond one six-pounder being dismounted, for what little ordnance the pink might provide would not be worth the time and effort to transfer.

As Jack studied his beloved brig, a slim female figure appeared on the quarterdeck. He strained to see if another, smaller figure accompanied Maria Cordero, but she stood alone, and Jack shrank with disappointment, frowning.

"First time she's been on deck since the fight," observed Josiah Smith, Jack's quartermaster and closest friend, who sat one thwart forward. "I'm surprised she left Helen below."

Jack's frown turned into a scowl as he said, "Archer's probably with her."

The pinnace reached the pink first, and with shouts and roars

5

meant to further terrify the coaster's crew, the pirates swarmed up the side of the vessel, bearing pistols, knives, axes, and cutlasses. The Rat—a small man with a penchant for racing rats—grabbed for the main chains, somehow missed, and fell unceremoniously between the pinnace and the pink. Laughter from his closest shipmates encouraged shouted taunts of amusement from the closing yawl. The Rat bobbed up and reached for the pinnace's gunwale, but the swell bumped the boat against the pink, pinching the Rat's arm. His howl garnered the aid of the last pirate in the boat—a huge block of a man singularly named Bull for his size, lack of wits, and the ring worn through his broad nose. Bull grabbed the Rat by his wild dark curls and hauled him high enough out of the water to flop him back into the boat like a fish. The unperturbed Rat started his climb all over again, this time with success.

Jack smiled, a reaction foreign to him over the past few days. Smith reflected the smile through his dark, wiry beard, blue eyes crinkled. Jack knew Smith's expression was more from relief at his captain's distraction than at the Rat's latest mishap. Like a concerned mother, Smith had fretted over him during the seven years spent together in Newgate prison. And since obtaining their freedom last year, Jack continued to give the older man plenty about which to fret.

Jack clambered up the pink's side with natural ease, followed by the yawl's party. The frightened seven-man crew bunched together in the waist. Their master stood slightly apart from them, harried by the Rat's cutlass as the soaked pirate demanded the man's clothing. The others from the pinnace laughed. The master, of course, was the best dressed of the crew—though not remarkably so—thus the Rat wanted to shift his clothes with this one. He already wore the master's tan felt hat smashed upon his dripping curls.

Jack waved a discouraging hand at the Rat. "Not now."

"But, Cap, we's the first boat here so we gets first pick, ye know." He used a particular scolding tone to remind his captain of the rules, as if Jack needed reminding.

Hiding his amusement, Jack responded with neither tyranny nor rancor, "Aye, but you'll leave him his dignity until I'm through here."

Crestfallen, the Rat frowned. He gave the relieved master a malevolent eye before sidestepping away, plucking at his own tattered shirt to draw attention to its woefulness, stained with blood from a superficial wound suffered in yesterday's battle.

Jack approached the master, a man probably twice his twenty-one years. He appeared afraid but not overly so; whether from the Rat or simply his situation Jack could not tell.

"We've no intention to harm you."

With Jack's assurance the pink's crew stood a bit easier.

"'Less you don't gimme them clothes o' your'n," the Rat interjected then backed away from Jack's glance with a weak, gap-toothed simper.

"We're in need of spars and cordage," Jack continued. "And a carpenter. Ours was killed yesterday. Which of you would that be?"

The men exchanged anxious glances but said nothing.

Jack scowled at the delay. "As I said, we've no intention to harm you...unless you're disinclined to cooperate."

Six pairs of eyes turned to those of the seventh, a man who did not appear pleased with their betrayal. He was the oldest, missing most of his light brown hair, the sun bouncing off his head, his mouth momentarily slack when Jack's attention rested upon him. He crumpled his hat in his weathered hands, shuffled a step forward, made a nervous, ridiculous bow.

"I'm carpenter," he mumbled. "Name's Hanse."

"Right, then." Jack nodded to a young black pirate. "Billy, fetch him back to the brig and get him working on the fore topmast."

Billy stepped over, but Hanse's round face fell into panicked despair, and he reached for Jack's sleeve. "Please, sir. I—I'll help you however I can, but you don't mean to press me, do you? I've a family to provide for."

Jack felt Smith's gaze upon him like a tactile conscience. It was not their practice to force married men. The *Prodigal* had had only two, and they were now free men at his stepfather's plantation outside of Charles Town, Carolina, awaiting the arrival of their families from England.

Refusing Smith's stare, Jack replied, "You do as I say, Chips, and you'll have more money for your family in a couple of days than you'll make in years on a tub such as this."

Anger darkened the man's green eyes. "And a noose to go with it. Then what will happen to my family?"

Joe Dowling, the *Prodigal*'s hairy gunner, warned, "If you don't like it, mate, we can arrange for that noose right now, can't we, lads? No trial holdin' things up, eh?" Grinning, he flicked his gaze to the yardarm above him.

The carpenter blanched and swallowed hard, then turned back to Jack, all impertinence gone. "You're just a boy. You don't understand what it's like to care for little ones, to put food in their mouths."

The words kicked Jack in the gut as he thought of his orphaned six-year-old half-sister aboard the *Prodigal*, silent and traumatized by the death of her father the previous day, and now frighteningly dependent upon him in all earthly ways. He growled at the prisoner, "I understand better than you think." He jerked his chin at Billy, and the black man grabbed Hanse by the arm, brandishing his pistol, and led him toward the entry port. Jack ordered Dowling to go with them then turned back to the master. "Your men will assist in the transfer of your spars, sails, and cordage. We'll leave enough to get you ashore."

"What about the cargo?" Sullivan—a red-haired, perpetually sunburned pirate—asked. "Hold's full of sugar. That'd fetch a fair price up the coast."

"No time for that," said Jack.

"Mebbe we should take the time," an unseen voice grumbled, but Jack ignored the dissenter.

"Now, Cap, now?" the Rat asked with a spark in his small eyes. When Jack waved his hand, the Rat chortled and jabbed his cutlass at the hapless master. "Drop them breeches." He never took his eyes off the master's fine gray coat with its gilt buttons on the cuffs. "You's gonna lose more'n yer carpenter."

Willie Emerick pointed out, "His rags'll be too big for you, Rat."

"I can sew, can't I?"

"Not without bleedin' all over."

Laughter roared across the desk.

"Lads, get the spars lashed together and floated across. Ned," Jack said to his enormous boatswain where he stood with sunlight shining upon his shaved head, "see to the cordage. Sully, you and Willie are in charge of the sailcloth. Let's get to it."

Jack stepped to the railing to watch Dowling and Billy give way in the yawl with the carpenter. The white-faced sailor looked with longing at the pink. Jack quickly pushed aside the weakness of sympathy. If they were to attack that convoy of merchantmen expected from England and if he was to locate the *Alliance* and exact his revenge, he would need a skilled man directing and accomplishing the repairs to the *Prodigal*. There was neither a minute to lose nor a man to be spared.

#

Maria Cordero did not catch the name of the new carpenter when he came up the side of the *Prodigal*, harassed and prodded by Dowling and Billy. Neither did she choose to think anything more of him since

8

his presence only served to remind her of the men lost in yesterday's fight.

Smith was one of the next men to return to the *Prodigal*. His stormy expression drew Maria near in curiosity, for he was not often cross, but—when he was—Jack was usually to blame. Maria greatly respected Smith; the older man was more like a surrogate father to her than simply a friend.

"I don't like where this is all takin' the lad," Smith groused more to himself than to Maria. "No reason for him to change our practices. That new cully there," he nodded forward to the carpenter, "he's married, for God's sake. He won't take to goin' on the account like an unwed lad might, and we need willing hands, not unhappy, affrighted ones what can cause us trouble." Then he turned away to mumble, "Already have trouble enough among us."

Smith's disgruntled intimation so surprised Maria that she was unable to respond with her usual quickness of tongue. He referred to David Archer, of course. The Prodigals had it in their heads that David was a Jonah—bad luck, cursed—because of the unhappy circumstances that had impelled him aboard. Some even claimed the death of James Logan had somehow been David's fault.

Smith moved away, no doubt wary of a response from her. But she forced herself to dismiss his superstitious comment and retreat below to the small wardroom to relieve David of his watch over Helen.

As usual when David's sapphire eyes met hers, the private sorrow that lived there fled to some dark corner to be replaced by hopeful friendliness (though not so hopeful as he once had been). As she entered the wardroom, he stood—an attractive young gentleman, the only son of a wealthy Carolina planter, so out of place here yet so trying to fit in among his rough mates, ever mindful of what was thought of him.

"What's happening with the pink?" he asked, and she told him all she had seen, not mentioning the new carpenter, not wanting to hear any further criticism of Jack's judgment nor wanting to consider it herself.

She moved to the hammock where Helen Logan lay. Though awake, the child made no sound nor paid any heed to the noises above her or to the people near her. Her fingers absently kneaded a toy—a soft bit of black bear hide that her mother had stuffed and sewn into the shape of a bear, adorned with buttons for eyes and a red neckerchief.

"He reminds me of my daddy," Helen had explained when she had first introduced Maria to Howard, "'cause Daddy growls in my ear just

9

like a bear. He keeps me company when Mamma and Daddy are away."

The girl's flaxen hair now lay lackluster and dirty against the pillow, her eyes devoid of their usual brilliant exuberance and gleam of life. She had neither spoken a word nor left the wardroom since her father's death.

David's words gained Maria's attention. "I had best get back on deck." But when he turned for the door, Helen's tiny voice halted him and caused Maria's heart to skip.

"Mr. David," the child said, hoarse and barely audible.

David disguised his astonishment. "Yes, Helen?"

Her fingers fondled the stuffed toy. Her eyes—paler blue than David's—focused upon him, upon another human being for the first time since being brought aboard from the *Alliance*. Tenuously she asked, "Have you seen my daddy?"

David's alarmed glance flashed to Maria then back to the child. This time his recovery was not so quick, and his hesitation weakened the girl's focus. She looked back down at the bear.

"I am sorry, Helen," he softly said. "I have not seen your daddy."

She did not look up again from the toy, squeezing the furry hide stronger. Her gaze dulled, and she said nothing more, as if she had never spoken at all. Bereft, David looked to Maria who quickly stepped over to escort him out.

"It's something," she whispered, and he nodded, dubious.

"Should I tell Jack when he returns that she spoke?"

"No. He has enough to occupy him. When he next visits, I'll tell him."

#

Within two hours the *Prodigal*'s topsails filled, and the brig resumed her journey up the coast toward Carolina, leaving the pink sad and nearly stripped under the hot June sun. After the crew had been fed, work resumed in earnest upon the damaged masts and yards, the hands directed by the morose, anxious new carpenter. Jack lent his aid wherever he could but—unlike every Prodigal—Jack was relatively new to such tasks. While his men had been aboard sailing vessels most of their lives, he had only months of experience. His skill lay in sailing the brig—a natural ability recently broadened, thanks to his stepfather, James Logan—not in the intricacies of setting up new rigging to replace that which enemy fire had shredded.

During a moment of respite, Jack leaned on the taffrail. The breeze coming in off the starboard quarter—right where the *Prodigal* preferred it—tried to tug some of his near-black hair from its queue. He frowned when he remembered Helen playing with his hair while they sat on Leighlin House's rear portico just a few days ago. So many things had happened in the past weeks, making days seem more like years: his mother's death, her funeral, meeting the half-sibling he had never known existed, then Helen's kidnapping and the subsequent search that he and James Logan had undertaken together in a bizarre twist of irony—Jack striving alongside a man whom he had once devoted his life to hunting down and killing. Then had come Logan's murder, but not at Jack's hands.

Prior to Logan's death, Jack had never considered his stepfather's mortality. Until Jack had found him nigh three weeks ago, he had viewed Logan as more of a mythical demon than a mortal being. A mortal being who—sensing his demise yesterday—had unexpectedly bequeathed the care of his beloved daughter to Jack, a last-minute transference that frightened Jack to the core, though he loved Helen dearly, for what did he know of raising a child?

Not wanting to think about the heavy familial burden, Jack gazed across the busy, harried deck, hearing but not listening to the shouts and orders of the work crews. David Archer—the unfortunate, unlucky son of Logan's duplicitous business partner and little more than a passenger—sat cross-legged in the waist, busily, unskillfully splicing under the tutelage of Josiah Smith. Jack noted a circle of empty deck around the young man, how the other men cared not to share space as they worked. Smith, as much governed by superstition as the rest of them, toiled with the boy only out of duty. The residual effects of a gunshot wound David had suffered weeks ago, as well as a recent beating from his father, caused him to move stiffly, though he attempted to hide his physical weaknesses. Jack scowled at the determined young man and wished he was not so affable. Even more so, he wished that the one person who had befriended David was not Maria.

At the thought of the beautiful young woman, Jack started for the aft hatch.

#

Maria listened to the feverish work above on the weather deck and frowned as she followed conversations that drifted through the wardroom's skylight. The tarpaulin that provided privacy had been

11

removed so light and air could reach this lonely, sad space. She wished she were up in the sunlight and breeze with the rest of the Prodigals, her mind occupied with work and setting the brig to rights instead of sitting here, suffocated by thoughts of her near future and the sufferings of the child who lay in the hammock.

Helen had said nothing since David had left. Now, as Maria sat alone, she wondered if she had fallen asleep and dreamt that Helen had spoken. Still the girl seemed not to notice her presence, a distance that pained Maria greatly, for she had grown very fond of the child during her brief time as governess at Leighlin. She thought of Helen's question to David. Did Helen truly not know her father was dead? Or was she simply refusing to believe it? Everything had happened so fast when the two boats had met between the *Prodigal* and the *Alliance*. Helen had resisted being separated from her father, and her struggle had caused Maria to tumble in an unbalanced heap with the child in her arms, so when the fatal shot had been fired neither Maria nor David had known in all certainty if Helen had witnessed her father's murder.

A quiet knock rapped upon the wardroom door. When Maria invited Jack in, he closed the door but hesitated, his attention upon his sister as if Maria were not there. The shadows that draped him took her back in time to the night when he had walked into her father's tavern in Cayona. A brooding, haunted young man, slender, almost graceful, sculpted cheekbones set high, eyes as dark as Maria's hair. He had stood there inside *La Piragua*'s door much as he stood in the wardroom now, as if waiting for his vision to adjust, to make sure nothing within would take him by surprise. His unrealized animal beauty had gained Maria's interest and curiosity from that first sight of him among the rabble of *La Piragua*, yet his demeanor had been anything but inviting and had been a portend of their stormy relationship.

When he stepped toward the hammock, the turmoil in his gaze struck Maria speechless. She despaired, for she had seen such agony there before and had known its influence over him.

"Has she said anything?"

Maria remained in her seat, kept thus by recent tension between them. She started to answer, but suddenly the truth did not seem like a good option, so instead she shook her head and moved her gaze encouragingly toward Helen, who had yet to stir since her brother's arrival. Jack turned to the girl, his brow wrinkled, mouth slightly pursed amongst his sparse mustache and thin beard—traits that belied his youth no matter the layers of maturity in his eyes. Upon his entrance, he had removed his battered hat and now held it in one hand while the other reached for the edge of the hammock. His fingers slipped restlessly along the edge of the canvas, drew Maria's attention to the narrow leather bracelet that Logan had given him before his death, a bracelet Jack had fashioned for his mother when he was only a boy in London.

"Helen? Are you feeling better?"

No response. Maria could hardly bear to look at his pained face. This child had once been able to bring more joy to Jack's visage than any other person, at a time when he had so desperately needed it. While Logan had stolen Jack's youth seven years ago, Helen had recently restored it; Maria had witnessed the restoration when she had arrived at Leighlin and first saw the siblings together. Happiness had so transformed the young man's face that Maria had not immediately recognized him.

Now Maria stood beside him, reached for his arm. "Jack…"

He in turn reached for Helen, but the child rolled onto her side, her back to him in a gesture—whether conscious or not—that took away what strength he had brought with him to the wardroom. The girl curled up with the furry toy in her embrace and buried her face in the pillow, closing her eyes. Jack's shoulders slumped, and he returned his hand to his hat.

"Jack."

He turned away, saying flatly, "I'll be back later."

She let him go, knew he did not want her to see the magnitude, the vulnerability of his hurt. For some time she stared at the closed door, again debating whether or not to tell him that Helen had spoken to David.

"Helen." She forced a tone of mild rebuke. "Your brother loves you very much. You have him worried sick."

Silence from the hammock. Maria was unsure if the child was even still awake. But something told her Helen was keenly aware of her presence and had been painfully aware of her brother's.

#

Ketch lay in a hammock that was farthest to larboard, gently swinging to the *Alliance*'s sea-bound rhythm. The larboard watch—nearly forty men—shared this forward space between decks in their closely packed hammocks, yet he felt very much alone. The solitude did not disconcert him; he preferred it no other way. The men talked, but Ketch did not join in, never had, nor was he ever invited to do so.

13

The Alliances had been suspicious of him from the start of the voyage when he had come aboard with Helen Logan. Word of the child's identity had quickly circulated, and while some may have admired his boldness in snatching James Logan's daughter from her very bed, most viewed the act as low and disreputable, however much it may benefit them in the end. And benefit them it now would with Logan dead at the end of Ketch's own pistol. The Alliances would receive a healthy bounty for the success of their mission to rid Carolina waters of its most notorious pirate. But even Ketch's contribution to that reality did nothing to endear him to them. Any such chance had been extinguished when the triced up, mutilated body of one of their shipmates was found in the hold yesterday, a man previously thought to have fallen overboard. Of course they suspected Ketch, and rightly so. But the bastard had deserved death for frightening Helen Logan.

Ketch rolled onto his side and stared at the snow's oaken timbers. He would be glad to leave her once they returned to Charles Town.

When he closed his dark eyes and wished for the oblivion of sleep—an elusive and often unkind friend—Ketch's thoughts returned to Helen. He had not wanted to kill her father in front of her. But Captain Wylder's weakness had left him no choice; Ketch could not hazard Wylder allowing Logan to stand trial in Charles Town where he had allies. Ketch greatly regretted any trauma he may have caused the child, not only because he cared for her but because he had cared deeply for her mother. The thought of Ella Logan's reaction to his part in these recent events troubled him more than he had ever anticipated, for he was not often a man of conscience.

"You are very kind to come see me, Ketch." Ella Logan's words echoed in his head as clear today as they had in her bedchamber two years ago, for no one save his own mother had ever used the word "kind" to describe him. Ella had lain nearly motionless in her bed, her pale yellowish face slick with sweat, her blonde hair—darkened by dampness—lifeless against her goose down pillow, her blue eyes heavy-lidded and faded by fever. The bedclothes were pushed back except for a sheet for modesty's sake in his presence, a presence he ruefully knew was not always a comfort to her. Not only did her illness disturb and agitate him, but his sympathetic reaction to seeing her thus shook him; sympathy was an emotion usually foreign to him and best not cultivated in his line of work.

From across the chamber, the uncanny stare of James Logan made Ketch even more ill at ease. Uncomfortable, he dropped his gaze from Ella, cautiously aware that Logan's insane possessiveness might make

14

the man think his attention inappropriate or presumptuous for his station in their world, especially here in this inner sanctum where Ketch had never before been summoned.

But indeed he had been summoned, by Ella herself. One of the household servants had delivered her note, which he had received with great curiosity and astonishment. Although he knew how to read and write, it had been some time since Ella had taught him, so he had great difficulty interpreting the letters on her stationery. And now here he was, awkward and at a loss, bewildered by Ella's very invitation.

Never a conversationalist, Ketch was helpless to conjure even a few simple words at the pitiful sight of Leighlin Plantation's mistress lying so helpless and drained. His attention caught upon a nearby basin of water in which a rag soaked, and he remembered the relief such a thing had brought to him as a boy beset by the smallpox fever. In a moment of nervous energy, he wrung most of the water from the rag then hesitatingly wiped her brow, not daring to glance at Logan who remained watchful but motionless, like a camouflaged serpent.

Ella's eyes showed surprise, almost shock, at Ketch's gesture, but then she made an effort to hide those emotions and whispered, "Thank you."

He wanted to remind her of the same kindness she had bestowed upon him when he had been near death the day they had first met, but again words failed him.

A quiet double knock sounded at the door, and Logan crossed over to answer it. A servant on the other side whispered, "It's Mizz Helen's bedtime, Cap'n."

Logan glanced back at his wife, who was listening intently, then his suspicious gaze slid to Ketch.

"Go to her, James," Ella urged. "She will expect a story from you tonight since she did not get one last night. Give her a kiss for me." A small smile teased the corners of her mouth as she closed her moist eyes. Ketch started to turn for the door to avoid being alone with her, expecting Logan to order him out, but her voice halted him. "Ketch will keep me company while you are gone."

Ketch was unsure who was more bemused by this—he or Logan. But with another wary glance his way, Logan left with the servant. Ketch turned back to Ella, but she appeared to have fallen asleep, breathing swallower. He frowned and was about to round the bed and go to the chair Logan had vacated, but then Ella's eyes opened partway. She studied him until he looked down at the mattress and swallowed hard.

"Before my husband returns, I must ask something of you." Her attention lay upon him, but he could not raise his head. "If I am to succumb, whether now or at another time, you must promise me that you will always protect Helen."

He stared at her, blocked the very thought of her dying.

"Do you understand?"

He nodded, both disturbed and flattered by her faith in him. "But Miss Helen has her father—"

"You and I both know the dangerous life my husband leads. A myriad of things could happen to him. So you will promise me?"

"Of—of course. I promise."

She closed her eyes and sighed as if with great relief, then she fell into a long, deep sleep.

As the memory faded, so did Ketch. He rejoiced when sleep took him away from the disjointed sounds of the *Alliance*'s berthing deck, the music of the water along her timbers lulling him.

Before hearing or seeing them, he sensed them coming. Evil had a way of taking up space, like a living entity, displacing air and dimming light, bearing a heaviness Ketch could always feel like a wet sail falling over him. The sensation brought him awake a moment too late. The men cut the nettles of his hammock, and he crashed to the deck. With the hammock flung over his face, the lynch mob rained blows and kicks from all directions. He cursed them, cursed himself for having let down his guard, and fought back as best as he could; capitulation had long ago been expunged from his persona by the brutality of others.

His struggles ended with a well-aimed thump to his head by something heavy, something wooden, a handspike perhaps. He fell through time, battered by a harsh, wet wind, a hurricane roar, until monstrous ocean swells swept over his head and momentarily drowned all sound. He surfaced, saw Ella Logan, heard her shouts amidst the wind's demonic shrieks. He knew where she was even before he escaped the depths and broke the violent black surface. A swell lifted her up and up before him, her arms flailing, fighting not to be carried farther away from the *Medora*. To reach her required Herculean strength against every element the sea and sky could hurl at him, and though his lungs burned and his muscles throbbed, weighted down by soaked clothing, he reached her as she went under a final time, her struggle lost. And this time he went down with her.

16

# CHAPTER 2

Jack burst awake, flailing and gasping. With wide eyes and hair dripping sweat, he sat upright in his hammock, nearly spilling himself upon the deck if not for Smith's steadying hands. An outcry died upon his lips. Reality rushed at him in the form of his quartermaster's concerned face and the morning sun through the stern windows. He followed the rays of light to where the sun bulged above the hazy horizon like a fresh orange, a blinding, distorted orb. He forced his breathing to slow along with his heartbeat, thankful that the images that had assaulted him had been but a bad dream.

"Easy there, lad," Smith said, stepping back, troubled yet certainly not unfamiliar with Jack's nightmares.

Jack slipped from the hammock, naked and sweaty. "What are you doing here? Is something amiss?" Embarrassed to have been rescued once again by his friend, he padded across the cabin to the small quarter-gallery to splash himself with water from the basin there.

"Nothin' amiss but you. I heard you a-shoutin' so I came."

Often Smith's mothering irritated him, but this time he appreciated his comrade's presence. In a daze Jack relieved himself then staggered back into the cabin to dress. The brig's energy beneath his feet, the sensation of live timbers, her voice around him, gave him a welcomed surge of comfort. He saw the question on his quartermaster's face.

"I was dreaming about my mother." Jack dragged his fingers through his thick hair, pushing the damp strands from his face. "It was just like that day she came aboard from the *Medora*." He stared at the padded stern locker where his mother had sat after he had rescued her from Logan. "Just like that day, she begged me to return her to Logan." He shook his head.

"How many times must I tell you, lad? She was just tryin' to protect you. She knew if Logan caught up with you, he'd try to kill you."

"Aye, but maybe she had feelings for him. After all, they had a child together." He sank upon the locker, toying with the bracelet upon his scarred wrist. "I should've asked her, but I was afraid to, and how would I know if she was telling the truth? I thought when I went to Leighlin I might learn the truth, but..." He shook his head again.

"'Tis nothin' to flog yerself over, lad. Both she and Logan are dead, God rest 'em. You have to let this die with 'em."

"I can't, Smitty. I want to know that the path I chose to find her was the right one, that she was pleased with me for those few hours of freedom from Logan. How many men did I kill to get to her? Was it all folly?"

"Of course not. But you have to let it go or it'll eat you alive. Yer priority now is yer sister. Remember that was yer mother's dyin' wish."

Jack's shoulders slumped. "Helen won't speak to me; I'm not even sure why."

"Give her time. She's had quite a shock."

Patience was not a natural trait in Jack; it chafed him, especially when he remembered Helen turning away from him. He nodded toward the door. "Go on deck, Smitty. I'll be up in a minute."

Reluctantly Smith obeyed. Jack remained on the locker for some time, twisting the bracelet with a finger and staring back along the lazy, sun-emblazoned wake of the *Prodigal* where a pair of terns ducked and swooped. A beautiful morning, he realized, a morning that would be fresh and invigorating on deck, enough to breathe life back into any man...or child.

With inspired determination, he went to the wardroom door and knocked, not gently like he had since Helen had come aboard but with force and urgency. He did not wait for Maria to answer; he had the door halfway open when she reached it, nearly knocking her back. Surprise widened her brown eyes, her long hair tousled from sleep. The man's shirt she slept in revealed her elegant neck, tanned in contrast to her shapely legs, though her natural dark skin tone made such a contrast minimal. Her hand closed the gaping collar, depriving him of a lovely view, and took unmindful hold of the gold locket that always hung around her neck. He tried to ignore his aggravating physical reaction to Maria, to the scent of her after a warm night of sleep.

He forced his gaze to his sister's hammock. "Has she been awake long?"

"Just for the past few minutes or so."

Helen paid them no heed. She was too busy peering over the side of the hammock, intent and worried about her stuffed bear that had fallen to the deck. With a doleful whimper, she wobbled in the hammock as if trying to figure out how to escape its height. She pressed her chest against the edge and used her weight to tip the hammock, stretching one arm in vain while the other clutched the side to keep from tumbling out. When Jack hurried to pick up the bear, Helen snatched it from him as if she feared he would keep it. She hugged it to her chest, half turning from him.

Jack faltered but summoned his resolve back to the surface. "Helen, you must come on deck with me. The fresh air will do you good."

Helen made no answer, not looking at him, her long blonde hair draping forward to hide her lowered face. Absently she stroked the stuffed bear.

Maria stepped closer. "Let's get you dressed so you can go with your brother."

But Jack refused to allow any delay or chance of repudiation. He extricated his sister from the hammock. Helen gave a small gasp, nearly dropping the bear, but she did not struggle as Jack pulled her close. She put one arm around his neck, not tightly as she used to do but instead with a lukewarm hold, her other arm smashing the bear between them, her chin on his shoulder, staring behind him.

Maria reached for her own clothes; on board the brig she wore the breeches and plain shirt of a common sailor. "I'll go with you. Just give me a moment."

But Jack did not wait. He headed for the aft companionway and climbed into the morning sun with his small burden, just as the Rat hailed, "Sail ho!" from the mainmasthead.

"Where away?" Smith called from the quarterdeck.

"Two points on the starboard quarter!"

Jack's heart leapt with anticipation, hoping the vessel was somehow the *Alliance*. If not for Helen, he would have sprang aloft for a better look, but instead he hid his excitement for fear of agitating her and joined Smith on the quarterdeck. The curious eyes of the Prodigals followed him. Jack wondered if carrying a child somehow tarnished their image of him as commander. One of them, however, was not perturbed by this sight—Samuel, who had sailed with Logan since being freed from bondage in Barbados. The African held great affection for the daughter of his dead captain. Seeing her at last outside of the wardroom brought a smile to his broad face where he stood near the mainmast.

"What do you make of her, Rat?" Jack called.

"A ketch, Cap. Crackin' on right well. Won't take her too long to overhaul us."

Jack hid his disappointment. "Angus, furl t'gallants and take in stuns'ls. Spill some of the wind from the tops'ls."

Angus MacKenzie, his shockingly yellow hair captured beneath a blue cloth, gave one of his unconscious grins. "And what do you plan for her once she's up with us, Long Arm?"

"We'll see if she's worth taking as a consort," Jack replied. "Help even the odds if we meet the *Alliance*." He caught Smith giving Helen a hopeful grin, but the tactic did not break the girl's veneer. Instead she buried her face into Jack's shoulder. "Smitty, we'll clear for action. Tell Dowling to get up here."

Before Dowling reached the quarterdeck, Maria arrived, hair pulled back into a queue, a floppy-brimmed hat upon her head. With a quick glance at the sudden activity, she seamlessly freed Jack of Helen, relieving and disappointing him at the same time, for he wanted to get through to Helen, not be distracted by this new development astern. He had hoped taking her about the brig would brighten her, for she had loved sailing upon her father's *Medora*.

As he relinquished Helen, Maria avoided his gaze. Something told him her evasion had nothing to do with the recent events in their personal relationship. No, this was something new, something she wanted to keep hidden. But there was no time to figure that out now, for his gunner mounted the quarterdeck.

"Dowling, once the ketch is within a couple of leagues of us, get the crews to their guns, enough to fight one side."

Dowling drolly grinned and responded with his usual habit of questions, rhetorical or otherwise. "Well now, that's about all we got left, in'it?" His gaze darted toward Helen. "Shall I draft yer wee sister into one o' me crews? Powder monkey perhaps?" He gave a quick laugh, his dark eyes anything but mirthful, never pleased about having a woman on board and a child even less.

"Keep the gunports closed until I give the order. We'll let 'em think we're a coaster."

"Aye aye." Dowling glanced between Jack and Maria then hurried away, bawling out to the gun crew captains.

Maria sat on a nearby locker with Helen on her lap. The girl kept her focus either downward or at the bear in her grasp, not at the brig's sails or active crew as Jack had hoped. "What are your plans?" Maria asked.

He turned his attention to the men laying aloft. "Might take her as a consort."

"We've barely enough men to sail and fight the *Prodigal*."

20

Her tone—though curious, not insulting—managed to nettle Jack here upon his quarterdeck. "I'll press the ketch's crew."

"All of them?" There was a hint of displeasure in her voice as her fingers brushed back Helen's flowing blonde hair.

"If they're any kind of sailor, aye." He tried to infuse finality into his words, but as usual even blatancy could not dent Maria's forthrightness.

"Even if they're married?"

He turned fully toward her, tried to suppress his irritation; he must not take out his own frustration on her, especially in front of Helen; neither should he assume she was being anything more than inquisitive. "I don't have the good fortune of being selective right now. After the convoy is dispatched, I'll release them."

Maria rose, easing Helen down next to her. "Come along, Helen. Let's get you properly dressed. I must fashion you a bonnet today to keep away the sun."

The girl stayed close to Maria, reached blindly and with a hint of apprehension to take her offered hand. Then the two descended the quarterdeck, leaving Jack alone with the two men at the tiller who were careful not to make eye contact with their perturbed captain. Jack paid them no heed, staring after Maria's small form, wishing simultaneously that he could take her into his bed as well as throw her overboard. A common frustration since they had left Cayona months ago in search of James Logan.

#

Maria was no great hand with a needle, but she had fashioned a simple dress for Helen from the meager stores found on the brig. The little creation would have to be sufficient until they returned to Leighlin. Ketch had carried the child off in her nightclothes, out from under Maria's very nose, but when Helen had been rescued she had worn a rough-hewn sailcloth dress. When Maria had helped her disinterested ward remove the garment yesterday before bed, she had asked Helen who had made it for her but of course received no response. Maria guessed Ketch to be responsible. Brute though he was, she had witnessed the man's affinity for Helen, something that made her wonder if he actually would have allowed her to be killed as the *Alliance*'s captain had threatened.

As Maria gently tugged the new dress over Helen's head, the girl kept a close watch on the stuffed bear nearby. Neither of them paid

21

attention to the noises outside of the wardroom as the crew made a clean sweep of the gun deck in preparation for battle. Maria's fingers combed the tangles from Helen's golden hair—hair the color of her mother's—then tied it back with a black ribbon. The somber color reminded her of the mourning bands all had worn for Leighlin's mistress. Helen retrieved her bear. Maria gave the dress one last smoothing over and, kneeling in front of her, smiled and tapped her nose.

"It would make me very happy to see you smile again, *osita.*"

No response, eyes upon the bear, fingers poking absently into its hide.

Maria frowned and stood. "Come along then. We'll go back on deck and show your brother your new dress."

They found the bedraggled carpenter just outside with Willie Emerick and Sullivan, waiting impatiently to remove the bulkheads, for those were all that remained standing. The carpenter swiped the hat from his head, held it along with a mallet in his right hand. If the existence of a woman and a child aboard a pirate shocked him, he hid his feelings well.

Willie, captain of the fore top, smiled a gap-toothed smile at Helen. "Good to see you out and about, young miss." He winked. "A right fine dress you're wearin'."

Helen said nothing, eyes downward. Maria introduced the men, hesitating until Hanse provided his name. He showed Helen a hint of a smile, as if the presence of a child eased some of his misgivings about his circumstance.

"Mr. Emerick and Mr. Sullivan are musicians," Maria explained to Helen. "Perhaps tonight they will play for you."

"'Twould be our pleasure." Willie crouched in front of Helen, his balding pate ashine with sweat. "Do you like to dance, miss? I can show you a jig or two if you'd like."

Helen's large eyes met his, showing a glimmer of life as she pressed against Maria's leg.

"No need to be shy," Willie assured. "We don't bite. Well, Sully might but I keep a close eye on 'im." He chuckled.

Maria smiled her thanks for their indulgence, then led Helen toward the aft hatch. The child traversed the moving deck with no misstep, as if she had lived at sea all her life. Indeed, she had been born and raised upon her father's brigantine until her mother had insisted upon a land-based life for her daughter, to avoid the perils of the open ocean as well as the dangers of Logan's piratical career.

Back upon the weather deck, Maria saw the ketch far in their wake but closer than before she had gone below. To be sure, she was a fast sailer for a ketch, probably traveling at twice the *Prodigal*'s reduced speed. The activity on the *Prodigal*'s deck had settled down to a patient wait, the brig carrying only topsails, the sheets started to reduce their drawing power. The coaster would not be up with them for nearly three hours, so men now lounged about on deck, casually talking about the ketch and what might happen, others continuing with speculation and anticipation about the convoy of merchantmen they were hoping to intercept off the Carolina coast and what they would do with their purchase. Rum and whores in Charles Town was the general consensus. Some men suspended conversation when Maria led Helen forward among them. Some smiled and spoke to the unresponsive child, others simply watched, a few of those with uneasy, resentful looks. Two men formerly of Logan's brigantine spoke briefly and fondly to the girl. She made eye contact with them, but nothing more did they gain from her. Jack's voice sounded from the foremast crosstrees where he roosted with Smith, a telescope in hand to study the coaster.

Upon the forecastle, David Archer idly polished one of the brass swivel guns, his back to Maria, very much alone even with others on the forecastle, others who kept the usual wary distance. Samuel had first brought the belief aboard that David was bad luck, and men like Joe Dowling kept up a steady stream of subversion above and below deck to propagate David's unpopularity. He claimed the boy's presence was responsible for the damage suffered by the *Prodigal* and thus the delay caused by it, possibly depriving them of the convoy's riches. Dowling and others had no appreciation for David's efforts to learn his duties and carry his weight aboard the brig.

Jack had promised to take David to England to escape his father's tyranny, a promise made not to David—the boy wanted no part in running away from his troubles—but to his sister, Margaret Archer. The way things were looking, Maria doubted if such passage aboard the *Prodigal* was possible. And if not, what would become of David? Returning to his family's plantation was not an option after he had shot and wounded his father during a struggle to protect Maria.

At the sound of Maria's footsteps, David turned, and the easy smile she was so accustomed to in good and bad times alike blossomed upon his florid, clean-shaven face. His eyes—as sharp as the blue sky above them—held a brightness reserved only for her. When his attention lowered to Helen, he left the gun to crouch in front of her, his

23

smile broadening for her benefit.

"What a fine new dress you have, Helen. And I am so happy to see you on deck today."

Maria tried to match his lightness of voice. "We've come in hopes of seeing dolphins."

"There were some yesterday, playing in the bow wave. Perhaps we shall be lucky and see them again today." He offered his hand to the child. "Shall we have a look together?"

Maria was astonished when Helen took David's hand. The girl hesitated slightly as he stepped forward, then she went along with him, the bear held against her chest. Passing the fore bitts and the bell, David sidled up to the pin rail and picked Helen up. Unlike her lukewarm hold in her brother's embrace, Helen snugged her right arm around David's neck and looked forward over the bowsprit which rose and fell with the long, following swell, a swell that liked to push the *Prodigal* far leeward if allowed. She brought one of her feet up and curled her toes upon the spritsail yard lifts. David leaned to peer downward at the push of white water surging around the stem.

"I do not see any of our friends today, do you, Helen?"

The girl lightened her grip enough to stretch forward to see over the rail, the breeze tugging some of her hair loose from the ribbon to writhe about her head like a serpent. Maria stayed a few steps back, consoled by David's natural interaction with the child. The two were no strangers—Helen had known David since Leighlin had been founded two years ago, for the Archers' Wildwood Plantation was the next plantation upriver. No doubt her mother's fondness for the young man had also nurtured Helen's affection for David. When he had been recently secreted at Leighlin, his presence had lifted Helen from a melancholy brought about by her father and brother's absence and had also appeared to have deepened their bond. Helen had seemed to sense the tragedy behind the young man and perhaps felt akin to it because of her mother's murder…and now her father's as well.

Within a few minutes, Helen tried to squirm from David's grasp, stretching her arms out toward the railing as if to climb upon it, but the young man took a step back. "We would not want you to fall overboard, now would we? What would your brother say to that, eh?"

Wistfully Helen eyed the bulwarks, then her attention went to the fore top, and she pointed. "Take me up there," she said, not as a request but as a gentle order.

Maria started at the unexpected sound of her voice, as she had in the wardroom, but she refrained from verbally reacting. Her attention darted up to Jack where he stared downward at Helen. From his height he could not have possibly heard her through the muting voice of the wind in his ears and in the rigging. But he said something to Smith and passed off the glass before using a standing backstay to descend.

David asked, "Are you not afraid to go so high, Helen?"

Vigorously she shook her head. "Daddy used to take me aloft."

He grinned. "Oh, yes. I recall your mother saying how that nigh gave her the vapors."

Jack dropped to the deck and hurried toward them, but Maria reached for his arm to discourage his eagerness.

"Jack, wait—"

"She spoke. I saw her—"

"Jack."

His rush of words halted when Helen put both of her arms around David and faced away. Her physical rejection of him stopped Jack's forward momentum more abruptly than any words from Maria.

Hesitant, David said, "Helen would like to go into the fore top. With your permission—"

Jack scowled. "Are you out of your mind? You aren't taking her aloft."

"She said her father used to—"

"She's my responsibility now, and I'll not take the chance of her...of you missing a ratlin' and—"

"Jack," Maria softly interjected as the attention of everyone aboard turned their way. She kept her grip firm upon his taut arm. "The brig is quiet; there would be no safer time. If it makes her happy, maybe it'll draw her out more."

He managed to hold his reflexive rebuke, perhaps so he could consider her hopeful logic. Turmoil colored his eyes black. Composing himself, his attention went to her hand upon his sleeve. She freed him, and he took a step toward his sister, saying, "Helen, if you'd like to go to the fore top, I will take you."

To Maria's dismay, the girl did not respond, did not stir, humiliating her brother, for all the men upon the forecastle and just abaft the foremast could easily see and hear everything.

Jack spoke louder, as if the child simply had not heard him, "Helen, would you like to go aloft with me?"

The girl shifted so she could see David's face, but she did not make eye contact with anyone and instead stared at the well-traveled bear. Quietly—but loud enough for Jack to hear—she said, "I want to go home." Then she glanced at Jack as if to see if he had heard before she looked at David. "I want to see my daddy. He must be home by now."

Jack paled, and his jaw loosened. His stark gaze went to Maria's frown.

Helen squirmed to the deck and scurried down the fore hatch.

#

The *Prodigal* flew English colors, and so the unsuspecting ketch pressed toward her with little caution, closing the gap to only a mile. Jack had not left the quarterdeck since talking to Helen, and he had few words for anyone during the hours of impatient waiting as the sun climbed higher upon the flawless blue shield above him.

While neither Helen nor Maria returned to the weather deck, they were there in the Prodigals' conversations held just beyond Jack's hearing. Although he felt foolish for allowing his sister's rejection to embarrass him, something far more troublesome irritated him—not only had she publicly cast him off but had figuratively and literally embraced the most unpopular man on board. Those who did not relish the thought of the captain's sister aboard were perturbed even more by her alliance with David, and those softened to her now had their doubts. Jack knew all of this without hearing more than a few, incautious comments; he sensed it like an ill wind blowing. He clenched his teeth, hands upon the taffrail as he watched the swirl of the *Prodigal*'s wake and the roiling bow wave of the closing ketch. He did not want these men set against him because of crazy superstition.

Smith mounted the quarterdeck, stood to leeward, and said, "Everyone's to his station."

Jack considered the ketch off the starboard quarter. She was a fine sailer, nearly the length of the *Prodigal* but narrower of beam, her hull newly painted dark green, her sails also appearing recently renewed. Her sail plan was unusual for the ketches to which Jack was accustomed—except for her small square main topsail she bore fore-and-aft sails, accounting for her ability to sail closer to the wind than the *Prodigal*. Jack's glass swung over her deck and located six guns neglected amidst plentiful cargo. A dozen curious men dotted the deck, a couple of them staring through telescopes as the vessel cut a pleasing line through the swells. She was no scrub like the pink.

Jack observed, "If she's seen our stern close enough, apparently *Prodigal* signifies nothing to them."

Smith grinned. "All the better for us. Shall we heave to?"

"Aye. Back the fore tops'l." He was unconcerned that they were to leeward of the coaster, for the *Prodigal*'s well-served guns were within a quick, accurate killing range. Even with the weather gauge, the ketch's master would be a fool to offer resistance. Jack glanced over his shoulder to where Willie stood at the halyard, ready to hoist the *Prodigal*'s ensign, his face alight with the anticipation of a spider on its web. On the gun deck below, the starboard crews stood to their pieces—four six-pounders and two eight-pounders—awaiting the signal. Jack realized he gripped the taffrail too tightly, his fingers tingling. His heart had picked up its pace. The Rat stood casually near the quarterdeck's starboard swivel gun, ready to man it at a moment's notice should the coaster resist. With eager expectancy he glanced at Jack. Jack, however, thought not of the Rat's enthusiasm but instead hoped Maria had gotten Helen to the safety of the hold.

At first the ketch hesitated at the *Prodigal*'s hoisted invitation to speak her, but then she allowed her large gaff mainsail to luff.

Someone in the *Prodigal*'s waist gave a loud chuckle, saying, "Aye, c'mon, you dogs. Spill yer wind and let's have you."

A tall, thin man upon the ketch's quarterdeck took a speaking trumpet in hand. As he did so, Jack clapped shut his glass and exchanged it with Smith for a speaking trumpet.

Jack hailed, "The ketch ahoy! What vessel is that?"

The tall man answered, "The *Fortune*...out of Barbados! Bound for Charles Town! What brig is that?"

Jack glanced at Smith whose every muscle tensed with anticipation, blue eyes ashine with excitement, a rapacious, encouraging grin showing through his dark beard. Drawing his lungs full, Jack turned back to the coaster and boomed out his answer, "*Prodigal!*"

With great zeal, Willie hoisted the black flag. It snapped sharply as the breeze caught the cloth and shook it out like a raven taking flight. The clamor of six port lids and the rumble of guns being run out gave Jack and those on deck a lightning charge of energy. Muskets appeared along the brig's railing and in her tops. A challenge roared from the throat of every Prodigal. The men upon the *Fortune*'s deck recoiled, and a wild, confused scramble ensued; to what purpose Jack could not tell. Then their master barked commands, heard across the water without the aid of a trumpet, and the mad dash ceased.

"Strike and you will be given full quarter!" Jack cried. "Run and we will destroy you!"

Again the hesitation, and Jack caught the impatient chatter below on the gun deck. Dowling's staccato voice incited his crews in hopes of plying their trade, the guns loaded with bar shot and chain shot, the gun captains instructed to fire for the rigging only. Then the *Fortune*'s master addressed one of his men, and their colors slowly glided downward. The Prodigals cheered, and the boarding party, led by Jack, headed for the stern ladder to descend into the pinnace being towed behind.

# CHAPTER 3

When Ketch awoke he guessed it was afternoon but could not be sure. He lay in the warm, quiet forepeak with five other invalids of the *Alliance*, cut off from all light except for a single lantern and snippets of sunlight filtering down through the deckhead or through the hawseholes. The stench of bilge water reached him, but he was so accustomed to the odor that it offered no offense. He raised his head from the pillow and looked around with one eye; his right eye was still swollen shut from yesterday's beating. The other patients—all wounded during the confrontation with the *Prodigal*—lay asleep, a couple snoring in the small, airless space. Ketch was glad to have a reprieve from their moans and groans. It was not that the sounds unsettled him or drew pity; instead the men's obvious weakness irritated him.

His mouth was still sore. His tongue had found another tooth missing when he had regained consciousness deep in the middle watch. As he had then, he now tested his limbs—everything responded slowly because of the bruising. His hand drifted to his sizeable nose. Broken again. Well, he had never been one to worry about appearances. Any natural redeeming quality to his face had been lost long ago among the scarring left by the smallpox, overwhelming anything of value to a woman's eye. He reached up to check the swath of bandages around his torn scalp. Of course the wound had bled prodigiously, no doubt shocking the first mate whose approach had interrupted the assault and scattered the assailants, or so the surgeon had told him. Ketch remembered little of the attack.

"I had heard you are a difficult man to kill, Ketch," Caleb Wylder's statement gained his attention. "It would appear that is true." The officer drew nearer from the gloom aft, bent considerably beneath the beams.

"Don't look so disappointed, Captain," Ketch said in a thick, cottony voice.

Wylder, tall and handsome—a gentleman—produced a small, disconcerted frown. "If you but tell me the names of those who attacked

29

you—"

"Why?"

Wylder clasped his hands behind his back as if not knowing what to do with them. "Those who did this to you should receive just punishment."

"I never seen punishment cause a man to stop his ways. I got scars what prove it."

"While I did not subscribe to your tactics in kidnapping Helen Logan, there is still the fact that because of it James Logan is dead, and my family's business—and that of others'—will survive and prosper because of it. Due to that fact I feel...beholden to you." His Adam's apple bobbed with distress; he did not like the taste of his admission of gratitude. Or was the distaste from profiting off the kidnapping of a child? Or perhaps the unpleasantness originated from the knowledge that he had faltered in his resolve to summarily execute Logan aboard the *Alliance* and thus had unwittingly forced Ketch's lethal hand.

When Ketch offered nothing in response to his admission, Wylder's frown deepened. "I must admit to my curiosity, Ketch—I am not fool enough to believe you killed Logan for the same reasons that motivated me to hunt him down. Did you not serve him for some time?"

"Aye, I served him," Ketch growled. "And he showed his thanks by butcherin' me brother and lettin' that bastard Mallory live."

"Mallory? Why are you concerned with him?"

Ketch scowled and said nothing more.

Wylder waited an uncomfortable moment, but when he received no response he said, "Well, if you change your mind and wish to speak against your attackers, send for me." With a curt nod he left the forepeak.

Ketch lay back and stared at the deckhead as his hammock gently swayed. He dismissed thoughts of Wylder, Mallory, or Logan. Instead he thought of Helen.

On the night he had stolen into the child's bedchamber at Leighlin Plantation, he had stood above her for a long moment. Her peaceful countenance had put a chink in his armor of resolve, the same that the child had later put into Wylder's plan to kill Logan outright. She slept soundly on her side, facing him, small hands clasped together near her chin as if in prayer or perhaps as if imagining she held the oddly absent bear. Ketch did not waste time searching for the toy, though he had wanted to take it with them to provide comfort, to keep Helen quiet. Instead he listened again with the acuity of a bat for any stirrings in Maria Cordero's adjoining bedchamber, but no sound came. So he bent over the child and carefully—with a gentleness that did not come naturally to him—encircled her slight form with his arms and drew her toward him. She awoke, but not fully, her eyes mere slits of confusion.

"Shh," he softly hushed. "Go back to sleep."

She fought against his command, her lips attempting to form a question, but she floated too close to deep sleep still and so drifted back into its drug-like protection. She did not wake again until they were in the skiff upon the broad Ashley River, headed for Charles Town. He had made her a nest-like bed among a coil of rope at his feet. From amidst her blanket, she brushed the hair from her face and blinked through the darkness at him, taking her time as if wondering if she were in a dream. Then she sleepily inquired, "Daddy?"

The word startled Ketch, causing him to almost let go of the oars. Of course the girl was disoriented, not used to seeing at night like he was, and his shape would be similar to Logan's with his strong build and hair of similar length. Indeed earlier that evening he had purposefully trimmed his recent growth of beard along the same lines as Logan's.

"I'm takin' you to yer daddy, Miss Helen. Recollect he's out to sea?"

On her knees she struggled closer to him. To his dismay, she shrank back when she recognized him.

"Go back to sleep now, child. When you wake up I'll have you aboard a ship what will take you to yer daddy."

"Where's Maria?"

"She couldn't come."

"Why not?" Instinctive anxiety in her voice. She had never been so utterly alone with him before. She looked around as if to get her bearings and seek escape.

Not a man accustomed to lengthy conversation, especially with a child, he impatiently said, "She just couldn't," in a voice that cowed the girl.

Helen dragged the blanket around her more for comfort, he suspected, than for the need of any warmth on the humid, ghostly mist-shrouded river. Her uneasiness agitated him. While fear was something he cultivated with purpose in other people, he did not desire it in this child, not only because he did not want her causing trouble or resisting him once they reached Charles Town but because he had never wanted her to fear him and had done everything he could think of in the past to make her not avoid him. He esteemed the child not only because of her mother but because of his infant sister of whom she always reminded

31

him. It was for that reason that he had killed that sailor aboard the *Alliance* the other day below deck. The man had frightened Helen with intimation of the real reason why she was aboard the *Alliance*. Ketch had pulled her away before the man could reveal more, and so he had seen to it that night that the fool had no further opportunity to loose his tongue.

Helen's eyes reached to the shoreline beyond a broad, impenetrable marsh from which bullfrogs and other creatures sent up an uninviting night chorus. Afraid that she might call out, Ketch quickly diverted her attention. "You want to find yer father, don't ye, Miss Helen? You said yerself he shouldn't have left you behind."

As she looked out at the black, rippled water, her eyes caught the glimmering reflection of stars in the clearing sky. She nodded.

"We're goin' to find him then. Together. So you go back to sleep now an' don't fret 'bout nothin', hear?"

Perhaps fatigue pulled Helen back to sleep or perhaps the soothing movement of the boat, expertly handled. But Ketch liked to believe his words of comfort had lulled her.

Now as he lay in his hammock, he pressed his eyelids shut in a sharp moment of anguish. Helen looked so much like her mother that it often pained him since Ella Logan's death. He tried not to think of the girl's mother, of the condemnation she would have had for his recent actions. As much as he had loathed the idea of kidnapping Helen—an idea that had not originated with him alone—he had recognized the necessity if he was to avenge his half-brother's murder and thus free himself of the nightmares in which his sibling haunted him, demanded retribution. Aye, Dan Slattery had deserved death for killing Ella Logan, but he had not deserved Logan's wanton butchery nor the unholy indecency displayed when Ketch had simply wanted a respectful burial for his kin. True, Logan could not provide such a burial for Dan's sake, but he should have at least done so for Ketch's sake, for his years of loyal service.

He thought of Helen aboard the *Prodigal*. He must get to her. He must not allow Jack Mallory to keep her away from the genteel life her mother had so carefully, tenaciously secured for her.

At the thought of Mallory, his hands balled into fists of potent rage. Everything, all of this misery, was driven by the arrival of that wretch of a boy in these waters. That scrawny, piss-poor excuse for a seaman. His death would not be a quick one, but instead a long, cruel process. Only Logan had stayed Ketch's hand, but now...now Logan was out of the way.

#

The trucks of the *Prodigal*'s larboard battery created rolling thunder across the deck, mixed with the throaty noise of the men. Each of the six crews had a new hand from the *Fortune*, all uneasy-looking fellows who fearfully followed orders and kept their mouths shut. The lack of bang, recoil, and smoke tempered enthusiasm, yet the Prodigals attended to their duties well enough to suit Jack. In order to conserve ammunition, he had decided only the *Fortune* would fire live during this exercise, giving Dowling the opportunity to judge his new crews' attributes.

While the Prodigals reloaded, Jack peered through a gunport to where the *Fortune* cruised under the brig's lee. Angus, the *Fortune*'s newly-elected master, stood upon the ketch's quarterdeck, surveying his new command. He had been happy to attain such a lofty position and took with him men most familiar with sailing fore-and-aft rigged vessels. That morning, before the gun exercise, the bulbous-eyed, stuttering pirate and his men had enjoyed testing the ketch's ability, their delighted shouts reaching across the water to Jack as the vessel sliced across the *Prodigal*'s bow several times in a show of speed and maneuverability that nearly put the brig to shame.

Now Jack watched the prize's gun crews—a mixture of Prodigals and unfortunate Fortunes pressed from their quiet coasting life—work their pieces, firing to leeward. Joe Dowling's stumpy form darted back and forth along the row of six-pounders, gesticulating, shouting, now and then delivering a cuff or a kick to some unworthy. When the gunner had first gone aboard the *Fortune*, he had complained vehemently and cursed the merchant sailors about the guns' neglect, and Jack had gladly left Dowling to see to their renewal under whatever means necessary.

Returning his attention inboard, Jack thought of the four wounded Prodigals forward, protected slightly from the noise by bulkheads. He regretted not having them here to lend a hand or above deck to handle sail. Even with the additions of the Fortunes, he felt woefully shorthanded when he considered the anticipated five vessels of the convoy. Though no doubt manned by typically small merchant crews, the convoy could still out-muster the two pirate crews, even if the merchantmen were unescorted.

He distracted himself by watching David Archer at the number three gun as he went through the dumb show of worming the piece.

Concentration weighed upon the young man, as if they were amidst a pitched battle. His crew were the least lively of all, almost sullen. Jack scowled. What to do with this fool boy?

A light voice spoke Jack's name, so incongruous and seemingly distant among the guttural male voices that at first he thought his hearing played him false. Then someone plucked his sleeve where he stood near the aft-most gun. He found Maria at his elbow, looking at him with concern, an expression all too painfully familiar. And like so many other times, her beauty momentarily robbed him of his verbal skills.

"You must stop," she beseeched.

"Stop?"

"Yes. The guns. The noise has Helen in a terrible fright."

"But we're not firing."

"There's still the noise and there's the guns of the *Fortune*."

"Helen's heard guns before. She was aboard the *Medora*—"

"Jack." The frown turned to exasperation. "It's not the same for her, not now, not after what she went through."

Jack bore his own frown, half frustrated by the intervention, half embarrassed by his own ignorance, for how could he forget that the guns of both the *Alliance* and the *Prodigal* had roared right over Helen's head when she had been in the yawl?

When he glanced back along the battery, several faces turned his way, none of them pleased, most of them comprehending without hearing the conversation. And what one man saw he passed along to his mate and he in turn to his mate until activity on the deck slowed and grew uncoordinated as Jack struggled with indecision. Meanwhile the Fortunes stared in shock at Maria, for this was their first sight of her.

"Jack, please," she implored, now keeping her voice low, for she too had seen the change among the Prodigals. When her gaze reached beyond Jack, he ground his teeth together, for he knew it was Archer to whom she looked.

Quietly Jack sighed and turned to the men. "We'll call that well for today, lads. Rat, jump on deck and signal the *Fortune* to cease firing."

With a mumbled, begrudging, "Aye aye, sir," the Rat obeyed while behind him the crews reluctantly stowed rammers, sponges, and worms.

"Thank you," Maria said near a whisper and quickly returned to the wardroom.

Jack wanted nothing better than to retreat to the solitude of his cabin and escape the stealthy waves of gossip that would spread throughout the brig, but instead he returned to the weather deck. Looking across to the *Fortune*, now silent, the last of the guns' smoke drifting westward, he caught sight of Dowling facing his way, hands upon his hips, before turning back to his duties.

A cloud descended over Jack, and he barked forward to Samuel near the starboard foresail sheet. The Negro came rolling aft in an amazingly smooth way for such a burly man, like a large predator on the hunt, low brow even lower than usual, as if expecting something unpleasant.

Jack ordered, "Tell Maria to come to my cabin. Stay with Helen while she's gone."

When Jack reached the aft cabin, he found Smith and Hanse at the table, charts spread before them. The carpenter jumped to his feet, but Smith remained low over the charts as if reading them put considerable strain upon his eyes. When the quartermaster looked at Jack from beneath his wiry dark eyebrows, he slowly sat up.

"You look like you could use a drink, lad," Smith said.

"Several," Jack muttered.

Hanse took a step back from the table, his attention never leaving Jack.

"Me and Mr. Hanse here was a-lookin' over these charts from the *Fortune*. He's been plyin' these waters for three years now. Knows a thing or two that might help us."

Jack considered the sweating carpenter. "And why would Mr. Hanse care to help us?"

This appeared to injure the man's pride and take away some of his usual trepidation around his new captain. "Reckon I don't fancy pilin' up on some reef any more'n you do, sir. There's that family of mine to provide for what I mentioned before."

"And if you keep mentioning them, Mr. Hanse, you may never see them again." An idle threat, of course, but one Jack could not contain in his agitated state and thus delivered with menace sufficient to intimidate the older man.

Jack moved to open two of the stern windows, and the cabin filled with the much-needed sweet sea breeze, ruffling the charts, which Smith started to gather.

"Well, Hanse, let's give the Captain his privacy. Looks like he needs some."

Jack turned. "No, stay. I mean, Smitty, you stay." Exasperation rang through the directive.

Smith glanced at him in curiosity. Hanse started for the door, no doubt eager to leave before he could get himself into any more trouble. Smith continued to roll up the charts.

"Leave 'em be, Smitty," Jack said as the door closed behind Hanse. "You can show me what that bugger told you. But first—"

A knock upon the door chopped off his words and chilled him. Judging by Smith's glance of inquiry, he must have paled considerably.

"Come in."

Maria slowly opened the door and looked about as if for others. In a painful flash, Jack remembered her last visit to his cabin and what an unholy mess he had made of that.

Seeing Smith and his welcoming expression, Maria returned his smile and stepped farther into the cabin. "Samuel said you wanted to see me."

Smith started to leave, but Jack scrambled to insist, "Stay, Smitty. This'll only take a minute." Actually he had no idea how long the conversation would last, but he desired an ally near, the person Maria esteemed more than anyone else on board, just in case she baulked at what he was about to present. Jack came around the table. "Sit down. Please."

Uncertainty crowded Maria's large dark eyes as she sat at the table. Smith remained standing, as if in preparation of swift departure. To sit was impossible for Jack, so he paced the width of the cabin, undisturbed by the brig's lively capers. He prepared his words, trying to draw calm from the soothing language of the brig, the water racing along her sides like a caress.

"Hopefully, we'll spot the convoy within the next couple of days, but before we do, I want to send Helen ashore." He turned back to Maria but a moment, determined not to be swayed from his resolve. "I want you to take her."

"Take her where?"

"Back to Leighlin. We'll stand in near Charles Town and send you off in one of the boats."

Smith said, "Who'll go with her?"

Jack cleared his throat uneasily. "I can't spare anyone, Smitty."

"Someone should go with her. That's a long journey—"

"'Twill be a near-run thing with these small crews once we come up with that convoy. I can't afford sending someone off." He forced himself to look at Maria and was thankful—and not surprised—to see her less concerned than Smith.

"I don't need anyone else, Smitty," she assured. "We'll be fine."

Smith scowled. "And what about when you make it to Leighlin? David Archer's father—that bugger Ezra Archer—might hear tell o' yer return. That man bears you a grudge for meddlin' in his affairs with his son, recollect. And wouldn't it be convenient for him with you there by yer lonesome."

"Dell and Rogers are at Leighlin," Jack reminded him of their former shipmates. "And the overseer, Defoe, won't let anything happen to Maria for Helen's sake if nothing else." Jack halted his pacing in front of his quartermaster's stormy countenance, unable to contain a small, satisfied smile. "Besides, we've both seen that Maria can take care of herself."

"But it won't be just herself, mind. She'll have Helen with her."

"Helen insists she wants to go home," Jack said regretfully. "And home will be the safer place for her once we fetch that convoy. Simply exercising the guns today nigh frightened her to death."

The truth silenced Smith as he stared gloomily at the deck. Then his glance flicked to Maria, and he grumbled, "If I didn't have to watch out for this muttonhead of a boy, I'd take you in meself."

She smiled her thanks. Jack wished her warm gesture had been directed his way, for he felt increasingly empty at the thought of her leaving.

"And what's to happen afterwards?" Smith pressed. "Once we've dispatched the convoy? Thought of that, have you?"

Maria's curious eyes latched onto Jack with tactile force. Obviously she had been thinking about the future while he had been immersed in commanding his small flotilla. If only he knew along what lines those mysterious thoughts of hers ran.

"I'll go to Leighlin," he answered.

"If they don't catch you and hang you in Charles Town after we plunder them ships o' Peter Wylder's."

Jack scowled in exasperation. "What is it you'd like for me to do, Smitty?"

"Go to Leighlin with 'em. The lads and me can—"

Although Jack's sensible parts told him Smith's words were out of concern for his captain, his sister, and her governess, all he heard was a lack of faith in his command.

"Is that what they want, the men? Is that what they've told you?"

"'Course not."

Jack wished he could believe him, but he found it difficult, especially after seeing the disgruntled faces when he had silenced the guns. Perhaps, once Maria and Helen were safely away, the balance would return. He shuffled around the table to the windows where he studied the brig's ribbon-like wake.

"I mean to see this through, Smitty."

"And what exactly is 'this,' eh? Yer hopin' the *Alliance* is escortin' that convoy, aren't ye? Revenge; that's what yer lookin' for, not purchase. Haven't you had enough of the revenge business, boy?"

"I said I'll go to Leighlin, damn it." Jack's harsh tone succeeded in stifling Smith's lecture and making Maria shift her weight uncomfortably. Jack settled and dragged a hand across his furrowed brow. "Helen has no desire to even look at me. Perhaps this time apart will mend that. Perhaps, by then, she will forgive me."

"Forgive you?" Maria echoed.

"Isn't it plain? She blames me for her father's death. Maybe even her mother's for all I know...for all she should."

"Nonsense. We don't know *what* she thinks right now. Her world's been turned upside down."

"If she doesn't think that, then why does she reject me?"

"She doesn't speak to me either. Just give her time. Things will settle. There's just too much right now for her to understand."

"Neither o' you should take any o' this to heart. After all," Smith gave a clever grin, "she's not speakin' to me neither. And you know how the little miss thought so high of me. Called me *uncle*, ye know. That's worth more than a wayward brother, sure."

Wistfully Jack smiled to himself, thankful for their reassurances. "Well, hopefully going back to the quiet of Leighlin will help her. Time will tell. That's what you say about everything, isn't it, Smitty?"

Smith winked at Maria. "Since when do you listen to me, boy?"

# CHAPTER 4

The *Prodigal*'s rigging still wept from that evening's gale, but the night sky was now clearing and the wind had settled. The swells slowly lost their angry white dressing and settled into black undulations that reflected the lantern lights from the two vessels. The *Fortune* displayed but a scrap of canvas while the *Prodigal* sailed under single-reefed topsails. The dampness on deck, however, did not spoil the Prodigals' enthusiasm for their music, provided on the forecastle by Sullivan's fiddle and Willie's tin whistle, both a little strained by the wet, but the half-drunken pirates did not notice their tonal imperfections. The pressed men of the *Fortune* lingered in the shadows in a small knot, the libations greedily withheld from them. Those upon the *Fortune* had been secured below hatches so they could not overpower the three men Angus had left behind. Light glowed from the skylight of the *Prodigal*'s aft cabin where a council of war had been convened, keeping Angus, Smith, Jack, and Dowling from enjoying the revelry.

Although the wardroom stifled after the storm, Maria hesitated to bring Helen on deck amidst the drinking. But when David came to invite them, Helen clambered from her hammock and into his arms, and the two looked so pleased in each other's company that Maria could not disappoint them. She was concerned by the child's indifference to the news that they would be returning to Leighlin— nothing more than a fleeting upward twist of her lips had greeted the announcement. But now the girl blurted the information to David with some amount of enthusiasm. Caught unaware by the news, his surprised gaze reached for Maria with disappointment and sadness, a sadness she suddenly shared at the realization that she might never see him again once she left the *Prodigal*.

Melancholy cloaked them both as they brought Helen on deck and sat next to one another on the larboard gangway near the main braces. Helen, in David's lap with her bear, watched the dancing gyrations of a couple of the men on the forecastle. The music prompted a slight of interest in the child that had been lacking since she had looked for dolphins yesterday. But perhaps her lingering sobriety was the reason

Helen said nothing and now refused to leave David when Samuel and another former Medora invited her to dance. Before turning away, Samuel's displeasure in seeing the girl cling to David was enormously evident in his glistening brown eyes.

David's voice reached hollowly through the night to Maria. "I am rather surprised Jack would send you off on your own."

"There's no one to spare."

Uncharacteristic anger darkened his sapphire gaze. "There should be someone. I should go—"

"David, you can't, especially after what happened. Your father will—"

"My father will cause mischief for you if he knows you are at Leighlin. He might hold you responsible for my leaving or at least for my being at Leighlin previously."

"I'll be careful." She smiled at his solicitude and leaned toward him to make sure he could hear. "I'll be fine."

To defuse his anger, she put her hand over his, and surprisingly he clasped it. Dozens of unsaid words pressed behind his lips and filled his eyes. Helen's attention drifted down to their hands then up at David's shadowed face. He freed Maria and looked away in frustration.

Footsteps sounded along the gangway, and Angus, Dowling, and Smith came forward. Men on the forecastle hailed Angus and Dowling, but the two men waved away the invitations and headed down the step to their waiting boat to return to the *Fortune*. Smith, however, took a bottle offered by Ned Goddard before approaching Maria and David. He crouched next to them, unexpectedly grave, and said to David, "Captain wants to see you in his cabin."

David hesitated. Smith refused to meet his gaze, looking off toward the musicians. Then David forced a small, insouciant smile before saying to Helen, "Sit with Maria, and I will be back directly."

He lifted the unresponsive child and transferred her to Maria's care then stepped aft.

"What does Jack want with him?" Maria asked Smith.

Smith affectionately tapped the end of Helen's nose and smiled before standing.

"Smitty—?"

He finally met her gaze but only for a second. "I'm sure David will tell you when he comes back." He tipped the bottle to his lips and moved away.

A couple of Prodigals quickly went to him and spoke close, eager, their eyes darting aft, watching David disappear below. Then one of them splintered off and moved to others, talking with obvious satisfaction. Exasperated, Maria wanted to badger Smith for the truth, but Helen stirred in her lap with a yawn. Maria searched for the moon and frowned. She should put Helen to bed so she would be rested for the long journey across Charles Town harbor and up the Ashley River, but instead she decided to wait for David's return.

#

Jack sat hunched at the table in his cabin, eyeing the bottle of Madeira that sat within easy reach, nearly empty there among the scramble of charts. He toyed with the leather bracelet upon his right wrist. The object was braided and dry. The two blue beads woven into the center of it caught the lantern light and assumed the color of an angry sea. In the natural light of day they were a bright, lively blue like his mother's eyes had been, like Helen's had been before her father's death. He could still remember the effort he had put into the bracelet's creation in his father's tannery. Better still he could recall the pleasure on his mother's face when he had presented it to her. She had retained the keepsake throughout her years of captivity with Logan, solid evidence that she had not forsaken her son, that she—like Jack—had clung to their shared memories. Jack had been dumbstruck when Logan had bequeathed the bracelet to him instead of either concealing it or destroying it for what it symbolized.

The expected knock came at the door. He stared at the bulkhead, his jaw tensing, then he invited David in.

The young man no longer walked with the aid of a crutch as he had when he had first come aboard. Jack thought of the heinous stripes that covered David's backside from shoulders to calves, caused by a rattan wielded by Ezra Archer; wounds that—much to Jack's chagrin—Maria tended to every day in the wardroom, in privacy, away from the eyes of ridiculing shipmates. Privacy... Indeed Maria had spent too much private time with David over the past weeks, first tending to him after Jack had shot him—a stranger then—aboard the *Alliance*'s sister privateer, *Feather*, then later in secrecy at a Charles Town physician's house until Ezra Archer had gotten wind of his son's return and dragged him home, only to have him escape his designs and seek refuge at Leighlin where Maria once again had gone to his aid.

"You wanted to see me, Captain," David said with unusual coolness.

"Aye." As Jack came around the table, he did not invite David to sit; instead he leaned back against the table, crossed his arms. He thought again of the Madiera but—as he had all night—he refused the temptation to drink, for he wanted his wits fully about him come morning. He looked the younger man up and down, acknowledged that he would be attractive to women; perhaps Maria found him so. Again Jack wished he disliked him, but he felt only an annoyance with his presence as well as with the trouble David had caused him and Maria since they had crossed paths.

"I'm sure it comes as no surprise for me to tell you that you are not a popular man aboard this brig."

"'Tis no secret, Captain."

"You don't seem to bridle under it."

"I only regret it."

"As do I. Unfortunately for us the others do more than regret it." He paused, feeling somehow uneasy with what needed to be said.

David's arched eyebrows raised slightly. "Unfortunate for *us*, you say?" His tone carried a touch of cynicism.

"Aye. You are aware of the promise I made to your sister."

"A promise to Margaret is not a promise to me, Captain. I have no desire to go to England."

"Then perhaps you will not so regret my decision."

"Which is?"

Jack tried to gauge the young man's attitude. There was something underlying, some hostility perhaps. "My men want you off this brig. They feel you are bad luck, that with you aboard we won't succeed against that convoy." Verbalizing this made it suddenly sound ridiculous, but he forced himself to hold David's gaze.

David barely flinched or faltered. "Very well. You are sending Maria and Helen off before dawn, are you not?"

"Aye."

"Then I shall go with them. It seems to me they should not be left to fend for themselves. A man should escort them."

His inference riled Jack, and he stood square, away from the table's edge so he was closer to David whose chest now rose and fell more deeply. "Don't think that sending Maria and Helen back to Leighlin was an easy choice for me."

"Helen makes the men uneasy, as do I."

Jack growled, "'Tis not the same—"

David held up a hand, and his veiled insolence nearly set Jack off. "You have no need to explain, Captain. I will be gone as you have asked, and I will see Maria and Helen safely to Leighlin."

42

"And there you will leave them."

David revealed nothing but a tiny, challenging spark deep in his indigo eyes. Somewhere the young man had gained personal fortitude with the renewal of his physical strength. Perhaps shooting his tyrant of a father had given him this newfound confidence.

"Maria has been a tireless friend to me. I will offer her whatever assistance she requires."

Jack nearly laughed. "I'd think your time spent with her would've taught you she needs very little assistance in anything. She's more capable of commanding this brig or running that plantation than you or I."

One corner of David's mouth went up in amusement, but the expression also revealed something suppressed, something very privileged that made Jack regret Angus's demand to shed them of this young man. "I would think you would be pleased to know Maria will have someone at Leighlin to help her in any way."

"You aren't afraid of what your father will do to you if you linger? Surely he'll hear about your presence."

"'Tis my sister and mother who begged me to leave Wildwood. They were the ones who were afraid, not I."

Bravado, Jack figured, thinking again about the vicious marks upon the boy's body. Well, bravado would do him no good once Ezra Archer caught wind of his rebellious son's return to land. So actually he had no reason to be jealous of David accompanying Maria to Leighlin; he would not be there long.

"If you see your sister before I'm able to return to Leighlin," Jack said, "I hope you'll convey my deep regret that I was not able to keep my pledge to her. And let her know I'll call upon her as soon as I can."

"I shall."

Jack stepped back around the table. "The *Fortune* will take you in, so be ready to ship aboard her at six bells in the middle watch. You'll have a long journey, so I suggest you leave the merriment on deck to others and get a bit of sleep beforehand."

"Sound advice." David bowed. "Good night, Captain."

Once the door closed behind the young man, Jack sat back down at the table and stared at the bulkhead. David had changed since they had first met. In that short time he had matured certainly. But he was different even from a few days ago when he had come aboard the *Prodigal*, weak and shaken from not only his physical wounds but from the trauma of having shot his own father, a prominent man in the province. He had not wilted under the scrutiny and harsh expectations of his shipmates as Jack had expected but instead had simply endured in relative silence, like one used to abuse, so much so that he had grown hardened to it. Or perhaps his strength was not from within but instead from without. Jack frowned and stared at the taunting Madiera. The fool was smitten with Maria. Margaret Archer had told him as much before the *Prodigal* had sailed in pursuit of the *Alliance*, and though he had seen the young man's attentiveness to Maria on board, there had also been enough distance between them to make Jack wonder about Margaret's revelation. Yet that breach had started to mend since Helen had opened up to David, forging a bridge between the boy and Maria as she had done between Jack and Logan.

Jack frowned at the thought of Helen in an open boat upon the dark waters off Charles Town harbor. He sighed. Maybe it would be just as well that damnable boy would be going with her.

With a scowl, Jack cursed his weakness and reached for the bottle.

#

"Lay aloft! Lay out!" Jack's voice seemed deeper than usual to Maria as he gave orders to have the *Prodigal*'s yawl hoisted.

The night's clouds had cleared by six bells in the middle watch, the moon and stars now shining pellucid light upon those aboard the *Fortune* to leeward. There was some grumbling among the Prodigals, mainly from those who had drank far too much during their frolic upon the forecastle, but most proved productive in their duties, eager to remove David Archer from the brig.

Standing next to Maria, Helen—dressed in a boat cloak hastily fashioned from tarpaulin—tipped her face upward to watch the men upon the yards, the night's illumination painting her face a pale white. The benevolent sea breeze tugged at her bonnet.

"Trice up! Brace in!" Jack ordered.

David's silent manifestation startled Maria, for she too had been engrossed in watching the work, half wishing she were part of it instead of the cause of it. He crouched in front of Helen, drawing her attention.

"Not afraid of going in the boat, are you, Helen?"

She shook her head convincingly.

"Brave lass. Looks like the sea will be agreeable as well. All the better."

"Is John coming?" Like her mother, Helen always used Jack's Christian name.

"No. He has business to attend to first."

The bonnet hid her expression, hand cold in her governess's gentle grip.

As yard and stay tackles were rigged to the boat, Jack came forward, the Prodigals avoiding his eyes. David took a step back from Maria as Jack halted in front of her and gave her a tight smile. The anxiety on his face penetrated the shadows. He knelt on one knee by his sister. Helen's grip upon Maria tightened as did her hold upon the bear folded in her other arm.

"You will be a good girl for Maria, won't you?"

Helen lowered her face, her chin touching the bear.

"I'll miss you." He lifted his hand to touch her but stopped himself. "I promise I'll come back to Leighlin as soon as I can."

Helen looked at him, and though Maria could not see her expression she could easily see Jack's reaction to it—a sudden, powerful wave of sorrow that kept him from rising.

Desperate to offer him hope, Maria said, "She wondered if you were coming with us."

This seemed to sustain Jack a bit, and he started to lean forward to embrace the child, but she pressed away from him against Maria's leg.

"Very well," he allowed in half-hidden frustration, standing. "Maria and...Mr. Archer will take good care of you. Mind them, hear?"

"Come along, Helen." David touched her shoulder. "Let me get you into the boat so they can sway us up. Give me your hand now."

Jack watched Helen step to the yawl where David lifted her over the gunwale. Maria thought Jack's eyes had a particular glisten to them, but his rapid blinks made it nothing more. She had been angry with him when David had told her of his orders, not only because of the ridiculous reasons behind David's banishment but because of the possible dangers that awaited the young man on land. But now, seeing Jack's torment, she felt nothing but sympathy for him.

"She'll be fine, Jack. Taking her home may be the best thing."

"But what if she really expects to find her father there?"

"We'll cross that bridge when we get to it."

"We?"

"Well...I mean...me."

He frowned. "I'm sorry this falls on your shoulders, Maria. Truly."

"Don't fret. Just come back safe as soon as you can."

Ned called to the crew, "Man the stays!"

"Maria," David called.

She gave Jack a final, tight smile, but before she could move around him he took the half step necessary to cover the space between them and kissed her. The gesture was so rushed and apparently spontaneous that he damn near missed her lips. They stared at one another, and Maria was unsure who was more surprised by his action. Jack opened his mouth as if to speak then quickly fled. Maria could not move, not until David spoke her name again. At last she shuffled over to him, a pinched expression on his face. His eyes flicked after Jack with an aberrant enmity. David took hold of her right hand to help her into the yawl and someone else took the other. She turned to see Smith grinning through the night.

"You keep yerself out o' trouble, hear?"

"Of course, Smitty." She wondered exactly what that grin of his was for, if he had seen Jack's impetuous display.

She settled upon a thwart and gathered Helen to her to keep her still during the hoisting.

"Walk away with the stays!" Jack cried from somewhere behind her.

As the yawl rose from the deck and slowly swung out over the water, an aching pit grew in Maria's stomach while her gaze traveled across the *Prodigal* and her shadowy crew. David fended the small craft away from the brig's side as the *Prodigal* rose and fell on the long swell. Maria could no longer make out faces, but she could distinguish Samuel's blocky form at the main yard tackle and Jack on the quarterdeck, hands behind him. She felt his attention upon her. What would become of him, of all of them, once they met with the convoy? She did not fear the merchantmen, but she feared the *Alliance* if she was there to protect them. The guns of the snow could throw nearly four times the weight of the *Prodigal*'s guns. Sure, there was the *Fortune*'s armament, but that would not be significant enough to conquer the privateer. So if the *Alliance* confronted the pirates, Jack and his men would be victorious only by boarding, and that would be a risky venture, considering they would be outnumbered.

The yawl settled into the water, and Maria hurried to free the tackles while David manned the tiller. The boat sheered away. Maria shipped the oars and pulled for the *Fortune*. Once free of the *Prodigal*'s shadow, David traded places with her, and they moved quicker through the water. A moment later the *Prodigal*'s main topsail filled and returned to life, and the fore course appeared in a ghostly fall, and when the yards swung 'round the brig started off on her larboard tack, presenting her stern to the boat. The moonlight momentarily caught the name upon her transom before darkness claimed it again. Maria could make out Jack's silhouette at the taffrail, backlit by the binnacle lamp. She felt the awkward press of his lips against hers and wished the kiss had never happened.

# CHAPTER 5

The yawl rode the tidal flow up the Ashley River with ease, assisted only by two pairs of oars, for the early morning breeze was too contrary to allow Maria and David to set the sail. The tide was nearly at flood, the water riding high up the stalks of the marsh grass and reeds that made up the broad expanses separating the meandering river highway from its banks. The river provided the only means of transportation to the various plantations inland from Charles Town, for swamps and dense forests impeded travel by wagon or horseback. Only Indians—the friendly Cusabos of the region—traveled among the ancient forests and lowlands. The Ashley, David told Maria, was named after Lord Anthony Ashley Cooper, the First Earl of Shaftesbury, an Englishman who had never been to the American colonies as a whole, let alone Carolina, though he was one of eight Lords Proprietors who owned the province.

At one point on the journey a dogger—a low, broad vessel— passed the yawl, no doubt carrying supplies and other items upriver, items that had originated in faraway England. Certainly from somewhere within the realm, for—as David explained—the Navigation Acts allowed the colonies no commerce with foreign countries.

"My father, you see, used Logan to circumvent the Navigation Acts," David continued. "As a pirate, whatever Logan plundered, including—strategically—my father's own exports, he could sell wherever and with whomever he so desired. Or he could smuggle the goods elsewhere in the colonies and sell them to people who were all too happy to buy goods that were cheaper than those whose prices were inflated by import and export fees, duties, and the like."

As he spoke, David remained turned away from the dogger to avoid being recognized, for he was well known on the river. Fortunately Helen—asleep beneath a protective awning—did not see the passing vessel and thus could not call greetings to the crew and garner attention.

Maria had traveled the Ashley only twice before, so she was not familiar enough with landmarks to know how close they were to Leighlin or to recognize the other plantations that they passed on the journey. Humble affairs mainly. Only one came close to offering a resplendency akin to Leighlin, and that was the Draytons' Magnolia Plantation where the manor bore a striking resemblance to Leighlin House.

"Mrs. Logan thought the Drayton home so remarkable that Captain Logan had Leighlin built in the same design," David informed. "The Draytons have been here since 1676—almost as long as my family."

"Speaking of your family," Maria seized upon the topic she had pondered all the way up the river and had been waiting for him to address, "what do you plan to do? Surely you won't go back to Wildwood." She watched the muscles of his back work beneath his thin shirt. The wounds inflicted by his father's rattan had reached a stage of healing that allowed him to ply the oars with little discomfort. She had asked him of the pain earlier, which of course he dismissed as insignificant.

"If you will suffer it, I think I should stay at Leighlin with you and Helen," David said, "at least until Jack returns."

His gallantry as well as his bravery in the face of his father's possible discovery pleased her. She was not surprised, though, for through the many trials he had endured since meeting her, he had almost always maintained that quiet courage, and Maria admired him for such fortitude in one no older than her eighteen years. Often she had compared him to Jack, finding so many contrasts, both physically and emotionally, yet even in their disparity both men attracted and intrigued her. Perhaps those differences interested her the most, and she thought of what an appealing man the two would make if their better qualities were meshed into one being. The main divergence of the two was how each reacted to the various tribulations that confronted them. Where Jack responded with anger, emotional withdrawal, and overt action, David answered with inner determination and almost fatalistic resolve. He was more willing to accept the hand of cards dealt him, whereas Jack was one to hazard trying to alter the inevitable, perhaps ending up with worse troubles than those with which he had started, demonstrated now as he sought revenge upon the *Alliance* and Ketch for his sister's grief.

"David, I appreciate your concern for us, but I don't want to be the reason for any more trouble between you and your father if he finds out you're at Leighlin."

The young man rested on his oars, water dripping from the paddles like liquid diamonds through sunlight to water. He allowed the tide to control the boat, his shoulders rounding with fatigue. "My father may use me unfairly—"

"Unfairly? Criminal is more in it."

"Maria," he quelled her outburst before she could expand upon it. "What I did to my father was wrong. It never should have gotten to that point. I never should have allowed my sister to have me removed to Leighlin. The minute I realized you were there, I should have had them take me back home."

"What you did wasn't wrong. You were protecting me. Your father deserved—"

"'Tis not for us to say what he deserves. 'Twas selfish of me, not honorable as you think. I must consider my sister and mother in what I have done. I love them more than anything else in this world yet I have shamed them and done something unforgiveable. They are why I have never left."

"What will your father do if he finds you? You can't put yourself in danger for us. You can't allow him to—"

"Maria, you do not have to worry about my father charging me with a crime." Cynicism rang through his tone, quieting her again. "My father would never suffer the humiliation of publicly admitting that his son shot him. He has designs for me that I have never told you about. To forfeit me as his son would be to possibly forfeit his own inheritance and reconciliation with his father."

"What do you mean?"

David hesitated, and at first Maria wondered if he would refuse an explanation. "My father is eldest son in his family. He and my grandfather had a falling-out years ago. My cousin Elizabeth in James Town is a favorite of both of theirs, and my father is determined we shall wed, and through those designs he will curry favor again with his father."

Surprised by this revelation, Maria held her tongue for a moment. Since meeting David, she had wondered—especially after his harmless kiss at Leighlin—if he had a sweetheart, anyone in the past or present whom he favored, for regardless of his attentiveness to her, Maria knew that no gentleman of David's breeding would deign to consider someone of her station. Not that she had encouraged his attention, but...

"You have no feelings for your cousin?"

"As an adult, I have seen her but twice. She seems a fine young woman, yet what does one see but outward appearances when with someone so briefly? And how does one know if what you see is not simply conjured? I do not think she is privy to my father's intentions, but there is no way for me to know otherwise. Besides," he pulled anew on the oars with particular force, "my intentions are to marry whomever *I* want, not someone my father chooses for me."

The sun's heat grew stronger, magnified by the murky river's surface. Maria's shoulders ached from the hours of work, and her stomach growled, but she could not choke down any more of the water and biscuit they had brought for the journey. More than anything she wanted a dram of rum.

"There's the bend," David said, looking upriver. "Leighlin is just the other side."

The river took a sweeping westward curve and disappeared around a forested spur of land. On this side of the spur lay Leighlin's southern-most rice field adjacent to the river, separated by an earthen dyke, where Negro slaves worked, some stopping to turn and look riverward, but they were too distant for Maria to distinguish faces. The new rice plants provided a pale green hue in their orderly rows. A thinning of trees closer to the spur revealed the place where Helen liked to play near the water, a place where the child had often gone with her parents to swim with her father and catch frogs and fiddler crabs from the dark, muddy banks to show in triumph to her mother.

As if sensing the proximity of her home, Helen stirred on her makeshift bed near Maria's feet. She crawled over and reached for the gunwale, peering shoreward. Maria expected to see a happy expression, to perhaps hear a joyful exclamation, but Helen said nothing. Her eyes, however, grew wider and showed a light of uneasy anticipation, her lower lip caught between her teeth, her fingers kneading the wood as if to squeeze more speed from the vessel.

Leighlin's landing bustled with mid-morning work—slaves unloading supplies from the small ketch *Nymph*, others loading a dogger with wood to take downriver on the coming ebb. Accustomed to seeing traffic plying the river, none of the slaves paused in their work when the yawl came into view. Maria's breath caught in her throat at the beautiful vista beyond the landing. Two ornamental ponds appeared as unmoving and reflective as looking glasses. Upon the path that separated the ponds, an egret preened its stunning white plumage; a second egret stood at the water's edge in patient wait for a late breakfast of unsuspecting prey. The path continued upward over green terraces and split an emerald sward into two equal halves, flanked by bloom-filled gardens. Beyond rose the austere brick manor house with its white-columned portico. A manor now devoid of both mistress and master.

Helen crawled over Maria's thwart and into the bow, standing with one hand clutching the painter. The golden-haired child's figurehead-like appearance turned many at the landing. Arms raised and fingers pointed. Greetings drifted to Maria's ears. Some waved to Helen who waved back. Great excitement stirred all who saw the child. Several of the men went running off, shouting news of Helen's rescue and return. Farther up the river in the north rice field, word seemed to magically reach the slaves, and many stopped work to stare toward the boat.

The tide was reaching slack water when the yawl glided up to the dock. Dark, grinning faces welcomed them, and all work had ceased. The glances of those more observant showed bemusement at Helen's escort and looked downriver as if for another boat.

"Welcome home, Mizz Helen! Welcome home!" those who spoke English exclaimed, bobbing their sweaty heads, straw hats clutched to their chests.

Helen's unresponsiveness in the face of such celebration surprised Maria, the girl's eyes glued to the distant house. As soon as the yawl touched and was steadied by eager black hands, Helen amazed all by clambering up unaided onto the dock and darting through everyone.

"Helen!" cried Maria.

David encouraged, "Go ahead after her. I will see to the boat and our dunnage. Jupiter, bear a hand here."

Maria struggled so quickly to get out of the yawl that the boat's respondent instability slowed her and nearly sent her falling backwards onto a thwart. Confusion furrowed the slaves' brows, curious glances taking in her unladylike shirt and breeches. Beyond a line of birch trees, Helen raced up the path. The startled egrets lifted silently upon the breeze to sail away. Maria rushed after her, not wasting her breath by calling out to her again.

She nearly caught Helen before they reached the portico, but with a burst of speed the child flew up the steps. Defoe, Leighlin's overseer, loomed in the doorway, his expression at first puzzled then split by an anomalous, broad, gap-tooth smile. But it was as if the welcoming Frenchman did not exist to Helen—she barely broke her rhythm shooting around him and into the house where she called for her father. At a loss Defore stared after her then turned to Maria for explanation as she halted in front of him, panting. Defoe's gray gaze went beyond her to the river then fell upon her with familiar wariness. Maria had never felt comfortable around the tall, formidable Frenchmen, not only because of his stoic nature but because of his undying loyalty to James Logan and the inherent suspicion such loyalty caused him to have toward Jack.

"Where's the Captain?"

Maria gathered her breath and her wits. Defoe's attention reached to David making his way up from the landing. The Frenchman's low, overhanging brow grew stormy, and the mistrust deepened.

"Logan is dead."

"Dead?"

Maria expected her revelation to garner shock from Defoe, but instead the overseer regarded her with angry skepticism.

"How?" The ex-pirate's attention flashed between David's unwelcome figure and the interior of the house where Helen ran about, searching, calling.

"Ketch killed him."

"Then why does the child call to her father?"

"She doesn't seem to know or believe he's dead. We weren't able to recover his body. She hasn't spoken to anyone except David since. Now you must excuse me, I need to see to Helen—"

Defoe took a firm hold of her arm, and the dutiful veneer fell away to reveal grief...and still the angry suspicion. "Where is Mallory?"

"Aboard the *Prodigal*. He's going after Ketch and the *Alliance*."

"How do I know it wasn't Mallory who murdered the Captain?"

Outrage nearly lifted Maria onto her toes. "How dare you? Jack risked his life, his brig, and the lives of his men to rescue Helen. He didn't want Helen orphaned any more than you do. Now, damn your eyes, unhand me and let me go to her."

She tore from his grip and hurried into the house. With Helen's return, servants huddled in the Great Hall near the rear portico doors, all atwitter, the sunlight pouring through the windows and upon the shining faces, smiles flashing white in their black countenances. When Maria entered, all four stopped speaking and stared at her unorthodox clothing before they made hasty bows and curtseys and scattered to their tasks. Maria could no longer hear Helen's voice. Instead she heard footfalls from the stair hall and returned to the front of the house just as a pregnant servant descended from the upper floor as quickly as her distended body would allow. When her troubled eyes caught sight of Maria, they widened with relief.

"Rose." Maria rushed to meet the slave at the bottom of the left-hand flight of stairs.

"Mizz Helen is upstairs in her daddy's chamber with Mary, a-crying. What's wrong wit' her, Mizz Maria? I was so happy to see her, but she just runned right past me." Then through the closest window she saw David on the portico with Defoe. "Mr. David?" she said near a whisper. She turned back to Maria in question and with unrest across her brow, perhaps remembering the bloody form of Ezra Archer upon the floor of her cabin after David had shot him.

"I must see to Helen," Maria said, rushing up the stairs. She passed through the ballroom—this floor's central room off which four bedchambers lay—and hurried into the master bedchamber.

Helen huddled upon one of the riverside window seats, legs drawn up beneath her dress, arms wrapped around them, the toy bear squeezed against her chest. Mary, one of the servants, hovered near, but the child ignored her solicitous inquiries. Helen's attention was upon the distant river as she rocked to and fro, face distorted with grief, tears wetting her cheeks. She made almost no sound as she cried, lips aquiver. Her hair had either escaped her ponytail or she had taken it down, and now it draped about her pink face, sticking to the moisture. Maria slowed her own racing heartbeat and approached Helen.

"Mizz Maria," the servant asked, distraught. "What's wrong? Why is she carryin' on so?"

"Please leave us, Mary," Maria gently ordered.

The servant hesitated with a glance at Helen then obeyed.

Maria sat near the child on the broad window seat. The edges of the gauzy curtains rippled slightly with the breeze off the river, pulled back and secured to allow as much air inside as possible.

"Helen...sweetheart..."

When David came to the doorway, Helen asked him, "Why isn't my daddy here? Where is he?"

Maria said softly, "He's with your mother now, Helen...in heaven."

The girl's angry gaze went from Maria to David. "No. He was in the boat with me and Mr. Ketch. Where is he? Where is Mr. Ketch? He'll know how to find my daddy."

"Helen," she tried again.

David's hand upon Maria's shoulder stopped her, then he took Helen into his arms. "We should get you to bed. 'Twas a long night, and I am sure Howard would fancy taking a nap in his own bed or perhaps having some breakfast."

His light, unaffected tone seemed to throw Helen off her focus and take away her indignation. "We're not hungry," she insisted stubbornly.

"All the same I shall have some small trifle brought to your chamber to tide you over until dinner." He started for the door, the girl clinging to him. Maria trailed after them, miserable and at a loss.

Mary hovered in the adjoining ballroom, wringing her hands in her white apron. "Mizz Maria, what's got that poor child so upset? Where her daddy?"

"Mary, please… Could you get something for Helen to eat? Something small. Maybe just biscuits and milk. And bring it up to her chamber."

Mary frowned ruefully and nodded.

Once in her bedchamber, Helen's distress seemed to catch up with her, draining her, and she stood without protest as Maria washed her face and dressed her in a clean shift. However, she would not look at her governess. Maria knew not what to say as she helped Helen into her four-poster bed. Moving to the three south windows, she angled the wooden blinds to mute the sunlight then went to the riverside windows to pull the sheer drapes, filtering the light yet allowing the breeze to penetrate.

When Mary arrived with corn biscuits, honey butter, and warm milk, David met her near the door and took the tray, thanked her, and sent her away. To Maria's surprise, he set the tray upon the bed then began to butter one of the biscuits as Helen watched from where she sat against a pile of pillows. All the while he carried on a monologue about nonsensical subjects like what he liked to eat and drink best, asking Helen about her own preferences, distracting the child from her troubles. Maria watched from the window seat, suddenly realizing how haggard and tired David looked—russet hair unruly and barely held in check by the black queue ribbon, his face dirty and shadowed by patchy stubble, his clothes equally soiled, the collar of his shirt untied, gaping to reveal his strong chest. She glanced down at her own grubby clothing but forgot about her appearance as she watched the young man and the now-settled girl. Where had he acquired such skill with children?

Maria touched her locket, which contained a lock of her father's hair. She recalled similar scenes when she—a motherless child—lay in bed, listening to her father's stories, sometimes in Spanish, sometimes in English, or his songs. Then drifting to sleep, secure in his protective company.

Her heart grew heavy at her failure to reach Helen. What would she do when David was gone? How would she help this child? She was beginning to believe that Helen truly did not know her father was dead. Would she wait forever for a reunion that would never come? Would she eventually despair of it and succumb to some fatal melancholy?

To conceal her fraying nerves, Maria fled the room. She avoided her own chamber, which adjoined Helen's, and instead crossed diagonally through the ballroom to the farthest bedchamber. There she fell upon the bed, exhausted and afraid. She removed her battered shoes and loosed her hair then lay upon her stomach to refuse the sobs that threatened her.

She did not know how long she lay there, but she sensed someone's presence an instant before she felt David's hand upon her shoulder. Startled and ashamed, she struggled to sit up.

"Maria..."

Not wanting him to see how wretched she must look or how deep her misery, she got to her feet, avoiding his eyes, wiping her own. Gently he gripped her arms. Too close to avoid him any longer without seeming ridiculous, she whispered, "Thank you...for taking care of her."

"Maria, it is time you let someone take care of *you*." Then he kissed her, softly, fleetingly, and she began to cry, making no sound, not even realizing the tears flowed until she tasted them upon her lips. He folded her into his embrace, and she capitulated, clung to him, felt the cruel wounds through his shirt. His warmth and strength seeped into her, eased the tension from her tired muscles.

"You must get some rest while Helen is sleeping." He loosened his hold. "Promise me you will try."

Tentative, she nodded, wishing he had not freed her. He removed his neckerchief and wiped her streaked face.

"David—"

"Hush. You have done so much for me; you must allow me to repay your kindness."

He silenced her protest with a second kiss, this one longer, then he gave her a small smile and retreated.

#

Jack's dinner fare was not expansive—cold beef and cheese, shared in his quiet cabin with Smith. During the *Prodigal*'s search for Helen, when Logan had been in command of the brig, a large portion of supplies had been ordered over the side to lighten the vessel. Except for the goat and half a dozen chickens, all of the fresh meat was gone—

eaten rather than jettisoned. This was the last of the beef.

"They should be at Leighlin by now," Smith surmised.

Staring out the stern windows behind his quartermaster, Jack replied, "Let's hope so."

"Well, the lads are a happier lot with that boy gone. And, of course, Helen too—they was worried you might not put up the same fight if you was frettin' over yer sister bein' on board."

Jack scowled. "Maybe so, but it don't set well with me, Smitty, especially breaking my word to Margaret Archer."

"You did what was best. Besides, you probably did Miss Archer—and her brother—a favor."

Jack grunted skeptically. "How so?"

"The lads may have eventually fed that boy to the fishes if bad luck continued to plague us."

"Somehow I don't think sailors' superstitions will be a convincing excuse to Miss Archer."

"And why should you fret about what that lass thinks of you anyway?"

"I consider her a friend, Smitty, as my mother obviously did."

Smith snorted. "Remember what Logan said about that minx. She's sly as a fox and not as helpless as you seem to think she is."

"Logan may have had reason to think ill of her, but I have none. Her letter to Wylder, after all, did help free Helen."

"Aye, for a price." Smith raised one cynical eyebrow. "Don't concern yerself with Margaret Archer no more, lad. You have two other females to occupy yer time, somethin' you need to remember once the metal starts flyin' when we meet up with that convoy."

Jack tossed a dismissive glance at his friend. "I'm to lead these men, Smitty, not follow them."

The old parental tone colored Smith's response: "You know what I'm talkin' about. I know what's in yer head—the same poison that's been there for years: revenge. You've gotten too bloody attached to the practice. But you need to put Maria and yer sister ahead o' that now."

Jack's knife sliced more cheese from the wedge. "I won't do anything foolish."

Smith scowled. "Somehow I find that hard to believe."

The excited voice of Willie Emerick—high above at the mainmasthead—shot down through the open skylight, "Sail ho!"

Jack leapt up and, with Smith close behind, sprinted from the cabin in such haste that he carried the cheese wedge with him to the quarterdeck.

At the tiller the Rat grinned at his captain and his traveling dinner. "Mighty kind o' yous to bring us lads slavin' out here in the God-awful sun somethin' to quiet our bellies. Forgot the rum, I see."

Distracted, Jack stared at the cheese then handed it off to snatch his glass from its becket and race to the starboard main shrouds. By then several others had clawed their way up the shrouds to see what had gotten Willie roaring down to the deck. Voices echoed all around. Some called the news to the *Fortune* under their lee whose shorter masts did not allow the same vantage point.

Willie made room for Jack at his perch, a smile on his sun-toughened face, then he looked back to starboard through his glass.

"Where away?" Jack's heart beat high, his glass already to his eye.

"One point afore the beam. Two sail." Willie chuckled warmly. "And we'uns with the weather gauge."

There was enough haze on the horizon to make Jack's vision unreliable for a time. He blinked and cursed and stared again. Then he saw them, not quite hull up. "Looks like you've won yourself that fine pair of pistols from the *Fortune*'s old master, Willie. Good eye."

The sailor chuckled with delight as Jack watched the topgallants of a third vessel climb just into view.

"Three." Jack tried to curb his excitement, not wanting to be disappointed or—worse yet—alarmed if one or more of those happened to be Royal Navy.

"Three, by God!" Sullivan cried from the foremast crosstrees, inciting further jubilation below.

In time the magic number climbed to five, and a general shout went up aboard both vessels. Jack's blood began to race, and his hands grew sweaty upon the telescope.

"Willie, swing down and relieve the Rat. Tell him to put that damned cheese down and get his beady little eyes up here where I need 'em."

"Aye aye, sir."

Jack cupped one hand around his mouth and shouted downward, "Clear for action!"

Once the Rat arrived, a lunatic grin upon his face in anticipation of riches and the flow of alcohol and strumpets to follow, Jack handed over his glass and said, "Logan said there would be two ships and three smaller vessels, hear? The minute you're certain those are nothing but merchantmen, you let me know."

With mock seriousness, he replied, "Aye, Cap. The very minute!"

Once back on the quarterdeck, Jack watched the last of the boats rise up from the booms and swing outboard on the tackles so they could be towed behind, out of the way of enemy fire. The men's swift efficiency pleased him. Indeed there was none of the sullenness that had existed when Archer had been aboard. He turned to Smith.

"Set t'gallants. The minute the Rat confirms they're merchantmen, we'll change course to nor'east by north to intercept them. Once that's done I want fore weather tops'l and t'gallant stuns'ls."

"Aye aye, sir."

Jack hid a small smile of amusement at Smith's sudden shift to formality, common during a time of action. He figured Smith did it more to encourage the crew's respect for their captain rather than for any deference the quartermaster might have for him.

Within twenty minutes the Rat and his renowned eyes confirmed that two of the vessels were indeed ships, and none bore the paintwork or colors of a naval vessel. Jack took the helm himself, and the *Prodigal* swung sweetly four points across the compass to her new course, as if keen upon the long-awaited quarry. Sails were trimmed anew, and men swarmed aloft to rig the studdingsail booms. Once their white, trapezoidal canvas billowed out, the brig quickened her pace, though the wind was now a bit closer to her beam than she liked it.

Jack climbed to the foremasthead with his glass and remained there for half an hour, taking his eyes off the convoy only long enough to study the trim of the sails for any flaws. Where was the *Alliance*? Not in Charles Town harbor; this he knew from Angus's reconnaissance when the *Fortune* had stood in to send Maria and Helen ashore. Perhaps the snow was one of those five sail yonder. But Jack discounted the theory, for as an escort the *Alliance* would no doubt range farther out in order to spot and meet any threat.

By now the captains of the convoy obviously feared the intent of these looming strangers. Jack held his breath as the convoy did exactly what he expected—it split into two groups. The three smaller vessels— two brigs and a brigantine—sheered off to leeward, two of them putting the wind upon their starboard quarter, the first floundering behind while the crew scrambled to complete the maneuver. With that welcomed flaw in sight, Jack signaled to Angus upon the quarterdeck of the *Fortune* and still under his lee. Even from this distance Jack could make out Angus's astonishingly manic, pleased grin, but the breeze—brisker here aloft—took the pirate's commands to his men away to the northwest. Jack watched in delight as the *Fortune* crowded on canvas and surged ahead, her bows cutting through the swells, sending spray across her deck, rainbows flashing amidst the white curtain. Joe Dowling jumped from gun to gun, ensuring all would be ready when they came within range of the merchantmen. Satisfied, his excitement building with every moment, Jack returned to the deck.

Before he ordered the gun crews to their pieces, Jack summoned them aft. He eyed the merchant sailors among them, hoping he projected sufficient menace when he said, "Any of you Fortunes who doesn't do his duty, your gun captains have orders to shoot you. Understand?"

The pressed men paled; the gun captains grinned.

"This will all be over soon enough, then those of you who wish to leave us may do so, but until then you'll stand to." He gave them one last scowl and barked, "To your stations!"

From the weather rail of the quarterdeck, he focused his attention upon the two ships of the convoy. Surprisingly enough, the two not only held their course, but within the next few minutes they backed their main topsails and hove to.

"What the devil?" Smith said from beside him. "Are they meanin' to fight?"

"They haven't run down their colors, so it appears they mean to do something other than hand themselves over to us."

"They won't have crew enough to handle sail and guns." In quick order Smith's amazement turned to suspicion.

"Maybe they haven't smoked us yet. After all, they can see we're not the *Medora*, and that's the vessel that's commanded these waters."

"But the smaller ones have run."

Jack nodded, trying to piece together the puzzle. "Perhaps just a precaution because of their size."

"Deck!" the Rat shrilled from above. "Three points off the starboard quarter!"

Jack whipped his gaze away from the convoy to see another vessel, flying up on a north-northwest heading, a course that would take her to the same destination as the *Prodigal*—to the first ship of the convoy; she was too far away to intercept the *Prodigal* before then. If that was indeed her plan. The Rat gave him his answer.

"She's the *Alliance*, Cap! As sure as I'm born!"

# CHAPTER 6

An electric current of excitement ran through the *Prodigal*. Voices raised in immediate debate as to whether or not the Rat had correctly identified the *Alliance*.

"That bastard Wylder knew any threat would hang to windward o' that convoy," Smith speculated quietly so no one but Jack could hear him. "So he stayed to windward of us."

"And now he has the weather gauge," Jack lamented. But little alarm touched him, for these were all things he had considered with Smith, Angus, and Dowling the night before. "Maintain your course," he ordered Bull and Sullivan at the tiller in answer to the question in their intensely interested eyes. Then he yelled aloft, hands cupped around his mouth to preserve his words, "Rat! How fares the *Fortune*?"

"She's nigh up with that brig what missed stays and fell behind!"

Again Jack looked back at the *Alliance* and the starkly white bow wave she threw, belying her speed and determination. Then he looked forward off the *Prodigal*'s weather bow where the first merchant ship awaited them, guns run out but hands so few that only three could be manned. Jack glanced back at the charging snow then up at the *Prodigal*'s sails.

"Take in stuns'ls!" he commanded, for setting them had not given the brig the speed for which he had hoped. He berated his poor judgment and sent word below to have the number one gun fire a warning shot at the ship. They were within a mile of her now.

"The bugger's no fool." Smith stared at the ship. "By heavin' to he made it so we can't lay a broadside into him 'less we keep yawin'; can't train the guns 'round that sharply."

"But once we're up with him we can rake him from stem to stern. We'll sweep his deck if he don't strike."

"I reckon he only wants to buy time 'til the *Alliance* comes up."

"Aye. And that's why we need to do this quick. I hope Logan was right about the gold."

"And about what ship carries it," Smith said with concern.

"Brown hull. Green portlids. That's the first one." Jack turned his glass upon the *Alliance* and burned with regret—regret that he lay to leeward of her, regret that to appease his crew he needed to give the convoy precedence over his personal vendetta. Too far away still to see detail, to see Caleb Wylder upon her quarterdeck or that turncoat Ketch. But he would see them, he would find them. Let the bastards come. By the time they closed, the *Fortune* would be able to beat back and assist the *Prodigal*.

At a word from Jack, the *Prodigal* yawed, and the number one gun sent an eight-pound solid shot over the heads of the ship's gun crews who ducked. The Prodigals laughed in derision. Jack waited. The red and gold colors of Wylder Shipping continued to fly, undaunted, from the masthead. The ship's guns fired simultaneously along with three guns from the ship astern of her, but the shots—poorly aimed—passed harmlessly to starboard. More mockery from the Prodigals. With this show of defiance, the brig's forward-most guns threw back her acceptance of the challenge in smoke and flame.

"Lay us athwart her hawse, Smitty. We'll take out her bowsprit and board her. Let's do it smartly; we'll only have half an hour at best."

The ship astern of the lead merchantman showed no signs of coming to the other's aide beyond firing her guns, something she would not be able to do once the *Prodigal* closed with the other. They were apparently content with letting their consort suffer in her stead, waiting for the salvation of their escort plowing up from the south.

Jack left the helm to his quartermaster then went forward to organize the boarding party.

"I want the two best shots in the tops with every musket already loaded and a second man with him. As one man fires, the other reloads," he ordered, the pirates now serious and determined, eyes flitting from him to the closest ship, hungry for the purchase aboard her. No one seemed concerned about the stalking *Alliance*. Jack wished he had David Archer with those muskets at his disposal; that is, if the boy was indeed the crack shot he was purported to be. Then Jack's thoughts progressed to Maria and Helen, and he cursed the distraction. "Leave at least one survivor in case we need help finding that gold." He gave a small grin. "I'm sure it won't be laying about where we can see it. Now get your weapons about you and man the swivels until we board."

Willie Emerick made a great show of handling his newly won brace of pistols, drawing irreverent remarks while the men prepared themselves. Many wore broad ribbons around their necks to hold multiple pistols. Others tested the sharpness of knives and cutlasses, though there was no need since they had been carefully prepared the night before. The chosen four scaled the shrouds to the tops as the brig yawed again and the starboard battery threw another shower of metal at their prey. The Prodigals had already fired two shots to the ships' one, and with great satisfaction Jack noted the accuracy of the *Prodigal*'s gun crews. The last round had been chain and bar shot; several blocks now swung uselessly aboard their victim, and a large, tenuous gap had been torn in the larboard shrouds halfway up the mainmast. But the three crews still feverishly worked their guns, running them out again for another crack at the brig. Fools, Jack thought. Why should they forfeit their lives so freely for another man's ship and goods? The *Alliance* may save the vessel but she would not arrive in time to save her crew.

#

The excitement on deck filtered down to the forepeak and awoke Ketch. He felt the *Alliance*'s lively race across the following seas. She must be making at least seven knots. Instinctive anticipation raised Ketch to a sitting position, though his bruised form protested such movements.

"What's happening?" one of the wounded men asked no one in particular.

"Mebbe they spotted the *Prodigal*," another surmised, eager for revenge, having talked nonstop about it these past days. "I thought I heard guns."

Determined to find out or at least to avoid the bravado that was sure to follow his shipmate's remark, Ketch stepped down from his berth with a false appearance of stability and strength. The others regarded him with bemusement, no doubt surprised he could stand.

Ketch stumped his way up the fore companionway, ignored the complaints of his body and the driving thump beneath the swath of bandage around his head. He paused on the ladder to allow his squinted eyes to adjust to the sunlight. The brightness sent shards of pain into his swollen eye, but he dared not close it lest he lose his depth perception as he finished his climb. On deck, men who flowed around him either ignored him or cast him baleful glances as they passed, busy in their tasks. Ketch surveyed the great spread of canvas, surprised how much she bore in this breeze. He staggered forward as the snow's stern rose up on a swell, the wave slow to pass beneath her, lifting the vessel up in an exalted push forward as if making an effort to move in complete harmony with the *Alliance*. When the wave passed under her bows, she settled little in the shallow trough before another swell encouraged her ever forward.

Ketch saw all that lay before him like a painted canvas—the two ships of the convoy, the smaller vessels to leeward of them, one of them beset by an unfamiliar ketch, and in the foreground the familiar shape of the *Prodigal*. As the brig lay athwart the merchantman's bow, her starboard battery roared out a final salvo that devastated her deck with grapeshot. The *Prodigal*'s sharply steeved bowsprit nosed over the ship's bowsprit, and the forward thrust left upon the pirate finished off the merchantman's foremost spars, snapping stays and sending the bowsprit and spritsail topmast into the sea.

From the *Alliance*'s quarterdeck, Captain Wylder exhorted those at the braces to gain another fraction of a fathom, to reach the ship before all was lost and the *Prodigal* could escape. A wave of agitation and rage welled in Ketch as he stared at the brig and thought of Jack Mallory. If they were able to close with the *Prodigal*, he would personally see to that whelp's end, and it would not be with the quick mercy of a pistol. Then he would take Helen back to her home as her mother would want.

Ketch watched the Prodigals board the merchantman. Ten thousand pounds in gold and silver lay aboard her, or so the Alliances reported. He wished he had a telescope to watch closer, to see if he could spot Mallory or even the Cordero girl, but surely the girl would be safeguarding Helen below. He considered Maria's fate once the *Prodigal* was captured. He had seen many a man hanged, especially as a child in Southwark when he and his half-brother had gone across the Thames into London to witness executions, but he had never liked seeing a woman hanged, no matter the crowd's enthusiasm, including Dan's. It would be a shame if the Cordero girl met that fate, for she had seemed a comfort to Helen at Leighlin. He also remembered how she had ministered to the Archer boy after his wounding in the fight with the *Feather*, how kind and attentive she had been, like Ella Logan had been to him when he lay near death aboard the *Medora*…

#

Jack climbed through the forward wreckage aboard the merchantman, followed closely, hungrily by his men with pistols, axes, and cutlasses in hand. But they found little to oppose them. Between the well-aimed, deadly fire of the starboard battery and the musketeers in the tops, all that remained of the merchant crew were three frightened men, men who apparently expected death at any moment. Through the debris and blood upon the deck, they retreated before the pirates, aft toward the mizzenmast. Two held pistols, the other—wounded badly in one arm which hung uselessly at his side—half-heartedly brandished a cutlass. Perhaps they hoped their comrades aboard the ship astern of theirs would strike down the Prodigals with musketry, but the range was far too great.

"Ground your arms!" Jack snarled and aimed his pistol at one of them. Impatience seared his brain as he fought to keep his eyes from the closing *Alliance*. The three men hesitated. One injudicious fool raised his pistol, and Jack killed him with an unflinching shot.

"Damn it, Cap'n," Willie Emerick complained. "I wanted to try out these here new pistols of mine."

"You'll get your chance if these two don't do as they're told."

The two sailors glanced in panic at one another and at the blood pooling around their fallen comrade. The wounded man swallowed hard and dropped the cutlass. The other cautiously lowered his pistol to the deck.

"We would've struck our colors," the trembling man insisted. "But the Cap'n wouldn't let us. Said he'd shoot the first man what reached for the halyard." He glanced hopefully toward the *Alliance*.

Jack advanced upon them, his men at his heels. "Where's the gold?"

The two fell back a couple of steps, eyes wild and white in their dirty faces. Terror stayed their tongues. Jack again glanced toward the *Alliance*. Too damned close. There was no time for this nonsense.

"Where is it?" he roared.

"We—we don't know," the older of the two said. "Only the captain and the supercargo knew, and they're dead."

"Stow your lies and tell us." Jack raised his second pistol. "The first of you to help us will get himself a bit of shine as well as his life."

"Please, sir…if we knew, we'd tell you, share or no."

Smith spoke near Jack's ear. "He's tellin' the truth, lad."

Again Jack gauged the distance to the snow. "Smitty, take four men with axes to the master's cabin and find that gold." Smith and his gang were gone before Jack's orders continued to Samuel, "Man the guns. Aim for their rigging." He knew the *Prodigal*'s starboard battery would already have been muscled around and trained upon the snow. The *Alliance*'s bowchasers were only six-pounders, and Wylder would be reluctant to fire even those with the *Prodigal* lashed to his father's ship. Before he turned away, Jack glanced at the two anxious sailors who seemed to hold their breath, eyes shifting between him and their salvation to larboard. "Willie, take 'em for'ard. The rest of you search the hold. Make it quick. We're about to have company."

Jack moved to the leeward side of the quarterdeck as a gunshot sounded from below, followed by the noise of the master's cabin succumbing to enthusiastic axes. His focus turned to the *Fortune*, which had fallen farther to leeward than anticipated. Angus had separated from the brig they had overtaken and was going about onto the starboard tack to begin beating his way back, but Jack knew the ketch would not arrive before the *Alliance*. The odds had grown even longer. True enough, Caleb Wylder would be loath to fire upon his family's asset, heavily laden—indeed his guns remained silent still as the snow closed to within two miles—but he had a crew twice the size, and Jack's men were now spread between the *Prodigal* and *Fortune*, so if it came to boarding—which Jack was certain lay in Wylder's plan—then their chances looked bleak.

With the blast of the guns, now manned by Prodigals, Jack turned back to windward. The shots, of course, fell short, skipped across the waves and disappeared well ahead of the snow.

"Save your powder until your shots can count," he shouted to Samuel's gun crews. "Give it a couple more minutes. Wait until the *Prodigal* opens fire." He scowled up at the sun as it slid behind a fuliginous cloud, a single smudge upon the blue dome above. He would give his men five more minutes to search for the specie, then they would have to flee, to run down toward the *Fortune* and join forces before the *Alliance* could take them one at a time.

Right before the *Prodigal*'s guns belched metal and flame, joyous shouts erupted below Jack, hoots and hollers, whistles and cheers. Then the pounding of feet up the aft hatch, and Smith stood before him with a wide grin as the sun reappeared; his blue eyes were afire like the wave tops beyond him. Four Prodigals emerged after him with two small reinforced chests between them, their faces also lit by broad, delirious grins.

"Take 'em to the *Prodigal*." Jack left the quarterdeck. "Smitty, recall the others from below. Get 'em back to the *Prodigal*, and cut her free." As his quartermaster rushed to obey, Jack moved to the gun crews with conjured calm. "Keep up your fire until we have her free, then fall back to the brig. Understand?"

Samuel nodded solemnly, almost grudgingly. Jack knew getting a crack at the *Alliance*, at the men responsible for Logan's death, infused

66

Samuel with a cathartic energy, a much-needed release. Like Jack, he would not be happy to run away from the snow, but there was no other option—they needed Angus's men and guns.

As the rest of the boarding party abandoned the search below and rushed back to the *Prodigal*, Willie remained near the two prisoners.

"What about these two coves, Cap'n?"

Jack paused to consider the two frightened, sweaty faces. "Take him," he gestured to the unscathed sailor. "He can tally onto a line when we need him."

"And the winged one?"

The wounded man quivered in fear and pain but said nothing, his eyes saying enough. It seemed an eternity to Jack that he stood there in deliberation when in reality it took no more than the blink of an eye. All he needed for motivation was the remembered sight of Helen's father being shot. Here he saw not a simple, innocent man who had followed orders but instead a man employed by Caleb Wylder's father, and it was Caleb Wylder who was as responsible as Ketch for Logan's death and Helen's grief.

"We have no need of a one-armed man." Turning away, Jack ignored the pleas of the condemned sailor. Willie's new pistol cut short his entreaty.

Even with the grapnel lines cut, the *Prodigal* still clung to the merchantman, held prisoner by the chaos of the ship's bowsprit and rigging. The spritsail yard had managed to thread through the brig's starboard hawse hole and become wedged and entangled. As Jack crossed over from the merchantman, he saw Hanse among the Prodigals, working with little urgency until he noticed Jack draw near, and then he quickened his pace.

The *Prodigal*'s guns that were able to bear upon the snow fired again, their target now well within range but providing only a narrow head-on outline. One ball struck the fore top of the *Alliance*, nearly destroyed it, and killed a man there, showering the deck with debris. Jack held his breath in hopes that the lower yard ties and halyards had been damaged or parted, but the large spar remained in place. With a broadside view of the snow, Samuel's crews let fly another blast, but the shots struck the privateer harmlessly above the waterline amidships. Within the next minute, the snow changed course two points to larboard and provided more of a target for all. She was going to swing around the *Prodigal*'s stern and either try to board or cut them off before they could free themselves. Jack's attention went to the *Fortune* again. She would come about soon, onto the larboard tack, which would eventually bring her to the *Prodigal*'s aid. He knew Angus was squeezing every fathom he could out of her, and Jack regretted not having the *Fortune*'s original master aboard her, for he would know how to coax even more thrust from her sails.

Imprecations and shouts of frustration forward told him that the struggle to free the brig continued. The growing bulk of the snow loomed near. Jack recalled Samuel and his men as the *Alliance* swung astern.

The *Prodigal*'s gun crews rushed to the larboard battery the minute the *Alliance* luffed up to leeward. The guns roared and swept the deck of the snow with grape. The large crew provided ample targets, ample casualties. The musketeers in the *Prodigal*'s tops opened fire as did the men with small arms along the rail. Jack left Hanse and three others to continue their feverish effort to free the brig while the rest raced to their predetermined stations.

Caleb Wylder stood upon the *Alliance*'s quarterdeck, speaking trumpet in hand. His words—no doubt demands for them to strike their colors—could not be heard over the crack of small arms, the bellow of the guns, and the higher-pitched bark of swivel guns fore and aft. The snow's guns remained silent; apparently Wylder planned to take the *Prodigal* a prize, as undamaged as possible, confident in the weight of his boarding party haphazardly massing upon her deck. The helmsmen of the *Alliance* put her hard over, and the snow nosed in against the *Prodigal*.

"Prodigals, to me!" Jack cried and charged forward along the larboard gangway. The gun crews poured up from below to rush forward with those on deck, to leap—armed to the teeth—onto the forecastle of the snow. The bloodied crew of the *Alliance* faltered, harried by the *Prodigal*'s sharpshooters in the tops and taken aback by the pirates' bold and seemingly foolhardy move. Jack sensed a weakness there, one he had anticipated and hoped for; some Alliances glanced at one another almost in question, obviously shaken by the unearthly shrieks of their enemy, the brief, gory slaughter wrought by the grape shot, and the dead and wounded men on deck.

"Hold!" Jack cried to his snarling men, a pistol in each hand, aimed aft. The pirates bunched around him, swelled with battle rage, their hair-raising howls prickling the back of his neck. Just a moment longer, enough time for the indecisive Alliances to crowd ever tighter together and provide an even greater target for what was to come.

Caleb Wylder—dressed in the fine dark blue coat in which Jack had last seen him—pushed through his men, and at his appearance some of their uncertainty passed. Then Jack caught sight of Ketch a few ranks back, to the right of Wylder. He almost had not recognized the man because of the bandage about his head and the fresh bruises on his pock-fretted, scowling face. Yet even the puffiness that nearly closed one eye could not conceal the burning hatred in the man's dark stare.

"You are outnumbered," cried Wylder. "Lay down your weapons. Quarter will be given to those who do."

"Damn your quarter," Samuel growled from next to Jack, and his pistol cracked. The ball struck Wylder in the chest, sent him reeling backward into his stunned men. Jack watched him fall, both satisfied and disappointed that Samuel had gotten to him first. Well, no matter; there was still Ketch...

An explosion in the midst of the tightly packed Alliances knocked men flat, mutilated them, sent screams into the air. Smoke blanketed them. Another explosion then another as the Rat and Willie lobbed four-inch grenades down from the *Prodigal*'s tops into the Alliances. Confusion dispersed the men, leaderless now and shaken, diving for whatever cover they could find. Some fled aft, others ran forward in blind panic where the Prodigals cut them down. After two more of the hand bombs wreaked havoc in the waist, Jack led the charge aft. He fired his pistols then resorted to his cutlass and boarding axe. With shouts and curses, he struck down all before him.

Smoke wafted away to leeward, passing over and around him like a ghostly cloud. Through its veil he caught sight of Ketch near the mainmast, wielding a handspike. The stout man parried a blow from one of his old shipmates from the *Medora* then bashed the man alongside the head, dropping him in an instant. His wild glance and scythe-like weapon went around him but found no one in immediate range. Then through the struggle he saw Jack. Unexpectedly he wheeled and fled down the main hatchway.

"Coward," Jack said amidst the din around him. With a new will and the power that accompanied it, Jack sliced his way through the battle. Just as he reached the hatch, the *Prodigal*'s bell rang frantically—the signal that Hanse and his men had freed her. Jack did not curb his chase, though—he plunged down the hatchway.

Just as his foot touched upon the planks of the dark 'tween decks, something solid crashed against the back of his head and knocked him flat. His weapons clattered away. Dazed, he crabbed his hands across the deck to either side in search of the axe and cutlass. A kick to his jaw flung him onto his side. His ribs ground upon a wooden handle—

his axe. Desperate, he scrabbled for it in a blind fog, but his attacker delivered a sharp blow to his arm. The limb went numb. Another kick, this time to the ribs, but Jack grabbed hold of the foot and twisted in an attempt to fell the man. All he gained for his effort was another bash to the head from the wooden weapon—the handspike—driving him closer to senselessness. His face struck the deck, bloodying his nose.

Through a haze he felt the man grab hold of him by his hair and by the waistband of his breeches to half lift, half drag him away from the hatch and farther into the darkness of the deck. Try as he might, he could not induce his muscles to fight back, could not voice his curses. Maintaining consciousness was struggle enough. The assailant threw him against something wooden. One corner of the object ripped through his breeches and gashed his thigh. He fell to the deck, emitting a groan that sounded faraway, as if from someone else. The man's heavy weight slammed down upon him, one knee buried into the small of Jack's back. Ragged, foul breaths, not his own. Muttered words, oaths, incomprehensible. The attacker twisted Jack's arms behind his back. Excruciating pain flashed in his injured arm and drew another moan from him, a pitiful mewl that angered him, made him fight to regain his senses and strength.

From a foggy distance he recognized Ketch's quiet, raspy voice in his ear: "Yer goin' to wish you was dead, boy. And when I'm through with you, that's exactly what yer gonna be."

A garrote encircled Jack's neck, twisted and tightened from behind with something wooden—a marlinspike perhaps or a belaying pin. He gasped and spluttered as his airway closed. His bound hands twitched in an impossible effort to remove the device. His eyes bulged but saw nothing. He tried to twist his body away but Ketch had pinned him. A heavier wave of unconsciousness crept toward him, turned gray to black. A knife pressed at the back of his neck. He heard the rending of his shirt then his breeches. The blackness stole nearer, crawled over him. And as it claimed him, he thought he heard Josiah Smith's voice— loud, enraged—and the garrote ceased tightening, but it did not loosen, and a nightmare pulled him away from reality, back through time…

# CHAPTER 7

"Pay or strip," the wardsman growled.

"But I have no money," Jack's thirteen-year-old voice rang hollow in Newgate's stony gloom.

"Then strip it is, mate."

Jack backed away from the wardsman's reach, but there was no escape. The man's hands clamped upon his wrists like the manacles that would soon encompass them. Jack struggled and kicked. But a boy was no match for a surly man and his villainous cohorts bent upon extortion and worse, once his clothes had been peeled away.

But amidst his outcries and his tormentors' laughter, an older man's roaring curses broke through, and Josiah Smith's wiry form cut the cruel sport short. His charge bowled the wardsman off Jack and sent the two others tumbling away in confusion. Smith pinned the wardsman and pummeled his face into a bloody mess as Jack scrambled to a dark corner. He stared in horrified disbelief as the two other men tore Smith from their comrade and beat him into submission.

"Rest easy there, Jack." Smith's voice now, but not from the prison memory; seven years of incarceration in Newgate's damp hell had sanded down Smith's voice, left it a bit raspy.

Sunlight against Jack's closed eyes chased away Newgate's grays and blacks, but he refused to open them, afraid he would see the wardsman. He still felt the perverse man's heavy weight... No, not the wardsman. This time it was Ketch. The terrible similarities of the two attacks made separating the memories difficult for his muddled, awakening mind. Manacles clanked. The one on his right wrist pressed something into his scarred flesh. His mother's bracelet. He had not had that in Newgate... The confusion thinned. Jack felt the sunlight more intensely now—a rarity in Newgate. It blazed against his naked torso. His thigh throbbed, and he remembered the gouge from being tossed like a rag doll by Ketch. His battered arm moved, though reluctantly and with great discomfort. Pain pulsated at the back of his neck and in his head, the sun making the agony worse. Dried blood from his battered nose crusted his mustache, but when he lifted a hand to rub it, a length of chain brought him up short. He opened his eyes.

"There you are, lad." Smith's voice above him again, as it had been that first day in Newgate when he had crouched over Jack's hunched, bloody, naked form.

From where he slumped on the deck Jack looked to the clewed up main sail, noted the slender mast abaft the mainmast, and knew even without the shackles that he was a prisoner aboard the *Alliance*. The vessel was hove to, pitching on the swell. Smith sat next to him, also in irons, secured to the fife rail. Smith offered a wan smile, deep blue eyes regretful. Splashes to larboard drew Jack's attention to the last of the dead being tossed overboard. One shrouded form they did not heave, however, and Jack recognized Caleb Wylder's gold-trimmed cuff peeking from beneath the canvas cover. Then he followed Smith's interested gaze to the knot of Alliances on the quarterdeck. Occasionally voices rose in anger, glances shot his way. Others spoke and gestured to leeward. Ketch stood beyond the group, leaning against the taffrail, arms crossed, bearded face scowling toward the two prisoners, apparently not vested in the discussion and infinitely unhappy with the current state of affairs.

"Bastard," Jack grumbled, struggling to sit up and push the memory of the Newgate wardsman far from him.

"Son of a bitch had you right where he wanted ye, lad…'til I knocked him on the head with that handspike o' his. Would've killed the whoreson sure but his mates grabbed me up."

"Where's the *Prodigal*? Did she get away?"

"Aye. The lads got her free just as you went below. They're with the *Fortune* there to the north." He grinned. "Hopefully they feel bad 'bout leavin' us behind and will come to fetch us."

Ketch stepped toward the debating group of men. The pirate's unexpected movement caused some to turn toward him, others to step away. As he spoke in a voice too low for Jack to hear, Ketch kept his stare upon him, his unruly brown hair whipped back by the breeze, giving his battered face a stark, disturbing quality. Jack looked away, hated himself for the weakness even as he did so. He knew Ketch blamed him for everything that had happened these past couple of weeks—Dan Slattery's death, the death of Leighlin's mistress—just as he knew Ketch would have killed him long ago if not for Logan's restrictive orders. Though Ketch's attempted murder had been foiled today, he would have all of Charles Town behind him tomorrow.

The men finished listening to Ketch, exchanged some final words of decision and then, led by an armed man who appeared to be in charge, marched toward the prisoners.

From a half circle of glowering faces, the first mate—young, sandy-haired, and commanding—flicked his green eyes toward his dead captain then to Jack. "It appears your mates are beating towards us with an idea of chasing us from the convoy or getting you back."

"And if I was you," Smith said lightly, "I wouldn't wait for 'em. They're a right nasty parcel."

In one seamless move the mate took the pistol from his waistband and pressed the end of the barrel against Smith's temple. Jack tried to lunge for the man, but his chains drew him up short.

"If you don't want to see your friend's brains blown against this mast," the mate warned, "you'd best do as we say."

Jack glowered at him. "What do you want?"

"You're going to call off your men. They're going to sail away from this convoy and let us continue unmolested. If they don't, we'll turn your quartermaster over to Ketch here to do with him whatever suits his fancy. You we'll save for the hangman at the pleasure of Governor Ludwell and Captain Wylder's father."

"Don't do it, Jack," Smith said, undaunted. "Let the lads come."

Considering his friend's bravery, Jack knew if anyone had the courage and wits to protect Maria and Helen, it was Smith. They would trust him. Helen had taken a shine to the old pirate, and there was no question about the affection between Maria and Smith.

Refusing Ketch's hope-sapping stare, Jack said to the mate, "I'll call them off, but Smith here must deliver the message."

"No, Jack," Smith began.

"I promise you they will stand down." True enough, he reflected. After all, they already had that which they had sought—the money. "But I'll only agree to it if you give me your word that you will let him go free. You will have me and my pledge that I will offer you no resistance."

"Damn it, boy—" Smith's manacles rattled sharply against the fife rail.

"Your word?" The mate started to scoff but cut himself short when he caught Ketch's glance. Whatever he saw there made his skepticism fall away, yet he hesitated, glanced once to leeward. "And how do we know your quartermaster won't send your men down upon us still?"

"He will give you his word, as I have given mine."

"The hell I will," Smith sputtered.

Jack held his gaze. "You will. Otherwise I fancy our friends here will turn us both over to Ketch."

Ketch shifted his weight as if in anticipation. Smith mumbled a curse.

"So what'll it be?" the mate asked.

Jack gave Smith a shallow, poignant nod to prompt him.

"Damn it, Jack—"

"Josiah…" He never used Smith's given name, so the deviation succeeded in silencing his friend's protest.

When the mate pressed the pistol even harder against his temple, Smith ground his teeth together and said, "Aye. You have me word." As the pistol withdrew, he beseeched, "Jack. Listen to me…for once in yer bloody life…!"

"Bring the boy to the cabin," the mate said. "He can write his message. Get the other into the boat. O'Brien and Foster, you'll take him over. Landon, signal the pirates."

"Jack—"

One of the Alliances unchained Jack from the mast, grabbed him by his uninjured arm and hauled him to his feet.

Jack held Smith's wretched gaze and said, "Take care of Maria and my sister."

The sailor jerked the manacles and pulled Jack toward the aft hatch.

#

Jack shivered in the night, still shirtless, the breeze moist from the rain that had passed over the *Alliance* half an hour ago. The downpour had soaked through his breeches. His arms and shoulders ached. The first mate dared not shelter him below deck where one of his crew might decide to take justice into his own hands, safely out of sight, so again the manacles secured Jack to the mainmast's fife rail. Alliances who came near to handle bunt lines or clews and leeches occasionally directed an offhand kick his way. High above the black outline of the mast and the billow of gray canvas, a handful of stars made a brief appearance through a cloud break. The storm had whipped up the seas and tried to press the snow far to leeward on her trek back to Charles Town. How many hours to daylight? They should reach town sometime in mid-morning.

During the previous afternoon he had watched with both relief and utter despair as the *Prodigal* and the *Fortune* bore away from the *Alliance* and left him in their wake. Though he kept an eye on the horizon the rest of the day, he knew he would not see his old comrades in pursuit. They had their money. A wry smile tugged his lips; with their captain out of the equation, they had his share of the purchase to split.

Word would reach Leighlin of his arrest, his trial, his execution. Hopefully Maria would not be brash enough to risk intervention of any kind. She must realize that she was now even more valuable to Helen, that she should not chance exposure or entangling herself in his fate. She would know he would not want it so. The thought of never again seeing them filled him with overwhelming pain, especially because of the chasm that had opened between them before their departure. But he tried to force away the anguish, for he needed to remain vigilant for an opportunity to escape, to see them again, even if it meant for the last time.

"They're better off without the likes of you." Ketch's voice rolled through the night, and his blocky form halted above him. He stared downward like a sledge about to fall, his loose, long hair keeping the lantern light on deck from his ragged features. Then he crouched in front of Jack who stirred warily. Ketch's eyes were black pools of hatred. He no longer wore the bandage about his head, and Jack could just make out the scabbed gash that disturbed his already disheveled hair. Jack watched him closely, ready to defend himself, though Ketch appeared to be without even a knife; no doubt a precaution taken by the mate. Keenly he remembered the garrote; if he looked in a mirror surely he would see its mark upon his neck.

"You think sendin' yer quartermaster back will keep 'em safe."

Jack said nothing.

"You should've taken Miss Helen back to Leighlin, not kept her on yer brig. Mebbe yer quartermaster will have better sense."

"You damned fool, she's not aboard the—" Jack choked off the rest of his impetuous words.

Ketch's expression opened in surprise, then a sly grin gleamed. "So you sent her ashore. And the Cordero girl, too?"

The manacles rattled as Jack stirred toward him. "Stay the hell away from them."

Until Helen had been kidnapped, Jack had paid little mind to Ketch. He had been nothing more than a shadowy presence—Logan's shadow, his guard dog at the end of a tether. Now things filtered back to him, images he had been too dazed to think much about before now: Ketch's display of grief over the death of Jack's mother; his brooding, silent presence in Leighlin's parlor as the plantations' mourners filed past the coffin; his tears falling in a rush down his cheeks while bearing the coffin to the grave.

"You claim such loyalty to my mother, yet you kidnap her daughter and try to murder her son."

"I told Miss Helen I was takin' her to her father, and that's what I did. She wasn't affrighted but once, and I killed the bastard what affrighted her. As for you, what good was you to Miss Ella but the death of her? Well, soon yer goin' to be danglin' from a rope, and I'll be the one lookin' out for Miss Helen, better than you ever could. I made a promise to Miss Ella, and I aim to keep it. If you hadn't come here, none o' this would've happened."

And there was the painful truth, a truth Jack did not need Ketch to bring to his attention. Such guilt had been going through his head since his mother had fallen, bleeding, into his arms.

"Ketch!" The first mate materialized out of the night. "Get away from him, damn you. Peter Wylder will want him alive to see his neck stretched right and proper."

"Aye, and I'll be there to watch you drop, Mallory. And if ye'd like I'll bring yer little harlot to watch. 'Less you'd like her to go with you."

Jack lunged for him but only succeeded in bashing his sore head against the fife rail and wrenching his wrists, the manacles biting into him. He writhed like a chained bear, striking out with his bare feet, but Ketch moved out of reach, anger gone, replaced by a cold look of satisfaction.

# CHAPTER 8

Leighlin was not the same to Maria. The house rang hollow compared to those short days when Jack and Logan had been there with her, when she had been getting to know Helen among this unimaginable splendor—the magnificent Georgian-Palladian house, enchanting gardens, mysterious swamps, and fertile fields. She had not been there of her own free will, but Helen had been unaware of the events that led to Maria's indenture and had welcomed her new governess with an open heart. The child had been starved for adult female companionship, a need even greater after the death of her mother. Helen's spirit and laughter had driven away Maria's own anxieties and disappointments. Now there was no laughter, and the gardens and house lay in a torpor.

So today when Helen had expressed a desire to see her pony, Maria happily accompanied her along the oak-lined lane leading to Leighlin's stables. The giant, gnarled trees with their wads of dangling moss provided a canopy of shade while the sandy soil produced tiny puffs of dust beneath the pair's feet. Mockingbirds called amidst the noise of insects and tree frogs, answered occasionally by the hair-raising cry of the peacock that liked to strut about, iridescent tail touching the ground, as if he ruled all of Leighlin. To Maria's right, out upon the broad rear greensward, a flock of sheep grazed placidly along with milking cows of white and fawn. Lambs cavorted about their mothers or lay in exhaustion in the shade of the bordering live oaks. They were an oddly speckled white with dark legs like their mothers' and homely to Maria's eyes. Gray squirrels scurried among the oaks, a pair chasing each other in dizzying circles before darting up a tree, a display that normally would have delighted Helen, but she took no notice.

Maria passed a familiar bench near the edge of the lane. The very sight of it pained her. Quickly she diverted her eyes, for it was all too easy to remember Margaret Archer there in Jack's arms, her lips pressed to his. She thought of Jack's awkward, parting kiss aboard the *Prodigal* and of the comfort of David's recent kiss. The usual comparison of the two young men tangled her thoughts.

Small clapboard cabins that bordered the far side of the stable yard were quiet here in the worst of the day's blistering heat, a time each day when work on the plantation halted for several hours. The slaves who lived in these cabins were Leighlin's skilled tradesmen—the carpenter, blacksmith, cooper, and the like. Those men and their wives now sat outside in the shade offered by a line of hickory trees that stretched the length of the cabins, but no laughter or loud talk could be heard as on other days. Even the three small children playing nearby seemed subdued. The blacksmith's shop opposite the cabins was silent, the forge cold. Maria frowned. The slaves did not work, yet David, Hugh Rogers, and Brian Dell chose to do so—even now they were in the west woods, chopping wood to be sold downriver. But she was glad David had a way to keep his mind off his troubles and uncertainty about his future; she envied him.

Maria admitted ignorance of the assignments of the slave workforce required for Leighlin's daily operation. The field hands, David had told her, were very unsettled and anxious since word had spread about Logan's death, and the same appeared true of the house servants. Of course the slaves' daily duties did not rely upon Leighlin's master but upon Defoe as overseer and the various drivers, for in the past Logan had been at sea more than at Leighlin. So in that sense their lives had not changed, yet they seemed restless nonetheless, perhaps unsure what their long-term fate might be. Maria wondered who could ease their concerns, for it certainly was not her place. Indeed, what would happen to Leighlin now that master and mistress were dead? She had never considered the legal ramifications but now worried that perhaps Ezra Archer—as Logan's business partner—might hold some sway over such matters. And what would it mean for Helen?

At the open doors of the barn, Maria asked Helen, "Why don't you bring your pony into the barn and give her a good grooming? I'll go find some brushes while you fetch her."

Without a word Helen started for the pasture where the mares— one enormously pregnant, one with a foal by its side—dozed with the pony in the shade of an ancient oak, side by side, head to tail, languidly swishing flies from each other.

Maria entered the tack room in the cool, silent barn. She had expected to see Jemmy, the mulatto stable-boy, but he was strangely absent. When she returned to the aisle, she heard the quiet, rhythmic clop of the pony's hooves, then the bay mare rounded the end of the barn with her small mistress. But just as they entered, Helen stopped in her tracks, attention riveted to the far end of the aisle. Maria followed her stare and softly gasped.

There stood Ketch, backlit by sunlight from an intersecting aisle, his face almost in complete shadow. When he slowly drew adjacent to the first stalls, light through the windows detailed his bruised face. Then he halted as if afraid of frightening them off. His dark eyes—one blackened—showed a profound lack of sleep, his hair loose and trailing in greasy strands about his dirty, bearded face. His expression lacked the usual menace and instead radiated a certain subtle desperation. He stood with rounded shoulders, appearing stiff through his entire body. Blood stained his shirt—old blood, days old perhaps, the very sight of it directing Maria's thoughts to something she feared greater than anything.

She regained her senses and turned to Helen, forced calm into her voice, "Helen, sweetie, put your pony in her stall."

Helen did not move immediately, but the pony knew its business and started toward the stall regardless of the girl's immobility. Helen mechanically unhooked the lead rope. Quickly Maria latched the door after the pony then drew Helen close, yet her touch did not break the child's spell.

"Helen, why don't you run back to the house for now while I talk to Mr. Ketch? You can come back later to brush your pony."

The girl moved away from her as if to obey, but she did not leave, nor did she stop staring at Ketch whose face now bore a troubled frown. She hugged the ever-present toy bear to her chest.

"Mr. Ketch…did my daddy come back with you?" Her question was genuine and bore no accusation.

Ketch's forehead smoothed with surprise, and his gaze flicked to Maria. He advanced a couple of steps but halted when Maria pulled Helen back to her. At last he answered, "No, Miss Helen."

"Where is he?"

The open discomfort on his battered face stunned Maria. She bent down to speak into Helen's ear. "Go back to the house now, sweetheart. I'll be there directly."

Helen gave Ketch one last, peculiar look, as though she did not believe him, then left the barn.

Maria wished she had more than horse brushes near at hand; a pitchfork would have been comforting. "How dare you come here?"

He scowled. "This is me home now, more'n yers. I made a promise to Miss Ella, to keep her daughter safe."

"Safe? You kidnapped her!"

"To get Logan to come out. You should be thankin' me."

"Thanking you? How can you—"

"You wanted him dead, for murderin' yer father back in Cayona. You told me yerself after Logan killed Dan that I should get to him afore he got to me."

Maria was struck speechless. Surely this man could not think he had done her a favor by making Helen an orphan? Unwittingly her gaze dropped to the base of his neck and the strange scar he bore there—two small, round discolorations set an inch or more apart above his sternum; his beard hid a matching scar under his chin which she had seen before. Quickly she refocused. "You were aboard the *Alliance*. Where is she now?"

"In Charles Town harbor with her captain dead and yer captain in chains, bound for the hangman's noose."

"What?" She produced the question with very little volume before continuing with false resolve. "I don't believe you."

As if insulted that she would think him a liar, Ketch answered coldly, "You don't have to believe me; you'll hear 'bout his arrest from others soon enough."

Maria desperately needed to lean against something, but the closest support was the stall door just out of reach, and she refused to reveal so much weakness to him, here with the two of them alone; she could only hope that Helen would tell someone at the house of Ketch's presence. She could not find her voice and felt foolish just standing there, staring at him in horrified disbelief. He stepped closer to her but not within reach. Her agony over Jack's circumstance overpowered her fear, killing her innate desire to stay physically distant, a fear reinforced by the memory of when Ketch had once nearly choked her to death.

"Yer boy captain said to tell you don't come to Charles Town; he said stay out o' his business and stay with Miss Helen."

"You're lying."

His expression darkened. "You know he don't want Miss Helen to lose you. You and me is all she has left."

She scoffed at his presumptuous words. "You and me? Defoe will have you dead the minute he sets eyes on you. I'd do it myself if I had a gun right now."

One corner of Ketch's mouth twitched upward in a smile likened to a man privy to a secret.

"If Jack was arrested, what about the others?"

"His crew, ye mean? Aye. They left 'im. Took the gold out o' that merchantman and killed Captain Wylder, then left Mallory behind. He

80

came after me when they boarded the *Alliance*." He gave a small grin. "His mistake."

"What did you do to him?"

"Not nigh what I wanted."

Somehow she kept from charging him with fists flailing. He had to be lying. She must run to the house, find Defoe, find David. David... She must not let Ketch know he was at Leighlin, for he would inform Ezra Archer.

When she tried to flee, Ketch grabbed her wrist in a painful hold, his cold gaze demanding. "Yer not goin' to leave Leighlin. He told you to stay. *I'm* tellin' you to stay. And if I have to, I'll *make* you stay...'til that boy's on his way back to England to hang." The chill in his words, the iron clasp of his fingers froze Maria to the spot, his brown eyes hypnotizing her. "'Tis for Miss Helen's good. You can't abandon her to yer foolishness." He pulled her closer into his unwashed smell. "She needs a woman's care. She needs protection. That boy can't help her no more."

From deep within herself Maria found the strength to rip herself from his grasp. Surprisingly he did not reach for her, nor did he chase after her as she raced from the barn.

#

Ketch shadowed Maria as she rushed back to the house. She was unaware, of course; he was skilled at keeping out of sight when needed. He had moved along the inner square of the stable yard, observed by slaves who would be too fearful of him to report his movements to anyone. From there he sidled down a wooded slope that fell away to a sluggish creek. Cloaked in shade, he watched Maria disappear at a run into the house. He settled there on his stomach, his eyes just clearing the top of the slope, and waited. Would the girl stay here or rush off headlong for Charles Town to try to help that stupid boy? Surprisingly he had not been able to predict her ultimate reaction to the confrontation in the barn. She was attached to Mallory; that much was certain, but her compassion for Helen was equally evident. Everything rested upon her belief in the false warning he had given her.

Within minutes of Maria entering the house, he heard Defoe's voice as the Frenchman emerged upon the rear portico along with one of the servants, Nahum. After receiving instructions, the young slave bolted off in a direction opposite what Ketch expected—not to the river but instead toward the interior of the plantation, back along a lane that led to the slave settlement and beyond. Frustrated, he scowled and settled for a longer wait as his stomach needled him. He had not eaten in twelve hours, for once he had left the *Alliance* he had forsaken the opportunity of a meal in Charles Town and instead hurried to secure passage up the Ashley River.

At the memory of Helen's questions in the stable, he grew morose. He had been prepared for her to be angry with him, frightened perhaps or repulsed, had steeled himself to accept her hate—as he accepted the hate of so many others—but the animosity had not come. Instead there had been hopeful curiosity in her blue eyes. Hatred would have been easier to endure. How could she not have seen him shoot her father? Had the Cordero girl shielded her?

His gaze lingered upon the house. Leighlin would not be a welcoming place for him now; not that anyone there had ever held any affection for him. The white men had merely tolerated him; the slaves had always feared him, not for what they had seen but for what they had heard about his ways from slaves at Archer's plantation as well as from Leighlin's drivers who conjured up Ketch's image like some Beelzebub to keep them in line if needed. Then there had been the incident with Jemmy after Mallory had first come to Leighlin. If they had any doubts about his reputation before that day, they did not afterward.

Soon Hiram Willis emerged from the lower level of the house with two other white men, ex-Medoras who worked at Leighlin. All were armed. Ketch flattened himself even closer to the ground, though he knew they could not see him in his concealed position. Willis was second in command to Defoe when Logan was not there; he also served as driver and physician to both man and beast, having spent years in the Royal Navy as a surgeon's mate. Ketch despised Willis most of all among Leighlin's ex-sailors. Willis was a suspicious man and had resented Ketch's position with Logan. He also carried a general bitterness toward life for his fall from the *Medora*'s fore topsail yard, an accident that had left him with a limp and a back that pained him still.

The men listened to Willis's instructions then fanned out in different directions. The youngest, Gabriel, left the portico at a quick pace and circled the house in Ketch's direction. Ketch pressed his face to the ground, though he was certain the fool boy would not cut through these trees. When Ketch chanced a slight movement to locate Gabriel, he saw him down to the right, headed along the lane that paralleled the creek and led to the main landing. Ketch relaxed again.

Time passed, and no one else emerged from the house, not even Maria. Foolishly he almost fell asleep amongst the fallen leaves from years past, soft and inviting. But the jangle of harness called his attention to a mule-drawn wagon emerging from the trees far across the rear sward, driven at a fast clip—that is, fast for the lazy mules in this heat anyway. Three men in the wagon—two he recognized from Mallory's crew, and the third... Ketch knew him well. He could not help but grin at the boy's audacity to be at Leighlin. Obviously he had developed a loyalty to the Cordero girl, for what else could have brought David Archer back within his father's reach?

Within half an hour of entering the house, Dell and Rogers emerged onto the front portico, followed by Maria who hovered about them, talking with animation. Then they hurried to the landing while Maria remained on the portico, pacing, glancing toward the river, chewing on her fingernails or toying with her locket. Ketch was partly surprised that she remained behind, for she was brasher than any woman he had ever met. He was relieved. Her decision to stay behind told him much about her, about the depth of her feelings for Helen as well as her sense of feminine duty. And perhaps it also had something to do with that damned Archer boy.

Once the two men set sail downriver, Ketch waited until Maria at last stepped hesitantly inside the house. Then he retreated into the dark, swampy forest beyond the creek. From there he made his way back down below the south rice field where he had concealed the skiff he had stolen from Charles Town's waterfront.

\#

The tide was against Ketch, but his strong arms forced the boat upriver. Thankfully the breeze was in his favor, for his muscles still ached from the beating he had suffered aboard the *Alliance*. He paid no attention to the forests and marshes to either side; he concentrated only upon his strokes, making them deep and broad, the creak of the oars giving him a metronome with which to monitor his consistency. He had been this way many times in the past two years, accompanying the Logans whenever they traveled to Ezra Archer's Wildwood Plantation or when attending to errands for his captain, so only occasionally did he now have to glance upriver to find his way. A shallop belonging to Wildwood passed him early on, nestled deep in the water with the weight of cargo bound for Charles Town markets. The boatmen— Negroes and a single white man—paid him no heed.

The rhythm of the oars lulled him into wandering thoughts, thoughts that—as so often happened since Ella Logan's death—took him back to his time spent with her. One golden day with her upon this river stood out in a contrast of happiness and sorrow. She had been summoned to Wildwood by the Archer children, for their mother had fallen gravely ill, and they—like Ketch—knew Ella's great gift of comforting those in need. Only severe pneumonia kept Logan from accompanying his wife, and so on that day—unlike any other before or after—Logan had been absent when Ketch escorted his mistress to Wildwood.

The journey had infused Ella with a unique giddiness; she talked of anything and everything that captured her fancy, many of them subjects Ketch did not understand, words she did not necessarily direct at him and sometimes said to the two slave boatmen; carefree chatter the likes of which Ketch had never before heard from her, a girlishness he was happy to witness. She did not seem to mind that he rarely responded to any of her comments, too bewildered by her behavior and Logan's absence to do so. She even insisted upon taking the tiller once. He would never forget her broad smile of satisfaction as she guided the yawl, sitting there in the stern-sheets in a beautiful blue dress and matching hat.

Yet by the time Ella's visit at Wildwood had ended and she returned to him at the landing, the gaiety had fled her face, and her eyes showed red rims from crying. As he helped her into the boat, she said nothing, wiping self-consciously at her streaked face. He tried to credit her sadness simply to the seriousness of Anna Archer's illness, yet he knew her to be stronger than that. After all, Mrs. Archer had been unhealthy for a long time, so seeing the woman laid low was nothing new. He wanted to inquire but knew it was not his place, nor did he have the ability to properly verbalize his concern. The boatmen stared wordlessly at one another, uncomfortable with their mistress's demeanor, until Ketch growled at them to shove off.

She said not a word for most of the return trip, her gaze lost upon the passing marshes, nearly unblinking even in the glare of sunlight off the water. Her skin was pale and tight, hands pressed together in her lap. The closer they came to Leighlin, the more anxious she grew, her fingers spasmodically grasping the fabric of her skirt, her eyelids blinking as if in another battle with tears. Her distress agitated Ketch.

When they were almost to Leighlin's busy landing, she turned to him, and the emotions on her face stopped his breathing as did her touch when she boldly took hold of his calloused hands. She leaned in, her voice too quiet for anyone but him to hear.

"There is something you must do for me, Ketch."

He feared her request, for what could make her so desperate that she dared touch him and speak intimately to him? And what of the slaves witnessing such an exchange? If they misconstrued the moment and word got back to Logan, his captain would have his head on a plate.

"Once we are at the dock," she said, "you must go to the house and find Helen. Bring her to me at the landing. Do not say anything to anyone."

His unease grew to an unbearable level, and he wished he were anywhere but in that boat.

"Do you understand?" she emphasized near a whisper.

He wanted to plead with her to reconsider whatever it was she planned to do.

Quieter still she said, "You will then take us downriver."

Although the knowledge that he would not be left behind to answer to Logan eased his anxiety, he feared for her well-being even more once Logan realized she was gone.

"You must hurry," she said the instant the boat touched the dock. "Go."

He did hurry, his heart pounding in his chest until he could hear it in his ears, sweat pouring down his body from more than just the sub-tropic sun.

Instinctively and with dread he knew where to find Helen—in her father's chamber. When he softly knocked on the bedchamber door, the child answered then stood with the door only half open, as if to protect her bedridden father from all intruders. Ketch put a finger to his lips and beckoned for Helen to come into the ballroom.

"Who is it, Helen?" Logan croaked from the darkened interior, freezing Ketch's blood.

"It's Mr. Ketch, Daddy."

"Ketch… Did my wife's visit go well?"

"Aye, sir. I—I'm sure she'll be up to see you soon, sir."

"Very well."

"I'll fetch Mamma," Helen pronounced.

"Thank you, lamb."

As Ketch led the way downstairs, he wished he could pick Helen up and carry her for the sake of expediency, but he knew the child would not let him touch her. So instead he had to endure her childish dawdling as she prattled about her father's illness on their way outside and down the portico steps.

"Why is Mamma still at the landing?"

Ketch winced, certain the girl's voice carried over Leighlin's every acre. "I'm not sure, Miss Helen, but she wanted me to bring you to her."

It seemed to take forever to coax the child past the gardens—she lingered to chase a particular butterfly then to pluck daisies that she said she would take with her when she returned to her father. Once near the ponds she stalked a brown stork until it flew away. By then Ketch was beside himself with frustration and apprehension, so much so that he nearly snatched the child up to carry her the rest of the way, but he knew that would cause an outburst and draw too much attention. Yet surely her mother must be frantic by now.

When they reached the landing, he found the boatmen had been dismissed, but other slaves bustled about, loading wood and deer hides onto a dogger. Helen charged forward when she saw her mother, calling happily to her.

"Look, Mamma, I picked some flowers to take back to Daddy. He wants you to come see him. He said if you come and kiss him, he's quite certain he'll be well again."

With a forced smile Ella carefully stood in the moored boat and stretched out her arms. "Come into the boat first, Helen. We are going for a ride."

"But what about Daddy?" Helen stopped just out of reach. "You must go see him. He said you've been gone too long."

"I shall. But first I want to take you for a ride."

"Can't we go later with Daddy?"

"Daddy is not feeling well enough to take us out." Ella's eyes flashed with concern toward Ketch where he stood uneasily behind Helen. "Come along now. We will not be gone long." She held out her hands again. With a reluctant frown, Helen stepped forward and let her mother lower her into the boat.

Ketch quickly cast off the lines and stepped into the yawl. He reached for a pair of oars and struggled with uncharacteristic ineptness with the tholes. Without thinking of his gentile companions, he loosed a string of oaths that made Helen gasp and rebuke him.

"Boat those oars, Ketch," Defoe's harsh voice sent dread flowing down into Ketch's limbs like hot tar. With Helen on her lap, Ella stared at Ketch, her face as white as the furled sail upon the yawl's mast. Defoe towered above him on the dock, a pistol in hand, his broad face fierce with outrage. Then a flutter of white caught Ketch's eye as Logan descended the terraces in nightshirt and dressing gown, moving with the awkwardness of an invalid but with deadly purpose, pistol in his grasp, its dark metal contrasted against the brilliant jade of the terrace grass.

Helen struggled to stand up. "Daddy!" She waved. "We're going for a boat ride!"

Ketch sought direction from his mistress, but sorrow had turned her face gray, and despair drained strength and resolve from her. With shoulders bent, she blinked away tears and flatly said, "We are not going anywhere, Mr. Defoe. There is no need to threaten anyone."

Helen frowned. "Why do you have a gun, Mr. Defoe?"

Defoe's lethal stare never left Ketch as he shoved the weapon into his waistband and closed his coat over it. "I heard there was a dog down here that might need shooting, Miss Helen."

"There's no dog, Mr. Defoe. Ahoy, Daddy!"

Her mother freed her, and she hopped up and down to see her father, chancing a fall between the dock and the boat until Defoe lifted her out of the yawl. She ran to Logan as he drew near, his hazel eyes ablaze, workers falling quickly out of his path. The man looked like death after two weeks in bed, his bearded face ashen, gait uneven but determined as he came forward, ridiculous and undignified in his dressing gown and bare feet.

"Defoe," he growled. "Take my daughter back to the house."

"But, Daddy, we're going for a boat ride."

"Helen," Logan said. "Go with Mr. Defoe. There will be no boat ride today."

The confused child knew her father well enough to obey without further question when he was vexed, though she appeared crestfallen at the inexplicable change of plans. She glanced back toward her mother and Ketch, then allowed Defoe to take her hand and usher her back toward the terraces. Logan glared at Ketch, his fingers restless upon the stag-horn ivory pistol. Ketch steeled himself for death. Ella slowly stood.

"And just where was you headin' with my daughter, madam?"

"For a short ride down the river, down to where Helen likes to swim."

"Did I not tell you to come directly back to the house once you returned from Wildwood?"

"Yes, James, but—"

He exploded, "Then what the hell is this?" He aimed the pistol at Ketch.

"James! James, no! 'Tis not Ketch's fault. I told him to do it. I told him to fetch Helen."

Ketch held his breath, eyes locked with Logan's, knowing there was no escape.

"Get out of that boat," Logan ordered her without lowering the pistol.

Ketch knew Logan would not shoot him because of what he had almost done, for he would know Ketch had only been doing what he did best—following orders. No, Logan would kill him because he could not physically take out his anger on his wife.

Ella placed herself between the two men. "James, I beg you, do not—"

"Get out of that boat. Go up to the house, damn it."

"James…" She struggled onto the dock, still shielding Ketch from Logan's aim.

"Go, I say! Damn you, go!"

But still she did not leave, and when he attempted to step around her, she placed one hand on the gun and took his other hand in hers, pressed it to her bosom, and began to cry, drawing Logan's attention to her. She clung to him, using her nearness to lower his arm, to immobilize it, all the while saying words Ketch could not hear but words that had the amazing power to mollify her husband. Ketch remained unmoving. Where could he go? If he stirred now, he could very well end up dead after all. So Ketch waited until at last Logan separated his wife from him, not unkindly yet with resolve. He slipped his arm possessively about her shoulders and turned her toward the house. With one backward glare at Ketch, he left the landing with his wife.

When Ketch stole up to the house, he saw neither mistress nor master. No doubt Logan had returned to his sick bed and Ella would remain with him, whether she wanted to or not. Two days passed before Logan emerged from his chamber, not completely well and still angry. Ella, however, did not appear, and the servants all whispered nervously. Ketch stayed out of Logan's sight, skulking about the house and the immediate vicinity, noting the oppressive atmosphere that had overtaken the house, everyone fearful and miserable, including Helen. Ketch waited that entire day to see his mistress, but still she remained in the master bedchamber. He knew she was there, for the servants had told him as much. Desperately he wanted to seek her out, tortured by the thought that she believed he had betrayed her. Yet he feared that to knock upon her door would bring Logan down upon the both of them again. So he eventually went upriver to Wildwood where he got drunk with Archer's overseer. Then he had gone to Wildwood's slave settlement to vent his anger and torment on those who could seek no retribution.

Late the next morning he returned to Leighlin, and as he came up from the landing he saw Ella upon the portico where she often spent evenings, rocking her daughter in a chair he had made for her. But now she was alone. Logan was nowhere to be seen, so he went straight up the steps and over to her, removing his hat and smashing it against his chest. He started to speak but choked upon his words because of what he beheld. The woman before him looked wooden and mechanical as she rocked ever so slightly, vacant eyes staring toward the river, dark circles beneath them, her skin pale, a shawl oddly around her shoulders on such a hot day. She did not seem to notice Ketch at all. The pitiful sight of her crushed him with guilt and took the strength from his legs. He sank to his knees before her.

"I didn't tell him," he said. "I swear, Miss Ella, I didn't tell him. Miss Helen was in his chamber when I went to fetch her."

Recognition dawned in her dull gaze, and she studied him for a long moment. At last, distantly, she said, "It does not matter now. I shall never see my son again."

Her words stunned him even more than her appearance, for up until that moment he had known nothing of Jack Mallory's existence. At first he had dismissed what she said as something conjured in a confused and devastated mind, similar perhaps to the strange musings that had fallen from the lips of his own mother after his sister had been murdered. He had never before considered that Ella had a family prior to Logan claiming her as his own. And so, many months later, when Ketch saw his mistress dying in the arms of her son and heard her address the boy as such, he recalled what she had murmured that sad day upon the portico.

Well, Ketch sullenly vowed as his oars cut deeply through the surface of the Ashley River, soon Ella would have the reunion with her son that she had so desperately longed for the day she had tried to flee Logan.

"So," he said aloud to her memory, "I'll bring you together after all." The thought, of course, gave him only bittersweet satisfaction.

At last Wildwood Plantation's landing slid into view. Ketch knew that the black slaves working there recognized him when he was still some distance off. They spoke among themselves, fleetingly, and when Ketch's skiff reached the shore they moved away like a flock of sheep from a wolf. The Wildwood slaves feared him even more than those at

Leighlin, for at Leighlin he had never been allowed the liberties that Ezra Archer permitted, those times when Ketch's demons drove him to unrelenting agitation and the only way to momentarily banish them was through violence. Ketch ignored the Negroes now as he pulled the boat from the water. He crouched to wash his face the best he could in the river. Maybe if he was halfway presentable—a long stretch, he knew ruefully—Archer would at least tolerate him long enough to feed him.

Wildwood was a poignant contrast to Leighlin. At Leighlin the rising land between the river and the house was open and breathtaking, while at Wildwood a small, sparse forest of palmettos, pines, and other trees upon flat land hid all but the roof of the distant manor house. Precisely straight allées set at right angles crisscrossed through the pruned trees and shrubs where slaves tended the plant life. Ketch traversed one such path from the landing to a second lane that branched to the right and stretched toward the very center of the distant house, to the steps of the front door. Any slaves who saw him fell away like shadows at midday. Far short of the house, the trees ended along a moat-like ditch that limited the range of the sheep grazing in a cloud-like formation upon the sweep of lawn. Ketch's battered shoes rang hollow upon the planks of a small footbridge. Beyond, the two-story manor stood, connected via latticework arbors to two flankers. The dark brown brick was a sobering contrast to Leighlin House's vibrant reddish masonry.

When he reached the front door, a servant met him before he could knock. Archer's black servants were always stoic, never revealing anything, even in their eyes, but this one blundered and showed a spark of alarm, taking half a step backward in the foyer.

"I came to see yer master."

The servant dropped his gaze and backed up to allow Ketch into the foyer. Then he retreated to the interior. Ketch knew to wait, that he would not be invited farther inside the dwelling, the inner sanctum in which he had only ventured once when the wayward, wounded David Archer had been dragged home from Dr. Knight's in Charles Town. This was a particularly cold home that emanated an air of detachment he had felt the first time he had come here. It was not like Leighlin where Helen's presence always gave the home liveliness, a lightness, where a family lived, where servants performed their tasks in an atmosphere of duty, not oppression and fear. Archer and Logan both had a brutal side, but Logan had had a sense of justice toward the lesser classes because of his own humble background. True enough, a family did live here—minus the son currently, of course—but there was no familial warmth, especially since the daughter was the only family member who occupied the house; the mother lived in one flanker and the father in the other.

The servant returned to the foyer. "The Master awaits you in the south flanker, suh." He did not need to add that Ketch was to find his way there not by traversing the short distance through the cool, vine-covered arbor but by going outside to take the circuitous route to the flanker's back door. The servant did not move—though he did waver slightly—no doubt under orders from Margaret Archer to make sure Ketch left the house immediately. The beautiful, headstrong young woman hated the very thought of him, Ketch knew, especially since his last visit here.

Ketch stepped back into the late afternoon swelter. At the flanker door another servant allowed him entrance—a gray-haired slave named Jeremiah who alone catered to his master in this dwelling, even sleeping in a bedchamber adjacent to Archer's. In silent slippers, he stepped to his master's darkened office just off the parlor in which Ketch stood.

Ezra Archer was a tall man, but he did not display his height by rising from behind his desk when Ketch entered. Instead, his eyes—the color of the ink upon his quill, nothing like his children's eyes—stared over reading glasses set low upon his slightly bulbous nose. His expression revealed nothing as he straightened, calling attention to a bandage and sling on his left arm. Archer's small lips had a perpetual purse to them, his face clean-shaven and devoid of sweat even in the stuffy room, darkened by heavy drapes. He stabbed the quill into an inkpot, then removed his glasses and disdainfully tossed them onto the desk amidst papers. His long face bore more lines than when Ketch had last seen him, marring his natural handsomeness. And physical pain lived there, too, from whatever sort of injury he had suffered. He swiped his free hand across his thinning sable hair—no gray to be seen—then he reached for a glass of lemonade. His Adam's apple bobbed as he downed the drink while Ketch salivated and swallowed with want and envy.

"Well?" Archer said when he finished, loud in the silent room before the curtains absorbed the sound. "Is Logan dead?"

"Aye."

Tempered surprise and satisfaction cleared some of the scowl from Archer's tanned face.

"And I run across yer son, too."

"What do you mean?" The scowl deepened.

91

"He's at Leighlin."

"What?" Archer rose from his chair.

"The Cordero girl came back to Leighlin with Miss Helen, and the boy came with them."

"How long has he been there?"

"Couple days mebbe."

Archer glided around the desk, eyes now distant, but he did not approach Ketch or invite him to sit. As usual his clothes were impeccable—spotless cravat and white linen shirt, tan riding breeches showing not a spot of dirt, even after undoubtedly having spent several hours in the saddle today, black boots shined to a mirror-like quality.

Archer asked, "And what of Jack Mallory?"

Ketch hid his surprise at Archer's interest in the boy. "*Alliance* intercepted Wylder's convoy and was escortin' 'em in when Mallory showed up."

"Escorted? So the *Alliance* is indeed employed by Wylder as I suspected?"

"His son Caleb captained her. But you don't need to fret about Caleb Wylder."

"Why not?"

"He's dead. When we engaged the *Prodigal* he was killed."

This confirmation of the Wylders' involvement in hunting down Logan and of Caleb's demise brought pure astonishment to Archer's middle-aged face and agitation to his body; he paced to the outer wall then back. At the desk he stared down at his drink, silent for a long moment before the distraction left. "How much damage was done to the convoy?"

"One of the ships and one brig was knocked about right well, and Mallory's men got away with Wylder's money."

A ghost of a smile touched Archer's lips for an instant only. "Mallory's brig was not taken?"

"No, but her captain was." Ketch could not contain a small, gloating smile. "He's under arrest in Charles Town."

This news did not elicit the expected response. Instead Archer appeared perturbed, muttered, "Is he?" as if to himself.

The planter's interest in Mallory irritated Ketch. He should be glad the boy was no longer a threat to his family's commerce.

Archer snapped back to the moment and stepped behind the desk to shuffle his papers into an orderly stack. "At the turn of the tide I will accompany you back to Leighlin."

Ketch frowned deeply. His hope for food faded.

# CHAPTER 9

Jack was incarcerated in a small storehouse near the busy Charles Town wharf, bound not only by manacles, which had not come off since first acquiring them aboard the *Alliance*, but now also by fetters. A length of chain secured him to a stanchion in the middle of the building. One of the town's militiamen had begrudged him a shirt shortly after his arrival that morning and an insignificant bit of food and drink, but other than that he had received nothing. His body still ached from Ketch's beating, but his hunger outweighed those troubling pains. The building stifled in the heat, smothering him in the stink of animal hides stacked in the building where they awaited shipment. The noxious odor reminded him of his father's tannery. He wondered if any of the hides had come from Leighlin.

Leighlin. Had Maria and Helen made it there without trouble? Would they learn of his capture? If only he could get word to Maria to stay away, to remain safe and unobtrusive, to protect Helen from the truth of his crimes; the child had never been cognizant of the piratical practices of her father and brother.

What would become of him? First a trip across the Atlantic, a stay in the Marshalsea or a horrifying return to Newgate, then trial and death. Since the *Alliance* had reached the harbor, he had been vigilant for any possibility of escape, but none had presented itself. He held out hope that Smith would come up with some way to rescue him, but how? He was only one man, and surely the Prodigals were too busy spending their money elsewhere to risk themselves in some hare-brained attempt to recover their captain. They would have already elected a new captain...

For a time he listened to the sounds beyond the building. Charles Town—protected by wooden palisades—was only a small frontier town, but he had not needed Logan to tell him how the port was growing. The wharf hummed with activity beyond these walls, the voice and smells of the sea and the freedom it offered so tantalizingly close. If he could get free, he could steal a boat and ride the Ashley upriver to Leighlin. Or at the least he could stow away on an outgoing vessel then eventually work his way back to Leighlin, anonymous and undetected. But he had no friends here, so whatever he did would be done without aid. Everyone in town knew who he was—the captain of the *Prodigal*, the pirate brig that had plagued shipping in and out of the harbor for weeks and had cost many of the inhabitants a considerable sum in goods. The new governor, Philip Ludwell, was no friend to pirates, something that could not always be said for the young province's former governors or some of the citizens. No doubt Ludwell would use him as an example to please his benefactors, the Lords Proprietors, who wanted all piratical trade eliminated.

Jack dozed fitfully, but his dreams of Helen and Maria shook him awake. Death he did not fear, but leaving them behind, his feelings for Maria unspoken and Helen believing him responsible for her father's death—or was it that she was disappointed he could not make her father materialize?—were things he could not bear.

Sometime in the early afternoon, he awoke from one of his dozes, awoke because of a nearby buzz. As he shook his foggy head clear, he realized the dull drone originated from outside. Voices... They blended together in excitement. Then he saw them—faces in the single window, young and old alike, men and women, some holding up children, pointing, some laughing, but all keenly curious. He stared back at them, wondered what fascinated them so until he realized he was the object of their interest. The attention made him feel like a caged animal, like a monkey he had once seen at Bartholomew Fair; the creature had looked mangy and pitiful, intensely unhappy and unhealthy, devoid of awareness of the children who gaped at it and poked through the bars. Jack scowled at the Charles Town citizens, but his ferocity only drew pleased smiles and encouraged remarks among them. Drawing up his knees, he leaned his forehead against them, closed his eyes and was thus able to avoid the sight of the gawkers if not to become deaf to them. After a time the herd tapered off, but whenever he looked toward the window he saw at least one face pressed against the glass, staring, hands shading away the sun.

Late in the afternoon the click of the door latch drew his attention. A militia guard admitted two men dressed in black, one middle-aged, the other younger, then remained in the doorway behind them, sunlight glinting on his musket. The two strangers' stares fell hard upon Jack. Mourning bands encircled their right arms, and because of that Jack knew who stood before him, though he had never seen them prior to this minute. The fresh grief was unmistakable—Jack had seen the same when staring into a looking glass after his mother's death—as well as

94

hate and anger.

They approached Jack, the older man's slow pace not dictated by trepidation or feebleness but by that draining sorrow. Beneath his black hat, he wore a fashionable wig, and his clothes bore the same tailored perfection as Caleb Wylder's. His hazel eyes were small but intelligent, slightly moist now and heavy-lidded, either naturally or from mourning, Jack could not know. Tiny wrinkles in their outer corners bespoke a good nature that was currently lacking. His fair skin bore a slight sunburn.

Jack forced himself to hold their gazes. The younger man appeared to be about thirty years old or a little more. He stood slightly taller than the other and was slimmer, but otherwise his features revealed his lineage with no doubt—he was the man's son. As if to safeguard against his parent stumbling or falling, he kept his hand on his father's arm.

When the older man considered Jack—here where he could see him in more detail—astonishment replaced some of his anger. His lips started to form words then failed. When he did speak, his voice was soft with wonder and a bit hoarse: "Why…you are just a boy!"

"I'm one and twenty, sir." The senseless words came out defensively, though Jack knew not why he felt the need to say such a thing.

"Old enough to be a murderer," the son said.

"You're Peter Wylder?"

"I am," said the older man. "And you are the man…the boy…who killed my son."

"I wasn't my pistol that killed him."

"Does it matter?" the merchant asked. "You commanded that brig in an act of piracy. That alone will see to your death."

"So it might. But if there was true justice, Caleb Wylder would be a prisoner here with me."

The son bristled. "My brother was guilty of nothing but protecting our family's interests."

"James Logan's daughter was kidnapped and taken aboard his vessel. Logan used my brig to find the *Alliance* and his daughter, and when he did he was murdered by one of Caleb's men; I saw it with my own eyes. 'Tis my understanding that your family has suspected Logan of piracy all along; Caleb took it upon himself to lure the man to sea and kill him without trial."

Wylder's back straightened. "How durst you accuse my son of such a thing?" His insult was genuine; Jack could see that the man truly believed in his dead son's morality.

"Why don't you find the *Alliance*'s first mate and ask him?" Jack challenged. "Although I'm sure he's been sworn to secrecy, as was every man aboard the *Alliance*. Or better yet, find Logan's man, Ketch. He's the one who killed Logan, but it just as well might have been your son; he condoned the kidnapping."

Outrage colored Peter Wylder's face. "You besmirch my son's good name to deflect the guilt of your own crimes. I believe none of it."

"Logan was a pirate," the son snapped. "Everyone knew it. If what you say is true, then good riddance and huzzah for my brother. Someone should have stopped Logan long ago. He was responsible for countless attacks on Charles Town shipping, including and especially my family's."

"Seth," his father cautioned him, obviously unsettled by the young man's slanderous talk.

Seth Wylder. Jack remembered the name. This was the man betrothed to Margaret Archer. A man, Jack could see, who had a quick, close-minded temper.

Margaret. The memory of her unparalleled beauty and strength of character came to him. Did she know of his arrest? Would she somehow try to help him in gratitude for what she would view as his assistance in her quest for Logan's demise? Or would she forsake him since he had not delivered her brother to England as promised and had instead helped kill her future brother-in-law? Did she even know her own brother was at Leighlin?

"Logan didn't come aboard my vessel as a pirate; he came as a father to retrieve his daughter from an evil design. A father, just like you."

"If Logan was not a pirate," Seth shot, "why would he seek the help of a scoundrel like you? And why would you help him?"

Jack had already vowed to say nothing to anyone about Helen being his sister. For all he knew the only people outside of Leighlin who might be aware of his relationship to Helen were those who had attended his mother's funeral. And even then Jack had no idea if Logan had exposed his true identity to anyone other than the Archers; Jack doubted Logan would have wanted to proclaim something so distasteful. Seth's statement alone made it clear that at least he was ignorant of the family connection.

Jack ignored Seth's questions and instead asked, "Why did you come here?"

Peter Wylder's gaze dropped to the hard-packed floor then to his son's scowl before he looked at Jack again. Jack could tell he had placed a seed of doubt in the man's mind, no matter how much his emotions rebelled against the ideas presented to him. When he spoke, his voice had regained the calm that he had first displayed. "I came here to see and know what kind of man could cause others so much pain. Instead I found a boy." He hesitated and coldly asked, "Have you ever lost a child, Captain? Or are you too young to have offspring?"

Seth growled, "None that he would admit to having fathered, I am certain."

"I've not lost a child, but death and grief are no strangers to me. My father and mother were both murdered."

Wylder faltered, a faint reaction. "Perhaps under different circumstances I would offer my sympathy, but I am afraid I will keep such sentiments to myself on this terrible day." Confusion and sorrow furrowed his brow, and he took one shuffling step closer, inclined slightly forward. "You have willfully thrown your life away. You may never feel the pain of losing a child, but neither will you experience the joy of having a son of your own. Perhaps that is justice, more so than simply your death."

The wretched truth of the man's words knocked back any sharp reply Jack may have made. Instead he held his silence as Wylder gave him one last judgmental look then turned to leave with his glowering son.

#

Maria ate little of her supper, and David and Helen who sat at the table with her were mere shadows. Her thoughts hovered over images of Jack in chains. How could this have happened? She glanced toward the dining room's river windows where failing sunlight grayed the paint of the frames. The tide would be turning in another half an hour. Hopefully Rogers and Dell would return from Charles Town with some news, some miracle. If they did not, she contemplated taking the next tide to town herself. How excruciating it had been to watch them go earlier and not be able to accompany them, to *do something*. No matter how much David tried to convince her that her decision to stay at Leighlin was a sound one—the only possible one—Maria still felt as if she were abandoning Jack to condemnation. "You must think of Helen," David had said. "Jack would want it so."

From across the table, she found Helen's blue eyes fast upon her, probing. Her intensity startled Maria and sent a wave of cold fear throughout her body. She forced a smile to hide her anxiety and guilt. Helen knew nothing about her brother's fate. Maria had told only David, Defoe, Rogers, and Dell. Defoe had not been moved or motivated to explore assisting Jack. Of course his first and only concern was for Helen and this plantation, and to tie Leighlin to an accused pirate would bring only ruin, so his lack of action and his argument against her helping Jack had not surprised Maria. He had been more interested in finding Ketch, a search that had proven fruitless.

"Maria," David's voice pulled her from her thoughts. From next to Helen, he gave her a tenuous smile of empathy. "You must eat something."

Helen's attention was still upon her, so she forced herself to choke down a mouthful of beef. Tentative, the girl followed suit. David nodded his satisfaction and went back to his own meal.

Maria knew he was troubled, not necessarily about Jack's fate beyond its implications for Helen but about her agitation over it and the possibility that she might still attempt to help her captain. Then there was the news she had brought from the stables about Ketch. True enough, no one had seen the rogue since, but his disappearance was nearly as troublesome as his presence, for what if he had seen David and carried such news to Wildwood? David had waved away the subject like a pesky insect, but she knew the dangers lingered in his thoughts.

A knock upon the front door summoned Thomas, one of the servants, into the stair hall to answer. Maria exchanged a curious glance with David. Who on earth would be calling this late in the day? Someone who had heard of Logan's death perhaps? In hopeful anticipation, Helen left her chair and rushed into the adjoining Great Hall, a cavernous room that commanded the house's main floor and allowed access to all other chambers on this level.

A man's gruff voice distantly demanded, "Get out of my way, you black ape." Then heavy footfalls advanced into the Great Hall and toward the dining room.

Thomas called in warning, "Mizz Maria!"

David instantly paled, like an hourglass drained of sand. Even before turning toward the doorway, Maria knew...

Ezra Archer's blunt advance avoided Helen who had fallen away from his disappointing presence. The coat draped about his shoulders bore a drooping, unfilled sleeve, a sling peeking from under his collar to remind Maria of when David had shot him. Behind him like a shadow drifted Ketch. Both Maria and David got to their feet as Archer entered the dining room, the hapless servant hovering in his wake.

Ketch stood to Archer's left as though to compensate for the man's disabled limb. His attention, however, lay not upon David and Maria but instead upon the food. His jaw moved as if to chew, and he swallowed, dark eyes ashine with yearning. His stomach loudly protested.

"Pip," Maria said to the young servant girl who had waited upon them at table. "Please take Helen to her chamber."

The black girl seemed relieved, yet she hesitated, for Ketch and Archer blocked the doorway. Maria waved her toward a spiral staircase hidden behind a door next to the hearth, a passage used by the servants to access the three floors. Pip eagerly herded the crestfallen child up the stairs.

By then David had left his chair and surprised Maria by taking her arm and urging her away from his father.

"You need not shield the girl," Archer growled. "I came not for her." He scowled at David, oddly composed. "You will come with me back to Wildwood. Then by the end of the week you will be on your way to Virginia to escort your aunt and cousin here for Margaret's wedding."

"I am going nowhere, Father."

Archer's indulgent look was no doubt meant to disarm. "Dear boy, will you never give up your foolishness?"

David took Maria's hand in his. "Captain Logan is dead, so for now my wife and I are staying here to care for Helen."

"Wife?" Archer choked.

Maria was glad the two intruders stared at David and not at her, for surely her own face reflected the same amount of disbelief as theirs. When Ketch's gaze swung to her, she lowered her eyes. Yet she feared that, too, was the wrong reaction to display, so she forced herself to look at Archer, to neither blink nor flinch. She gave David's cold hand a supportive squeeze.

Black rage flared in Archer. "You are out of your mind if you expect me to believe this trumpery. You are not of age to marry without—"

"You are mistaken, Father," David answered calmly. "My birthday was a fortnight ago."

"Who married you? No man in Charles Town would durst—"

"Caleb Wylder; when we were aboard the *Alliance*."

Archer hesitated only an instant. "How convenient for you that

Caleb Wylder is dead."

"I would not know that, Father. He was quite alive when last I saw him."

David's poise amazed Maria, and she wished she could do something to aid him, but the very idea of them being married and his quick thinking to fabricate such a lie left her helpless. Or perhaps the scheme was not so quickly conjured after all but instead planned.

When Archer took a step toward them, David tried to guide Maria behind him, but she was too dumbfounded to comply.

"This is an outrageous lie. You know very well that I will get to the bottom of this."

"He's not lyin'," said Ketch.

Archer wheeled upon him. "What did you say?"

"I was there, aboard the *Alliance*."

"You mean to say you witnessed this?"

Ketch nodded laconically, his gaze locked with Maria's shocked stare.

"Yet you failed to mention it to me at Wildwood."

Ketch shrugged. "Slipped me mind." His attention slid to Archer now, unafraid, almost flippant, and Maria saw in that instant that Ketch had no strong attachment to Archer as she had feared. He was challenging him the way he had challenged Logan after Dan Slattery's death.

Archer glared at his son. "If this be true, you know what this means."

"If you are referring to my inheritance...yes, Father."

Archer's face grew ever more crimson. "You would forfeit all of that and your family for...for *that*?" He jabbed a finger at Maria who refused to react in any way other than to elevate her chin slightly.

"I shot my own father over her. Does that not tell you all you need to know?"

Archer appeared on the verge of an explosion, but instead he held his temper in check and forced out, "You will not make a fool of me, boy." When David put his arm around Maria's waist, Archer gave her a most lethal look. Then he wheeled, his coat skirts whirling about him, and left the room, barking for Ketch to follow him.

Smoothly Ketch swiped as much food from the table as he could, including a decanter of wine, then tossed Maria an enigmatic glance before leaving.

With the sound of the front door closing, Maria slipped to the river windows to watch Archer and Ketch stride down the sward between

the two gardens, back toward the landing. Their formidable shapes—
one dressed in color and taste, the other battered, ragged, and dirty—
threw long evening shadows. Ketch devoured the stolen food, and the
sunlight glinted upon the decanter as he tipped it up to his mouth just
before disappearing below the grass terraces. Numb, Maria sank upon
a window seat.

"Maria...forgive me." David sat across from her on the broad
wooden seat. "I did not mean to put you in this position. The words just
fell from my mouth. I know not what I was thinking."

"There's no need to fret, David. I understand." She looked back
toward the landing. "But what I don't understand is why Ketch lied for
us."

#

Ketch and Archer reached Charles Town late in the night when all
good citizens were abed and those more questionable inhabited the
waterfront taverns and brothels. Ketch knew not where Archer was
bound and did not care, knowing only that the planter would be
spending the night in town. After four silent hours upon the river with
the man, Ketch was happy to leave his presence for a gaming table.
Ensconced at his most frequented establishment, The Grey Pelican—
small, dark, smoke-filled, across from where Jack Mallory was held—
Ketch settled at a table with six other men, all sailors, to play One-and-
Thirty and spend the Judas money Archer had paid him for Logan's
death.

He drank heavily for the first hour, the coins falling easily from
his hands, for he found himself eager to be shed of such a tangible
reminder of what he had done. But after that, he allowed himself no
more liquor; he needed enough of his wits about him to take the skiff
back upriver in the cloudy night.

Usually the strumpets who worked the tavern knew from past
unpleasant experiences to stay away from him. Near the bar they
chattered among themselves, their laughter reaching Ketch through the
greater noise of patrons and a fiddler. He knew he was a curiosity
among the Charles Town whores, someone to challenge their skills at
seducing a man who always, without fail, refused their attention. After
the first few months the challenge had lost its charms, but apparently
tonight's show of wealth gave them incentive to try their luck again.

The first one hovered about him, but Ketch did not look at her.
"You're a lucky man tonight, love. Why don't you spend your

101

winnings on some frolic upstairs?"

Ketch said nothing, concentrated on the three cards in his hands.

"If that bastard didn't keep takin' my money, sweetheart," one of the sailors said, "I'd take you up on some of that frolic." He and the others chuckled; Ketch remained silent and attentive to his cards.

The dealer asked him, "Stick or have it?"

"Stick."

The dealer moved on to the next man. The strumpet put her hands on Ketch's shoulders. He forced himself not to react as her fingers worked upon his sore muscles, her body pressed against the back of his chair, her breasts brushing him. He won the hand, but the next one he lost. And the next.

"Get away from me," he growled and stared at the new hand of cards.

"Come now, love," the woman crooned in his ear. "Let me sit on your lap and I'll bring you good luck."

"You can sit on *my* lap," the sailor to Ketch's right grinned.

The strumpet ignored the near-penniless seaman. As the dealer went around the table, asking the others if they desired another card, the blonde dipped a hand down Ketch's loose shirt, unmindful of the blood stains upon it. When she pressed upon his hidden bruises, he did not wince. He tried to dismiss her, to not feel her touch, to not smell her, but his resolve was growing weak, and the old agitation swelled in him as memories crept out from the darkness. He lost another hand and most of his money. The relentless whore's fingers drifted ever downward.

"Damn you, woman," he snarled, startling her back a step. "Can't you see you've brought me ill fortune?"

She pouted, considered the dwindling money on the table.

"Well," said the sailor on Ketch's left, "she's made me a quick fortune, so I reckon it's time to call it a night, eh, lass? And to repay you for your kindness." He stood, unsteady from too much rum, and reached clumsily for her breasts. She giggled and slapped at his hands in a vague display, then kissed him and led him away.

Cursing, Ketch snatched what money was left him and stalked out of the tavern. He paused on the dark street, his breath coming in a short, deep rhythm, his mind at war with his body. He swore an oath at the unseen wenches before turning to the wharf.

Distracted from caring where he stepped in the darkness, he stumbled along the strand. It was slack tide—he smelled it more than saw it—so when he reached the skiff he had to drag it across the shingle to the water. Cursing himself, he half fell into the boat, then shipped the oars and pulled with violent, frustrated force along the shore and toward the mouth of the Ashley, which flowed south of the Charles Town peninsula.

Four endless hours of solitude up the river; too much time to think, to remember. *Damn that wench!* He pressed his eyes shut, rested on his oars. Her face flashed before him—not the Charles Town whore but the one in the Plymouth brothel long ago. He had not meant to hurt her; the horrible memory she had awakened had triggered the violence, violence he had not even known he committed until the screams of Dan Slattery's wench had jolted him back to his senses. The young prostitute's wide, dead eyes stared down at Ketch from where she straddled him, his hands still tight around her throat. Horrified and panicked, he bolted from the establishment.

Dan had caught up to him in an alley black from a moonless night. "What the hell was that?"

Ketch paced, mumbling, "I killed her."

"Aye, and you spoilt me fuck by doin' it. Now you best hope we get back to the *Harwich* afore the law catches up with you."

"I'm not talkin' about the girl."

"Then what the hell are you talkin' about?"

"My mother," he said, low and dismayed. "She was strangled, like what I did to that girl. What if I did that to her, too, and didn't know it, like now?"

Surely his half-brother had not forgotten the marks upon his mother's neck or her wide, disbelieving dead eyes when they had found her in her bed, naked and violated. It was Dan who had thought quickly and rushed him away, not only fearful of Ketch being suspected in the murder but to keep him from an orphanage or worse; it was Dan's idea for them to disappear into the anonymity of the Royal Navy. He had always protected his younger sibling, leaving Ketch with a moral debt he could only repay by avenging his half-brother's death at Logan's hands.

"What if," Ketch murmured, "I did it and I just don't remember."

Dan stepped closer and put a hand on his shoulder with a grip almost painful. "I wouldn't doubt if ye did, lad. But she got what she deserved. If anyone had knowed the truth of the matter betwixt her and you, they'd have said you was right in killin' her."

Ketch stared at his brother, distressed that Dan did not try to convince him of his innocence. If he had indeed killed his mother, he knew there was no justification for the killing, no matter what Dan said.

The things his mother had done, the person she had become...Ketch felt at fault, for he should have kept his stepfather's secret from her. Instead his revelation of his infant sister's murder had cost his mother her husband...and her sanity.

Ketch continued to ply the oars deep into the surface of the Ashley River. There was not a wisp of breeze in the deep, haunted night to make hoisting the sail profitable. Strange animal cries from the distant shore on either side made him think of another world, an afterworld where horrible retribution awaited those of his ilk. He thought of the Charles Town whore, and the anger and frustration again welled up. The unrest would grow, he knew; it would build all the way upriver and would not be quelled until he could physically purge the torment.

# CHAPTER 10

Jack spent an uncomfortable night in the storehouse. The chain that tethered him to the stanchion was not long enough to permit him to recline, so he dozed in the same position that he had been in most of the previous day. His muscles protested the confinement, his wrists raw and his mother's bracelet frayed from his attempts to free himself from the manacles. The harbor's dampness that had crept into the building added to his discomfort. Although he had been given a meager supper of fish and water, the food was long gone from his belly by the time night invaded the storehouse. His stomach's grumblings provided lonely echoes to contrast with the scurry of mice and rats. When he slept, dreams troubled him—dreams of Maria and Helen, of his parents, of Smith and Logan, of Ketch's assault, of Newgate.

In the morning he welcomed the busy sounds of the wharf that rescued him from the nightmares. Sunlight streamed through the eastern window but did not reach him to ease the lingering clammy chill upon his skin. He listened to the crunch of wagon wheels, the rhythm of hooves, men's voices, and the brush of placid water against shingle and wharves. Beyond the window men moved to and from the docks, no one pausing to look in on him, to gawk. Apparently the excitement of Long Arm Jack's capture had waned.

The calls of seabirds made him long to be aboard the *Prodigal*, away from the stench of fly-covered hides, out on the open water, free, feeling the rise and fall of the deck beneath him. He remembered how he had shown his mother about the brig, the pride he had felt in doing so, the touch of her hand light upon his arm, the music of her voice—interested and pleased. She had been proud of him; of that much he was certain. But the rest... He should have pressed her for the truth when he had the chance. Yet would she have answered honestly?

In the early afternoon the militiaman guarding the door entered, musket in hand, holding the door for someone else to follow.

A tall man stepped inside the building, and when he moved away from the blinding backlight of sun, Jack could see him better. He was middle-aged and gaunt, but the gauntness looked natural, not due to poor health. Small, squinted black eyes peered out from a narrow, hawkish face. Indeed, he reminded Jack of a bird of prey with those piercing eyes and slight hook to the end of his beak-like nose. His wig and clothes proved him to be a man of means. At first Jack thought perhaps this was the governor, yet surely the governor would not come to a smelly warehouse but would instead summon him. And there was something familiar about the man. Jack, however, said nothing to give away his curiosity as the stranger halted in front of him and sized him up with a bit of displeasure.

"I am Malachi Waterston. I have received permission to have you removed from this place."

"Removed to where?" Jack asked with neither fear nor great interest.

"To my home."

"Why?"

Waterston gave him an indulgent, small smile as if Jack were a wearisome child. "Would a private home not be more comfortable than sitting chained to a post in a dark, smelly warehouse?"

Cautiously Jack eyed him.

"You must first give me your word that you will not attempt escape. Guards will be at the doors, true enough, but your word of honor is required."

Jack's mind churned in an attempt to place the man. "Why would you trust me?"

Waterston's dark eyes took on a twinkle of amusement, and he started to turn away. Then Jack remembered...

"Wait."

Waterston turned back, one thick gray and black eyebrow raised.

"You have my word."

#

"Mizz Maria!" Rose called from the kitchen house's porch to the lane where Maria carried flowers from the garden.

At first Rose's voice did not register upon Maria, for a plethora of worries clouded her mind. Had Rogers and Dell discovered a way to help Jack? Yesterday she had nearly left for Charles Town but for Helen's pained expression when the child heard David arguing against such designs. Afterward Helen had inquired of Ketch's whereabouts, as if she needed to find something solid from her quickly vanishing extended family. Maria also wondered to where Ketch had vanished.

106

Why had he lied for David and why had he been with Ezra Archer to begin with? Did Archer not realize Ketch's kidnapping of Helen had led to his partner's death? Or was he ignorant of Ketch's part in it?

"Mizz Maria!" Rose hailed again.

The smile upon the pregnant slave's shining face, easily detected even from this distance, pulled Maria from her perplexity. She altered course and crossed over the cropped grass—a brilliant emerald green from the early morning rain that had given way to breaking clouds and a strong breeze off the river. When she climbed the porch steps, Rose's grin widened, surprising Maria after the deep grief of the day before.

"Please come inside," the slave beckoned.

Curious, Maria followed her into the kitchen which took up the whole front half of the brick building. A passage led to back rooms where the slaves who worked there lived, except for Rose who dwelled with her husband in the settlement back among the trees to the northwest. The four other kitchen slaves now lined the rear of the room, the dark women smiling and the younger two giggling behind their hands. Breakfast was long past, and the beginnings of dinner had begun, but for now all work had stopped.

"What's this?" Maria asked.

Rose's happy, mischievous expression never faded, her hands resting upon her swollen belly. From a counter behind her, she presented a large blackberry pie. "We made this special for you, to congratulate you on your marriage to Mr. David."

Speechless, Maria stared at her, not because of the pie but because of her words. Marriage. To David. Since the eldest Archer's unheralded visit yesterday, Maria had thought little about David's deceit, for to her it had been a momentary thing, a ruse to send Ezra Archer away and provide David immunity so he could remain at Leighlin. Apparently the ever-present ears of servants had picked up the conversation and spread it as gospel among the slave population. Marriage!

Rose waited, the pie still held out. Her smile waned in puzzlement. Maria managed to return the smile, though tenuously, when she realized she needed to propagate this fiction for the sake of David and Helen, for she knew gossip traveled readily up and down the Ashley River as sure as the tide. And though she trusted Rose implicitly—the slave owed her life and her own happy marriage to David's past benevolence—Maria did not trust any other Leighlin slave not to spread word of David's falseness if she shared the truth of the matter, not out of maliciousness but simply as a part of the natural transfer of information among the region's slaves. And, she considered for the first time, if Leighlin's slaves believed the marriage to be true, it would only be a matter of time before Helen learned of it. What should she tell the child? Helen would not understand that the union was anything but genuine.

Maria managed to take the pie while still holding the half dozen roses in one hand. "Thank you. This is very kind of all of you."

"Mr. David...he a good man, Mizz Maria," Rose said. "A kind man. You is very blessed, and so is he."

"Thank you."

The front door opened, gaining everyone's attention. Nahum entered in a rush and slid to a halt when he saw Maria. His eyes lowered in deference, yet his whole being radiated urgency.

"What is it?" Maria asked.

"I was tol' to come here, lookin' for Mr. Defoe."

"Here?"

"Yes'm. No one's see'd him today. Mr. Willis sent us 'round lookin' for him."

Rose's gaze went from the young man to Maria. "He not been here."

Cold memories of the day Helen had been kidnapped flooded Maria. She urged, "Keep looking."

"Yes'm." The servant quickly left.

Maria handed the pie back to Rose. "Would you serve this after dinner today, Rose? I'm sure David and Helen will both enjoy it very much, as will I."

After thanking the women again, a troublesome foreboding pushed her outside, something that told her she had been forewarned of this new mystery. Hurrying into the manor house, she found Hiram Willis in the Great Hall talking to David and the other white men of Leighlin. All turned when she entered.

"Where's Helen?" she asked David.

"She's with her playmate upstairs."

"No one's seen Defoe?"

"No, ma'am," Willis said, hat in hand. He was a stumpy, grizzled man with flecks of gray in his light brown hair and beard, but Maria knew he was not as old as the grayness portrayed. "We're goin' to organize search parties. Not like Defoe to come up missin' without tellin' one of us where he's bound."

Logan's death had already shaken these men, but now Defoe's mysterious absence left them even more leery. Considering her familiarity with sailors' propensity for superstition, Maria hoped these men did not attach any part of Defoe's disappearance to David's alleged bad luck.

"He rarely leaves the plantation," Gabriel offered with apprehension. "None of the boats is missin' neither."

"That rules out his going to Charles Town," David said, "or another plantation. He must be somewhere on this property."

"Is there anything I can do?" Maria asked.

"Stay here with Helen, close to the house." David's tone carried a warning, as if he feared something or someone—whatever had caused Defoe's disappearance—to perhaps prey upon Helen as well. But Maria did not hold that fear. In fact, if her growing suspicion was true, Helen was safer than anyone at Leighlin.

#

Even with his fetters removed, Jack's three-block march to Waterston's home was unpleasant. The painful attention he drew far outweighed the physical discomfort of the gash on his leg. Most of the time he kept his eyes lowered, his dark hair flopping over them like a dirty curtain, his tie ribbon long gone. Townspeople paused in their daily business to point and stare, to whisper or catcall. Children darted near, some teasing, some wide-eyed with curiosity, some ignoring Jack to talk instead to Waterston or to the militiamen who escorted him.

At one point, when Jack glanced toward the row of buildings on the right-hand side of the street, he nearly stopped in his tracks. Quickly gathering his wits, he managed to hide his interest in the two men loitering in front of one tavern. He dragged his attention away from the troubled expressions of Rogers and Dell. Had Maria sent them? Or were they merely in town on business or pleasure and had heard the news of his capture? They would follow him, he knew; they would see where he was being taken. This chance glimpse of his old shipmates gave him a brief breath of hope.

Waterston's home was a two-story structure, narrow like so many of Charles Town's wooden buildings, but made of brick, proving to Jack that he was a man of means. At the front door, the militia officer begrudgingly removed Jack's manacles. One of the guards disappeared around a corner to undoubtedly cover an unseen second entrance.

The ruddy-faced officer asked, "Would you like me to post one of my men inside, sir?"

Indulgently Waterston smiled. "Thank you, Captain, but that will not be necessary."

The officer did not appear convinced. He gave Jack a warning look before turning away.

A white servant met Waterston inside the door and took his hat; Jack had lost his aboard the *Alliance*. The girl flashed Jack a nervous glance.

"Brandy in the parlor, Jenny," Waterston directed. "Is my wife home?"

"She should be here any minute, sir."

Waterston's home was lavishly furnished, and its neatness and style bespoke an attentive wife. The windows yawned open enough to welcome the sweet sea breeze that was freshening over the harbor, the sheer, lacy curtains drawn inward with the unseen breath.

Waterston gestured to Jack. "Come. I will show you to your bedchamber upstairs. There is a fine view of the harbor. My wife took the liberty of laying out some clean clothes for you. You look to be about the size of my eldest son when he left for England."

Jack followed him up the stairs, still trying to comprehend what was happening, thankful to be out of the stifling stench of the storehouse. "Do I know you, sir?" he asked, not wanting to give too much away in case his memory served him falsely.

Waterston did not halt his march upward. "You do not know me, but you have seen me before, as I saw you once before." Reaching the top of the stairs, he glanced at Jack and confirmed his conjecture: "At your mother's funeral." He led the way down the short hallway and into a small room at the end of it. "This used to be my son's bedchamber. For now it is yours."

Jack hid his alarm over Waterston's knowledge of his parentage by drawing near to the low window that looked over the rooftops and palisades toward the harbor, toward the dozens of masts that bristled against the azure sky and spoke freedom to him. Yet the harbor might as well be as far away as England for the good its proximity did him.

"In the chamber across from us, you will find a bath drawn. That cut on your thigh needs tending...and your wrists. I can send for a doctor—"

"No...thank you." Jack turned and tried to force an appreciative smile but fell short.

"In the least you must clean and bandage the leg," Waterston said with unquestionable authority. "I will fetch some bandages for you. When you are washed and dressed, come downstairs for some refreshment."

Jack started to thank his host again, but Waterston was gone, his footsteps receding down the stairs. He considered the room—a small bed, a desk, a chair, and a nightstand. Beautiful dark wood. That single, tantalizing window. He pushed the sash up higher and stuck his head out. Below him, near the front door, one of the guards leaned on a musket and chatted with a curious citizen. No sign of Rogers or Dell. Frowning, Jack pulled himself inward. He started to undress, wondering what the appearance of his old shipmates would mean for him if anything. After all, what could they possibly do to help him? He certainly would not want harm to come to them just for his sake.

Once washed and clad in fresh clothes slightly large for his slim frame, damp hair hanging loose and limp, Jack descended to the main floor where Waterston—now without a wig to cover his salt-and-pepper hair—escorted him to the parlor. There, upon a settee, a woman in a pale blue dress bounced a baby upon her knee, the white lace of her cuffs floating behind each movement. Happiness lit her face, her fingers holding the tiny hands of the child who gurgled and chortled with delight. When she saw Jack, her knee did not stop in its movement to entertain the baby, as if there was nothing more important in the world, not even a criminal in her home. Her open smile of welcome surprised him. He recognized her from the funeral as well, had thought at the time how much younger she looked than her husband. Though plain and rather shapeless, her obvious warmth made up for any physical commonness.

"Captain, this is my wife Sara. Sara, my dear, perhaps you remember Captain Mallory from Mrs. Logan's funeral."

"Yes, of course. Who could forget such a striking young man? But, alas, we were never introduced."

Jack gave a slight, rusty bow. "An honor, ma'am."

"Pray sit down, Captain," she encouraged. "We have tea or brandy, whichever you prefer."

The parlor was bright and cheerful from the sunlight dancing in through the windows. Furniture of polished wood and luteous upholstery with welcoming cushions provided great comfort to Jack's sore body. The brandy Waterston offered further eased the aches. As Jack relaxed into a chair, his host sat next to his wife and grinned at the baby, the expression so incongruous with what thus far had been a stoic nature. He spoke quietly in the boy's ear and received a reply of nonsensical sounds save for something close to "papa." Jack thought of the last time he had held an infant—a sibling, a brother, days old and only days later dead.

Without even raising his head, Waterston seemed to sense Jack's attention upon the child. "Truly 'tis Robert you should thank for your being here, Captain, not me."

"Sir?"

Waterston sipped his brandy. "A year ago I was called away to England on an emergency; our eldest son was gravely ill. Sara was close to her confinement, and I did not want to leave her, but she insisted. Your dear mother was kind enough to take her into her own home and care for her, and Robert when he arrived."

"It was a difficult birth," Sara said, her expression serious now, her leg no longer bouncing. "I would not have survived, nor Robert, if not for Mrs. Logan's help." She shifted the boy onto her lap. "So I have a beautiful son, and we both owe your mother a debt of gratitude."

Her admission—like her husband's—of the knowledge that he was Ella Logan's son astounded Jack, and he sat in stunned silence.

"I lost my first wife to childbirth, Captain; I could not have endured the loss of Sara."

"So…Logan told you that his wife was my mother."

"Yes," Waterston said. "Fear not, however, for we are the only ones who know, and we will respect that you want to keep this quiet for the sake of your half-sister."

"Aye."

With a hopeful smile and significant nod to her spouse, Sara said, "I am happy to inform you, Captain, that my husband practices law. That was his occupation in England."

"But here it is only secondary," Waterston continued. "Obviously Charles Town is not large enough to warrant many lawyers. My main occupation here is broker in the fur trade. And your stepfather is one of my biggest clients. I will help you in any way I can to prepare for your trial; I can petition for it to be held here instead of in England. The governor, as you saw by your release into my custody today, favors me." He chuckled. "However, he might not favor me overly much when he hears that I will represent you."

"But how can you possibly help me? There will be a score of witnesses against me from the *Alliance* alone."

"Leave strategy to me, my boy. That is my arena." He drank more of the brandy, and a shadow passed over his tanned face. "Speaking of your stepfather, I have heard nothing of his whereabouts. I saw him before he last left Charles Town. He told me he was embarking on a dangerous voyage but nothing more. I have sent word to Leighlin for him, to tell him of your plight when he returns or in hopes that Mr. Defoe will know how to contact him."

Jack paused with his glass midway to his mouth, and his expression brought concern to Sara's face. He composed himself and said, "Logan is dead."

Sara gasped so sharply that little Robert halted his squirming. The child looked up at her, then reached to touch her pale face. Slowly Waterston set his glass down as if afraid he might drop it.

Jack continued, "It would appear Charles Town remains ignorant of the *Alliance*'s true mission. Well, she was no simple escort for that convoy, if that's what has been said. Caleb Wylder set sail from this harbor with Helen Logan aboard, kidnapped from Leighlin. He used her as bait to lure Logan to sea. Logan sailed with me aboard the *Prodigal* to rescue her and died in the attempt. Caleb Wylder is responsible for his murder."

"Good heavens." Sara put a hand to her mouth. "Why would Caleb Wylder want Mr. Logan dead?"

"The Wylders suspected Logan to be a pirate, but I don't think Peter Wylder knew of his son's plan."

Waterston's gaze held Jack's for a long moment. Secrets reflected there, but what were they and would Waterston ever trust him enough to reveal them? Then the shadows were gone, and the man said, "We knew James Logan only as a planter."

"And a good man," Sara said with a tremble in her voice. "Oh...Helen... That poor, poor child. Is she safe?"

"Aye. I was able to rescue her. She's at Leighlin now, and she's the reason why I must find a way out of this. She shouldn't be made to suffer for my sins."

"But, Captain Mallory..." Sara hesitated. "Pardon my impertinence, but you are accused of piracy. They say you have attacked others ships before that convoy. Certainly you are not capable of such crimes."

Jack's attention drifted to the scar upon his right wrist. Before his bath he had removed his mother's bracelet to keep it from irritating the abraded flesh and had left it upon his bedside nightstand; he felt weakened by its absence. As he considered his next words, his index finger traced the lip of the nearly empty glass in his hand. Here was his chance to let Logan's past sins be known—his piracy, his duplicity, his crimes against Jack's own family—to reveal him for what he truly was and the sorrow he had caused. Yet this couple appeared to esteem Logan highly; it would not be to his advantage to insult their memory of him, especially with the shock of Logan's death fresh upon them.

Carefully Jack began, "When I was younger, I was falsely accused of a crime and imprisoned in England. My mother didn't know of my fate. Perhaps she even thought me dead. When I was freed, I began my search for her. I learnt that she was with James Logan and heard that he was a pirate who cruised off the Carolina coast; I knew nothing of Leighlin. So to find him, I needed a vessel of my own. That's how I became a pirate."

"I am confused, Captain," Sara said. "Obviously you found Mr. Logan and your mother, so why attack Mr. Wylder's convoy?"

"I wasn't interested in the convoy. I suspected the *Alliance* would be escorting Peter Wylder's ships. It was Caleb whom I sought—and another man who sailed with him. I wanted retribution for what they had done to my sister and my stepfather." He wondered if Waterston knew Ketch. Perhaps Ketch could be found and arrested for Logan's murder, yet who would speak against the man or take Jack's word as a witness? No, if he could get out of this current mess, he would find Ketch himself and mete out his own justice. The Waterstons were studying him closely, no doubt weighing the truth in all this, so Jack continued, "You mustn't think ill of my mother. She didn't abandon me, nor I her. Our separation wasn't by choice."

Sara hugged her baby close and murmured, "How happy she must have been to see you again."

Eager to leave talk of Logan and his own shortcomings behind, Jack probed, "Did you see my mother often?"

Sara glanced at her husband as if expecting him to answer, but he appeared distracted still. "We occasionally shared dinner with the Logans—here or at Leighlin House. Helen—poor child—she loves to play with Robert. I think she would have liked a sibling of her own." She blushed. "How astonishing to think she now has just that."

"I'm afraid a sibling fifteen years older is not much good to a six-year-old."

"Why, she seemed quite enamored of you the day we saw you at Leighlin."

Jack frowned and stared at his borrowed stockings.

"We often saw your mother and stepfather at gatherings held at any one of the plantations along the rivers or here in town," Sara said. "Your mother enjoyed herself so much, and Leighlin's social events were the most talked-about of all. Ella had such a way with organizing, and she was the most gracious hostess in all the lowcountry." Her eyes, heavy with sudden moisture, lowered to Robert as she brushed his thin hair from his forehead. "I miss her so very much…and now her husband. I considered your mother my particular friend, though we did not spend as much time together as I would have liked. She and her husband traveled often." Suddenly she raised her head, as if just realizing the connection. Then just as quickly she covered up her amazement. "Now and then they left Helen with us when they would travel. Helen enjoyed coming to town. It was probably quite lonely for her at Leighlin when her parents were gone." Her voice caught upon the last word, and her husband expertly handed her his handkerchief. Sara stood. "Pray excuse me, Captain. You must be famished. Let me get you something to eat to tide you over until dinner."

Of course the servant who had met him at the door could see to this chore, but Jack realized Sara needed an excuse to remove herself so she could allow her tears. Waterston's eyes followed his wife and child before turning back to his guest.

"It was wise of Caleb Wylder to lure Logan to sea to do his evil work. Although Logan has enemies here—businessmen who suspected him of piracy—he also has many friends."

"Like you." Jack smiled in gratitude and finished his drink. "Perhaps it would be better if the trial was to take place in England. I don't want Helen exposed to it. The way news seems to travel like lightning up and down the river..."

"I urge you to let me petition for it to be here. You will have allies here, Captain; albeit none who will say so under oath, but allies just the same."

"How do you mean?"

"These are things best left unsaid, my boy. You must trust me on this."

Jack frowned. "'Tis Helen I'm worried about. There can be no way my blood can be traced to hers. I don't want anyone trying to take what is hers; her father's wealth is all she has left. I won't see men coming forward for reclamation of losses from my piracies or Logan's once they learn he is dead. You must give me your word that no matter what happens at trial, no matter what anyone may say, you will protect Helen even if it means sacrificing me."

"Surely it will not come to that, Captain. As far as I know from Logan, besides myself, only the ex-sailors at Leighlin know of your blood connection to Helen. And his men are loyal and discreet."

Jack's fingers drifted to the garrote mark on his neck. "It would seem there is one among them who is not so loyal any longer."

#

While the search for Defoe continued, Maria and Helen ate dinner alone. Sustaining a steady stream of distracting conversation proved difficult when all Maria received from Helen was an occasional nod or shake of her head. Because of this Maria's thoughts often turned to Ketch. She suspected him of being responsible for Defoe's disappearance, especially when she harkened back to her warning in the stables that Defoe would never let him linger. Could this have been her fault, or had Ketch already had a malicious design upon the Frenchman? Was Ketch somewhere upon the property still? Would he harm David or the other searchers?

Helen was aware of Defoe's absence, so she grew attentive whenever she heard a sound from outside, but both she and Maria were always disappointed. So many acres to cover, many of them swampy. It would be nightfall before the search parties returned. Frustration took away Maria's appetite. She had told Rose to keep the pie for later when David and the others would be famished and in need of a hearty meal.

Watching David depart with the others hours ago—a boy always ready to take on the same responsibilities as the men around him—had stirred her in an unexpected way, and she had realized how afraid his leaving made her, even if he was to be gone only a short while, especially when she knew not where Ketch lurked. What if David turned up missing like Defoe? She had almost asked him to stay at the house but knew he would not. Only a boy, she reflected again, yet no immaturity existed in him. Indeed, he could no doubt run Leighlin as his father ran Wildwood. David had said little about his deception with his father yesterday, and Maria avoided bringing it up. Although he had apologized to her, she had seen no regret in his blue eyes, only that spark that had flared whenever he had kissed her in the past, instances she had not found distasteful and in fact had taken great comfort in.

She considered Helen's troubled expression at table. She and David had yet to share the marriage masquerade with her, uncertain how to even broach the subject. And for now there was no need; it would only confuse her. Hopefully the servants' gossip would not reach the child's ears.

If only Rogers and Dell would return from town... What if something had befallen them? She must send someone else to Charles Town. But surely none of the white men would break away from their search in order to help Jack Mallory, a man responsible for the chain of unhappy events that began with the death of Leighlin's mistress. She should go herself; the desire had kept her awake all last night. She looked at Helen and frowned.

The anxiety of the past days drained her energy, so in the late afternoon, with the big house depressingly quiet and Helen napping in her chamber, Maria retreated to the library on the main floor. The empty fireplace on the interior wall opposite Logan's large desk commanded the room. Logan had left his desk in chaos, but David had set everything into some semblance of order. Behind the polished mahogany expanse, windows looked out upon the rear greensward where Maria gazed in hopes of seeing the searchers return, but only sheep and cows moved about in the weakening sun.

She turned back to the books lining the shelves against the south wall. Hundreds perhaps. Logan had said he obtained many of them from vessels he had plundered, not for his own pleasure but for his wife who had been an avid reader. Maria could imagine Ella in that room, sitting on one of the window seats for light, reading to escape her reality. Shakespeare perhaps. Although Maria did not know all of Shakespeare's works—her father had only two that she had read—her eyes traced the bindings of the volumes shelved together and figured they were all here. For a moment she considered a comedy but instead decided upon *Romeo and Juliet*. Its pages were well worn; by the original owner or by Ella? If Ella, what had drawn her to the story?

Once stretched upon a settee across from the fireplace, Maria found that she could not concentrate upon the book; sleep pressed at her eyelids. In less than half an hour the book lay unread upon her bosom and she asleep in the warm room.

David's voice rescued her from a terrible dream of Jack being hanged by Ketch. With a gasp, she sat up, her movement so quick and unexpected that the book slid to the floor and David stepped back. As she regained her wits, he bent to pick up the book, then sat on a small, squat table in front of her, his clothes dirty as were his hands and face.

"My apologies. I did not mean to startle you."

Maria swept her hands over her disheveled hair to secure it back into its pins. The library had grown even warmer in the early evening, for the breeze had melted completely away. "Did you find Defoe?"

"No. We found some strange marks, perhaps from someone being dragged across the ground, but they were intermittent and did not lead us to anything. Mr. Willis was talking about borrowing my father's hounds to search or soliciting a tracker from the Indians they trade with."

"Have Rogers and Dell come back?"

David's expression changed ever so slightly, and he seemed to withdraw a bit. He set the book upon the table. "No. Not yet."

117

"I must go to Charles Town. Maybe something happened to them."

David frowned. "Maria, please—"

"Mizz Maria! Mr. David!" Thomas's alarmed voice echoed in the Great Hall. They turned to see him with Jemmy. The stable-boy appeared beside himself, eyes wide and white, straw hat in one hand, Helen's bear in the other. Maria's heart went cold.

David crossed to the doorway. "What is it?"

"It's Mizz Helen, suh," Jemmy stammered. "She went away on her pony. She say she goin' to find Mr. Defoe. I tried to stop her, but you know that li'l girl. Then just now her pony...she come runnin' back without Mizz Helen, just her bear tied to the saddle."

# CHAPTER 11

The search for Defoe and Helen involved every able-bodied man on the plantation...and Maria, for she refused to stay behind this time. She joined Hiram Willis and two slaves while other groups fanned out into all regions, from open fields to cultivated acres of corn, beans, and other crops, from swamps to forests and along the stretch of river.

Willis sat astride a trusty mule while Maria rode a big bay gelding named Curly, formerly Ella Logan's mount. Although no great equestrienne, Maria remembered her recent lessons under Helen's tutelage and reminded herself not to clutch the reins too tightly. Tethered to the sidesaddle, Helen's toy bear bounced along.

They retraced the tracks of Helen's pony from the stable. The trail wound through Leighlin's western forest where occasional breaks offered grazing for a modest herd of rangy, russet-colored cattle, sluggish from the heat, many lying in the shade, chewing, wispy tails flicking constantly. The landscape grew swampier the farther into the interior the searchers traveled. The grotesque cypress and tupelo trees with their gnarled knees and finger-like bases lent an unearthly quality to Maria's surroundings. Sometimes Helen's pony had trotted, sometimes cantered, so perhaps it had not been too long since the mare had lost her small rider. What had caused the child to become unseated when she was so natural astride the stubborn little beast? Maria studied the washed out blue sky from which light drained as the sun slid toward the horizon. Desperation brought new strength to her tired voice as she continued to call out into the wilderness for Helen.

As twilight closed in through the foliage like the fingers of a clenching fist, Maria detected uneasiness in the quiet words exchanged by the two slaves trudging behind her, some words in English, some in their native tongue. Their worried gazes rolled about them, particularly toward the rear as if afraid something followed them. Undoubtedly the foreboding disappearance of Helen and Defoe had sent their thoughts into a realm far more frightening than anything related to Ketch's reputation. But Maria did not attribute the supernatural or anything mysterious to Helen's disappearance. She told herself that the girl had simply wanted to help with the search for Defoe and had somehow fallen from her fractious pony. Maria prayed the answer was that simple, and soon they would find her. With a deliberate mental struggle, she managed to banish images of bears and panthers.

Willis eventually noticed the slaves' anxiety as well. When he pulled up alongside a sluggish creek to let the mule drink, he studied the pink streaks of evening across the sky and said, "You boys can go on back now. Miss Cordero, you should go, too. 'Twill be nigh dark soon."

"I'm not going back until we find her, Mr. Willis."

He sighed and nodded to the impatient slaves who quickly started back down the brushy trail, never looking back. Studying the mule's tawny muzzle buried in the water, he murmured, "I wish that girl didn't have her father's stubbornness. She needs to be afeared of some things. 'Twould serve her better in this country. Too many wild things out here to do her harm." Then he caught himself and glanced at Maria. "But I'm sure we'll find her soon. She probably just lost her way or had the sense jarred out of her when she fell off that damned pony."

They continued along the narrow path and again called out into the still air, pausing between shouts to listen above the chorus of insects, frogs, and birds. Bats made their faint, high-pitched noises above, mainly unseen. Black waves of humming mosquitoes caused Maria to fan her hand in front of her face and let down her hair to protect her tender ears from the hungry annoyance.

"You should go back, miss. These bugs'll eat you up in no time. My skin's a mite thicker and tougher than your'n," he grinned through his bristly beard.

Maria ignored his remarks, considered instead Helen's soft, tender skin exposed to the bloodthirsty vermin.

Absently scratching his barrel-like chest, Willis muttered, "Whatever possessed that child to come out here? Her father told her she was never to ride alone."

"How long has Helen known Defoe?"

"Nigh unto five years, I reckon."

"She's lost so much lately; I'm sure the thought of losing Defoe has her desperately worried. I'm afraid to know what it'll do to her if…" She frowned.

"Defoe watched over her when her parents was gone. That damned Frenchman will ne'er admit it, but he has a soft spot for that mite. Who don't? She's always enjoyed tormentin' him; playin' jokes on him to get him to crack a smile on that damned wooden face of his."

120

He grinned. "One time she put frogs in his bed."

Maria abruptly raised her hand for silence, pulled the gelding to a sudden halt. The horse tossed his head at the rude command and took a step backward, but Maria kicked him forward onto the bit. "Listen," she said to the horse as much as to Willis, as if that would persuade the animal to behave. She strained her ears. "Did you hear that? A ways ahead. Listen."

The sound drifted to her again. Not strong but persistent. A small, frightened voice. She booted the gelding, surprising Curly into a forward lurch. When the horse considered going from the trot back to a walk, Maria kicked harder and slapped the reins against the thick neck, startling him into a careening canter along the overgrown trail where brush scraped at her face and arms. She stayed on by sheer will and by her focus upon the sounds ahead. She called Helen's name as she went, then forced herself to pull the bay back down to a brisk walk so the air did not whistle past her ears, blocking her hearing. Then she heard the voice clearer, closer, but not strong: "Daddy, help me!"

The trail widened as the brush fell away to either side, and Maria found herself on a spit of sandy ground between two swamps. A hundred feet ahead she saw a dark creature struggling just off the left-hand bank. In the falling darkness, it took her a moment to understand what she saw: Helen—tarred in black muck and sunken up to her chest in it—cried out, barely able to struggle any longer, sobs low and hoarse.

"Helen!" She leapt from the horse as Willis crashed up behind her on the mule.

"There's a snake!" Helen cried. "A snake in the water!"

Maria raced forward, her eyes never leaving the child as Willis shouted caution to her. Then the shadowy blur of a man bolted across her path, staggering her. "Get back!" he snapped and threw himself into the morass next to the child. He sank up to his knees. An ominous ripple creased the black surface of the water within three feet of the girl. The long, thin object flashed at the man before he flung the snake far from them. With curbed curses, he pried the sobbing child from the sucking ooze as Maria stumbled to the swamp's edge. She took Helen from her rescuer so he could better extricate himself. The mud had claimed his shoes and caked his stockings and worn breeches. Ignoring Helen's unbelievable filth, Maria pulled her to her bosom where the girl clung to her, trembling violently and crying.

Helen's savior struggled upright as Willis drew near. Maria stared in utter disbelief at Ketch. In those few seconds his face paled as he grasped his right hand. Two fang marks showed where the snake had bitten him. The skin around it began to turn an angry red. He fell to his knees, mouth pressed against the bite to try to suck the venom out. Maria stood in helpless shock, unable to set Helen down, hardly able to comprehend what had just happened. She half expected Willis to draw the pistol from his waistband, but he seemed to weigh the action against Helen's immediate well-being and instead took the child from her.

"Let me check her over," he said calmly. "Miss Helen, let's make sure you're all in one piece."

Maria wondered if she should take Willis's pistol, but she knew she could not dispatch Ketch unarmed and here in front of Helen, especially after what he had just done. Ketch, however, was not concerned with anything but his effort to draw forth the poison. His dark gaze revealed fear where she thought none could ever exist. His left hand tried to untie his neckerchief but shook too badly. Without thinking, Maria pushed his hand away and struggled with the dirty knot, cursing until it came free. Then she used it as a tourniquet high on the arm. The hand had swollen in that short time, and pain whitened Ketch's face.

"Mr. Willis," she called. "We need your help."

Willis felt Helen's limbs for any broken bones where she sat in limp exhaustion. Flatly he said, "There's no help for him. He'll be dead afore morn and good riddance; saved me some powder and shot, that snake did. We need to take Miss Helen back home where she can be tucked away in bed, washed and warm."

Helen's tired, frightened eyes went from Willis to Maria. Tears trailed down her smeared face as she looked with a silent plea upon Ketch's bent form.

"He saved her life," Maria said. "We should *try* to do something. We owe him at least that."

Maria's request and Helen's obvious concern irritated Willis. He threw a hot glance at Maria. "If you've any hope for his life the arm must come off, Miss Cordero. And the bloody bugger will likely be unconscious in a short while, so gettin' him back to Leighlin won't be easy."

Without another word, Maria hurried over to Helen and swung her up upon one hip then prodded Willis over to help Ketch to his feet. Not an easy task, for he was already unsteady. Amazingly he did not regard them with any caution or threat, his senses too muddled. Maria hurried over to Curly.

"Up you go, *osita*." She forced calm into her words as she lifted the child. "Look here." She untied the stuffed bear. "Look who came to find you." Helen clutched the bear to her befouled frock and looked at Ketch as if in consideration of imparting the object to him. Maria wiped the tears from the girl's cheeks only to see new ones forming. "You're safe, sweetheart. We're going to take you and Mr. Ketch home."

# 

"Wake up, young man." Malachi Waterston's curt voice drifted through Jack's dream of Maria, soft in his arms. He ignored the voice, but then it came through strong enough to dissipate the lovely image. "Wake up."

Begrudgingly Jack awoke from a sleep deep and restful, cultivated by Sara Waterston's dinner and her spouse's fine brandy. When he opened his eyes, the daylight in the chamber had faded considerably from when he had retired here earlier.

"Supper will be served within the half hour, and our guests will be arriving any minute," Waterston informed. "My wife insisted that I let you sleep as long as possible."

"Supper?" Jack sat up, realizing his stomach was indeed empty again. He glanced through the window. Evening already, the sunlight fading away in the saffron sky, turning the harbor a deep indigo. He looked at Waterston's fresh cravat and clean white linen shirt. "Guests, did you say?"

"Indeed." Waterston smiled. "Guests who are very eager to meet the notorious Long Arm Jack."

Jack frowned, dragging a hand through his flattened hair. Was he to continue as a sideshow for these townspeople?

"Do not fret, Captain. I deliberately invited these guests for your benefit. Not that they know of my motivations, but..." He winked. "James Moore is a friend of your stepfather and of Irish blood like Logan. He, too, was at your mother's funeral and will, I assure you, be discreet. He is a powerful man in the politics of Carolina, one who has profited in the past from piratical trade here in our fair town. His wife is a tender-hearted soul who will no doubt lend her persuasive talents to your cause. The second couple I invited are Charles Johnson, who is a member of the Assembly, and his wife, Grace. Truth be told, Grace has greater influence in this town than her husband in some ways. She can bully or exhaust anyone over to her opinion better than any politician I have met, so if you beguile her with your youthful good

123

looks and charm, my boy, you may help temper opinion about your plight. She also has a brother on the Assembly who, like Moore, has profited from the pirate trade, not that Moore will admit it to you tonight, especially in front of our other guests, whom I believe you already know."

"I know no one in Charles Town."

"True enough, they do not live in town; they live up the Ashley River. Whenever in town overnight, Ezra Archer stops here, in that chamber across from yours. He and his daughter will be joining us for supper."

#

The Waterstons' dining room was a bit too small for nine people, but no one seemed to mind the close quarters and the settling of the day's heat in the house. The Waterstons' two indentured servants busily kept food coming and removed emptied dishes seamlessly, nor was a wine goblet ever wanting. Duck, quail, and fish provided the main courses while fresh vegetables from the country imparted color and variety, all in abundance for Jack's never-flagging appetite. Early conversation was polite and safe: commerce, crops, and the weather. Never a loquacious conversationalist, Jack forced occasional comments. His thoughts, however, were anywhere but upon the subjects at hand.

He tried to stay focused on his plate as much as possible so as not to stare across the table at Margaret Archer, but it was nigh impossible. She wore a pale yellow dress that he had seen before, on the day he had first met her at Leighlin, when she had entered the Great Hall and taken his breath away with her sultry beauty. Now the evening candlelight played upon her flawless skin, the slight, wavering shadows giving it a darker tone than on that sunny day at Leighlin. Her blonde hair was swept up upon her head, allowing tendrils to fall on either side of her high cheekbones and dangle alongside silver earrings that dripped from delicate earlobes. He found himself wanting to reach out and touch them, yearning for softness. Her eyes were a lighter blue than her younger brother's but held the same dazzling quality, a power that made him never want to look away from her. Her bow-shaped lips enticed him anew with the memory of her passionate kiss, even now stifling his breath. Of course at the time Logan had berated him, claimed Margaret was simply manipulating him for her own designs to get her brother away from her father's oppressive regime. Jack, however, had never felt manipulated, had never doubted that Margaret held a certain affection for him, as he did for her, an affection that often—considering Maria—left him in a quandary. Where, though, would her affection lie now that he was incapable of fulfilling his promise of transporting her brother to England? At least he had accomplished one thing for her—though admittedly not his goal at the time—and that had been the death of James Logan. If nothing else, perhaps that would have proven his worth to her.

Margaret's troubled gaze often sought his across the table. He liked to think her concern was solely for him, but he figured in truth it was for her brother, for with Jack Mallory a prisoner in Charles Town—a man without his brig—where could that possibly leave her brother? Still aboard the *Prodigal*? Killed during the fighting? Or did she know he was at Leighlin? He wished he could ease her worries.

During the evening's introductions, it had been obvious that the Johnsons were unabashedly enthralled to be sharing a meal with a celebrated criminal, especially—as Grace Johnson had pointed out with little veneer—one so astonishingly young and eye-catching. Sara Waterston, whose seat was at the end of the table opposite her husband and to Jack's right, had strategically placed Grace and her matronly bulk on Jack's other hand.

"So, Mr. Waterston," Grace said with great eagerness, "have you heard the rumor about James Logan?"

"I have." Waterston's face betrayed nothing.

On the other side of Grace, Charles Johnson—a thin, reedy fellow somewhere in his early thirties—leaned slightly toward Waterston. "Do you believe it?"

Waterston took his time wiping his mouth with a linen, the single vertical crease between his eyebrows conveying displeasure. "Believe what, Mr. Johnson? That he is dead?"

Johnson nodded. Judging by his attentiveness, he highly valued Waterston's opinion. "They say pirates killed him."

James Moore, across from Johnson, added, "I heard that Governor Ludwell himself fitted out a privateer against Logan and had him killed at sea, that the Lords Proprietors ordered it so, that they had money in the venture as well."

Ezra Archer scoffed. "We have heard all this talk before. I discounted it then and I discount it now. Utter nonsense. James Logan a pirate! Forsooth! He was no pirate; he was a gentleman."

"From whence have these rumors of Logan's demise come?" James Moore's wife asked. "I have heard them from no one of authority."

Grace, round face shining with a slight sheen of perspiration, reddened a bit, as if she had just been accused of something. "Sailors," she admitted. "There has been talk along the waterfront." Quickly she added, "Not that I have spoken with any of them myself, of course, but that is where the talk has originated. Surely they would know, if anyone would, especially if Captain Logan did die at sea."

"Well," Johnson said with the sudden excitement of an epiphany, "we have a genuine pirate in our midst, do we not?" His enthusiastic gaze swung to Jack. "Perhaps he knows the truth about James Logan. Planter or pirate, Captain? What say you?"

When all eyes turned in anticipation, Jack froze. Of course he wanted to blurt out the vile truth about James Logan but...

Waterston rescued him. "Mr. Johnson, you must remember that the Captain will be on trial for his life. It would not be prudent of him to speak of anything that might incriminate him."

The Johnsons seemed to deflate with sheepish disappointment.

"Of course," Johnson murmured. "My apologies, Captain."

Jack smiled his acceptance.

"You did business with Logan, Mr. Waterston," Johnson persisted. "You suspected nothing?"

"Of course not. This is all idle gossip. I refuse to hear any more of it. I am a man of the law, as you know. I require hard evidence, proof without a doubt, and we have none, have we?"

Johnson appeared cowed this time and shrank in his seat, dropping the subject and paying attention only to his food. His wife touched his arm in solace, then—as if to ease the tension—she beamed across the table at Margaret Archer, the wine adding to her florid complexion, "How are the wedding preparations coming, my dear?"

Margaret's smile appeared forced. "Everything is coming along well."

"I am sure it will be the talk of the whole province. Charles and I are so looking forward to it. I do hope the weather is not too withering."

"Yes. Perhaps we should have waited until fall."

"Oh no, my dear!" Mrs. Moore protested. "You would not want Seth Wylder to slip away, now would you? A fine man, he is. And the pickings are none too plentiful here on the frontier, are they?" Her conspiratorial wink with Grace drew a self-conscious smile from Margaret.

"That is the sad truth," Grace said. She gave Jack a sly, sidelong glance that surprised him with its coquettishness. "The men in Charles

Town far outnumber the women, but the quality...well, for a young woman of Miss Archer's breeding..."

At first Jack took her insinuation to be an insult directed at him and his social standing and those like him. But when her fleshy hand had the audacity to touch his leg under the table, he realized those men of lesser quality did not offend her after all. He nearly jumped when she inadvertently pressed upon the hidden gouge on his thigh. Margaret bounced an inquiring glance from him to Grace and away with a faint smile in the corner of her lovely mouth, apparently not surprised by the woman's attraction to her young supper companion.

"What of your family, Captain?" Wine-emboldened, Grace ignored the waning patience of those around her. "Are you married?"

"Mrs. Johnson!" Mrs. Moore scolded. "Of course he is not. He is just a boy." She smiled soothingly at Jack, as if he were one of her five children of which she had earlier spoken.

Grace scoffed. "And was not my Charles just a boy when he courted and won me? Perhaps the Captain is not as young as he appears. After all, a mere boy could not have committed the robberies and murders of which he is accused."

"Mrs. Johnson," Sara Waterston interrupted, handing her a dish. "More yams perhaps?"

"It seems an injustice almost," James Moore said. "Considering how Charles Town benefited from pirates in the past, and now with Ludwell at the helm suddenly the same men who came to these shores to trade with our citizens—and grease the palms of certain officials like our former governor, Seth Sothel—are looked upon as from the devil himself. It seems to me you cannot have it both ways."

Hopeful Mrs. Moore said, "Maybe the Captain did not willfully commit any crime. Perhaps he was forced. I have heard pirates do that—take men from merchant ships and force them to become pirates." She looked at Jack as if hoping he would reinforce her belief.

"Well, Mrs. Moore," Jack said with a wry smile, "with my legal counsel sitting here, I must hold my tongue and beg you to forgive my inability to address your speculation."

Mrs. Moore blushed, adding youthfulness to her appearance, though she was already some twenty years younger than her spouse, Jack guessed. He wished circumstances were different, and he could speak openly to the Moores, to learn more about their relationship with his mother and to know if Logan had revealed his past to them as he had to Waterston. As Waterston had said, he needed as many allies as he could find.

127

"Well," Sara Waterston said with a warm smile, "it would appear that it is time for dessert."

#

During the short gallop back to Leighlin, Maria warred with herself. Perhaps Willis was right and they should let Ketch die after what he had done to Leighlin's master as well as perhaps Defoe. If Jack were here, no doubt he would hurry Ketch on his way. She told herself that Jack would indeed make it back to Leighlin soon, then Ketch's fate would be in his hands. But for now it was in hers. She tightened her hold around Helen in front of her, the girl's troubled gaze upon Ketch, who was slumped over Willis's mule, staying on only with the reluctant help of Willis's strong arm. The child urged Curly and the mule to greater speed. The concern in her voice sealed Maria's decision not to willfully allow Ketch to perish.

By the time they neared Leighlin House, all light had fled the sky and left behind a deep purple above the rear sward across which the horse and mule galloped, scattering sheep to either side like a parting white wave. The servants congregated upon the rear portico, and Thomas began to ring the bell that hung at one end. This would carry across the still evening air to the searchers to let them know Helen had been found.

Maria reined Curly in at the portico steps and dismounted, leaving Helen atop the gelding as she called to Mary to take the child inside.

The black woman rushed down. "Oh, Mizz Helen. What happened to you?"

Maria hurried to help Willis with Ketch who miraculously clung to a thread of consciousness. With a moan, he half slid, half fell from the mule. Jemmy gave him a wide berth as he ran to take charge of Curly and the mule. Sharp whispers broke out among the servants upon the portico.

"Thomas!" Maria snapped. "Nahum! Get down here!" They scurried to her side. "Carry him up to Mr. Rogers's chamber. Hurry. Mind his right arm."

"They should take him to the lower level," Willis protested stridently. "He don't belong in the house proper."

In confusion the servants hesitated.

"Do as I say!" Maria barked.

Thomas and Nahum looked from Ketch to one another with something between fear and revulsion. They eyed the swollen, discolored arm.

"*Now*, damn you!"

Hearing a woman curse shocked them into action, their glances flashing white at her as they bent to their task. Ketch groaned softly as they carried him up the steps.

Helen lingered on the portico, ignoring Mary's urgings to come inside, her attention upon Ketch as he passed. When Maria and Willis ascended the steps, she asked, "Is Mr. Ketch going to die?"

Willis turned a weary look upon Maria. "Mr. Ketch is very sick, Miss Helen."

The hint of tears returned to Helen's eyes. "Is he going to die?"

Willis hesitated, then started to speak, but Maria insisted, "Mr. Willis won't let that happen, will you, Mr. Willis?"

Again the unhappy man faltered, his face red with indecision.

"Miss Helen," Mary quietly spoke in her ear, "let's get you inside and cleaned up."

"Mr. Ketch saved me from a snake, Mary."

"Did he? Well, I'm so glad you is safe. Now come inside out of the damps."

"I want to help Mr. Ketch."

"You a sight, child. We must get you fed, washed and to bed."

Maria offered Helen an encouraging smile. "Go with Mary now. You can visit Mr. Ketch in the morning."

"I couldn't find Mr. Defoe," Helen murmured mournfully, rubbing her runny nose and smearing the dried mud on her face. "I tried..."

"Come along now," Mary urged with a gentle tug on her filthy hand.

As Willis started to follow, Maria took hold of his arm. "We must think of Helen and what she needs, not what you or anyone else wants."

Willis grunted. "I'm not makin' no promises. 'Tis in God's hands more'n mine. And I suspect God's no friend of Ketch."

#

Jack stripped off his clothes and pulled a nightshirt over his buzzing head. Warmed by an hour of drinking brandy with the men in the parlor and by a belly still delightfully bursting from his over-indulgence at the supper table, he crawled into bed. A cooling, gentle sea breeze brushed his face and brought the delicious scent of the ocean and of early summer rain through the partially open window. He could almost forget the armed guards at both doors.

His thoughts went to Leighlin, to Maria and Helen tucked away in their beds, safe. But were they safe? He remembered what Ketch had said about Helen. Jack groaned and tossed about. Surely Defoe would see Ketch dead before allowing the villain to set foot on Leighlin's land. And if Smith honored his request to safeguard Maria and Helen, his quartermaster would dispatch Ketch in no time.

The alcoholic haze cut his worries short and pulled him away into a deep sleep. But only minutes seemed to pass in this blissful state before a hand upon his shoulder awoke him. He expected to see Waterston, but instead he made out Ezra Archer's shape hovering close in the moonlight, an index finger to his pursed lips. Jack sat up, startled by the intruder's appearance and urgings for quiet. Archer's other arm—the one in a sling—held a substantial piece of clothing, something yellow and rustling and smelling of jasmine.

"Shave your face clean," Archer quietly ordered. "Then take off that shirt and get into this." He tossed the garment across Jack's bed. "Make haste…before the guards sober."

# CHAPTER 12

Maria had thought Ketch unconscious, but when Thomas, Willis, and she attempted to tie his ankles and left wrist to the bedposts to immobilize him for the amputation, the man suddenly roared to life. So violently did he thrash about to avoid their restraints that Maria feared he might fall off the bed or injure one of them, so she ordered them all to cease. Ketch's wild eyes stared at them without recognition. Perhaps his furious defense was purely instinct or perhaps he realized how helpless he was under the hands of a man who would like nothing more than to see him dead. His eyes rolled in agony, and he turned his head to vomit. Willis cursed. Ketch gave a soft groan and slipped into unconsciousness.

"Maria," David's voice from the doorway drew her attention from the mess she hastily cleaned up. "I must speak with you."

She gestured at Ketch, but Willis said, "Go on. He won't give me and Thomas no trouble now."

Frowning, she left the chamber and followed David toward the front of the ballroom, their footfalls sounding unusually hollow on the broad oak planks. Welcoming scents drifted upward from the dining room along with servants' voices.

He glanced at Helen's closed door. "It was you who found Helen? She is unharmed?"

"Yes. She had fallen into a swamp, but Ketch pulled her out; he saved her from a water snake, but it bit him."

David's blue eyes stared through the candlelit dimness toward Ketch's chamber. "Then he will be dead soon."

His cold satisfaction surprised Maria. "Willis is going to amputate the arm and try to save him."

"Save him? Dear God, why?" His restless hands moved along the seams of his breeches, as if unconsciously trying to wipe something from them. He had acquired a haunted appearance, something she had seen the night he had been secreted from his home to Leighlin and had lain exhausted, like one who had just endured a great physical and emotional ordeal. When he spoke again, he kept his voice quiet.

131

"Maria, you do not realize what that man is. Saving his life today will not guarantee that he will not slit our throats tomorrow." He stepped closer, almost desperate. "There is no one else on earth that I would say this about, Maria, but he deserves to die. And you must let him."

The pain on his face made her personal indecision all the worse. "I'm sorry, David. I'm sorry for whatever it is he did to you, but Helen...Helen wants him to live; Willis is doing this because of her, because she asked him to."

The frequent intensity of David's gaze often bordered on painful, forcing her to look away, but this time it was his turn to divert his eyes. "Why was he there, out in the swamp?"

"I don't know. I'm guessing he was watching out for Helen. He told me yesterday in the barn that—"

"Did you ask him where Defoe is?" Anger in the question. "Perhaps you will find him in that same swamp."

At a loss, Maria blinked away tears of confusion. David's expression softened, and he quietly sighed out his frustration.

"Forgive me, Maria. I know you are thinking only of what Helen wants, but in this instance what she wants could bring further ruin to this house."

"Willis says his chances of survival are slim. So perhaps this will all be taken out of our hands." She studied his dirty riding boots, perhaps once belonging to Logan and too large for David. "I'm sorry. I just didn't know what else to do with Helen standing in front of me, begging Willis."

"I know." He caressed her cheek with the back of his warm hand.

She smiled her appreciation. "Supper will be on the table now. Pip said they have been keeping it for you."

"Come with me."

"No." She offered a consoling touch upon his arm. "I'll stay with Helen for a while."

#

Ketch tracked his stepfather through the thick Southwark fog that crept up from the River Thames and shrouded the close lanes and alleys like pale serpents trapped among the tightly-situated buildings. Simply by smell, Ketch knew the nearby river rode high along its banks, the stench of low tide banished. Light shone only infrequently from the dwellings that he passed, and the angry bark of a dog or the fleeting shadow of a cat barely distracted him. The thickness of deep night and the palpable curtain of dampness helped conceal him and muffle the sounds of his feet as he slipped from doorway to doorway, eyes always upon his stepfather's dark figure many paces ahead of him, determined not to lose him. Now and then he caught the distant, quiet cries of his newborn half-sister, Sophia, swaddled in her father's arms.

Ketch remembered his mother weakly pleading with her husband from her birthing bed. "Please, Edward, let me keep this one."

"Keep this one and there won't be enough money to feed the one we already got." He threw a disparaging, guilt-inducing glance at Ketch. "No, she goes the way of the others. Mrs. Bennett will find her a good home. Don't fret."

No matter how much she had begged and cajoled—more so than over the four previous babies—nothing dissuaded her husband, and he had carried Sophia into the night. Leaving his mother to her tears, Ketch had trailed him, determined to find out where the mysterious Mrs. Bennett lived. He would go there every day, he vowed, until he could make sure Sophia did indeed end up in a good home with the loving parents he had imagined for his other banished siblings.

The fog thickened to near impenetrability as Ketch's stepfather drew nearer to the Thames. Ketch nearly bumped into a drunken man with equally drunken women under his arms, but he writhed out of the way before they could curse and call attention to him. He hurried on, barely able to see his stepfather.

At the end of the narrow, stinking street, he expected his stepfather to turn left, to go to the great bridge and cross over into London, but instead he continued straight on to the river. Puzzled, Ketch drew back into deeper shadow alongside a building, his stepfather's outline just visible, facing the Thames. Ketch shivered and clutched his threadbare shirt closer to his skin to combat the damp. Why had his stepfather stopped? To light his pipe perhaps...

A distant splash broke the quiet. Then his stepfather wheeled about, and Ketch flattened himself against the dilapidated wooden building and held his breath. With quick, purposeful strides, his stepfather drew away from the river. He crossed his empty arms against his chest to fend off the chill and disappeared into the gray, twisting mists, bound not in the direction of their home but no doubt to some alehouse.

A quiet voice reached Ketch; a sudden coolness touched his hot brow. A woman's voice...but not his mother's... The Southwark fog dissolved, and grayness gave way to black then dark orange. A suffocating wave of pain swept through him and slammed him back to consciousness, left him drenched in a fever sweat. He instinctively jerked against bindings that were no longer there. Her voice came again, and a wet rag upon his forehead soothed him.

"Miss Helen?" he murmured.

"She's safe. She's sleeping now."

His fuzzy mind played a cruel trick upon him, and the person who answered him was Ella Logan, but when he turned his head upon the pillow, he saw Maria. She frowned and reached for a nearby cup.

"Drink this." She slipped one hand beneath his head and put the cup to his lips.

Brandy. Logan's good brandy. He had always salivated when watching Logan drink it. How good it tasted. He closed his burning eyes and savored it as its dulling warmth spread throughout him, down into his arms... Hopeful, he looked but the right arm...it was gone, no matter how much it seemed to still be a part of him. There was only a swathed, throbbing stump. What had they done with his arm? He remembered taking the axe to Defoe's arms, throwing them to the alligators...

Maria took the cup away from his mouth, and the movement brought her scent to him. He studied her as if for the first time. It was easy to see what that damned Mallory saw in her. She was a beautiful girl in her own right, though many white men would disdain the dark complexion that she had acquired through the blood of her Spanish father and perhaps her French prostitute mother.

He cast one last look to where his arm should have been then turned away from the abomination that remained, refused to think about it. His violence against Defoe had nearly cost Helen her life—of course the child had been looking for the overseer; he had heard her calls to the Frenchman—so to pay with his own flesh was only just. The loss of his arm allowed him to absolve himself, and because of that he did not completely mourn its loss.

He stared up at the bed's canopy. "Miss Helen shouldn't have been in the swamp."

"She was looking for Defoe."

"Who let her do such a fool thing?"

Maria's tone grew stronger, insistent, close to anger. "What happened to Defoe?"

Her gold locket drew his hazy attention. He remembered his hands around that slim neck, pressing... He had regretted those actions; after all, she had only been speaking the truth about his half-brother. But he had not wanted to hear it, especially with Dan's and Ella Logan's deaths so fresh, so confusing and horrifying in their connection.

"Ketch," she refocused him. "Tell me where Defoe is."

Nausea reared up but he fought it off, felt his face pale with the effort. His sweat seemed to freeze upon his half-naked body beneath the sheet.

"Did you kill him?"

Pain tried to distract him, but he had learned long ago how to push it aside, compartmentalize it, make it wait. He studied her, remembered her kind treatment of David Archer aboard the *Prodigal* as well as her kindness to the other wounded after the battle with the privateer *Feather*...and her gentle way with Helen.

Frustration built in her, and she used added force to squeeze the water from the rag into the basin before soaking it. "Why did you lie to Ezra Archer about David's marriage?"

He closed his eyes. She was a persistent thing, he thought distantly as the agony drained his strength from within. Of course she desired answers before he could die on her. Yet even if he had intended to answer her questions, he lost the ability as well as his tenuous grasp upon consciousness.

#

To Jack's great embarrassment, Margaret's clothing fit his slender form in most places except the bosom, a fact he knew not how to obscure until Archer tossed a cloak upon the bed. Jack placated his humiliation with a brief, admiring thought of Margaret without her clothes. Was this scheme hers? No, not with her father's active participation. Jack did not allow himself to ponder Archer's motives, for there could be no answer to that at the moment. As he picked up the cloak, he hoped no one would look closely at him, that the night would completely conceal him, for any observer would wonder why this homely girl had so many nicks upon her face or why she was so darkly tanned.

Above the tap of rain against the bedchamber window, Jack whispered to Archer, "I gave Waterston my word when he brought me here that I wouldn't escape."

"And who expects a pirate to honor his word?" Archer scoffed.

Jack swallowed his pride. This was not the time to parry words with this bastard.

"You want to see your sister again, don't you, boy?" Archer donned a short cape. "Then put on that cloak. Follow me and say

135

nothing."

Leaving the house by way of the front door, they stepped into a steady rain. The guard there—sitting in a slump—climbed to his feet but nearly fell over before steadying himself against the house with one hand. He suppressed a belch and brought his musket up before Archer's voice halted him with an uncharacteristic lightness.

"All is well, my boy. No need to frighten my daughter with your gun."

"Beg pardon, sir," he slurred.

Jack kept his head lowered, the cloak's hood sheltering his face from the rain as well as from the guard.

"Come along, my dear." Archer offered his arm. Jack hesitated then inwardly cursed his confusion and reached for Archer.

And with that they were upon the dark Charles Town street, walking none too briskly—certainly not as fast as Jack desired but at least not faster than he could maneuver in his unwieldy disguise. Margaret's shoes were too small and pained him with each step. Fortunately it was a short walk to the wharf—only two blocks. The light and noise of taverns along the waterfront brightened their surroundings. Archer guided him to the opposite side of the street, close to the palisade wall, away from most of the wandering sailors and whores.

Archer eased him closer, disquieting Jack, then spoke in a low voice, "There is a boat awaiting you. It will take you to Wildwood. You will spend the night there, and I will rejoin you on the morrow. You are to go directly there, do you understand? Stop nowhere or you will lose the tide and—more importantly—my favor. Do you hear me?"

In a ridiculous falsetto that was not as quiet as he had hoped, Jack replied, "Aye."

Softer still and with an iciness that made the rain seem cold, Archer added, "If someone intercepts you and you implicate me or my daughter, you will never see your sister again."

Jack was unsure if Archer was threatening his personal safety or that of Helen, but again he forced himself to bite back his quick-tempered retort. He was already ill at ease for having to rely on this man's help.

Ahead of them, a familiar shape leaned in shadow, silhouetted by a distant lantern. Jack tried to see clearer through the rain, for he figured his eyes were playing tricks on him. When Archer led him up to the form, the obscure man showed a leg, swept off his hat, and made an elaborate bow.

"Good evening, m'lady," the welcomed voice of Josiah Smith penetrated the patter of rain. "Yer lookin' particularly lovely tonight."

Archer growled, "For God's sake, man…"

Smith's grin flashed through the night, startling Jack, for he almost did not recognize his old friend without his thick beard and mustache. But Smith quickly doused the expression for the sake of prudence. Jack restrained himself from embracing his quartermaster or at least from bantering back in his customary way.

Archer pulled Smith close. "You have your orders."

With an unhappy glance, Smith said, "Aye." Then his expression changed completely again, and the light from across the street showed the familiar spark of mischief in his eyes. He offered Jack his arm. "Allow me, miss."

Jack gladly let go of Archer and took Smith's arm. Smith patted his hand, chuckled, and turned them toward the wharf, leaving Archer behind.

"What say you to an old man examinin' yer wares, missy? I'm loaded with gold coin. Seems our captain has been indisposed, so me shipmates and me took the liberty of disbursin' his share."

Jack restrained his grin. "I'm afraid my wares may disappoint you, sir."

"Aye. I like 'em with more meat on their bones." He chuckled licentiously.

"You're never going to let me live this one down, are you, Smitty?"

"Not a chance, darlin'. Not a chance."

#

The steady, soft rain continued to fall as the boat shouldered the small waves off the tip of Charles Town's peninsula. The broad mouth of the Ashley River yawned before Jack, Smith, Rogers, and Dell, blended with the dark night as the incoming tide pushed them farther away from civilization. Jack welcomed the wilderness that would soon swallow them. The song of the water, the smell of it, soothed him there beneath the cloak's hood.

At the tiller, Smith called softly forward to Hugh Rogers on the bow thwart. "I'd say yellow's his color, wouldn't you?"

Jack hollowly threatened, "'Vast there, Smitty."

"That was quite a sight, him tryin' to get in the boat," Smith continued, close to laughter. "Lackin' a bit in female grace, eh, lad?"

"Damn it, Smitty. Stow that and tell me what the hell's happening. How'd you get here?"

"Didn't think I'd leave you to yerself, did ye? I know better than that. You get in too much trouble by yerself, sure. I convinced the lads to bring me back to Charles Town. In fact, the *Prodigal* is in the offing right now, waitin' to see if I'm goin' to bring you off."

"What about the *Fortune*?"

"Angus took her north along the coast, lookin' for some safer place to spend their purchase."

Jack asked of Dell and Rogers, "How did you lads find out I was arrested?"

"Ketch showed up at Leighlin with the news," Dell said. "He told Maria; she sent us."

Jack bristled. "Ketch at Leighlin? I trust he was shot on sight."

"I'm afeared not. No one saw him 'cept Maria, and she had no gun at the time."

Rogers quickly added, "She wanted to come to Charles Town herself, of course, but we told her no and to stay put like you told her to."

"Like I told her? I wasn't able to get word to her."

"Ketch said you told him to tell her."

"I never told Ketch anything." A sense of dread set his heel tapping as they hoisted the sail. "Damn it, Ketch should be dead. Maria and Helen shouldn't have been left alone there with him."

"She's not alone, Captain," Rogers said. "David Archer is there last we knew, and Defoe and Willis and the other lads. They won't let nothin' happen to Maria or Miss Helen."

Jack wished Rogers's words gained him confidence, but the thought of Ketch anywhere near Maria or Helen twisted his innards. "I should be going to Leighlin, not Wildwood," he lamented.

"Not tonight, lad," said Smith. "I'm afeared we need to follow Archer's orders for now. He got you this far. Maria and Helen is safe. 'Tis you we need to fret about. I'm not sure how everything happened, how you ended up in a dress and all, but…" His grin showed when he lit his pipe now that the rain was slacking. "What matters is that yer not goin' to get yer neck stretched."

Jack pushed back his hood as the marshlands and forests closed in on either side of the wide, placid river. "Why did Archer help me? That's the real worry, Smitty. Did he say anything to you?"

"Nothin'. Mebbe it was Miss Archer more'n her daddy. She's the one Rogers and Dell talked to about gettin' you sprung. But she didn't

138

tell them no details neither."

"Well, she won't be glad she helped me once she finds out her brother is at Leighlin instead of crossing the Atlantic."

"She knows," Dell said, handling the sheet with ease. "She asked us what had become of him. So we told her about him bein' at Leighlin."

Jack's gut tightened even more. He stared up at the clearing sky where now and then a star peeked through the ashy cloud cover. "What did she say?"

"She looked relieved actually...that he was safe and hadn't been arrested as a pirate."

Rogers added, "She was a mite worried, too, of course."

Smith grumbled, "She might have saved yer skin in the hopes that you'll help her cursed brother again. But I'm tellin' you—"

"Belay the lecture, Smitty. Right now I'm not in a position to help anyone. But I'll feel better once I get back to Leighlin. Rogers, once you return there, tell Defoe I want Ketch found."

"He was already workin' on that when we left, Captain."

"I may not be able to return to Leighlin and deal with him as soon as I'd like. First there's Archer to attend to. He wants something from me. He'd not have risked all this otherwise."

# CHAPTER 13

Maria awoke in the chair at Ketch's bedside, stiff and feeling as if she had not slept at all. The first pale light of morning grayed the interior of the bedchamber and removed the oppressive shadows of the long night. The gentle tap of rain against the windows had stopped; hours earlier its soothing melody had lulled her to sleep when nothing else could, not even brandy. Why had she lingered here through the night? Was it a deathwatch? She feared having to tell Helen that the man had died, yet she could not wish for him to live.

Regardless of Maria's conflicted interests, Ketch remained alive. Now, unconscious still, he squirmed restlessly in the bed, gripped by the worsening fever that darkened his unruly brown hair to sweaty black against the damp pillow, his lips moving in an incomprehensible mumble. He had kicked the sheet away from his bare chest. Sweat slicked his muscular, scarred flesh.

From just outside the chamber door, Mary's soft, excited voice called, "Mizz Maria."

Maria hurried into the ballroom and quietly closed the door behind her.

"Mr. Rogers and Mr. Dell is a-comin' up from the landing."

Maria's heart leapt. "Is Captain Mallory with them?"

"No'm. Just them two."

Maria's hopes sank; cold fear gripped her. "Fetch a fresh pitcher of water for Mr. Ketch. Send Pip up to fan him as well. We've got to keep his fever down."

"Yes'm," Mary said with reluctance.

Maria rushed downstairs and out onto the front portico as Rogers and Dell wearily ascended the steps. They both smiled at her, lifting her spirits.

"Did you find Jack?"

They removed their hats, and Rogers answered, "We helped him escape. He's safe now."

The air she had unwittingly been holding in her lungs escaped in a soft rush. "Thank you." She pressed a hand to her sweaty forehead.

"But...where is he?"

"At Wildwood."

"Wildwood?"

"Aye. Mr. Archer and his daughter got him free. He was bein' held in the house of one of Mr. Archer's friends."

"Archer? But...but why didn't Jack come here?"

"Mr. Archer ordered us to take him to Wildwood. Said he'd be safer there, in case someone had tied Jack to Leighlin."

Confused, Maria frowned with deep disappointment, thinking not only of her own desperate desire to see Jack but also of Helen.

Dell added, "I'm sure he'll come see you and Miss Helen as soon as it's safe."

"Perhaps we can go to him."

Dell and Rogers exchanged a glance, and Rogers said, "I doubt he'll be stayin' at Wildwood. I wouldn't think Archer would put his own family at risk by harborin' him. The militia and such will be lookin' for Jack."

"Of course. So you spoke to Archer?"

"No." Rogers wiped his ruddy face with one sleeve. "We spoke to Miss Archer. Smitty talked to him, though."

"Smitty?"

"Aye. He come back to Charles Town to try to help Jack. He's with him at Wildwood. If Jack's not able to get word to you in the next days, I'm sure Smitty will. When we dropped him off, Jack told us to tell you to be careful, not to fret about him, and to keep Helen safe."

Dell added, "He's vexed about Ketch bein' 'round these parts."

"But he sent Ketch here—"

"He said he never did."

Maria cursed herself for believing the lie. "Ketch is here. As a matter of fact, he's in your bedchamber and will be for some time. But he's in no condition to harm anyone, I assure you."

The two men looked at one another with alarm.

"He was bitten by a snake. Mr. Willis amputated his arm last night." She considered their haggard appearances. "Why don't you two get some breakfast? It should be ready in a few minutes. Please rest today; I can see both of you need sleep. Use David's chamber; he should be up by now." She touched Rogers's arm and bestowed a small smile. "Thank you both."

Once they had shuffled into the house, the world closed in upon Maria. Relieved anxiety over Jack's fate drained out of her like a rushing life stream, and she wilted against one of the portico's white

141

pillars. She slid downward to the sun-warmed black and white sandstone tiles. For a moment she remained there, voices in the house oddly distant—David had discovered the returning men. Her gaze traveled across the front sward and the landing far below, out along the river to the sweeping bend where sunlight changed the dull water to a beautiful orange canvas.

"Maria!" David's concerned voice. He hurried to her side and took her hand.

She offered a wavering smile. "I'm fine. I just needed to sit down."

"Jack is safe," he said with little emotion.

"Yes, thank God."

"You look tired; did you not sleep?"

"A bit."

"At Ketch's bedside?"

She frowned.

"So he lives?"

"Yes. But he has a bad fever. Perhaps we were too late and the poison has a hold of him."

"Then it will be the end of him after all," he said, almost to himself. When he caught Maria's look, he frowned. "Forgive me."

With David's help she got to her feet, said, "Go on to breakfast. I'll see if Helen is awake."

When she reached the girl's bedchamber, she found it empty. Turning back to the ballroom, she saw Ketch's door halfway open and heard Helen's voice. She hurried across and halted just outside Ketch's room to listen.

"What happened to your arm, Mr. Ketch?"

Maria had to strain to hear Ketch's reply: "They cut it off."

"'Cause of the snake?"

"Aye."

In the long pause that followed, Maria peeked around the door. Pip stood on the far side of the bed, tentatively fanning Ketch while Helen stood on the near side within arm's reach...if he had an arm to reach for her. He lay quietly, only a small clutching movement of his hand against the mattress proof of his pain. His wet, dark eyes were on Helen, unblinking, half closed.

Helen hugged the stuffed bear in her arms. "I'm sorry I got stuck in the mud and you got hurt."

"Don't fret 'bout that, Miss Helen. I promised yer mamma I'd protect you. Remember?"

"Are you going to get better?"

"I don't know."

The girl wavered. "You must get better. Then you can help me find my daddy like you did before. No one else can find him."

Maria hurried into the chamber. Surprised, Helen turned as if caught doing something that would garner a scolding. Forcing calm, Maria smiled to reassure her and said good morning. Helen shocked her with a small, sad, "Good morning," eyes downcast. It was the first time since her father's death that she had offered such a greeting to Maria.

"Are you keeping Mr. Ketch company?"

Helen nodded shallowly.

"Are you hungry?"

The child shook her head.

"Why don't you snuggle back into bed while I see to Mr. Ketch, then we'll go down to breakfast together? Pip, go with her."

Helen glanced from her to Ketch whose gaze still remained upon her as if his life depended on her presence. Then she slowly left with Pip. Ketch closed his eyes. Two vertical creases between his eyebrows revealed the pain he had masked while the child had been there; he could hold the dam no longer.

Maria came around the bed and soaked a clean rag in the basin's fresh water. "Why did you lie to me about Jack?" With agitated force she wrung the rag.

Ketch choked back a groan, his limbs moving again as though to escape.

"You told me Jack sent you. But he said he didn't. Why did you lie?"

Ketch stared at her in an instance of enraged clarity. "He's here?"

"No."

"But he's free?"

"Yes, damn you." Infuriated by her own stupidity, she glowered at him and withheld the cooling rag. "You'll not do to Jack what you did to Defoe."

He closed his eyes, writhed slightly, and rasped, "Jack Mallory don't care a damn about his sister...or you. If he did, he'd never have gone after that convoy; he'd be here, wouldn't he?"

"Damn you to hell. I should have listened to Willis and David." She crumpled the rag in her fist. "You can rot in that bed; it's what you deserve." With that, she threw the rag into the basin and left him.

#

143

The clock in the bedchamber where Jack awoke showed nearly noon. All was quiet save for beastly snores from Smith next to him in bed. Jack blinked his hazy eyes to make sure he had read the time correctly. For a moment he was unsure of where he was, then his glance caught Margaret's yellow dress draped over a chair, and he vaguely recalled being brought to Wildwood's south flanker in the waning hour before dawn touched the sky. Now the closed shutters and drapes blocked some of the sunlight and muffled a variety of birdcalls. He lay there for some time, trying to decipher all that had happened in the past twenty-four hours. Glancing at the sullied dress, he wondered how Margaret had explained the loss of her clothing to Sara Waterston that morning. Or had the Waterstons been in on the scheme?

Without disturbing Smith he got out of bed. A pair of brown breeches lay meticulously folded upon a dresser, stockings and a shirt neatly beside them. Once dressed Jack wandered about the deserted ground floor—a central parlor with two bedchambers on one side and a dining room and a locked room on the other. In the dining room where a breeze off the river trickled through the open windows, he found two place settings with immaculate linen and sparkling silver. Wine, dishes of bread, butter, and fruits had been arrayed on the polished table. With a furtive glance, he sat down and set to devouring everything there, reluctantly halting in time to leave something for Smith.

At any moment he expected to see at least a servant, but as time passed he saw no one. As far as he was aware the only other soul to know of his presence here besides Archer was Ethan Castle, a reticent white man who worked for Archer and had met them at the landing in those early hours. He had brought them here and told them not to leave the flanker, to wait for Archer's return. Jack thought of Anna Archer— Ezra's frail wife whom he had met shortly after his mother's death— and considered seeking her out but decided to obey Castle's directive.

The next few hours slipped by in slow boredom, putting Jack on edge. Eventually Smith dragged himself out of bed and demolished what was left of the food and wine.

Jack had never seen his friend clean shaven. The absence of his heavy beard revealed several small scars and a humorous pattern of lighter skin. Here in the filtered daylight his altered appearance somehow made him look younger and older at the same time. Already heavy stubble sprouted. Jack had considered his own nicked up, bare face earlier in a looking glass and scowled at his inability to cultivate anything respectable to mask and toughen his youthful, fine features. With humiliation he remembered the couple of sailors last night on the strand who had called out crude remarks as he passed in Margaret's dress.

Jack's pacing elicited protests from Smith who urged calm. As Jack twisted the bracelet upon his wrist, he thought of Maria, of Ketch. Surely after Maria told Defoe that Ketch was responsible for Logan's death, Defoe would have dispatched the son of a bitch. Perhaps he had nothing to worry about after all.

Around half past three that afternoon Archer arrived outside the flanker's front door, driven up from the landing by a liveried slave in a small, covered gig of highly polished cherrywood and shining harness. A ridiculous sight out here in the middle of nowhere, among little else but slaves and god-forsaken swamps. Archer looked more like a politician arriving at Parliament than a planter in the backcountry of colonial Carolina. Was he trying to impress or simply save himself from a hot walk up from the landing? He stepped down without assistance, unbalanced not in the least by his immobilized left arm. His clean clothes did not reflect the four hours he had just spent in a boat from Charles Town. Jack noticed with no small amount of curiosity how Archer never seemed to sweat much if at all, even in his layers of clothes. Jack's thoughts returned to Margaret's dress, and he wondered why she had not accompanied her father back to Wildwood.

When Archer entered the parlor, a black slave descended from the second story—gray-haired, thin, and dressed in spotless white. How he had thus far remained silent and unseen disturbed Jack. Seamlessly the old man took his master's coat and disappeared into the bedchamber at the front of the flanker.

"Gentlemen," Archer said in a voice lighter—but certainly not friendlier—than Jack had ever heard before. "I am pleased to see you heeded my direction to remain here. I trust you have spoken with no one outside these walls other than my man Castle."

"We have not," Jack answered.

"Pray sit down." Archer gestured to a maroon settee, then sat in a matching armchair across the Persian rug from them. Within seconds the same servant materialized with a pitcher of lemonade and a decanter of brandy with glasses on a blinding silver tray. He poured lemonade for his master and brandy for the guests. Then just as mysteriously the stoic slave vanished. Archer downed a considerable amount of his drink before he sighed with pleasure—the most pleasure Jack had ever seen upon his long, tanned face—and leaned back in his chair to consider them with his round, dark eyes, world's different from those of his children, more like Ketch's eyes.

"I will not mince words, gentlemen; 'tis not in my best interest to harbor fugitives on my property. You are wondering why I delivered you from your certain death sentence, Captain Mallory. As a businessman I am sure you know I would never do something so reckless for nothing."

"Was it Margaret's...Miss Archer's idea?" Jack asked in the hopes that the young woman retained her fondness for him.

Archer's smile held more sarcasm than warmth. "My daughter was certainly concerned for your welfare and solicited my resources to secure your release, but truth be told I had planned to assist you before she approached me."

Jack sensed Smith's concerns grow along with his own. Because of his unease, Jack forced levity and a bit of his own mockery: "So then you didn't rescue me out of loyalty to your dead partner—my dear stepfather?"

One corner of Archer's mouth rose. "I am afraid I cannot claim such an admirable motive, dear boy."

"Then why?" Smith took a healthy swallow of brandy.

"I have a proposition for Captain Mallory. Something that will ultimately benefit both of us."

Jack eyed him.

"I have two...tasks that I need you to accomplish for me. The first is very simple. My niece and her mother will be coming to Wildwood for my daughter's wedding, which as you may know is within a fortnight. I was to send my son and one of my own vessels to Virginia to fetch them, but that vessel has been delayed indefinitely in Boston. So instead I will send you. You will leave immediately, for it will be best if you are not seen in these waters or upon these lands until the...excitement of your escape settles." He sipped more lemonade.

"And how will I sail to Virginia when I have no vessel?"

Archer bobbed his glass in Smith's direction. "Your quartermaster tells me that your brig waits in the offing."

"My crew won't subscribe to an unprofitable cruise up the coast to pick up passengers. They're pirates, not a parcel of merchant sailors at your beck and call."

Archer raised a dark eyebrow at him. "I understand your men took several thousand pounds of specie from one of Wylder's ships. Why do they need to remain pirates when they possess such riches and could become honest men?"

Smith snorted. "Honest men? So they can work for rich buggers like you or give up half their money in taxes? At sea they're their own men; they answer to no one, not even to Jack in all things."

"You seem to forget something, Mr. Smith. They will always be under a sentence of death for the crimes they have committed. That makes enjoying their plunder dangerous business."

"And taking a jaunt up to Virginia will change that?" Jack scoffed.

"Captain Mallory." Archer pour more lemonade. "How do you think James Logan survived in his sea-going enterprise as long as he did? What other pirate has had such longevity?"

Jack glanced at Smith's unhappy face.

"My influence reaches throughout this province, to the Assembly and to Governor Ludwell himself. Indeed to the Lords Proprietors even." He swept his hand in a wide arc. "Much of what I have acquired on land is thanks to those…friends. You might be surprised at what I can accomplish with a few well-written and well-directed letters or audiences. Ludwell is new to office and, though his ascension is being contested by the deposed Sothel who turned a blind eye on piracy, he is bent on the eradication of pirates, so I am sure there is nothing he would like more than to hear that the crew of the *Prodigal* is willing to abandon their high seas thievery off his coast."

"Are you talking pardons?"

"Yes, Captain. Full pardons for all of them, if they so desire."

"And if they don't?"

"Then I will compensate them for their journey to James Town, and they can take their chances with the law." He sipped his drink. "They must hold *some* loyalty to you, otherwise they never would have come back. Certainly you can influence them."

"Their return may have more to do with Smith's silver tongue and Charles Town's whores than any loyalty to me."

"I understand the crew of the *Alliance* has been paid off, but that does not mean they will not speak up if they recognize one of your crew. If your men are wise, they will stay away from Charles Town for a while."

"Wise?" Smith grinned sidelong at Jack. "Aye, the Prodigals might be loyal. But wise? No."

"So, Captain, will you repay my benevolence and discretion with a quiet sail up the coast and back?"

"And if I don't?"

Archer's gaze hardened with the rapidity of a swat. "I have but to snap my fingers and the two of you will be in chains, on your way downriver. And if you would think to buy your freedom by implicating or slandering me, think again."

Jack did not attempt to conceal his discontent. "And who's to say we won't still end up in chains once we fetch your kin from Virginia?"

"Call me what you will, Captain, but I am no blackguard. I am a man of my word. Captain Logan could have attested to that."

Jack thought of his own broken promise to Waterston. How easily he had forfeited his honor...

"And there is still the second task for which I will need you."

Jack glanced at Smith, still seeing caution there but also a slight nod of encouragement, perhaps so slight that Archer could not discern it. "What is the second task?" With a flick of his wrist, Jack emptied his glass.

Satisfaction spread across Archer's harshly handsome visage. "I am afraid I cannot divulge that at this time. Not all of the pieces are yet in place. But I assure you, if you are successful in this last endeavor, you will be rewarded with more than just your freedom."

"And what does that mean exactly?"

Archer sank deeper into the chair, exuded self-confidence and satisfaction at how he was able to lay everything out and watch his quarry follow the trail like a baited animal to the hunter. "Your sister is at Leighlin, along with Miss Cordero, who—mind you—has caused me considerable trouble, which I am willing to overlook if you cooperate. I am sure you would like nothing more than to be permanently reunited with them, to stay at Leighlin and live without fear for your life."

Jack produced a small, noncommittal nod and waited with half-narrowed eyes. He wondered how Archer knew of his relationship with Maria, then realized—Logan, of course, for there could be no one else. Did Archer also know that his son was just downriver?

"You must know Logan would never have left Leighlin to you," Archer continued, "especially after you brought so much sorrow into his life."

The hard truth knocked away some of Jack's strength, but he tried to hide any reaction. He had not even considered the legal ramifications of Logan's death.

"The truth of the matter is this: in the event of his death and his wife's, the guardianship of Leighlin and his daughter falls to me. I retain power over the plantation until Helen is of age."

A growing unease soured the brandy in Jack's belly. "And if something were to happen to Helen, what would happen to Leighlin?"

Archer smiled pleasantly. "Why, Leighlin would become mine."

Jack's blood chilled under the power of that cold simper. The veiled threat was there, laid out skillfully before him, leaving him no choice but to placate this man by obeying his whims. "So if I accomplish these two...tasks, then you will see that I can safely live at Leighlin with my sister?"

"As safely as Logan did. You have my word. And further, when enough time has passed and Long Arm Jack has been sufficiently forgotten by the citizens, you will become Helen's guardian. I will maintain control over Leighlin, however. After all, what do you know of running such an operation?"

Although a part of Jack tried to accept the fact that Archer's proposition was almost generous, considering that his life had been in the balance just a few hours ago, he could not ignore the unrest in his mind and body, especially not knowing what the enigmatic secondary task would be. He sensed Archer had a particular reason why he would not reveal details beyond the vague explanation he had given. And would Archer demand more once the bargain was fulfilled? Jack had sold his soul to the devil once before when revenge had controlled his every thought and action for seven years—and had led him to his current unpleasant situation. He had paid the price the first time by losing his mother, and now Helen hung in the balance. He did not want to enter into an agreement with Archer that would compromise his future with his sister and perhaps Maria. At the moment, though, he had no choice. He would have to take his chances in order to survive, if for nothing else than to care for his sister as he had promised their mother; he would not fail her again.

"Very well," Jack said at last and leaned forward to offer his hand to Archer.

A satisfied and slightly surprised smile spread across the planter's face as he shook Jack's hand. "Excellent, Captain." He set down his glass and stood. "Now I will let you get some rest until the tide turns. At that time we will sail downriver to Leighlin. They are expecting us so that you may say good-bye; I know you are eager to see your sister. From there you will take one of Logan's boats and rendezvous with your brig to begin your journey to Virginia. I will be sending Mr. Castle with you. He will see to my niece and her mother."

Jack stood and smiled wryly. "And he'll make sure I comply with our agreement."

Archer's eyes took on an amused light, almost a twinkle. "Indeed, Captain."

# CHAPTER 14

As the magnificent sight of Leighlin House slipped into view, an unexpected lump formed in Jack's throat. Sunlight blazed against its windows and red roof, dazzled upon the portico's four white limestone columns. A flock of gray coots sped through the air from the forested banks upriver, across the expanse of Leighlin's sweeping terraces and ponds, and continued southward beyond the treetops. Along the banks of the ornamental ponds, long-legged snowy egrets hunted patiently, like timeless statues.

Jack wondered why he was so moved. Was it simply the anticipation of seeing Maria and Helen? Or had he developed some sort of attachment to Leighlin, though he had spent but a short time there before Logan's death? Maybe the fact that his mother had lived there gave him a certain fondness for the plantation. Whatever stirred these feelings also made him dread separating from Maria and Helen once more.

When he stepped from the boat with Smith close behind, he wanted to break into a run, but instead he waited for Archer. Ethan Castle, dutiful if not solicitous, assisted Archer in his awkward struggle to the dock. Jack had yet to form an opinion of Castle, for the man had spoken little during their brief encounters. He was an Englishman, perhaps from Liverpool, but his accent seemed a bit worn down, as if he had been away from his native land for some time. Jack guessed his age somewhere in his thirties. His physical traits had no resemblance to Archer or his family, so he undoubtedly was not a relation. Maybe he was indentured as were so many colonists.

Smith, Archer, and Jack left Castle behind at the landing. Jack could hardly contain his relief and excitement as they climbed the terraces and crossed the sward. The two slaves in the flanking gardens paused in their work to stand respectfully facing Jack, hats removed. He thought of his mother's grave beyond the right-hand garden. He would visit it before he left and take her some fresh-cut roses—her favorite flower.

When he caught sight of someone on the portico, his steps faltered.

Helen looked so tiny standing there alone, her black dress aflutter about her legs in the river breeze.

Smith said, "Looks like someone's a-waitin' for you, lad."

Jack broke into a run, his speed hindered by the healing gash on his thigh. Helen waited, toy bear held against her chest with both hands. Then just as Jack reached the steps, she wheeled and darted back into the house, calling, "Mr. David! John is here!"

Jack bounded up the steps two at a time. When David and Maria emerged from the house, Helen appeared in the doorway behind them, her wide blue eyes steady upon him. She offered no smile, but the brightness of her gaze made him believe she was glad to see him. Perhaps his uncharacteristic lack of facial hair took her slightly aback. He turned his attention to Maria, and what he thought to be tears in her eyes brought him up short. With a tempered expression, she smiled at him, and he could see that she restrained a flood of words.

David spoke first. "Welcome back, Captain," and offered his hand and an odd smile, standing close to Maria, too close for Jack's liking or comfort. After shaking Jack's hand, the younger man's attention shifted to his father coming up the steps with Smith, but he did not reflect the expected alarm.

"I'm so glad you're safe," Maria managed.

How Jack wished they were alone. Desperately he wanted to take her in his arms, to make up for his pitiful show of affection before she had left the *Prodigal*.

"Look who we have here," Smith beamed. "Back in a dress, I see."

Maria laughed nervously as Smith stepped next to Jack. "Smitty. I almost didn't recognize you."

Smith absently rubbed his scruffy chin as he was wont to do since shaving off his whiskers. "Hard gettin' used to, I admit. But I wager it won't take long to grow back."

David took on formality as he addressed his parent: "Father."

Jack was astonished to find no anger on Ezra Archer's face, though certainly no warmth or satisfaction either. He must have already known about his son being at Leighlin; yet regardless of that probable fact, why was there no hostility toward David who had—after all—shot the man? Was the sling not reminder enough to all?

"I hope you have time to stay for supper, Father. We decided to eat early to accommodate your visit since your missive said you will be traveling downriver afterward."

Archer looked between his son and Maria, as if mulling over something, and for a fleeting instant he smiled. "Actually Captain

Mallory and Mr. Smith will be the ones traveling downriver. I will only be going as far as the Draytons'. So in order for my companions to take advantage of the full ebb, they will not be able to tarry beyond our repast."

"You're leaving?" Maria's tone revealed her disappointment.

When Jack floundered, Archer answered for him, "To show his appreciation for my family's help, Captain Mallory will be seeing to an errand for us."

Helen quickly vanished into the house. The pained curiosity on Maria's face begged Jack for clarification.

"Do come in," David said in a way too familiar for Jack's tastes. The boy looked disturbingly at home in his surroundings, as if this place protected him from his father's ill will. "We can talk over supper."

As David turned for the doorway, Jack took the opportunity to ask, "How is Helen?"

Maria frowned. "She still says very little to me, but she talks to David and some of the others."

"Does she still not understand what's happened?"

"I don't think so. She speaks of her father simply being lost."

Smith offered cheerfully, "Perhaps seein' her wayward brother again will help bring her 'round."

The light fare eaten at Wildwood was long gone from Jack's belly by the time he saw the long, laden table in Leighlin's dining room. Logan's usual place was left respectfully empty. To Jack's consternation, David held out a chair for Maria next to his own. Then the young man further irritated by helping Helen into the seat on his other side. That left Jack with no choice but to sit between Archer and Smith on the opposite side. The boy's obvious control and assumption of power grated upon Jack. David's display of awkwardness while at sea, his deference to Jack, was nowhere to be found here on land.

As Mary, Rose, and Pip poured wine and served the food—beef slaughtered earlier today along with sweet potatoes, corn, peas, and cornbread—the uneasiness on Maria's down-turned face increased, as if she could sense Jack's growing displeasure.

"How did you come to be arrested?" she spoke suddenly, perhaps to avoid any possible lapse in conversation.

Jack described the attack upon the convoy, ending with the admission, "I was fool enough to fall for Ketch's bait and chased him below deck. That's when I was taken." An inner tremor silenced him when his senses relived that moment and the nightmare memory that had followed. He forced his attention to Helen, but the girl did not seem to attend to his narrative, using a finger to prod her warm beef; her father would have scolded her lack of manners, no doubt, but no one said a word.

"What about the *Prodigal*?" Maria asked.

"They freed her from the ship and sailed off, leaving me and Smitty behind."

"Aye," Smith said, his mouth full of cornbread, which he quickly swallowed so he could continue without spitting crumbs. "But the daft boy talked 'em into lettin' me go."

"What about Angus and the *Fortune*?"

"They sailed with us for a day 'til I convinced the Prodigals to come back here for Jack. Then they sailed north to spend their purchase."

"Are you going back to the *Prodigal* now?" Her gaze shifted from Smith to Jack just as Helen's gaze lifted from her plate to her brother.

Jack could look at neither of their disappointed faces. "I'm afraid I have no choice." He took a full gulp of wine, then set the goblet down and compelled himself to turn toward Helen. "I'll be back as soon as I can."

Helen revealed no belief in his words.

Maria said, "But it's too dangerous for you to sail right now."

Archer gave Maria an indulgent smile. "No need to fret, I assure you. If Captain Mallory is prudent on his journey, no one should molest him."

"Do you think the militia will look for you here, Jack?"

Again Archer interceded, "The only people in this region who know of Captain Mallory's ties are my family and the Waterstons—the couple who offered the Captain lodging while under arrest. Those who were at Mrs. Logan's funeral were told no details, and if they recognized him in town after his arrest, I trust those people have been discreet, as friends of the Logans."

This eased some of Maria's anxiety.

Jack sought to change the angle of the conversation to something benign. "I will need to speak with Defoe before I leave."

Silence dropped over the table, and the glance between David and Maria set Jack's nerves on edge.

David said, "The day after we arrived here, Mr. Defoe disappeared. We have search parties out looking for him still."

"Disappeared?" Jack stopped eating.

"No one has seen him, not the slaves nor any of Logan's men,"

David continued while Maria attended to her plate with fresh concentration. "Mr. Willis said Mr. Defoe rarely leaves the plantation, and when he does he tells the other men his business, and of course he would have to take one of the boats, which he has not; they are all accounted for."

"That don't make no sense," Smith said around another mouthful of food washed down by copious amounts of wine. "Defoe didn't strike me as the kind of cove what would wander off daft or drunk and fall into the river or a swamp."

"Indeed," said Archer. "He is a loyal and conscientious man. I often told Captain Logan how fortunate he was to have such an efficient overseer."

Jack's focus returned to the reticent young woman across from him whose sudden interest in her meal did not ring true. "Maria, do you have any ideas? Did he give you any clue as to where he might've been off to?"

Her mahogany eyes lifted to his, then she stared back down at her plate. "No. He addressed the slaves after we told him what had happened with Logan. He said good night to me later, and that was the last I saw of him."

"I tried to find him," Helen's small voice surprised all of them. She did not look at anyone as she tortured her sweet potatoes with her spoon, and she spoke as if to herself, like someone confessing a sordid secret. "But I got stuck in the mud after I fell off my pony."

"Fell off!" Jack cried with dramatic flair to draw her out. "Did you get hurt?"

Helen shook her head. "Mr. Ketch did."

"Ketch...?"

David spoke before Maria could, his tone and expression showing enough displeasure to rival Jack's own. "We did not know he was still on the property."

"He saved me from a snake," Helen murmured, "and it bit him instead."

This news provided Jack with some relief. "Then he is dead?"

A muffled, distraught outcry drifted down through the large chimney that connected every room on this side of the house. Helen gasped, her head lifting, eyes wide. All paused, some looking upward, some staring at others in alarm. Then Helen scrambled from her chair and bolted to the stair hall, ignoring Maria's calls for her return.

Quickly Maria set aside her linen. "Excuse me." As she came around the table, Jack stood and reached for her arm to halt her. She regarded him with a strange fear that caused him to retract his hand.

"You mean to tell me he's here?" he quietly demanded. "In this very house?"

"Captain." David pushed his chair back with a scrape.

"He *murdered* Helen's father," Jack continued, close to Maria, so close that her scent almost disarmed his outrage. "He would've killed *me* if it wasn't for Smitty."

Aberrant anger flushed David's face as he drew near.

"You don't understand," Maria said. "We didn't want to help him. It's Helen... She begged Willis to help him. She blames herself for him being bitten. And she thinks if he lives he can find her father."

"What?"

"I heard her say it to him. He must have told her before—when he kidnapped her—that he would help her find her father, and he did in her eyes. She thinks he can do it again." Her voice dropped along with her own agitation. "We couldn't just let him die in front of her."

David took a gentle, protective hold of her arm, drew her back, stirred Jack's ire in a new direction. Jack pushed the irritation aside. "So what did you do?"

"Willis amputated the arm that was bitten. But Ketch has fallen into a fever." She glanced upward. "And it sounds as if it's worsened."

"Mr. Willis!" Helen's distressed voice echoed through the stair hall, followed by the rumble of her running feet.

Maria glanced, askance, at David who stepped into the Great Hall. "Helen. Helen, what is it?"

"We have to find Mr. Willis. Mr. Ketch is very sick."

"Helen—"

"Please, Mr. David. Help me find him."

"Very well then. I will ring the bell so he comes to the house. You must not fret so."

The girl grabbed hold of his hand and tugged him toward the rear portico and out of Jack's sight. From the far overmantel in the Great Hall, the portrait of Jack's mother reached out to him, the dark blue of her dress turned almost to black in the weakening evening light through the west windows.

"I'm sorry, Jack," Maria said near a whisper. Hastily she left the room. Jack listened to her footfalls as she hurried up the stairs. Then the bell began to clang sharply.

"Come back to the table, lad," Smith cajoled. "You can't go up there and slit that bastard's throat in front o' the womenfolk. With any luck he'll be dead by nightfall."

Undecided, Jack stared a moment longer at his mother's alabaster face, at the golden hair so like her daughter's, so different from his own.

David returned to the dining room while Helen rushed back upstairs. "I tried to talk Maria out of helping Ketch." He reclaimed his chair. "I do not favor his presence here any more than you do, Captain, I assure you."

Jack shuffled back to his chair next to Smith.

"'Tis fortuitous that my son is here," Archer said, unaffected by all that had just happened around him. "As Ketch recuperates—if he does—David can make sure he causes no mischief while you are gone. And then there is the running of the plantation to think about. With Mr. Defoe absent, Leighlin needs someone well-versed in the duties of managing a large plantation." He gave a small smile meant for no one in particular before drinking his wine. "I have taught my son everything I know. You will find Leighlin operating smoothly when you return, Captain."

Jack's head swam. What in hell was going on here? He stared at David, not having considered him remaining longer at Leighlin or that his father would allow it, let alone encourage it. When David met his gaze, Jack realized he had underestimated the young man's strength as well as the extent to which he would go to remain near Maria.

"Surely, Mr. Archer, you have need of your son at Wildwood."

"Not at the moment. Perhaps when we harvest the indigo next month, but for now he is needed here with you gone and with his wife needing to stay near your sister."

Smith stammered, "Did you say...wife?"

Archer's last words echoed in Jack's head. Surely he had heard incorrectly. To whom was the man referring? He had never heard of David having a wife. Then he noticed David's steady, unblinking, triumphant look, and Jack felt suddenly sick. His left hand tightened upon his table knife.

"Wife?" he strangled.

"Yes, Captain," David said.

Smith clutched Jack's arm as if sensing his desire to leap across the table at the opportunistic son of a bitch. Slowly Jack sat straighter in his chair, his right fist clenching, the other fingering the knife.

"I find it difficult to believe your father would allow such a thing."

Archer wiped his mouth with a linen. "Unfortunately, Captain, my son is of age; he did not require my consent." A hardness edged his voice, his jaw tight. "Do not think I approve of the match, but what is done is done."

"Maria has cared for me," David said, "and now I will care for her. She needs a man who appreciates her, who loves her."

"A man?" Jack laughed harshly. "You're nothing but a boy who can't tell the difference between a bobstay and a back stay. You're no more of a match for someone like her than—"

"Than you, Captain?" Anger colored David's composed features, darkened the blue of his eyes to that of a stormy sea. "Perhaps you can tell me why she fled your cabin that night aboard the *Prodigal* and hid in the wardroom? If you were any kind of gentleman—"

Jack started to stand; Smith clung to him like a terrier.

"I think, Mr. Smith," Archer calmly but ardently said, setting his linen aside and standing, "it would be prudent if we three took our leave now, before we are acting as seconds in a duel. And I am living proof that my son can hit whatever he is aiming at."

David also stood. "Perhaps that would be best."

"I want you gone from Leighlin," Jack demanded. "Maria will stay with Helen, but you're to leave."

"And what of Ketch? You would have her alone here with him?"

"Rogers and Dell will protect her. Damn you, I want you gone."

"Jack." Smith yanked him toward the doorway.

"And Helen? I am the only person to whom she will speak. You would have me leave her now while you are gone once again? You may curse me but have you no compassion for her?"

"You insolent bastard." Jack lunged to escape Smith's grasp, but the older man threw him into the Great Hall and pushed him toward the front door.

"Jack. Let it go. Let it go for now, boy." With a powerful effort Smith forced Jack out onto the portico, Archer only steps behind. "Get a hold o' yerself, lad." He shook Jack a final time then freed him, staring him into submission and sensibility. Jack looked over his quartermaster's shoulder into the house, but David was wise enough not to follow. "Now let's go." Smith provided a strong nudge toward the steps, his bi-colored complexion blending into one of dark bad humor. "The sooner we're gone, the sooner you can get back here and straighten out this mess."

#

Maria found Ketch soaked in sweat, the bedclothes thrashed into damp wads, unintelligible mumbles falling from his parched lips. He had vomited again, this time unable to avoid getting the foul bile all over himself. For a long moment she did not move from the doorway. She struggled within herself, for she knew her wanton neglect had exacerbated Ketch's condition, and now she had to choose to either rectify that or allow it to continue and end in his death. Well, she told herself as she stepped into the bedchamber, the least she could do was clean him up. She retrieved the rag from the basin where she had left it after that morning's argument and proceeded, though the task proved difficult because of his agitation.

"Damn you," she quietly said in frustration. "Hold still."

She startled at the sight of Helen in the doorway, the child's anxious eyes on Ketch. To distract the girl, she said, "Helen, come take the pitcher and fetch fresh water for Mr. Ketch please."

The child darted around the bed as Maria tossed the warm contents of basin and pitcher out of a window. Helen tucked her toy bear into the black ribbon sash around her waist. When Maria handed the pitcher to her, the girl regarded her with a mixture of appreciation and deep worry. Maria smiled and touched her cheek.

Helen softly asked, "You're going to make Mr. Ketch better, aren't you?"

Her eyes held doubt, the first Maria had ever witnessed in her. How painful it was to see this child's continued suffering, and she realized with sudden clarity that no matter what her own desires she would not be responsible for compounding that suffering.

"Yes, I'm going to try. Now run along and bring Mary back with you."

The girl instantly obeyed, her feet loud upon the floorboards as she hurried out with the pitcher hugged to her chest.

"She's in danger."

Maria turned at the unexpected hoarse rasp of Ketch's voice. His eyes tried to focus on her. His struggles had halted but for his left hand clutching at the mattress.

Weaker, panting, he repeated, "She's in danger."

Composing herself, Maria recalled their earlier conversation, thought of Jack's safety and her promise to Helen. "You said you're supposed to protect her, but how will you protect her if you die…if I let you die?"

Her troubling words distorted his face, but he could not reply, for jagged coughs shook him, and he retched again. His eyes rolled back, and furrows dredged his forehead. His breathing increased, and Maria knew unconsciousness would reclaim him soon if not death itself. All these hours of inattention, of being left alone to suffer in the day's heat, had taken their toll on his body and, she hoped, on his mind as well. She needed to reap what she could before he would neither comprehend nor remember.

"There's only one person at Leighlin who gives a pin about keeping you alive. And if I'm going to do that for Helen's sake, I need something from you first."

He eyed her with distant suspicion.

"I need your promise, your solemn promise that you will do Jack no harm. Do you hear me?"

Ketch struggled to swallow, teeth clenched in displeasure at her words.

"You claim such loyalty to Ella Logan," she continued desperately. "You save her daughter but try to kill her son. What loyalty is there in that?"

He pressed his eyes shut, struggled with the pain that racked him.

"What do you think she would say, looking down on your pathetic, mangled self? What do you think she would do if she had to choose between your life and Jack's, even after all you did for her?"

"Fuck you," he feebly spat.

"She would see you to your end to protect him, as should I."

His anger seemed to fuel the fever, his face an alarming red, his head lolling back and forth in resistance. She could see his struggle to choose, could feel the rage in him, could see it in the pulsing of a large purple vein on his forehead. Although she knew he was powerless to act, she made sure she kept out of reach.

"Promise me, Ketch. You'll not harm him."

He glowered at her.

"You say Helen's in danger and you want to protect her; you want to live here. I can convince Jack to let you stay, but you must promise not to harm anyone else." Of course she had no idea if she could acquire Jack's permission; in fact, she was quite sure she could not, but...

Ketch's bared teeth showed palely. "Damn you..."

"If you survive and are banished from here, what will you do? No one will hire a one-armed seaman." She stopped, said no more, waited near hidden panic, for she could not bear to see anyone—not even Ketch—in so much physical distress. But she could not give in, not now.

Helen came to the doorway, pitcher in hand. She stared at Ketch's tortured expression, then hurried around the bed.

"I brought water, Mr. Ketch."

Maria took the pitcher and tantalizingly poured the contents into the basin, filling the room with liquid sound and the promise of relief. Ketch moaned.

Helen drifted over to the bed, her bear now held in the crook of one arm. Maria felt an instinctive urge to pull the child away from him, but instead she watched, mesmerized, as the girl took Ketch's hand. Before being kidnapped Helen had shrank away from Ketch during the one instance Maria had witnessed them interact; she easily recalled Ketch's humiliation over the child's reluctance. Now Helen's touch reflected none of her former aversion, and Ketch's anger and even the horrible discomfort momentarily left him. He wore a profound look of wonder and gratitude that stilled Maria's breath and made her suspect that no other human being had ever before touched him with such tenderness. His hand slowly closed around Helen's fingers, and he nearly smiled, his eyes moist.

Tears spilled down Helen's cheeks. "I'm sorry, Mr. Ketch. I shouldn't have ridden my pony out alone. Daddy told me never to do that."

"Don't fret so, child."

"Everyone keeps going away. You aren't going away, are you?"

Maria drew Helen back from the bed. "He's not going away, *osita*. He's promised to protect you…and your brother. Haven't you, Ketch?"

Helen waited hopefully for his reply, fingers kneading the bear.

At last he whispered, "Aye," with a begrudging glance at Maria before he closed his eyes.

Just then Mary appeared in the doorway. The slave's hands twisted in her apron as she stared at Ketch.

"Mary, have a wash tub taken out to the rear portico," Maria gestured. "Fill it half full with cool water. Do you hear?"

"Y—yes'm."

"Get the other servants to help you. Tell Thomas and Nahum that I'll need to have Ketch carried out to the tub once you're done."

"Yes'm."

"And tell Pip to bring up a fan."

The slave bustled off to comply, talking to herself.

"Helen, why don't you go back down to visit with your brother? I'm sure he's wondering where you are. Maybe he'll even stay long enough to tuck you into bed." When Helen lingered, Maria gently escorted her to the door. "Go on now. I'll take care of Mr. Ketch."

Willis's booted feet rang in the stair hall, and Helen ran to meet him. "Hurry, Mr. Willis." At the top of the stairs, she took hold of his

160

hand and tugged him into the ballroom.

Willis aimed a scowl at Maria as he allowed the child to drag him forward. "What's all this about?"

"Helen, run along now." Maria waited until the girl was at last headed to the stairs, then she turned to Willis with new-found urgency. "Ketch's fever is worse. I thought it would help if we put him in cool water. Mary is having a tub brought to the upper portico."

"This is why you called us back?" he growled with a glance beyond her into the bedchamber. "There's two more hours of daylight we could use searching."

"I've no need for lectures, Mr. Willis. If you won't help, then hold your tongue and leave."

He gave her a half-threatening glare and entered the bedchamber. Ketch lay unconscious, his skin glistening in the failing light.

"Have you changed the dressing?"

"Not since earlier."

"Fetch me fresh bandages."

Gladly she left, not wanting to see the horrid stump of Ketch's arm. When she returned with bandages as well as fresh towels and rags, Mary and Pip made a procession of buckets through the ballroom and out onto the portico where Thomas and Nahum had placed a washtub.

"Mind what I said, Mary," Maria ordered. "Only half full. We can't get his bandage wet."

Willis straightened up from his examination and announced, "The stump is not the issue. The fever is coming from elsewhere. Effects from the venom like as not. Bastard refuses to die. I can bleed him, I reckon." With a sigh, he continued, "Leave the bandages and go find something we can use around his chest to keep him from sliding down into the tub."

Mary brought her a length of rope, and Maria wound towels around it to pad its coarseness. By then the men had carried Ketch to the portico and lowered him into the tub. His eyes opened at the shock of the water against his hot flesh, then he drifted away again as Maria brought the rope. Willis, determined to shield her eyes from Ketch's nakedness, told her to remain at the portico door and give the rope to Thomas, but Maria scowled and stepped forward.

"I've nursed injured men before, Mr. Willis, clothed and naked. I'm not an innocent."

"Suit yourself."

Together they threaded the band under Ketch's armpits then tied the ends to the feet of the tub.

"You'll have to make sure it don't bind him," Willis instructed, "'specially that right shoulder, hear? And keep that bandage dry."

"Thomas," Maria directed, "I want fresh water coming all the time to keep the water as cool as we can. You and Nahum alternate taking two buckets of water out of the tub each time and replace them with fresh. Understand?"

"Yes'm."

"Mary, where's Pip with that fan? This breeze may die as evening comes on. Someone fetch me a chair." She took a cloth out of the nearby basin and began to pass water over Ketch's chest. She wiped his neck and carefully squeezed water over his bowed head.

"He needs water inside of 'im just as much," Willis said as Mary brought a chair for Maria. "You must try to wake him soon. If he's not able to drink and keep water down, give him a soaked cloth to suck on. When I get back later, I'll bleed him."

With that, Willis started for the doorway where he paused to cynically say, "You haven't asked me about Defoe."

Maria stammered and stumbled over an excuse.

He scoffed. "Why don't you just tell us so we don't waste our time and energy?"

"I don't know what happened to him."

Willis snorted and threw a distasteful glance at Ketch. "I reckon *he* does."

With that, he disappeared into the house. His desertion—though expected—made Maria uneasy. The other servants left as well, save for Pip who hesitantly drew close with the palmetto fan. With a smile Maria thanked her for the artificial breeze. The lowering sun had cleared the roof of the portico and now shone directly toward them through a thin veil of clouds.

By the time Thomas returned with fresh buckets, David came to the doorway.

"Can you take over for me, David?" Maria asked "I'd like to say good-bye to Jack and Smitty—"

"They left."

"Without saying anything?"

"They were pressed for time. And Jack was not pleased about…" He nodded toward Ketch's drooped form.

Mary appeared behind David, wringing her hands against her apron again, waiting for him to turn. "What is it, Mary?"

"It's Mizz Helen. She won't get dressed for bed. She just settin' in the window, looking after her brother and crying."

David vanished toward Helen's chamber, and Maria called Mary over to take her place by Ketch. The prospect horrified the woman, but Maria spoke sharply, her patience at an end. Then she hurried into the house.

Helen sat on the broad seat of one of the river windows, dressed only in her shift, her knees drawn up beneath it and her arms wrapped around her legs, the bear crushed against her chest. She looked just as she had the day they had returned to Leighlin, making Maria fear that any progress made in these past days was now lost. David, seated across from her in the window, quietly spoke, but she did not seem to hear him, her attention toward the distant landing. Maria hurried around the large bed and sat in a chair nearby.

"He didn't even say good-bye," Helen hiccupped, silent tears trailing down her cheeks.

Maria found these words difficult to believe. Granted, she knew Helen's continued refusal to communicate with Jack injured him, but she never would have imagined he would leave Leighlin without saying farewell to his sister and imparting some sort of encouragement.

"Helen," Maria employed a strong tone to overpower the child's desolate focus. "Remember how sick Mr. David was when he came to Leighlin not long ago? Remember how you helped him get better?"

Helen stared at her bear and nodded.

"Why don't you come out on the portico where Mr. Ketch is?"

"Maria!" David objected. "He is not wearing any...he is..."

"Mr. David can bring the rocking chair out and you can sit on his lap. He can tell us all a story while I try to bring down Mr. Ketch's fever."

David's uncomfortable expression drew Helen's curiosity. The young man sputtered a few more words but then succumbed to the insistent gazes of the two females.

# CHAPTER 15

The four-hour journey down the Ashley River seemed like four minutes to Jack, so distracted was he. He had started out at the tiller, but Castle took over when Jack's inattention nearly brought them under the bow of a passing ketch. Moving in a daze to the thwart forward, Jack watched light and color drain from the sky. Night settled down into the broad river around them, inking it black as the clouds thickened above. Smith handled the sail, conversing with Castle, but Jack heard none of their dialogue; it was mere babble that blended with the slosh of water against the hull, the breeze against the sail, and the creatures of the night. Not until the river spit them out into Charles Town harbor did he realize he had not visited his mother's grave as planned. The recognition of his negligence sank him deeper into despair.

He remembered a time aboard the *Prodigal* after he had rescued his mother from Logan, a time when he had watched her and Maria talking upon the forecastle. The scene had brought a smile to his face. He had been thankful that Maria could offer female kinship to his anxious parent. What had they talked about? His mother had known of his interest in Maria, seemingly more so than her son, so perhaps they spoke of that. When she had pressed him about the relationship, he had balked. Then, while she lay dying, she had looked from him to Maria and entrusted Helen to them. Well, Jack considered bitterly, there could be no "them" now.

With hours to defuse his temper now behind him, he regretted his outburst and hasty departure from Leighlin, for he had left not only without visitation to the grave but, worse yet, without saying farewell to those whom he loved. Selfish truth be told, he had wanted Helen to show excitement and happiness at his return to Leighlin, especially after his days of captivity when he had feared never seeing her again. Yet he could not expect her to understand his desires any more than he could expect her to be anything but distracted and devastated over the loss of her parents. But to witness her concerns for Ketch of all people... It had been a one-two punch for which he had not been prepared and still smarted over.

David Archer... It was foolish to be angry with him. Indeed, the anger had been misplaced. Jack knew he had no one but himself to blame for losing Maria. If he had listened to his mother, if he had listened to Logan, to Smith... But again blind stubbornness had been his undoing and the undoing of others, for now Helen would be deprived of Maria's nurturing once she left to live elsewhere with her...husband.

He asked himself again why Maria had married David now and so quickly and clandestinely. Was it simply to keep the event from his father until he had no choice but to reveal it? And why had Archer not mentioned it to them on the journey from Wildwood to Leighlin?

Jack stared beyond the harbor which they were about to cross, felt the choppier motion of the boat, felt a chill in the breeze as a wave slapped against the bow and sent a shower of spindrift over him. But an inner chill started him more than any cold spew of water, and his hand gripped the forward edge of the thwart.

What if Maria were with child?

His mind raced backward, back to the journey with Logan to the Outer Banks when they had been away from Leighlin for several days, only to return and find that David Archer had been there in hiding all along. Jack knew little about the mysteries of the female body, but he knew enough to realize the timing could very well be right. His stomach heaved at the thought.

"Two blue lights at the main," Smith's voice cut through the night some time later when the harbor was far astern. "There she lies."

At first the blue lights as well as a couple of other lanterns upon the deck were all Jack could make out of the *Prodigal*. A rush of anticipation filled him, and he itched to be aboard his brig again, to leave all of these disturbing, sad thoughts behind, to be free out upon the open water, captivity thrust into the past once again.

Ned greeted him at the entry port, light shining upon his shaved head and broad grin. The rest of the crew surrounded the boatswain in a crescent of welcoming hails.

The Rat stepped forward, his hair a dark, windswept cloud around his head. "We knowed Smitty would git you free, Long Arm." His words cut off when he realized a third party had accompanied his shipmates up the side. He advanced to his usual uncomfortable closeness, too close for Ethan Castle who retreated a step.

Castle—taller than Jack but almost as slight of build—always had a definite uneasiness about him, at least whilst among pirates, Jack had noted, and that uncertainty was more apparent now in his new surroundings. His smile was quick and nervous as the Rat sniffed at him and narrowed his small eyes. Castle often used his hands to express himself while conversing and now he raised them as if speaking, though no words came forth. Instead just a few syllables spilled out, and he looked to Jack for assurance.

"New member of the crew, Cap?" the Rat asked. "We just got rid o' them lubberly coves pressed from the *Fortune*."

"Just a passenger, Rat. Give way there. I'm sure Mr. Castle doesn't fancy catching any of your vermin."

The others laughed, including Castle who sounded more ingratiating than genuine. Reluctantly the Rat stepped back among his shipmates.

"Before I explain our passenger, I want to thank all of you for coming back for me."

"Wasn't you we come back for, Cap'n." Bull's simple voice. "Came to spend our money on Charles Town's ladies."

Lascivious chuckles followed, grins flashing through the night.

Jack cautioned, "I hope none of you were recognized."

"We only went in the dark," Sullivan said, followed by more laughter.

"Aye, an' we didn't dance with no sailors," Willie Emerick added, bringing more ribald mirth.

"Smitty, escort Mr. Castle below to my cabin. Ned, break out the rum—that is, if there's any left. Now, everyone lay aft."

With their lust slaked and their bellies full of Charles Town victuals and drink, they were all in a pliable mood, so it took less persuasion than Jack had feared to get them to agree to sail to James Town. With Wylder's money in their hands there was no need to hunt for fresh prey, and Virginia would provide new revelry with less risk. Archer's offer of future pardons seemed to hold little interest at the moment, but if the Royal Navy suddenly appeared on the horizon or if a constable clapped a hand upon someone ashore, Jack was certain that offer would instantly have more appeal.

Jack's rescue was as good an excuse as any to celebrate, so with the *Prodigal* hove to for the night, the men trailed off to begin their revelry, boisterous and in high spirits, calling for Sullivan and Willie to strike up a dancing tune. One man, however, lingered behind, hat in hand, feet moving uneasily upon the deck.

"Captain," Hanse spoke tentatively, taking Jack momentarily aback, for he had forgotten about the pressed carpenter. The balding man drew closer into the light offered by the binnacle, his eyes carrying the familiar worried look of a captive. "If you please, Captain; you heard the Rat—they let them pressed Fortunes go, but not me. It don't seem fair. I helped you set your brig to rights. Seems like I earned—"

"Mr. Hanse," Jack growled, for he was in no mood to be charitable. "Has the *Prodigal* acquired another carpenter while I was gone?"

Hanse's expression fell. "No, sir."

"And until we do, you'll continue to have the privilege of serving aboard my brig. If you consider what the alternative might be, you would hold your tongue."

Hanse's despairing frown bore a certain amount of anger, but he quickly fled to hide his resentment. It was then that Jack noticed another man nearby, a shadow much larger and darker than the carpenter, one that had perhaps lingered in case Hanse had given his captain any trouble.

"I didn't expect to see you still aboard," Jack said as Samuel stepped forward. He moved toward the leeward rail of the quarterdeck, drawing the man with him.

Samuel did not respond immediately, his gaze upon the black sea. Since Logan's murder, he had spoken few words to anyone. Maria had been his closest confidant on board, for their friendship dated back to her days in Cayona, long before Jack had known her.

With only a hint of a smile, Samuel said, "The money is good."

Jack grinned, pleased to find some humor still in the man. "Aye. But I half expected to see you at Leighlin by now."

The faint smile fled. Samuel stared toward the distant ribbon of the coast that was thrown into an orange and gold silhouette by the last flash of the day. "Perhaps I will go back, if I am wanted there, but not yet." His attention returned to Jack. "How is Helen...and Maria? Were you able to see them?"

"Aye." Fresh pain diverted his eyes. "They're both safe at Leighlin. I had supper with them before coming off." He paused. "Ketch is there, damn him. Hopefully he's dead by now—Willis amputated his arm because of a snake bite."

Though Samuel wore a small frown, there was neither alarm nor hatred in his expression. "It does not surprise me he's there."

"He wouldn't be if I was still there."

"You're not saying that because of what he did to Captain Logan."

Jack tried to decide if Samuel was insulted by his lack of compassion for his stepfather. "Don't misunderstand me when it comes to Logan, Samuel. True enough, I had my debt to settle with him, but as you saw I didn't...because of my mother and Helen. And 'tis Helen—and Maria—I'm concerned about when it comes to Ketch."

Samuel softly chuckled. "If that is your concern, then it is no concern at all."

Angry that Samuel would trivialize his fear, Jack growled, "And how would you know that? The man kills indiscriminately."

"Not so. True, Ketch will kill a man with little thought, but I can tell you confidently that he will not kill a woman." A small grin showed palely through the night, further consternating Jack. "And when it comes to Helen...well, you may rest assured that no harm will come to that child with Ketch there. But, a snake bite..." He shook his head. "Leighlin's slaves and the Medoras used to say Ketch has a demon in him that protects him from being killed by another man. After all, he survived the silver mines and torture at the hands of the Spanish; how many others could say as much? So if something is to kill him, more likely it will be a serpent than a man."

"How can you place such faith in a man who betrayed Logan...Logan, mind you, who was the very man who saved Ketch from the Spanish?"

"Ketch killed Logan not for himself but for Dan Slattery. Ketch had only two loyalties in his life—your mother and Slattery. Logan killing Slattery was crime enough to Ketch, but for it to happen at the same time he lost your mother..." Samuel shook his head. "He loved her very much."

Appalled, Jack said, "You pity the man?"

"I pity anyone who has lost as much as he has...as much as you have. As a boy, Ketch's stepfather deserted him, and his mother was raped and murdered. Slattery was all Ketch had after that until your mother came along. Ketch had a deep devotion to her, so deep that it clouds his judgment of you. I see you for what you are, and I understand why you came here. All Ketch sees is a man who destroyed everything he cared about—the same way you saw James Logan. And he resented Logan for allowing you to live and come to Leighlin."

Jack leaned back on the railing, uncomfortable with any humanization of Ketch or a comparison to him. "He may be devoted to Helen, but he has no devotion to me; quite the opposite, as you say. We tried to kill each other aboard the *Alliance*, and I doubt that will change when I return to Leighlin."

"If he survives."

"Aye. 'Twill make things easier and I'll sleep sounder if he does not." He studied Samuel. "You have no malice for what he's done to

Logan?"

"Of course. But killing Ketch will not bring Logan back. And for Helen's sake—for Leighlin's sake—she is better off with him alive. Logan knew that; that's why he didn't kill him that day aboard the *Prodigal* when Ketch insulted him and tried to bury Slattery with the others."

"Beneficial or not, I won't allow him to remain at Leighlin when I return. I'll be there for Helen. Her *family* will protect her. But if he's as devoted as you say, killing him sounds to be the only way to rid Leighlin of him."

#

Ethan Castle was a taciturn man until he had a sufficient amount of rum in his belly. Until then, the Englishman had been content to hold his tongue—something Jack figured he had learned to do well in the employ of Ezra Archer. Castle listened to the tales told by the Prodigals, many embellished for the sake of melodrama and their guest, including the attack upon the convoy. The more Castle drank, the more his anxiety over being among a notorious pirate crew seemed to ease. And by the time Smith escorted the passenger down to Jack's cabin for the night, there was little he or Jack could do to silence the man. He slouched at the table with Smith and Jack—who had not been without drink since coming aboard—and proceeded to tell them about his former life in England and about his life since coming to the colonies, first as an indentured servant to the Archers then as a hired hand.

"So you was always with Archer?" Smith tipped back another bottle, obviously enjoying this game of plying the newcomer with drink and watching his veneer crumble away.

"Aye. First in Virginia. That's how I know the Chesapeake and the James River to pilot you gentlemen. That's another reason why Mr. Archer had me come with you. Well, that and the fact that I know Miss Elizabeth and her mother, so they'll feel...safe...around the likes of you...er...your crew, that is."

Jack, who until now had sat back in his chair, content to let Smith and Castle do the talking, leaned forward, one hand using a bottle for support. "Is this the same Elizabeth that Archer wanted his son to marry?"

"Aye. Still does."

"Still?" Jack glanced at Smith who, to his surprise, did not appear as curious about Castle's revelation as he. Through his alcoholic fog he

169

realized Archer must not have told anyone of David's marriage; not surprising since Archer would be mortified over such a union and no doubt would seek a way to dissolve it.

"Mr. Archer has his heart set on patchin' up his troubles with his daddy in Virginia," Castle explained. "Sees Miss Elizabeth as a way to do it. She's a favorite of the old man, maybe seeing as all he has is troublesome sons."

"So what's Archer's story?" Smith slid the remains of his bottle toward Castle who had just emptied a mug of ale. "What makes him such a right awkward bastard?"

Castle downed a swig and grinned, his head drooping with signs of surrender to fatigue and the pull of the alcohol on his weary mind. But he seemed to enjoy having an audience too much to give in just yet. Jack figured remote plantation life surrounded by slaves and a fractured family of whites allowed for poor company.

"He wasn't always such a one," said Castle. "When I first met him, he was a strict bugger, true, but not like he is now. Rough with the darkies, aye; quick with the lash. But his family...that was somethin' different. You've seen his wife, eh? Lately, I mean?"

Jack nodded, refrained from drinking more for the moment, figuring something significant just might be revealed soon.

"Sickly now, eh? Taken a turn for the worst since her son left, she has." Sadness grayed his expression, made him seem older as he dragged a hand through his wind-battered brown hair. "Good woman, Mrs. Archer. Deserves a kinder man." He sighed and drank again. "When I met her, though, she was right healthy. Pink as a peach and quick with a smile, even when her husband was in an ill temper."

Smith prodded, "So what happened to her?"

"It started with Davy actually. He was always an unruly lad. Not in a bad way, if you know what I mean, but curious like, so he was always getting into mischief. Book-learnin' came easy for him and being a planter's son didn't always hold his interest, so he often strayed a bit, always finding ways into trouble and makin' his father powerful mad. Mr. Archer tried all sorts of punishments on the lad, but nothing worked. But then...after..."

Smith raised an eyebrow. "After what?"

Castle's voice dropped and his face lowered closer to the table, drew Smith with him. "Now, mind you, I wasn't there to see any of it with me own eyes, so I can't speak in total truth. But what I hear tell was young Davy got caught kissin' one of the slave wenches. He was only twelve. I'm sure he was just being...well, like I said, curious. Just

170

a boy, you know, with no brothers to play with and teach him right and wrong in such things, and stuck way out there away from other white folks. And that foul wench was older than him, old enough to know what she was a-doin'."

Smith flicked a sly grin and wink toward Jack. "I reckon Archer wasn't too happy about that, eh?"

"By Christ, no. Had that wench beat nigh to death and gave his boy the worst thrashin' of his young life. Sent him to his bedchamber for two days. Wouldn't let him out, wouldn't let him have nothing more to eat than bread and water. Had Mrs. Archer half out of her wits. 'This is the last straw,' said he. 'That boy has tried my patience for the last time.'" Castle smiled wryly. "I'm sure he was afeared his boy would end up bedding one of them darkies and having a baby out of her, or worse yet falling in love with one of 'em, if you can imagine."

The very thought of David's predicament gave Jack a macabre prick of satisfaction, no longer feeling the slight bit of sympathy for the luckless bastard that he had before the marriage.

"That evening I was passing by the house on my way to the landing when I heard right horrible screaming from Mrs. Archer. I thought someone was set upon her, so I ran inside. She ran past me, crying something terrible. I was dumbstruck and was just standing there like a slack-jawed fool when Mr. Archer came running downstairs, his hair and eyes wild like a crazy man. He asked where she had gone and I told him out the door. I expected him to chase after her, but damned if he didn't. Instead he went into the library and shut the door. Servants said he stayed in there the whole night, drinking himself into the next world."

"What in hell happened?" Smith prompted.

"No one knows, but it was something with Davy. After Mrs. Archer had run out, his sister found Davy's door unlocked and he was in there a-cryin'. Don't know if he ever told anyone what happened. His sister maybe; they've always been real close. From that day forward everything changed. Mr. Archer moved into the flanker. Don't know whether that was his idea or his wife's, but as far as I know they've never shared a bed since." He shrugged. "Reckon it wouldn't matter if they did. I hear tell since that night he can't…well, he can't…'" Embarrassment sent Castle reaching for the bottle and downing a large gulp, as if suddenly realizing he had said too much. "Whatever happened, he's been taking it out on that boy ever since."

"No wonder the poor bastard wants to get away from his father," Smith said with a touch more pity than Jack liked to hear.

"Is it true Davy's staying at Leighlin?" Castle asked hopefully. "That's what I heard tell on the river."

"Aye, he's there," Jack grumbled. "For now."

"They say he's with that girl—that half-caste girl what snuck him to Doc Knight's when he was shot."

Jack scowled and snatched the bottle from Castle. "Reckon I've had enough talk tonight, mate. Why don't you sling your hammock before you can't see straight enough to do it?" Jack stood, trying unsuccessfully to hide his own swaying movement, which was far beyond that of the *Prodigal*'s lively roll. "I'm going on deck for some air."

# CHAPTER 16

Jack knew little of James Town's history other than its notoriety as the American colonies' first English settlement. Ethan Castle expanded that knowledge a bit more during the journey up the broad James River, including the fact that the settlement had once been the official port of entry for Virginia. Fortunately for them this was no longer the case. However, to help ensure that no one along the James— on land or upon the dozens of craft plying the waterway—recognized the *Prodigal*, they had sailed to her current moorings with the very last light straining down the river from a weak sunset. From there, Castle had taken the yawl a mile upriver to Joseph Archer's tobacco plantation where he would spend the night and return at first light with Elizabeth and Caroline Archer. The Prodigals, meanwhile, had packed themselves into the pinnace and pulled enthusiastically across the river to partake in whatever pleasures the small town had to offer. Samuel and Billy had volunteered to stay behind, too concerned that their black skin might put them in an unsafe situation, for Virginia had well-established, extensive slave laws.

He had accompanied his men, but now—deep in the night—Jack sat alone outside one of James Town's taverns. The settlement lay quiet around him, the only sounds coming half-heartedly from the ordinary: music and the voices of drunken men and women—those somehow still semi-upright. The street before him was deserted and dark. His bleary eyes reached beyond the wharves to the few lights aboard the *Prodigal* where she lay moored far out, closer to the opposite shore. The lights seemed to dance, though no breeze stirred the waters beneath her keel, and Jack realized the alcohol clouding his brain caused the dance. Many other vessels of varied sizes and rig lay at anchor upon the river, but Jack knew the *Prodigal*'s precise location among them, even in the shroud of night through his fog of rum and ale. He could count on her to be there. She had been his escape in so many ways during their short history together. Perhaps he should have stayed aboard her tonight. But to have done so would have meant sleep, and sleep could again bring the nightmares back to him, as it had every

173

night since Ketch had tried to kill him.

Newgate continued to haunt him with renewed force, particularly the assault when he had first set foot in the jail. Often Ketch's visage replaced that of the wardsman. The memories also took him back to an even bloodier day in the prison, the day when he had become an animal of vengeance and violence, a day when he stepped away from the innocence of youth into the shadows of a criminal. Over the years he had told himself that he was not that man, that murderer, and once reunited with his mother he would regain the integrity of an honest man, and the nightmares would cease. And they had for a short time. Was it simply Ketch's assault that had revived the memories or was there more to it? Was it because he was indeed still a dissolute man no matter how he tried to convince himself otherwise?

"There you are." Smith's voice reached Jack just before the older man dropped down loosely next to him and relaxed back against the building's foundation. "Why'd you leave so early? Won't be sunrise for another two hours. Didn't that lass keep your interest up?" He chuckled and slugged back a short pull from the bottle Jack had next to him.

Jack thought of the rough wench he had left behind in the room upstairs. A sordid, hollow clash of mad release. At the thought of her, his head throbbed even worse. He was cursed now, he feared; Maria's face would torment him whenever he dared lay with another woman. With a crapulous groan, he pressed his hands to his temples.

Smith emitted a protracted, significant sigh and set down the bottle. "Well, I reckon I've let you suffer long enough."

"What are you talking about, old man?" he moaned.

"If you'd take five minutes outside of picklin' yerself since we left Leighlin, I'd tell ye." Smith started to take the rum bottle again, but Jack possessively snatched it back and shot him a threatening look. Smith sighed again and shook his head. "When we left Charles Town I had reckoned it'd be good for you to be miserable for a while—mebbe bring you to yer senses finally—but I can see if I don't speak plainly now, you'll end up livin' in a bottle from here on out and pickin' up the pox from some strumpet."

Jack took another swig just to defy his friend. "What in hell are you getting at?"

"I'm gettin' at you, you thick-headed swab. You've been mopin' for these past days, feelin' sorry for yerself, but it don't seem durin' all that time that you've done any thinkin'. Reckon that's why you keep *me* around—*someone* has to do the thinkin' when you stop doin' it."

Jack was struck speechless by the inference that their friendship was only for his personal gain. It injured him deeply to realize his behavior had led Smith to believe such a thing.

Smith leaned closer, the blurry edges of his face wavering then becoming more defined. "Did it never once enter yer empty head that just maybe Maria is simply tryin' to help David Archer? That what she's doin' she's doin' for him, not herself? Or is such selflessness beyond you and yer self-pity?"

"Smitty—"

"Maria likes to...fix things. You haven't realized that yet? 'Tis her nature to take care of others. You've seen it yerself. Yer mother, God love her, saw that right away; that's why she and Logan both wanted her near Helen. And that boy...why, he would've died more'n once if not for her. She barely knew 'im, but she took care of him. You pushed her away after yer mother died; I saw it. You wouldn't let her help you, so she helped someone else. And he appreciated her for it. What the unlucky bastard said at supper t'other night was true: Maria deserves someone who'll appreciate her."

Deflated by the truth of his friend's words, Jack mumbled, "Then she's got what she deserves. The bloody coxcomb loves her, God curse him. His sister told me as much, as if she needed to. I have eyes."

"But no ears, damn ye. Yer still not hearin' what I'm sayin' to ye. Maria don't need to marry the boy to help him; she only has to *look* like she's married to him. If you wasn't so wrapped up in yerself, mebbe you'd have thought of that."

Jack studied him, not daring to hope. Perhaps Smith was as drunk as he. "Why would she play everyone false? If they're so deserving of each other, then why not just go through with it?"

"Yer not seein' things clear, Jackie. Everyone but you seems to know Maria loves you. David Archer knows it. Why else do you think you ruffled his feathers t'other night? If he was truly married to her, he wouldn't have gotten so angry. He'd have nothin' to fret about when it comes to you and the lass, would he? But he knows you'll be comin' back, don't he?"

The idea was too much for Jack. He needed a clear head to believe this. He got up, paced several unsteady feet into the deserted, rutted street, stared toward the *Prodigal*. "If that's true, why wouldn't she have told me?"

"When did she have the chance?"

Jack's sodden mind tried to move faster, to go backwards, to remember.

"David wouldn't want you to know the truth 'cause he knows how you feel about Maria and how you feel about him. And you told him yerself how you want him out o' there, away from her. He heard plenty about you and her when he was aboard the *Prodigal*. Lads like Dowling took great delight in fillin' his ears with shit, true and untrue. And he saw you kiss her that night they left the brig. Yer in a competition, boy."

Jack stumbled toward him. "Maybe Archer doesn't believe Maria is married to David either. Maybe that's why Castle said what he did about Archer and his niece."

"Now yer puttin' two and two together. You said yerself it was odd how Archer accepted what he was told. Mebbe he's just bidin' his time, takin' a different approach since all t'other ways of bendin' his son to his will haven't worked. Maria's done somethin' Ezra Archer couldn't—she's given David a reason to stay in Carolina. And remember what Archer said—he wants the cousin stayin' at Leighlin while she's visiting. Oh, sure, he claims it's to keep Maria company and to get to know her cousin's wife, but I'm thinkin' Archer just wants that girl close to his son. She could be in on Archer's little plan, too. We don't know her. Why wouldn't she want to marry a rich planter's son? It'd get her away from this dismal place."

Jack produced a small smile as he sat back down. "You think any place on land is dismal, Smitty."

"Archer said this cousin took a shine to his son. Sounds like a willing partner for Archer's plans."

"Well, I will admit you're making sense. Except..." He frowned toward the rum bottle.

"'Cept what?"

"You may be right about the Archers and about the cousin, but you're probably wrong about Maria."

"What d'ye mean?"

Jack looked into the endless black sky with its hidden stars. "Maria probably isn't as fond of me as you think. I've not exactly done all the right things, as David Archer pointed out so clearly."

"No one knows yer faults better'n me, lad, 'specially when yer wearin' a dress."

Jack's smile twisted. "Thankee, Smitty. You're too kind."

"Maria's seen 'em, too, mind. But against all reason she still cares about you." He cleared his throat, stood. "But all that aside, lad, I've told you before—you can't wait forever. When we get back to Leighlin, you'd best belay yer pride and all the blame you heap on yerself and

176

talk to that girl. Find out the truth."

"And what if the truth is she's married to David Archer?"

"Then you crawl out o' yer bottle, get on with yer life, and take care o' Helen like you promised yer mother."

#

Ketch heard his half-brother's groans before he could ever hope to see him through the cramped, low darkness of the *Medora*'s hold. He hated the closeness, the lack of air and light; it reminded him of the silver mines.

"Dan," he called and lifted the lantern. The weak light reached out to the prone form there in chains, slightly awash in bilge water. Dan was leaner and taller than he, but lying crumpled in the hold he appeared small. Dan's mud-brown eyes squinted up at him, homely face bruised and battered, fresh blood smeared across his wide slash of a mouth. While Ketch's redeeming facial qualities had been lost to pockmarks, Dan's lack of good looks had come naturally.

"So what's the verdict?" Dan croaked out with his usual nonchalant self-confidence. He tried to sit up, but the damage caused by the handspike, which Logan had used against every region of his body, had left him too sore to accomplish this simple feat. Ketch hung the lantern upon a nail and reached to help him, but Dan cursed him off. "What's Logan have planned for me?"

Ketch crouched next to him. "Here. I pinched some rum for you." Dan grunted and allowed him to help with the cup. While trying to hide his anxiety, Ketch answered, "He's goin' to maroon you."

"Is he now? Well, minutes ago he was goin' to kill me, but thanks to your sway over his cursed wife, now it's down to maroonin'. Well, Ketch, me lad, why don't you try some more of your charm and see if you can get me another reprieve?" Sarcasm threaded through his words. He coughed and spat blood. "Lost a God damned tooth, I did. Bastard..."

"Dan, what in Christ's name was you thinkin'?"

The older man's mouse-colored, blood-crusted hair flopped into his eyes. "You know how I am; 'twas just a matter of time afore I went for her. And you, actin' like her trained dog or somethin'."

Ketch bridled at his ungratefulness. "She just now saved yer life by speakin' up, even after what you tried to do—"

"Spare me, mate. She didn't do it for me; she did it because *you* begged her to."

177

Dan's continued contempt for his loyalty to Ella Logan injured Ketch, for he knew not how to appease his brother and serve his mistress as well.

"Give Logan some time to cool down," Dan instructed. "Then in the morn I want you to talk to his wife again, ye hear? You aren't goin' to let your only kin rot to death on some God-forsaken island, are ye?" Dan dragged himself onto one unsteady elbow and eyed him. "You owe me, Ketch. If it wasn't for me gettin' you out of Southwark, they'd have strung you up, sure."

"Dan—"

"Then what about that sodomite aboard the *Harwich*? I took care of him for ye, didn't I? Eh? And who was it sprung your carcass from that Spanish hellhole?"

Ketch shifted his weight, avoided Dan's eyes.

"I've always looked out for you, haven't I? Takin' care of me little brother." He tapped Ketch's knee. "Now it's your turn, eh?"

"He won't let this go. You know Logan—"

"You saved his wife from drownin' just months ago, mate. He's not forgotten that. Neither has she. Use that."

"I already did. Yer lucky Logan don't hack you into bits and toss you over the side."

Dan's voice lowered. "Is that what *you'd* like to do? Just 'cause of her? I never touched her."

"You would've if not for Stephen Moore stoppin' you."

Dan pushed slightly away. "So that's how it's goin' to be, is it? Pickin' them over your own kin."

"Damn it, Dan, you shouldn't have done it."

"You owe me, Ketch." Unblinking, Dan grabbed his wrist. "I'm your brother, damn you. What are they? Someday Logan won't have no need for you, and then what'll become of you without me?" His manacles clanked as he freed Ketch with a shove and repeated, "You owe me."

A mockingbird's song drifted obtusely to Ketch. How could there be a bird in the *Medora*'s hold? No, he was not aboard the *Medora*... Dan's image faded, as did the dank, smelly darkness of the brigantine's hold. His brain worked on two levels—that of one drifting thoughtlessly from sleep and that of a mind searching for the reason a bird's voice sounded so loud and close.

Slowly his eyes opened. Morning sunlight angled into the chamber from the north window, the open white shutters letting in the remains of the night's sweet breeze. Whitewashed brick walls

178

emanated coolness. He remembered that he no longer resided in one of Leighlin's upper floor bedchambers; that had been reclaimed by Rogers and Dell while he had been relegated to the lower level, to the small quarters where Defoe used to sleep. When the fever had gripped him Maria said the hard-packed dirt floor and brick walls of Defoe's chamber would offer him relief. Ketch smiled wryly as he imagined the protests the other men put up at the suggestion of Defoe's abode being invaded by one suspected of murdering the Frenchman. Of course he could not remember if such protests had indeed occurred; he recalled little from the past days except his exchange with Maria about Jack Mallory—that remained painfully clear—and the soft, feather-light touch of Helen's hand in his.

Since he had come to this space, the child had brought him flowers; he smelled the roses in their nearby vase the instant he awoke and even sometimes before when he had not been fully conscious. She had even read a story to him last night after his fever had broken. Though her voice had barely penetrated his semi-consciousness, it somehow still soothed him. No one had ever read to him before. Certainly not his illiterate parents.

The bird's song came again, and Ketch focused on the yellow stare of a mockingbird on the north window's ledge, its grayish head twisting to get a better view of him. The bird's long tail feathers tipped upwards as it turned with a hop. Then—unimpressed with the man—it spun about and took flight in a flurry of dull colors.

Ketch lay back against the pillow, shoved the sheet away. His shirt bore an unfamiliar freshness. He could not recall when he had acquired it or who had put it on him. Undoubtedly the Cordero girl, for none of the men wanted anything to do with him; he did not need to remember a specific to know that was fact. Vaguely he recalled a small window of perspicuity when he had been immersed in a tub and realized he was naked, but at the time he had not cared about his humiliating vulnerability and exposure. All he had cared about was the wonderful relief given by the water's embrace, the trickle of it past his burning ears when the girl sponged his head, and the way the breath of a breeze increased the water's balm. But now, thinking of the young, beautiful woman hovering over his well-endowed nudity, he hoped she had not seen that particular scar, the nasty white one where no hair would ever grow again.

He looked at his bandaged shoulder where the sleeve had been cut away, at the offensive, swathed stump, and softly cursed. Then he closed his eyes and listened as above him and beyond his door Leighlin

179

House stirred to life. Much earlier Willis and the other white men would have left their beds in the adjacent chamber and gone about their morning duties. They had called off the search for Defoe yesterday after Wildwood's bloodhounds found traces of Defoe's blood near the west swamp. Aye, it had not been far from where he had found Helen that day. It seemed so long ago. Residual blood; all that was left, for the alligators had gotten every piece of the Frenchman that Ketch had tossed to them. The foregone conclusion followed that either by Ketch's design or the design of a natural predator Defoe was beyond reach, though Ketch knew no one truly believed it to be the latter.

Soon Helen, Maria, and that damned Archer boy would be in the dining room for breakfast. The smell of food actually appealed to him again, especially the hickory waft of pork coming from the kitchen house. He salivated at the thought of a heaping portion of the meat.

Again he stared at the bandages. He often swore the limb was still attached—a cruel, torturous sensation. He even experienced pain in it, pain in something that did not exist. His right arm. His dominant arm. His cutlass arm. Glowering at the low ceiling, he cursed the handicap, the weakness. How ironic that Ella Logan had once called him Logan's *right*-hand man; he had bragged as much to Dan the night when the crews of the *Medora* and the *Prodigal* had mingled to gamble, dance, sing, and drink—before Mallory had stolen Ella Logan away. Dan had tried to coerce him into joining Jack Mallory's crew. In an effort to persuade him Dan had mocked Ketch's accomplishment, his standing with Logan, and reminded him of his previous warning that Logan would use him up and discard him, that Ella Logan controlled him like a dumb beast. "Like your whore of a mother used to control you," Dan had sneered. "And we both know what she did to you."

Ketch pressed his eyes shut. Dan had never understood the empathy he had felt for Ella Logan. She had lived a captive, just as he had, though he for a much shorter, violent period of time. Even in her own misery she had shown him—and countless others—a compassion that he knew he would never possess. And so he had stood aboard the *Medora* that day long ago and sailed away from his brother on that lonely cay with nothing but a pistol with one shot and some bread and water. Dan had been correct about one thing: Ketch had owed him a debt, a debt repaid with Logan's death. Yet, he wondered, if he had somehow been able to spare Dan the marooning perhaps his half-brother would not have killed Ella Logan and ultimately caused Helen to become an orphan. It was a consideration that he knew would haunt him forever.

# CHAPTER 17

From the lower rear portico, Maria watched the two riders out upon the sward. Helen, mounted upon her pony, called to David astride Leighlin's bay stallion, urging him on in their game of keeping a lamb and its mother from the rest of the flock moseying in the shade of the bordering oaks. Maria was relieved David had volunteered to take her place when Helen had asked her to ride, for she had no confidence in her ability to stay on a horse while completing any significant maneuvers.

Her attention lifted beyond the trees to where clouds had begun to build in the southwest, warning of a storm to come with the climax of the afternoon's heat. She picked up a fan from the small wrought-iron table where she sat and fanned herself, sipping lemonade. Her admiring gaze returned to David. He sat a horse well, in natural balance and communication with the animal, hips swinging, hands light but firm upon the reins, back straight yet supple. A handsome, dashing figure; mature and confident. When he failed in his quest and the ewe and lamb darted to rejoin the flock, his laughter played along the breeze. The pleasant sound increased when Helen scolded his negligence. His continued willingness to indulge the child pleased Maria. If not for him, Helen would have little reason to smile or laugh. Having a man spend time with her right now was valuable beyond measure, especially considering Jack's absence and the way he had left without saying good-bye.

David had done wonders to deflect Helen's sorrow when they had explained that Defoe would not be coming back, that he must have fallen into the swamp like she had and perhaps drowned. She had not cried but had fallen silent and withdrew the rest of that day, but by the next morning they had managed to find things to keep the child's thoughts away from the loss of yet another familiar, constant person in her life. They took her to Charles Town where they bought her sweets, and Maria purchased fabric to make her a new play dress. Neither had told her about their sham marriage and had decided to stay silent on the matter until their hand was forced.

181

"Mizz Maria," Thomas's deep voice pulled Maria from her drifting thoughts and turned her toward the door. She had not heard his approach. He often displayed the same stealth quality Defoe had possessed. "Mizz Archer has arrived."

"Already?"

"She apologizes for her early arrival and understands if you can't receive her yet."

"No, please bring her here."

Maria had first met Margaret when David had been a patient at Dr. Knight's, following his wounding aboard the *Feather*. Her generous character and the way she loved her brother had endeared her to Maria, while Maria's diligence in caring for David during his injury had ensured that Margaret held her in the same high regard. Even the kiss Margaret had shared with Jack did not dampen Maria's opinion. After all, she could not hold the display against her, for she had never revealed her feelings for Jack to Margaret.

When her guest reached the portico, Maria met her in the doorway, both smiling their greetings. She thought Margaret the most beautiful woman she had ever seen and had always felt physically insignificant next to her. The two women were a contrast—one tall and fair, the other small and dark, and Maria found it easy to see why Jack was attracted to Margaret, who was her senior by two years. Margaret portrayed the grace of royalty, adorned with an astonishingly glorious wardrobe. Her flaxen hair was now pinned beneath a small, jaunty pink hat that matched her dress, white lace spilling from her neckline and sleeves. This splash of color clashed with Maria's dark mourning attire.

Margaret's blue eyes—so like her brother's—reached toward her sibling who just then spotted her and kicked the stallion into a gallop. Helen urged her recalcitrant pony into a following run until the two of them reined in sharply at the bottom of the steps. David leapt from his mount in one smooth, flowing movement that brought him up the steps and into his sister's arms. Laughing, he picked her up and spun her about.

"Put me down, you fool," Margaret scolded, also laughing. "You smell like a field hand."

Grinning, David obeyed. "What a fine thing to say to the brother you had banished and hazarded never seeing again."

"Hello, Miss Archer!" Helen called from her pony with a cheerfulness that warmed Maria.

"Hello, Helen. I see you have been keeping my brother busy."

"Yes'm. But he won't let me ride Curly instead of my pony. He's afraid I'd beat him in a race."

Maria laughed. "Well, it's far too warm now to race horses anyway, Helen. Why don't you ride back to the stables and send Jemmy for Mr. David's mount? Give your pony a good rub down."

Disappointed but not cowed, Helen reined her pony away from the house and trotted off down the lane toward the stables, her pigtails bouncing against her shoulders.

David held a chair out from the table for his sister then Maria. The warm scent of horse emanated from him as he claimed the third chair. Mary appeared with more glasses, which David filled with lemonade, too quick to allow the servant to do it. Mary gave him a look of false rebuke then returned to the house.

"We did not expect you this early, sister."

"I was able to leave town sooner than I had anticipated."

"Was it Father who told you I was here?"

"Yes. He is confident you will stay in the region now, no matter what I may say or do to remove you." She smiled at Maria who suddenly understood the inference and blushed.

David's smile lost some of its strength. "Ah, yes...well..."

"Is it true?" Margaret's eyes sparkled with mischievousness; her brother's continued defiance of their father obviously pleased her.

Maria opened her mouth but knew not what to say.

"Is it true you are married?"

David's hesitation surprised Maria, for surely he trusted his sister with the truth. Or was it something else that made him falter?

Margaret continued, "Father does not believe it."

"He doesn't?" Maria asked.

"He says it is a conspiracy."

David frowned, his shoulders rounded, his fingers played with the glass. His reaction drained the excitement from Margaret.

"We are not married," he murmured. "It was an impetuous, selfish fabrication on my part when Father arrived here. But I cannot desert Maria and Helen. Helen has taken her father's death very badly, as you can imagine, and for some reason she has become very attached to me. She begs that I stay."

"She hardly speaks to me," Maria added. "Or her brother when he was here. I'm not sure why. But she will talk endlessly with David."

"She has always taken to my brother, probably because of how much her mother cared for him. And maybe now because of the absence of her own brother." Margaret touched David's arm to pull him from his faraway thoughts. "So what do you plan to do?"

183

"I would rather wait to make that decision when Captain Mallory returns."

"Margaret," Maria said to deflect attention from David's discomfort, "I want you to know how grateful I am for your help getting Jack free."

A small smile touched Margaret's lips and displayed the dimples that made her particularly alluring. "I am afraid my dress had more to do with it than me personally."

"Your dress?"

"Captain Mallory wore my dress to disguise himself and leave Mr. Waterston's house in the middle of the night with my father."

"Jack...in a dress?"

Maria was the first to lose her composure, and when David and Margaret also succumbed, they spent a good long moment in mutual mirth before reality sobered them again.

"I was glad to help. But I do regret that he was not able to help my brother get away from Carolina. Perhaps when Jack returns from Virginia—"

"No, Maggie. I will hear no more of that. I am not going anywhere."

"Brother—"

"Things are different now. I know where I want to be, and it is not England. I want to stay here, with those whom I love."

Margaret frowned. "Father is having Captain Mallory bring our cousin Elizabeth to Leighlin. He wants her to stop here while she is visiting for the wedding."

"How utterly presumptuous of him," David protested. "Why on earth would he do that?"

"Is it not obvious? I told you he does not believe you are married."

"Then why does he not say so to me?"

"He knows forcing you has gotten him nowhere and almost drove you away. He needs you here. You know he has plans to acquire more land so the Proprietors will proclaim his estate a manor and grant him manorial rights. He could be nobility. He does not need scandal, and he will need you—and his father's money—to run the other plantations he hopes to establish in the province."

"I will not suffer him to force me into a marriage I do not want. One of us marrying the wrong person is enough."

"David!" Margaret rebuked.

He sighed and collected himself.

Maria hurried to distract. "Your wedding is only days away. You must be excited."

"I have not had time to be," she said with a wavering smile. "In fact, I should be going soon so I do not miss the rest of the tide to take me home. Mother has been working herself to the bone with preparations and the guests coming in soon. I fear for her health; she is not well." When David straightened in alarm, she rushed to assure, "I think it is mainly exhaustion. Once the wedding is past and the guests are gone, she will get strong again. Do not fret. I am watching her closely, but you know how she insists on being as busy as her health will allow."

"Does she know I am here?"

"Yes, though she is afraid to know exactly what is going on between you and Father."

"Did Father tell her that it was I who shot him? Is she angry with me?"

"She is not angry; she knows you had good reason. She was very happy and relieved to hear you are well, and she desperately wants to see you. You will come to the wedding? Both of you?"

"Of course, you goose."

"I shouldn't," Maria said. "I mean, I'd love to but…Leighlin is in mourning."

"But you are not a part of the family," David began then immediately halted, making Maria wonder if her face reflected the incongruous hurt his words had caused her.

"It wouldn't be proper for Helen to go, and I'll not leave her."

"She is right, David. We must think of Helen." Margaret's attention wandered toward the stables. "Poor child…"

As David considered his sister's distant expression, his own suddenly changed. "Maggie, there is something I have been wanting to ask you."

"Yes?" she said, still not completely back to him.

"How did you know Caleb Wylder was captain of the *Alliance* when no one else did?"

The sharp change in subject startled both women. Margaret blinked at her brother as if a bright light had been shined upon her face, her lips parted in surprise, but she quickly recovered and spoke with confidence. "Caleb told me, of course."

"But Father said he could find no connection between the privateers and Peter Wylder."

"Because there was none. Mr. Wylder knew nothing about Caleb's designs. Like Father, Mr. Wylder thought Caleb was returning from

185

England aboard one of the convoy ships."

"But why would Caleb risk tipping his hand to anyone, especially to the daughter of his quarry's partner? I mean, I know how Caleb felt about you, but…"

Margaret's gaze drifted down the sward.

David gently pressed on, "When I talked to Caleb aboard the *Alliance*, I got a distinct feeling that he was not alone in his venture, that you held sway over him and that is why you thought he would honor your request for Helen's release."

Maria slowly set her glass down upon the table, her thoughts rushing to keep up with David's intimations.

"Perhaps this is something you and I can discuss later, David." Still Margaret would not look at her brother, and a single furrow marred her forehead.

"I am not judging you, Maggie. If you had a part in Caleb's plan, I am not the one to chastise you. After all, I volunteered aboard the *Feather*, and she had the same goal as the *Alliance*. I just never guessed my sister would be so daring as to have a hand in the plot as well." He almost looked approving, though concerned. "So am I correct in my speculation?"

The distress increased on Margaret's face, and she nodded, turning away once again. At first Maria was horrified but then reminded herself that she, too, had sought to kill James Logan after he had murdered her father. If not for that desire, she would not be sitting at this very table with these two people, one of whom she now saw in a different, shocking light.

David asked his sister, "But what part could you possibly have played? Surely it was not simply a matter of you asking Caleb—"

"Caleb knew his father could not afford to nor would he agree on moral grounds to finance such a venture, so I put up half of the money to fit out those vessels."

David almost laughed. "And pray, sister, where did you acquire such funds?"

She pressed her lips tight together. Maria was unsure if she held back mirth or despair. "I got the money from Father."

Now David did laugh, his curious eyes bright over his sibling's industrious audacity. "However did you manage that?"

"I told him it was for the wedding; I had gotten it over a period of time. After all, I thought it nothing short of fitting that Father should finance Logan's downfall after all their partnership had gained him."

"Dear sister, what a fox you are." He tempered his delight when

186

her discomfiture lingered. "You regret your part now?"

"I do not regret its success, but I do regret what it has cost Helen. Maria, you must think us horribly callous. But Peter Wylder is a good man, an honest man, and my father's partnership with Logan was destroying the Wylder business. With his losses from the convoy, it is even more precarious. If Mr. Wylder does not make good next shipping season, his business may yet fail. But with Logan gone, he—and all the other merchants and those whose livelihoods depend on the shipping trade—has a chance to recover. With competitors' products not making it to their destinations because of Logan, my father's profits increased greatly. Of course politics had a hand in my father's grand plan. He sides with Proprietary control over the province, whereas Mr. Wylder sides with the opposition and wants Carolina to stand on her own and make her own way in the future. To drive the Wylders out of the province would weaken the stand made by James Moore and the other Goose Creek men." She paused and sighed as if exhausted. "I realize what this has done to Helen—it is an anguish I will take to my grave—but it was the grief of one against the suffering of hundreds of others, and perhaps the future of Carolina."

Maria's stare lingered on David's now shameful countenance. Perhaps this was also why he felt so compelled to stay with Helen—to repay the child for his attempted contribution as well as simply his wish for her father's death. And now he had his sister's verified role in Logan's demise to add to his guilt.

"I am concerned for Captain Mallory," Margaret said. "He is in my father's debt. I am sure you can guess that my father did not free him because of any affection for him. In fact, I believe he had planned to do so before I ever became involved. Now that he has lost his greatest ally, I fear he may coerce Captain Mallory into taking Logan's place."

"You said your father sent him to Virginia. Surely that's a far cry from attacking Charles Town shipping."

"For now it is. But he sent Captain Mallory on that errand to get him out of the region. I understand men were sent up the Ashley to all of the plantations in search of him."

"Yes. Militiamen stopped here. Of course we told them we didn't even know what the fugitive looked like but they were welcome to search the property, which they did."

"By now they will figure he has gone to sea, and they will wait to see if he turns up again, if he is bold enough to continue to prey on Carolina's commerce. I certainly hope Captain Mallory will not be seduced by anything my father may offer."

187

"He has no reason to be. He will want to be with his sister."

"Yes, but is Captain Mallory willing to settle down to life on a plantation? He knows nothing about it, but he does know the sea."

Maria closed her eyes and shook her head, wanting to clear the confusion and troublesome thoughts. She did not like the idea of Jack being beholden to Archer in any way.

"Dear Lord," Margaret's shocked voice opened Maria's eyes. "What on earth is he doing here?"

Ketch had emerged from the lower level and now stood between the flanking portico steps, looking out over the sward. Willis's shirt should have been too small on Ketch, but because of weight loss over the past few days, the shirt was not ill-fitting at all. The whiteness of his fresh bandage dazzled. His contrasting dark hair was a frightful, unruly mess, not accustomed to being clean. Two days ago Maria had shaved him, revealing under his chin a curious pair of marks that matched those near the base of his neck, but already he had significant new growth.

He turned at the sound of David's voice as the young man began to explain Ketch's presence to his sister. Maria hurried to the edge of the portico.

"What are you doing out of bed?"

Shading his eyes, Ketch appeared surprised to hear her so close. He wavered slightly, an awkwardness no doubt due to the absence of his right arm or perhaps simply from weakness.

"Stretchin' me legs." He craned his neck when he heard Margaret's scandalized voice speaking quietly to her brother. He scowled. "Where's Miss Helen?"

"At the stables."

He nodded to himself, not taking his suspicious gaze from the Archers.

"Are you hungry?"

"A mite."

"I'll have Rose fix something for you and have it brought to your chamber."

Apparently he took that as a directive to return inside, away from her guest, for he pulled his dark eyes from the Archers and reluctantly turned back to the door. His obedience surprised her, and she stood there for a long moment, blinking down at the empty space below.

# CHAPTER 18

"It is such a strange formation of land, is it not, Captain?" Elizabeth Archer's voice drew Jack's attention from the binnacle. She stood near the quarterdeck's starboard railing, just forward of the relieving tackle. Through Jack's telescope she studied the distant, vague ribbon of the Outer Banks, which gleamed in the early afternoon sunlight. The ocean swells rolled in upon the strip of low, sparsely-populated land, leisurely breaking in a creamy line as far as the eye could see. Ocracoke Inlet lay to the southwest, spilling into the broad, open waters of Pamlico Sound, which separated the southern Banks from the distant mainland. Just inside the inlet, the white of sails caught the sun; a coastal vessel perhaps, nothing large. Landward, gulls fluttered in pale groups while terns and an occasional petrel wheeled about the *Prodigal*'s rigging as she finished coming about onto the starboard tack, sailing away from the Banks.

The brig lay under all plain sail as close as she could to the southwesterly wind that pressed her over at an angle that would challenge any lubber, yet Elizabeth Archer stood steadfast with one hand on a back stay. An awning had been rigged to protect her from the sun, but she had left its shade for a better look at the coast, tying a double knot in the ribbon under her chin to anchor her blue and white, short-brimmed hat. Her dark hair—not as dark as Maria's raven mane—had been pulled away from her face and tied back with a blue ribbon. Her broad visage accommodated her generous mouth and easy smile as well as her green eyes and her arched, sable sweep of eyebrows. The quality of her smooth skin was startling to Jack, so accustomed to the weather-beaten faces of seafaring men. Elizabeth was not tall for her seventeen years; she was small like Maria, but her structure was not as refined. While not an overly beautiful girl, she was attractive enough to garner the attention of every man on deck, though she somehow seemed not to notice.

When Elizabeth had first come aboard on the James River, she and her mother had cast a concerned eye over the besotted, recalcitrant crew after the Prodigals' night of debauchery ashore. Jack had barked out commands to get underway, and the men obeyed, albeit slowly, but by the time they reached the open ocean, most heads had cleared, and the complaining died away. The women, assured by Castle that the *Prodigal*'s crew were quite capable of getting them safely to Charles Town, had finally begun to relax when Jack escorted them to his cabin. There he rushed the Rat to finish tidying what would henceforth be the passengers' berth.

"But where will you sleep, Captain?" Elizabeth had ruefully asked.

"I'll sleep for'ard with the men."

"With the common sailors?" Caroline Archer gasped, wide eyes the color of her daughter's.

Jack had hid his amusement, especially when he realized the woman was not condescending but more admiring of his selfless willingness to subject himself to what she considered hardship and debasement.

Elizabeth, now contemplating the sunlit beauty of the ocean and the brig's magnificent spread of billowed canvas, said, "I wish Mother could see this."

But Caroline Archer had no desire or ability to leave her cot in the aft cabin, prostrate with seasickness, tended by their maid. She had, however, encouraged her daughter to spend time above deck with Ethan Castle. Elizabeth was not bothered by the brig's motion whatsoever, too excited by all that was taking place around her to think of anything else.

Jack watched the flutter of the girl's indigo dress and her floating hem's agreeable revelation of small feet in velvet shoes and slim ankles in flawless stockings. All her clothes appeared new, as if made specifically for this visit to Carolina.

"It would appear you've sailed before, Miss Archer."

"Yes, Captain." The ready smile revealed a tiny gap between her two front teeth, a flaw that gave her an even younger appearance and made Jack think of the lower incisors missing from his sister's smile. "I have been to my uncle's plantation once before, and I have traveled up and down the Chesapeake a number of times. I have even been to England."

"Have you? Well-traveled then."

She blushed at his flattery, a demureness he had noticed when she had first arrived.

He stepped next to her at the railing. Today he felt more himself, happy to converse with others, particularly this young passenger.

Although he still did not know the truth of what he would return to at Leighlin, Smith's conjectures had provided enough hope to forestall his melancholy.

"How long has it been since you were at your uncle's plantation?"

"I was at Wildwood a year ago." Her gaze reflected the pleasure such a memory provided. "My uncle and I correspond regularly, especially since he and David—I mean, young Mr. Archer—last came to James Town. That was about six months before I came down here."

"Pardon my boldness, Miss Archer, but I understand your uncle would very much like to see his son wed...to you." Jack employed a small, wily smile to draw her out while he forced away the realization that such a wedding would not take place if his worst fears were true.

The pink of Elizabeth's cheeks from his earlier remark now deepened to crimson. But his charm made it impossible for her to take offense at his audacity, and she seemed to realize he was merely teasing her, not in an inappropriate way but in an effort at friendship. Her own smile shyly returned, and she looked down at the deck then back up at him from beneath long lashes, biting her lower lip. The girl was either naturally coquettish or she had already received excellent guidance in the art.

"Well, Captain, if you can keep a secret..." She cast a glance at Smith and Billy at the tiller. Smith tried to appear as deaf and innocuous as the piece of wood he manipulated to steer the brig but failed, of course, unable to hide the smile in the corner of his mouth.

Jack took a step closer to her and lowered his head. "Any secret of yours is safe with me, Miss Archer."

Barely loud enough for Jack to hear in the strong breeze, she said, "I have always been very fond of young Mr. Archer."

Jack could see that she was telling nothing but the bare, innocent truth, for her eyes brightened and softened even more. Self-conscious, she turned back to the Outer Banks. Jack hoped for both their sakes that her heart would not end up broken.

"Does your uncle know your feelings for his son?"

"Oh, yes. He has invited me to Wildwood several times since, but..." She frowned. "My grandfather..." She stopped to recover discretion, and her attention rose to the sails. "This wind is so stubborn. Is there any danger we will not make it to Carolina in time for the wedding?"

Jack gave a slight bow. "You have my solemn word, Miss Archer; I'll get you there in time even if I must row you there myself in one of our boats."

She looked at him in surprise, as if taking him literally until he grinned and chuckled, then she laughed, too.

From the mainmasthead, Willie Emerick hailed, "Deck, there! That sail has cleared the inlet!"

Jack took his telescope from Elizabeth and stepped over the relieving tackle to the taffrail. The murmur of curious voices around the brig joined with the wind's song in the rigging and the dash of water against the black hull. The distant vessel had not concerned Jack, but he had ordered Willie to keep him apprised should the stranger leave Pamlico Sound, and now that it had done so before the *Prodigal* could work to windward, he felt a nudge of caution. He wondered if any vessels had been dispatched along the coast to look for the *Prodigal* or the *Fortune*. To be snared now—with two of Ezra Archer's relatives on board—would be the end of him either from the law or from Archer himself. Perhaps, though, mere coincidence had impelled the stranger to leave Pamlico Sound just then.

"What do you make of her, Captain?" Smith asked.

The smaller vessel crowded on more canvas. She cut through the water with a salient smoothness, her fore-and-aft sail plan offering more efficiency in these airs than the square rig of the *Prodigal*. Once well free of the inlet, she altered course to take the wind upon the starboard quarter, a heading that would converge with the *Prodigal*. Even if he were to immediately change the brig's course and bring the wind more aft, there would be little chance of out-pacing the stranger. His only choices were to maintain his heading and wait for her to close and determine if she were a threat or to come up into the wind and lose time by waiting for her with guns ready.

"Maintain your course," Jack ordered over his shoulder.

An apprehensive Ethan Castle stumbled down the canted gangway toward the quarterdeck.

Elizabeth's excited voice flew to Jack on the wind. "What is it, Captain?"

"Probably just a coaster, Miss Archer. Or fishermen. Nothing to fret about."

Carefully she lifted her skirts and crossed the relieving tackle, obviously unconcerned with damaging or soiling her clothes and equally oblivious to the quick show of leg she provided. "Grandfather was hesitant about allowing us down here. He was worried about pirates."

Jack made sure he remained turned from Elizabeth so she could not see his grin. Smith choked off the beginnings of a laugh and converted it into a lengthy cough.

Castle drew next to Jack. His glance went back and forth from his female charge to the captain, and Jack could see his consternation in knowing the *Prodigal* was a pirate without being able to offer this knowledge to assure Elizabeth of their fighting capabilities against an adversary. It was also plain that he wished to acquire reassurance from Jack that—if the approaching vessel was a pirate—the *Prodigal*'s true nature would indeed be to their benefit.

"If she is a pirate, Miss Archer," said Jack, "I assure you the *Prodigal* will be more than a match for her."

In surprise, the girl asked, "Can we not outrun them?"

"We've nowhere to go but farther out to sea in order to attempt to outrun her, and even then it would only be a matter of time. She is a faster sailer as you can see by how quickly she's closing with us. Her sail plan allows her to lie closer to the wind than us."

"Oh, dear..."

"Perhaps Mr. Castle should take you to your cabin for now. If need be, I'll send word to fetch you and your mother down into the hold for safety."

Not a scrap of color flushed the young woman's countenance now as she gulped and stared at the stalking vessel.

"Now, Miss Archer," Jack continued while he gave her a hand down the steps of the quarterdeck, "don't tell your mother anything yet. No need to upset her in her...delicate state."

"But if those are pirates, what will you do?"

Castle's noticeably-paler face bore the same question.

"I hope to stave off hostilities. Once they get closer and see our guns, they will realize how foolish an attack would be. I will offer them some of our rum, and then I'm sure we will be on our way directly. Rest assured, pirates are nothing but drunken cowards, truth be told. Now hurry down with yourself. Stay in the cabin until you're told otherwise."

Her white face descended the companionway into the dimness of the gun deck, her eyes glued to his until he stepped back to Smith.

Jack returned his full attention to the unknown vessel, telescope pressed to his eye. The stranger was gaining even quicker now that she was farther from land and receiving the full strength of the wind on her broad sails. Then the significance of her ketch rig nudged Jack. A cautiously optimistic smile broke across his face as shouts forward told him that some of the Prodigals had the same conjecture as he.

Jack cried, "Rat, hoist the colors!" then to the helm, "Smitty, bring her into the wind."

"What is it, lad?"

"I think we may have found our lost shipmates. If I'm wrong and 'tis just a coaster, then the minute those fellows yonder see our colors, they'll bear away. Either way, we'll soon know the truth of her."

Once the black flag was hoisted and flapped out to leeward, the ketch neither altered course nor checked her way. Instead she responded with an ensign of her own—a plain black scrap of canvas. Shouts of recognition went up throughout the brig.

"Angus," Smith grinned. "An unimaginative cove with that simple rag o' his."

"Silence there!" Jack yelled. "Silence for'ard, I say!"

All raggedly obeyed, casting puzzled looks his way. Ned hurried aft, pointing. "She's the *Fortune*, Captain. Angus and the lads—"

"Aye, that she is." Jack winked at Smith. "But we don't want our passengers to think we're mates with those lads, do we? Wouldn't that spark some confusion and interest among the ladies?"

Realization smoothed the lines from Ned's broad forehead.

Flames belched forth from one of the *Fortune*'s larboard guns, followed a second later by the distant report. Through the aft cabin skylight, Jack heard the women's frightened voices, then quietly said, "Let's have a little fun with this, shall we, gentlemen? Imagine the stories Miss Archer and her mother can tell at her cousin's wedding of how the captain who transported them saved them from a horde of murdering, raping pirates."

Ned chuckled. "Aye aye, sir."

"Spread the word, Ned: no shouts between vessels. And lower away the yawl before Angus gets too close and throws our little plan to the wind with his prodigious gab."

#

When Jack and Smith hooked onto the *Fortune*'s mainchains, Jack called up to their waiting mates, "Now, lads, don't look so pleased to see us. I have a reputation to forge with the passengers aboard the *Prodigal*; they think she is an honest vessel. If they wander on deck and see you looking less than ferocious and menacing they'll start to wonder."

"*Female* passengers?" Joe Dowling flashed a hopeful grin at his mates. "Anything worth samplin'?"

"Not by the likes of you, Joe," Smith shouted, drawing laughter

194

from all.

Angus MacKenzie's stark yellow hair fell forward around his face as he peered down at Jack. "Passengers, Long Arm? Not turned into a-an honest man on us, have ye?"

"Maybe." Jack reached the deck and stood among the small crowd of pirates. He noticed a couple of the pressed men still aboard, but the rest of them were gone. Those who remained seemed at home among the others; apparently after partaking in the convoy's riches, pirating had suddenly appealed to them. Vaguely he thought of Hanse aboard the *Prodigal*—the unwilling fellow had been banished from the passengers and threatened with death should he reveal his status as pressed.

"How'd you escape?" Angus asked.

Smith clambered up after Jack. "That's a story to be told over a bottle, mate. Awful dry talkin' out here in the sun."

"Agreed," Angus grinned. "In the cabin there's rum what we took off that convoy."

"Ahoy, Rat!" Dowling roared across the short distance between the two vessels. "You fuckin' whoreson coxcomb, you still owe me from that last hand! Swim yer mop-headed, shitty-arsed self over here an' pay up!"

From the *Prodigal*'s main top, the Rat dropped his breeches and flashed his scrawny white buttocks in Dowling's direction. Laughter erupted from both sides.

"Pipe down," Jack ordered. "Mind what I said, Dowling. I don't need those women thinking the *Prodigal* is a pirate."

"Why don't I pull over there and show 'em a real pirate? You can come in an 'rescue' 'em after I'm done."

"Stow it, Joe," Angus growled. "No one leaves the barky. Now come along, gents. We'll get some rum into Joe and take his mind off his prick for a-a few minutes."

The *Fortune*'s cabin was barely large enough for a small table and the four men who sat around it, and the windowless stuffiness made Jack better appreciate the *Prodigal*'s cabin. Angus liberally doled out rum from an open pin at the end of the table.

"Now tell us how you came to escape, Long Arm," Angus encouraged.

Dowling added, "An' how you came to be a bloody tender."

Smith took a long swallow of rum, for Jack had limited drink aboard the *Prodigal* while the Archer women were on board; not a popular directive, of course, even with Smith. "Lemme tell the story,

Jackie." He grinned, and Jack rolled his eyes with a relenting wave of his hand. Smith chuckled. "Gents, lemme just say me captain here cuts a fine figure in a dress."

The two others eyed Smith.

"'Twas a disguise," Jack clarified. "I was held in a citizen's house in Charles Town. I used the dress to get away. Sailed under false colors, you might say."

A slow smile stretched through Angus's small, mangy beard. Dowling began to laugh.

"I had to beat the sailors off him," Smith insisted with great delight, flailing one arm to demonstrate. "They all thought he was quite the comely wench."

As the mirth increased, Jack scowled and drank away his humiliation.

"Imagine their surprise if they'd got to see 'neath that skirt," said Dowling. "Well, maybe not *too* surprised, considerin' Long Arm's not so long—"

"Now, now, Joe," Smith interrupted. "Don't be pokin' fun at the Captain's…ordnance."

"What? His swivel gun compared to my 24-pounder?"

Jack set down his mug with a thump that made Smith's words more insistent amidst the laughter: "'Vast that talk, Joe, afore Long Arm soaks yer head in that cask."

Angus managed to collect himself, wiping tears from his bulbous eyes. "So the dress explains you bein' here, but what about them passengers? How'd you come by havin' them aboard and bein' in these waters?"

Now Jack sobered, and his obvious discomfort likewise sobered his mates. He did not want to admit his dilemma, did not want to appear weak to these men by being beholden to another. But there was no help for it, and begrudgingly he explained his debt to Ezra Archer. As he did so, intense intrigue replaced the jocose atmosphere.

"So yer workin' for him now?" Dowling said in a tone that revealed neither disdain nor admiration but a great deal of opportunistic interest.

"I'm working for no one. I'm repaying a debt. Plain and simple."

Angus studied him across the table. "So what's the second part of this accord of your'n? What'll he have you do after you get back to Charles Town?"

"I don't know yet. He wouldn't tell me." Jack felt foolish admitting his ignorance.

"Sounds like he's testin' you." Dowling's dark eyes lay hard upon Jack. "Tryin' you out, eh?" He leaned over his pewter mug. "After all, he's a bit fucked without Logan, isn't he?"

"Joe has a-a point," Angus agreed.

"Not a bad idea really," the gunner continued. "That is, if Archer gives us the same protection he gave Logan."

"We won't need protection because we won't need to pirate," Jack said. "Part of the deal is that he will secure pardons for both crews—all my men."

Angus reared back. "Pardons?"

"Aye, to those who want 'em."

Angus stared at Dowling who did not seem as astonished. In fact, the short, hairy gunner appeared skeptical when he asked, "How would he get us pardoned?"

"He seems to have some sway politically in the province. He must, otherwise how could Logan have gone untouched for so long?"

"And we should trust 'im?" Dowling downed more rum.

"Whether you trust him or not would be up to each man," Jack continued.

"I say we lay low for a while and enjoy our latest purchase," the gunner said. "Then we see what Archer has to offer in the way of us takin' over Logan's place."

Jack shook his head. "I don't intend to keep pirating. I have my sister to think of."

Dowling laughed. "'Tis not that simple, Long Arm. You've been a right criminal—alleged and otherwise, eh?—for too long to make a quick switch to bein' a peaceful, law-abiding lubber. There's more of the rogue in you than you want to believe. I see it; you will, too, if you're honest with yourself. And if I was you, I wouldn't be so quick to trust no rich planter to just let bygones be bygones after whatever it is he's goin' to have you do. Run his own son off, didn't he? Who says he'll warm to you and hold to any bargain?"

"Unfortunately I owe him my life, Dowling. Don't think that I like it. But for now I plan to uphold *my* end of the bargain. After that, who knows what will happen? Besides, what good is the purchase from the convoy if you have to look over your shoulder every time you try to spend it? And staying at sea is no guarantee—probably less so—that you won't swing from a rope eventually. Some of the lads might welcome a chance to settle on land with enough money to start an honest life, raise a family maybe."

Dowling snorted. "Thinkin' 'bout that dusky wench o' your'n,

Long Arm? That boy what went ashore with her has his eye on her, you know. Belike you won't have her waitin' for you by the time Archer lets you try your hand at bein' a farmer, eh?" He laughed ominously. "No, sir, mate. Mark me, you'll end up with your true callin' in the end. And it's not farmin'."

Jack scowled, angrier at himself for the doubts Dowling seeded more so than at Dowling himself. But he forced those thoughts aside and returned his focus to the moment. "As I said, I'm not sure what Archer has planned for me next, but as soon as I know anything about the pardons," he glanced at the brooding gunner, "or anything profitable, I'll let you know."

"And how will you do that?" Dowling asked with a touch of sarcasm.

"Sail down to Charles Town in a few days. I can send Leighlin's ketch—the *Nymph*—to find you in the offing." He allowed a small, tempting grin. "In the meantime, don't get caught in Charles Town with your breeches down around your ankles."

# CHAPTER 19

"Mr. David, why won't you let Mr. Ketch eat with us now that he's feeling better?"

David sat on the edge of Helen's bed, having just finished a bedtime story. Maria turned down the lamp on the nightstand. Its golden flicker across the young man's face showed his displeasure at the unexpected question. Beneath the edge of her cap, a single line upon Helen's forehead seemed to challenge David, as if their faces were dueling in an effort to dissuade the other's stubbornness. Helen's fingers worked absently against the soft fur of her stuffed bear where she held it to her chest like a battle shield.

Maria knew David's refusal to allow Ketch to share meals with them stemmed not so much from societal hierarchy but instead from his personal aversion to the man. Perhaps Ketch's gradual recovery of strength increased David's concerns. The fact that the man was minus a dominant arm did not seem to diminish any of his menace from David's point of view. Again Maria wondered exactly what Ketch had done to cause so much humiliation that David could not even meet Ketch's eyes. And Ketch, of course, made no effort to allay David's anxiety. If anything, he viewed David with barely veiled contempt as an intruder at Leighlin. No doubt he shared Samuel's belief that David inherently brought bad luck.

"Well, Helen," David said at last, "Ketch is not..." His frown deepened. "Mr. Ketch is...well, a hired hand, you might say. Like Mr. Defoe or Mr. Willis. And a hired hand does not share the same...privileges that you as a family member share."

"But you're not family and you eat with me. And Mr. Dell and Mr. Rogers—"

David's jaw tightened. "True enough, but while your brother is away I am head of the household. Mr. Dell and Mr. Rogers are more guests than hired hands. You do not see Mr. Willis having dinner with us, do you?"

"No, but Mr. Willis has Gabriel and the others to eat with; Mr. Ketch eats all alone in his chamber. I helped him eat breakfast today.

It's so hard for him with just his left hand." Her well-rehearsed look of sympathy did not move David, so she tried another tactic. "Mr. Ketch is going to help me find my daddy again now that he's getting stronger."

David scowled. "Did he tell you that?"

Helen lowered her gaze to the bear and murmured, "No, but he found Daddy before, when Daddy and John went sailing and left me behind."

"Helen..." David sighed when Helen's worried eyes lifted to his, all pretense now gone. His unconvincing smile curbed whatever he had been about to say. "Enough talk for now. Time to sleep." He bent and kissed her forehead, something Maria had never seen him do before.

The demonstration brightened Helen who capitulated for now and gave him a sleepy smile. She whispered, "Good night," with the air of one who did not intend to give up her fight for Ketch's inclusion. She turned onto her side to watch him leave.

David gestured for Maria to accompany him. Reluctant because of the stormy resolve on his face, Maria followed him from the bedchamber and closed the door. Then he drew her toward the stair hall.

He kept his voice low. "We cannot let this go on any longer. Helen needs to know the truth about her father."

"But...we've both tried; she doesn't *want* to know the truth."

"Maybe she needs someone else to tell her, someone who is responsible for this happening. She seems to think so highly of Ketch now; she seems to think he will be her savior again, so let *him* tell her the truth. He deserves to do it, the murdering blackguard."

"I don't think she would believe him any more than—"

"Well, he should try. Helen cannot go on waking every day thinking her father is going to appear or that Ketch will fetch him. Think of your own father. What if someone kept you believing that he was alive, yet for some reason he never came back to you? Which is worse for her to endure: Logan's death or a lifetime of perceived abandonment?"

Maria touched the locket around her neck, the mention of her father bringing fresh sadness. Could that be why she had not pressed this matter—because of the pain her father's death caused her, shot in front of her as Logan had been shot in Helen's presence? An agony she would never wish upon anyone, especially a child who had just lost her mother, who had no kin around her. To witness that pain, that realization in Helen would only bring back her own grief.

"Ketch will not do it if I tell him to," David blunted his tone at the sight of her sorrow. "If anyone is to convince him, it will be you; he seems to hold you in some regard now. But do not try to appeal to his feelings; he has none. Ketch is used to taking orders—it must be an order."

Maria remembered Ketch's reaction to Helen's touch, and she knew David was wrong about the man's capacity to feel, but this was a point she certainly could never argue with David or anyone else upon whom Ketch had left his mark. Even now her humanizing thought of him disconcerted her; she should feel nothing but caution about the man. To consider confronting him was equally displeasing, as was the idea of him trying to convince Helen, for certainly the brute would lack the compassion necessary to do such a sensitive thing.

Toying with the locket, Maria stared at David's chest where a few faint hairs peeked above the opening of his shirt. He took her hand into the warmth of his own and gave her a wavering smile. In his blue eyes she saw much more than concern for Helen.

"You will talk to him?"

She frowned and nodded.

He raised her hand to his lips and gently kissed it, his gaze glued to her with that unblinking power that always disarmed her. She remembered the first time he had kissed her and how she had dismissed it, thinking he were only enamored of her because of her physical care of him when he had been hurt. Even when he had recently blurted his marriage lie to his father, a part of her credited the indiscretion to desperation regarding his own safety. His other physical advances—aboard the *Prodigal* and then the day they had returned to Leighlin—she discounted as mere products of the moment, of the events that had been taking place around them, drawing upon their weariness, their loneliness, and the circumstances.

But things had somehow changed since Margaret's visit. Maria saw it in David's absence from the house, from her, heard it in his voice, saw it in his eyes at the dinner table or when they sat in the evening with Helen on the portico, or...now. And though she saw it—this indecision whether to linger longer at Leighlin or to give up this masquerade altogether—she knew not what to do to help him with his struggle. So all she could do was stare at him until he freed her hand and descended the stairs.

#

That night thoughts of Jack, David, and Ketch kept Maria awake for several hours. Once sleep finally claimed her, it was loath to free her, and so, when dawn first broke, she was only vaguely aware of Helen leaving the bed they shared since their return to Leighlin; the child did not want to be alone at night, a fear she had displayed since her father's death. The servants, of course, thought that when Maria entered David's bedchamber in the evenings it was to share her husband's bed, but instead she would use the short connecting passageway to go from David's chamber to Helen's.

By the time Maria roused herself and went downstairs for breakfast, Mary reported that David had already eaten with Helen and was currently at Logan's desk behind the library's closed door. Helen had gone to play in the gardens with one of her slave playmates. Once through eating, Maria headed to the stables.

She found Willis in the barn with Jemmy, just as Mary had told her. A very pregnant chestnut mare stood calmly in her stall, head down, munching hay with an anxious Jemmy stroking her shoulder. At the rear of the mare, Willis had his arm up to nearly his shoulder as he palpated her. Maria felt scandalized for the mare, though the animal did not seem mortified at all. She wondered if a midwife or physician would do the same to a pregnant woman. It certainly made the thought of pregnancy less appealing.

"Mr. Willis."

"Ah, good mornin', Miss Cordero...er, ma'am." As if self-conscious of his position, he quickly finished his exam and withdrew his arm, reached for a towel and a bucket of water.

"How is she?"

"Oh, she seems fine so far. Hopefully we will have a new foal by this time tomorrow."

At the thought of a newborn, Maria smiled and hoped the foal would provide Helen with a distraction. Maria had never witnessed the birth of anything before. Perhaps it would be interesting to see...or daunting when she considered her own hope to one day give birth.

"What brings you here, ma'am? Out for a ride?"

"I wondered if you knew where I might find Ketch. He's not at the house."

"He came to me first thing and said he wanted work to do. Said he wants to earn his keep." Willis snorted skeptically. "First time I've heard the word 'work' come out of that lazy cove's mouth. And how much real work can a man do with but one arm?"

"Is he well enough to work?"

Willis laughed. "I don't care a farthing if he's not. He asked for work; I gave him some. I had him take a work gang out to finish the fencing by the west creek—keep them bloody cows out of the swamp. Lost two calves this spring, fool things. Gave him the six worst bucks for a gang. Lazy black dogs, the lot of 'em. I reckon if anyone can get an honest day's work out of 'em, it'll be Ketch." Willis chuckled. "Just bein' alone out there with him will scare the bejesus out of 'em so's they don't slack off."

Maria held the stall door for Jemmy so he could exit with the towel and bucket. "Jemmy, could you saddle Curly for me please? And tell me how to get to the west creek."

Willis raised an eyebrow at her. "You're not ridin' out there to Ketch, not without me or one of t'other men with you."

"Don't be foolish, Mr. Willis. He won't harm me. He's barely strong enough to walk twenty paces." She gave an indulgent smile. "I'm sure I could outrun him."

"What purpose do you have with him anyways?"

"I have a message to deliver from Mr. Archer. Now, Jemmy, if you please…"

#

Curly's laziness did not allow for speed, and Maria had not the heart to prod the beast much, for his golden bay coat was already dark from sweat before they left the stable yard. Judging the thickening gray clouds, Maria expected not to see the sun again today; it would undoubtedly rain later. She sniffed the breeze but caught no hint of precipitation yet. She rode through forests and past fields of corn and other crops, as well as past peach and apple trees, which Curly furtively attempted to rob. The slaves in the fields gave her only a glance. The white driver whom she saw—Gabriel—swept his hat from his head where he lounged beneath a tall pine. When she inquired, he assured her that she was headed in the right direction.

Once she reached the west grazing land, the trees through which she had been riding fell away, revealing cleared land no more than five acres in width and breadth. Cattle browsed mainly around the fringes to partake of the trees' protection, ears and tails busy in their constant war with insects. Some lay placidly, jaws rhythmically working. Two calves played half-heartedly with their mothers; others had already worn themselves out and lay in sweaty dark lumps. Curly made his way through those in the open, eying the creatures with great disdain.

At the far end of the pasture, a sleepy team of mules hitched to a wagon rested under the cover of hickory trees, long ears twitching, tails unproductively swishing, heads drooping. Curly blared a half-hearted neigh to his stablemates, but the mules looked his way with very little enthusiasm. Nearby half a dozen slaves worked upon a fence line, splitting logs with axes. Ketch sat upon the wagon's tail, pointing and barking an order at the slaves who swung their axes quickly if not efficiently. When the slaves—well-muscled young men—saw Maria, they hesitated in their work and removed their hats.

Ketch followed their gazes only briefly before chastising them. "Mind yer split, you bloody heathens. Don't want 'em too thin or the beasts'll go right through 'em, hear?" Then, trying to hide his surprise at the unheralded sight of Maria, he awkwardly shifted off the wagon, staggering slightly.

Maria marveled at the man's resilience considering the physical ordeal he had endured just days ago. The fact that he was out of bed, let alone in solitary charge of a work gang, forced her to admire his fortitude. Why did he not linger about the house in the relative ease it would allow him? Surely no one had been bold enough to attempt to shame him into working, and no doubt he would not have listened to such an effort anyway. Plainly Ketch intimidated all the white men at Leighlin and—no matter their hatred of him for Logan's death—none of them had the nerve to remove him or exact revenge, especially with Helen's new-found loyalty to him so evident. To think a small child could so thoroughly shield someone as fearsome as Ketch almost amused Maria.

She dismounted next to the wagon and secured Curly to it. Ketch watched her with suspicion, his hand against the wagon in a false display of casualness. Maria knew, in truth, he needed the wagon for support. His color still had not regained its normal dark hue since the snake bite.

"Where's Miss Helen?"

It was invariably the question he asked when the child did not accompany her. The veiled solicitude in his inquiries always left Maria apprehensive.

"Last I saw her, she was in the gardens."

"You ought to keep a closer eye on her," he grumbled.

"David's in the house if she needs anyone."

Maria's dread had been building during her ride, and in fact she had been glad that Curly had progressed at a mere shuffle. Facing Ketch now brought her unease to greater heights. If David discovered she had come here alone, he would be displeased and would surely ride out to ensure her safety, but she had purposefully told none of the servants where she was bound. Since speaking with David last night, she had been trying to think of a way to convince Ketch to tell Helen the truth, but everything she thought of left her feeling even more worried about the child's response, more so than her anxiety over Ketch's reaction to her demand.

Surreptitious glances from the sweaty slaves flashed her way still, and Ketch snarled, "Keep yer damn eyes on yer business, Zeke, or I'll take that axe to ye."

This thoroughly convinced the men to turn back to their work.

"I came to speak with you about Helen," Maria began weakly. She considered inviting him to sit but knew he would not. He watched her closely, the familiar vertical lines between his eyes being the only things that showed his interest in her words. Forcing bluntness, she continued, "It's cruel of you to let Helen think you're going to find her father for her."

This was plainly not what he had expected her to discuss. Revealing no anger, he avoided her gaze and looked at Curly who was already dozing, long, black tail swishing, the coarse strands whispering through the air.

Maria pressed on, trying to be firm but finding little strength. "It's time she understands—truly understands—that her father is not coming back, that you can't find him for her. You must tell her the truth."

His unhappy gaze snapped back to hers. "The truth?"

"Yes."

He shifted his weight, and sweat broke out upon his brow with greater definition. "She won't believe me no more than she believes you."

The quick readiness of his excuse astonished her, though his delivery did not completely convince her that he believed his own words. "She'll believe you if you tell her you're the one who killed her father. That was your choice; now it's your responsibility to make her understand. You can't keep up this lie about finding him. You've had your health as an excuse up until now, but what about tomorrow? Next week? Next month? How will she feel when she realizes you've been lying to her?"

"I've not been lyin' to her."

"Letting her believe otherwise is near enough the same thing."

His breathing had increased. She had expected resistance but not this level of distress; she took a discreet step away from him.

"In time," he said, "she'll forget. She'll stop askin' 'bout him."

"You know she won't."

His eyes wandered restlessly, as if considering an escape. "Tellin' her the truth will only hurt her; it won't bring her father back."

"You must tell her something so she doesn't keep thinking he's coming back. Her brother is returning home soon, and she needs to understand that her father's death was not his fault."

"It is his fault, damn him. If he hadn't come to these waters none o' this would've happened. Why don't you tell her that?"

Angry with herself for opening this door for him, Maria pushed onward. "Helen needs to grieve and heal. She needs to have a relationship with her brother. She needs him...and he needs her."

"I don't give a damn what he needs."

"Tell her the truth, Ketch."

"I won't." His hand ran through his unruly hair as he turned back to the wagon. "I can't."

"Then you leave me no choice." Purposefully she stepped over to Curly and tossed the reins back over the gelding's head. "If you won't tell her, then I will. And what I'll tell her will be nothing short of the whole truth—that you and you alone are responsible for her father's murder."

Before she could settle in the saddle, Ketch had a hold of the bridle, startling Curly fully awake and making the horse shy away. All weakness had left Ketch now, and a muscle along one of his scarred cheeks twitched with tension. And while there was menace in his eyes, Maria was startled by how well he managed to contain it, how desperate he was to stop her, to convince her.

"Please," he said quietly, jaw tight with control. "Don't."

"I have no choice." Maria glared at him, hiding her reaction to his conflict, not allowing an ounce of sympathy, ready at any moment to whip Curly into a run. "Let go of the horse."

"No..." Ketch struggled, glanced into Curly's uneasy brown eye. Then, as if suddenly exhausted, his hand fell from the bridle, and his head drooped. He stepped back, reached for the support of the wagon, mumbled, "I'll tell her."


#


Maria sat alone on the upper portico and watched the sun sink behind the trees at the far end of the long sward, just visible under a gray bank of clouds that would soon bring the rain she had anticipated all day. Songs drifted in from the unseen slave settlement—faint and sad—joining with the creaky noises of tree frogs and the chorus of their cousins in the swamps. The sheep had wandered between the kitchen house and the main house. Helen was abed. Maria had tucked her in some time ago and had expected David to join her on the portico as he did every evening, but he had not appeared. So she sat alone and waited for the rain.

At supper David had asked Helen if she had seen Ketch today. The child had not, nor had anyone else after he had returned to the stables with the mule team. His obvious avoidance chafed Maria, yet perhaps he would tell Helen about her father tomorrow; perhaps he had lacked the courage today. She marveled at how Ketch could so coldly torture his fellow man yet cower at the idea of confessing his sin to a child.

When the rain came at last, Maria stood from her chair. She breathed in its cleansing scent as it fell—straight down and soft, the darker clouds beyond the trees promising an increase in tempo. She was still not tired but decided to go to bed regardless.

A distant glow of light showed beneath David's closed bedchamber door. She gave a light knock as she always did to warn him of her entrance. She found him in a chair in the far corner, reading by lamplight. Closing the book, he gave her a weary smile and stood.

"Bedtime at last?"

"Yes," she replied. "The rain is making me sleepy."

"Did Ketch return?"

"I haven't seen him."

David frowned. "Perhaps he has decided to leave instead of tell Helen what he did."

"Perhaps," Maria said doubtfully then ventured, "Why didn't you come out to the portico tonight?"

The frown deepened, and he sank back to the chair. "I would not have been good company."

"Something's troubling you?"

His sapphire eyes studied her with that innate power of theirs, and she could tell he was debating whether to answer honestly or not at all.

"Are you worried about Helen—about Ketch talking to her?" Maria asked.

"Of course there is that, but…truth be told there is something else weighing heavily on my mind."

Maria moved to sit on the edge of the bed.

"I still feel a fool for using you to deceive my father."

"David—"

207

"I am a coward. I should have had the courage to simply ask you right and proper, and not because I needed a reason to stay here or to foil my father's designs."

Disarmed by what he meant, Maria could say nothing.

David hesitated then crossed the short distance between them. The sudden resolve on his face stole Maria's breath. He knelt before her.

"I want to marry you, Maria. And not to confound my father but because I love you."

She strangled on her response, finding no air with which to expel the words.

"You do not have to answer right now. I only ask that you think about it."

As he sat next to her, the rain increased and created a racket against the open west windows, but neither of them moved to close them. Maria felt drained and exhausted, as if having run a great distance. Before her, she saw not the weak boy who had lain near death aboard the *Prodigal* or in Rose's cabin but instead the self-assured young gentleman who had smoothly stepped into the role of temporary patriarch at Leighlin, who had displayed compassion and strength at every turn, and who had shown Helen as much love as could be hoped for from a child's own father. Even his aversion to Ketch's presence at Leighlin she knew had as much to do with her own safety and the safety of all at Leighlin as it did his own demons. As a young girl in Cayona wishing for deliverance from her mundane life, never had she dreamt of someone of David's standing and character asking for her hand in marriage.

His warm fingers touched her cheek. She could not keep herself from accepting the gesture and allowing him to cradle her face, his fingertips light upon her ear beneath the fall of her thick hair. He smiled nervously. "Will you not say anything at all? Have I alarmed you that much?"

"Of course not. It's just…I'm overwhelmed."

"But not totally appalled, I pray."

"Of course not. I'm flattered. You have no idea…"

He gently kissed her lips, weakening her further. "You will think on it then?"

Saying no was impossible with him so close, so intimate here in his bedchamber, the taste of his lips upon hers, that unbreakable gaze of his boring into hers.

"I will think on it," she whispered.

He smiled broadly with relief and hope, and she could see he desperately wanted to kiss her again and more, so she stood from the bed and bade him good night. As she crossed over to the side passageway, his eyes remained on her—she could feel them like hands caressing her back. She chanced one backward glance before she slipped away.

Once in Helen's bedchamber, she paused and leaned against the doorjamb. Her heart raced unabated. What had just happened? Only a fool would not have seen the inevitability of the moment. If she had, she could have been more prepared. But prepared how? Would she have said more—or less—than she just had? How could anyone prepare for such a thing?

Helen slept soundly, undisturbed by the rain. Maria frowned, fatigue gone. She could not go to bed; it would be impossible right now to lie here when on the other side of that wall was a man who had just taken a leap of faith and offered her his pledge, his life, and by doing so would forfeit not only money but family as well. This was not something to decide one way or another in just one night. But how long should she take? And how would she know her decision was the right one?

Craving fresh air and coolness—her clothes stuck to her sweaty skin—she silently left the chamber and fled downstairs to distance herself from David, to push aside the touch of his flesh against hers, to think clearly, without impetuosity and animal passions.

In the Great Hall, the white lace of Ella Logan's portrait gown seemed to glow in the darkness as Maria hurried past, making her think of her son. Jack had been there in David's chamber with her, in the back of her mind as David proposed to her. She had tried not to acknowledge him, for she did not want her feelings for Jack to taint her judgment of David. The fact that she had not outright declined David's offer startled her and made her wonder about her true feelings for Jack. Her previous fantasies were clear and painful enough to recall, but the reality of their relationship... Exactly what was their relationship? It had been nothing but muddled, the only clarity being the first kiss they had shared. Had she been a fool to cling to that memory, that brief passion when so much that had happened afterwards was anything but passionate? Was she letting that one moment cloud her present and future?

Carefully she opened the back door and stepped onto the portico where she stood for a long moment, breathing deeply, slowing her heartbeat as she bathed in the refreshing damp breeze that had sprung up with the heavier wave of rain. She closed her eyes for a time, settled herself, then opened them to the curtain of rain pouring off the portico eaves.

Light stretched outward from the lower level of the house, from Ketch's window. Curious, she wandered to the side of the portico and looked downward. The open shutters allowed the rain to course down the stone sill into Ketch's chamber. From there she could partially see his bed—empty and untouched. She frowned when she thought of the conversation she had had in the pasture with the man.

She glanced at the black sky. The high clouds were moving much faster than the wind here across the sward; the rain would pass soon. She hesitated then darted down the steps into the wet and through the door to the dry lower level.

Damp mustiness greeted her in the dark gloom of the common room, compounded by the fresh rainfall. She waited for her eyes to adjust. The common room was filled with foodstuffs and various necessities for the plantation, in casks and sacks nondescript in the darkness, surrounding a table and benches used by Leighlin's white workers for their meals and socializing. Snores rumbled, but she could not tell from which of the four bedchambers the noise originated or if from several. The two small chambers for the house servants lay off the common room on the south side—one for the women and one for the men. Female whispers drifted from the farthest, soft laughter and giggles behind the closed door. On the north side were two similar chambers—one shared by Willis and the other white men, the second formerly inhabited by Defoe.

Not wanting to disturb anyone, Maria quietly crept toward the latter where the door stood ajar. A skinny shaft of light fell through the doorway onto the hard-packed floor, guiding her steps. No sounds from within. Who had left the lamp lit and unattended? Perhaps Ketch had come and gone. Or maybe Willis or one of the servants had been in there. She shook her head at the neglect and pushed one hand against the door to open it wide. There she halted as if struck by a brick.

On the floor beneath an open window, in the small space between the foot of the bed and the interior wall, sat Ketch. Rain trickled along the sill and down the wall behind him where he leaned. A half empty bottle of rum sat beside him, but it took only one glance to discern that he had drank much more than half of a bottle. The length of his gaping shirt insufficiently concealed his arousal.

He held a bloody knife poised above his outstretched leg, the muscular flesh of his thigh a grid of gory slices.

# CHAPTER 20

Maria stared at Ketch's mutilated leg and breathed, "Dear God..."

Ketch made no move to get up or to cover his nakedness. Alcohol flushed his face, his loose hair damp and limp, framing frightening ebony eyes filled with rage and loathing. "Get out," he growled.

"What on earth are you doing?"

"Get out!" he roared, startling her in the small, low room. "I said get out, you meddlin' Spanish bitch!" Spittle flew with the stridency of his insult.

She remained frozen, horrified by his almost unrecognizable appearance.

He set the knife down and threw his bottle at her. His awkward left-handed throw came close to Maria's head, the bottle smashing against the doorframe and spattering her with rum.

Willis's voice came from behind her. "What in God's name...?" The glass on the floor discouraged his bare feet from stepping next to Maria. What he saw over her shoulder drove crimson color into his bearded cheeks, and he clapped a hand upon Maria's wrist and dragged her backward. Then he yanked the door shut.

Trembling from head to toe, Maria tried to pull from his grip. "Unhand me. What are you doing?"

"Keepin' you from gettin' your fool head taken off."

Willis's roommates stood in the adjacent doorway as dark shapes. In a surly tone, Gabriel asked, "What's all the damned noise about?"

"Just Ketch in his cups, lads. Go back to bed."

The men grumbled among themselves and shuffled back into the further darkness, closing the door behind them. Maria sensed the presence of the servants, peering out from their chambers as well, whispering, but then they quickly retreated, and the doors shut.

As Willis pulled Maria toward the table, he spoke close. "What the hell was you doin' in his chamber?"

"I—I didn't know he was there. I was out on the portico and saw his shutters open with the rain getting in and a lamp lit. I was just going to douse it and close the shutters."

"Was ye now?" Skeptical, Willis lit a candle on the table.

Maria shook free of her shock. "What else would I have been doing?"

"I think you've taken too much interest in that bloody bastard. He's no wolf you can tame. And now you've seen what you're up against." Willis tapped a blunt finger against his temple. "He's not right in the head."

"But did you see what he's done to his leg? We should stop him."

"Leave him be. If we're lucky he'll slit his own throat. He's dead drunk, and when Ketch is drunk you stay away from him."

She stared at Ketch's closed door. "Why would he do such a thing to himself?"

"I just told you why."

"Has he done that before? Hurt himself, I mean."

"Never seen the like. Too busy maimin' others, he is. Not natural, that one. Somethin' riles ol' Ketch, he goes off his nut. Hard tellin' what it is this time."

With sudden clarity Maria knew exactly what it was.

"Now do you see why none of us want him here? Only Miss Ella held any sway over him and kept him in check. Him hurtin' Jemmy the way he did, right under Captain Logan's nose, told me there'd be no controllin' the bugger after she died."

"What did he do to Jemmy?"

He cleared his throat. "Nothin' a woman needs to hear. Like I said, there's no controllin' him, not with him grievin' over Miss Ella and that damned Slattery. Now maybe you'll let us get rid of him. If you want to keep your own captain safe, you will. We all know Ketch bears him a grudge."

"He gave me his word when I helped him through the fever," she said weakly. "He won't hurt Jack—or anyone."

Reproachfully Willis eyed her. "After what you just saw him capable of doin' to his own self, are you really going to count on the word of a madman?"

Maria glanced again at Ketch's door and remembered when Helen had stood at his bedside and comforted him when no one else would. Never would Maria forget the reaction the gesture drew from the man, like the sun breaking over a black, stormy horizon. Because of that one compassionate moment, that one incongruous connection and Ketch's very human reaction to it, Maria could not believe the man was mad.

#

When morning came, Maria spent an awkward breakfast with David and Helen. She was unsure what to say or do in David's presence after last night's proposal, and he seemed equally uncertain, his efforts at conversation stilted. Helen appeared to sense the strain, glancing curiously between them. Maria toyed with the idea of revealing that Ketch had returned—she could not tell him the details in front of Helen—but she decided to keep silent, not wanting a potential argument about forcing Ketch's hand again. As soon as David finished his meal, he left, headed to a field downriver that was being cleared for rice cultivation. With bear in tow, Helen trailed off alongside Cuppy, a slave playmate, to hunt fiddler crabs down by the river.

When Rose came into the dining room with Pip to clear away the two settings, Maria stirred from her web of jumbled thoughts.

"Rose, do you know if Mr. Ketch is awake?"

"We fed the other men a bit ago, and he didn't join them. I heard them say something 'bout Mr. Ketch sleepin' off his ale." The curious, cautious light in her eyes made Maria wonder about the gossip already circulating. It would not be long before David discovered the truth.

"Pip, fix a tray of fresh tea and hominy and take it to the common room downstairs. Rose, I need you to fetch some of that balm you used on Mr. David's wounds. Do you remember it?"

Rose exchanged a glance with Pip then said, "Yes'm."

"Bring that and a pitcher of fresh water and lint bandages to me downstairs."

When Maria reached the lower level, no one else was there except two male slaves bringing in bushels of peaches. They bobbed their heads to her and replied good morning to her salutations. At the table she picked up the sweetgrass tray with the tea and hominy, and the slaves watched in unabashed wonderment as she approached Ketch's chamber. She tossed a rebuking look their way and off they went to retrieve more of the bushels from the wagon outside.

She paused at the door and listened. No sounds from within. She had a dreadful image of finding the man dead. "Ketch? Ketch, are you awake?"

She caught the faint protest of the bed frame.

"I've brought you some breakfast."

"Get away from that door," a thick, groggy voice croaked from within.

Maria frowned. She heard movement behind her and turned to see Rose with the requested items, her brown eyes intent with questions and concerns.

"Put them on the table," she said then dismissed the slave with thanks.

Once Rose had left and the two slaves had come and gone with more bushels, Maria balanced the tray upon her hip and reached for the door handle. She faltered, tried to gain some courage and put the vision of last night from her mind. Then she gingerly opened the door.

Ketch lay on the bed, his muscular arm crooked over his closed eyes as if to protect them from the light streaming in through the open windows. He lay on his back, still clad—much to Maria's chagrin—only in a shirt, but at least now a sheet covered his lower body, hiding the work of his knife save for blood stains. His ankles below the sheet displayed the fetter scars that she had first noted after the snake bite. He slid his forearm up to his brow and cracked his red-rimmed eyes at her, glowered down the length of his crooked nose.

"Get out."

Maria marched resolutely in, careful not to step on the broken glass. She wondered where his knife was as she set the tray on the chest next to the bed. Then she went to retrieve the articles Rose had set on the table. He looked surprised to see her return.

"Are you deaf, girl?"

Maria picked up an empty basin from the near corner of the room and gave it a quick wipe before setting it on the chest. "You best eat while it's still warm."

He covered his bloodshot eyes again.

She placed the bandages and jar next to the basin. "Put this salve on your cuts. If you need help with the bandages let me know. We should change the dressing on your...arm as well."

"Leave me be."

She contemplated his subdued but still combative mood. "Very well."

With that she started for the door but stopped when Ketch's quiet words reached her: "I couldn't tell her."

Maria turned back around, considered him and her own part in having trapped him into this predicament. Ketch's eyes remained hidden beneath his arm. Flatly she replied, "Very well."

A brief pause. "Are you goin' to tell her?"

Thomas hailed her from the common room, as if afraid to come too close to Ketch's chamber.

She closed the door and went to Thomas near the table. Anxiety furrowed the man's low brow, his hands pressed together in front of his chest, twisting. Was it because of what he had heard and witnessed here

214

last night? Or was it simply Ketch's presence that caused such distress? Surviving a snake bite when others at Leighlin had perished from the same had added to Ketch's terrifying mystique among the slaves.

"What is it?"

"Old Mr. Archer...he down at the landin', askin' for you. Say he need to speak with you by yourself."

"Why doesn't he come up to the house?"

"Don't know. He told Isaac he in an all-fire hurry on his way downriver on business and for us to fetch you straight away."

"Very well. Thank you, Thomas."

The slave drifted back through the door, passing the two hands who were still unloading the wagon. Maria thought of sending for David and warning him of his father's presence, but caution squashed that impulse and propelled her out of the house. Perhaps Archer had news of Jack's return.

She found Ezra Archer seated on a bench beneath the line of birch trees that separated the busy landing from the ponds. When he caught sight of Maria, he stood and doffed his hat, gave a slight bow, his demeanor taking her off guard, unsure if the gesture was sincere or satiric. As usual his clothes were impeccable—a golden brown coat of velvet trimmed with darker brown, a silk doublet of pale blue, heavily embroidered with the same golden brown, his cravat and lace cuffs dazzling white in the morning sun, immaculate silk stockings below his brown breeches, the gold buckles on his shoes shimmering. He wore a stylish wig. All she could imagine was how hot such a thing must be.

"Good day, Miss Cordero."

Maria hesitated, revealed no emotion. "Perhaps you've forgotten—it's Mrs. Archer now."

"Is it?" He gestured to the shaded bench. "Pray sit. I apologize for my uninvited intrusion upon your day. I am on my way downriver and thought it convenient to stop now."

Maria smelled a lie, for she had a feeling every decision Archer made was based upon calculation, not the whim of the tide. She placed herself at the far end of the bench from him.

"I wanted to tell you that Captain Mallory should be returning any day now. With him will come my niece Elizabeth. She will stop here at Leighlin through my daughter's wedding. I hope this is enough warning for you to prepare for her arrival."

"I should think this should be a request, not a demand."

"Miss Cordero, Captain Logan left Leighlin under my hand, not yours. 'Tis only through my benevolence that you are even allowed to live here."

The shock of this revelation momentarily silenced her. She had never considered this very crucial reality. Quickly recovering, she said, "This house is in mourning. We should not be entertaining guests—"

"Spare me the charade, Miss Cordero. Who is there to mourn Logan and his wife? A mere child, some heathen slaves, and a few invalid seamen? Surely Logan's tragic end causes you little sorrow, considering that he murdered your father."

His knowledge of her past unsettled Maria further. "It seems to me Wildwood would be a more appropriate place for your niece."

"Wildwood will soon be overrun by guests and we with little place to put them. Elizabeth is acquainted with David, and I thought you— being of similar age—would be a fitting companion for her. In fact, I am counting on you for your assistance."

"Assistance in what?"

His melanic eyes took on a resolute, dangerous glint with which she was more familiar. "'Tis obvious to me that you care a great deal for my son."

"Of course."

"So I would imagine you would want only the best for him and for his future."

Maria scowled in anticipation of a challenge.

"I do not believe my son to be married to you."

"Then why don't you tell him as much yourself?"

"What good would that do? You have witnessed for yourself how set my son is against my wishes and plans for a comfortable future for him. But he is not so foolish that he does not know deep within himself that what I want for him is best."

"What *you* want? Perhaps you should consider what *he* wants."

A wry twist altered his small mouth. "Let me show you David's future if he is foolish enough to cling to you: I will publicly disown him—no matter the pain that will cause my family—and I will reveal the shame he has brought upon us, shooting his father and marrying a half-caste island girl of no account, a girl who is little more than a common sailor looking to turn a profit by her new-found connections, certainly no spotless maiden fit for a gentleman. He will be cut off not only from my financial support but from his family and this entire community. No one will durst assist him, so he will be forced to leave Carolina, penniless, with you around his neck like an anchor, as well as any mongrels you may breed."

Maria started to stand, but Archer's hand clamped around her wrist like a manacle, and his eyes gleamed a warning.

"Or...he will marry his cousin, who is desperately enamored of him, and enjoy every familial blessing coming to him. I have plans to build an empire, Miss Cordero. I will soon be acquiring more lands on which to build additional plantations in the province, and David will be responsible for running them while my energies are focused elsewhere. He will be respected in this community as his father is. And when I pass from this earth, all will devolve to him."

"You only care about David marrying your choice of brides because of your own selfish aims."

Archer slowly freed her arm, apparently confident she would not bolt now. He smiled slightly. "True enough the union would be to my benefit. However, you will soon see for yourself that my choice for him is an appropriate, favorable one, not the choice he has made simply to spite me. Elizabeth is a fine young woman, one David would normally choose, I believe, if not for his stubbornness to do whatever is opposite his father's will. He has not given the girl an honest chance. That is where you come in, Miss Cordero. You will convince him to release you from his charade. Think of what is best for David. And while you are doing so, think of Jack Mallory."

She scowled. "What does Jack have to do with this?"

"You must remember that Captain Mallory is in my debt, that I am the only one who knows what, who, and where he is. It would be a shame for all of us if I was required to turn him over to the governor's men because of your lack of cooperation in this simple matter. Then what would become of his poor sister?"

"You bastard." She stood, drawing the attention of some of the slaves at the landing.

"A man who would risk all that Captain Mallory risked when he helped you escape my men in Charles Town...well, that is a man who cannot possibly be happy about that same young woman living a lie with another man under his family's roof, can he? So you see, Miss Cordero, you now hold the fortune of two men in your hands."

# CHAPTER 21

"Uncle!" Elizabeth Archer threw her arms around Ezra Archer the moment he entered Wildwood's withdrawing room, offering Jack an incongruous display, for he had never seen the patriarch of Wildwood accept physical warmth from anyone. Equally amazing was Archer's genuine reciprocation of the girl's gesture.

"Elizabeth," Caroline Archer scolded from where she sat near one of the windows, her plain form bronzed by the early morning sunlight.

Remembering herself, Elizabeth blushed and stepped back to curtsey.

Archer chuckled. "It is quite all right. I am equally happy to see the both of you."

"Oh, but whatever happened to your arm?" the young woman asked with concern. "Why is it in a sling?"

"A hunting accident, I am afraid. Nothing to concern yourself over, my dear. It is healing well. Now tell me, how was your journey?"

"Exciting! We were set upon by pirates. But Captain Mallory gallantly preserved us. He was able to fend off the villains without firing a shot."

"Indeed?" Archer raised a shrewd eyebrow at Jack who restlessly sat in the far corner of the room.

"Mother felt very poorly the whole trip. Seasickness, you see. But it never troubled me. Captain Mallory said I must have the sea in my blood."

"Perish the thought, dear girl," Archer responded as light footsteps neared the room. He turned as his wife arrived, even frailer and more sallow than when Jack had last seen her. "Madam, our guests have safely arrived."

Anna offered them a ghostly smile, and Jack caught Caroline Archer's startled reaction to the woman's appearance.

"You must all be exhausted," said Anna, "especially traveling up the river all night. Come, let me get you ladies to your chamber so you can relax and shift your clothes. I am having breakfast prepared for you. Captain Mallory, will you be joining us?" Hope raised her sparse eyebrows and lightened her tone.

"Thank you, ma'am. I—"

"Captain Mallory and I have some business to attend to," Archer interrupted. "Have his breakfast brought to the flanker."

Crestfallen, Anna offered Jack an apologetic smile before ushering the women from the room. He had seen more than apology in her sunken eyes—urgency perhaps, something pressing to be shared. Something undoubtedly about her cursed son. But then she was gone, and he followed Archer to the flanker where he and Smith had been secreted those days ago.

Smith already lay sprawled in bed, snoring from the long night spent on the river. Archer closed the bedchamber door and led Jack across the parlor to his darkened office.

Archer offered Jack a seat near the empty hearth, not far from the end of a massive mahogany desk. As he moved to open the curtains of the south windows, the familiar male servant entered, dressed in pristine white, blinding against the darkness of his skin. Jeremiah carried a tea tray to a long, squat table before Jack. The old man filled two china cups—both so delicate that Jack thought them better suited to a woman's hand—on matching saucers, one of which he carried to his master. Archer took it from him and sat in a chair across the hearth from Jack as the servant retreated.

"Upon the evening ebb you will escort my niece and her maid to Leighlin. Until then, you will remain in this flanker, you and your quartermaster. Is that understood?"

Jack leaned back, slurped the tea. "Since there's no need for your son to stay any longer at Leighlin, I'll send him back with the boat."

"In case you have forgotten our agreement, there is still one more thing you must do for me. And that will take you away from Leighlin for a short while more." He showed no interest in Jack's unhappy expression. "So my son will remain at Leighlin and keep it running smoothly. He will have time—undistracted time—to spend with his cousin."

"He has a wife to distract him."

Archer chuckled as he set the cup upon the table and crossed his legs with a confident air, like a man who watches pieces of a puzzle fall seamlessly into place with very little effort on his part. "You have seen enough of my son to know he will go to any length to defy me. I believe this latest scheme is but a contrivance. I have designs upon my son marrying *properly*, and Elizabeth is the one who will be his lawful wife in the end, and you, Captain, will do all in your power to see that

219

happen, and that includes keeping David and his cousin at Leighlin, away from the meddling of his mother and sister. I will tell Elizabeth that she may hear some nonsense from her cousin that he is married but that she should take no heed, that he is merely playing a stubborn game with me. Our…conflict is no secret to her."

"What makes you confident your son will show any interest in your niece if he hasn't already done so?"

"He has but to spend time with her. You have been with the girl over the past several days. Is there anything untoward about her?"

"No. I agree she's a lovely girl. Very bright and full of life."

"Like my son when there is occasion for it. And at Leighlin I am sure there is just such occasion."

Jack scowled.

"Now," Archer retrieved his cup, "on to the next order of business."

Jack tensed, swallowed too much of the tea at once and scalded his tongue.

Archer drank in distracted fashion, and his hardening gaze brought a chill to the room. "What I am about to tell you must go nowhere beyond this chamber. Not even your quartermaster must know, not until it is necessary and quite apparent. If word of this was to leak out, the success of it would most certainly be in jeopardy. And if that be the case, Captain Mallory, your very life will be in jeopardy also. You have agreed to assist me in exchange for your freedom; you have yet to disappoint me. Your game of making your recent passengers believe you are an honest man capable of fighting off pirates—men of your own ilk—tells me you are interested in remaking yourself in the image of an honest man."

Thinking of the troublesome nightmares, Jack growled, "I became a pirate out of necessity—to find my mother—not out of any desire for a criminal life."

Archer seemed amused. "Time will tell, dear boy, when it comes to your true calling. But if you wish to have the opportunity to rejoin the light of decent men, you must revisit the darkness one last time. And then—after you do—you will be free of your debt, and you will be able to live in peace with your sister."

"And what is it you want me to do?"

"The week following my daughter's wedding there will be a vessel leaving Charles Town for Barbados. A particular vessel that you will attack and destroy. You will kill all on board; you will not want any survivors to pin this crime upon you or the men you seem so nobly interested in preserving."

"Who will be aboard this vessel?"

"That is of no concern to you. The vessel will not be heavily armed, so it will take little effort on your part to destroy them. You will sink her to the bottom; you will leave no trace."

"What is the name of the vessel?"

"That will be revealed to you in time." He took a last long sip of tea, his tolerance of its temperature astounding Jack. "Now, I must be off. Your meal will be here shortly." He stood, as unemotional as if he had told Jack of a pleasure cruise instead of one bent upon massacre. "Mind what I told you, Mallory. Speak of this to no one if you want to secure what is left of your sister's family...and its holdings."

#

"You're trembling, Miss Archer," Jack observed as he assisted Elizabeth onto Leighlin's dock. He glanced behind him at Smith. The older man was grinning like a wolf at Elizabeth's young maid whom he handed with little gentlemanly aplomb down the gangplank from Wildwood's shallop.

Elizabeth laughed nervously. "'Tis just excitement, Captain. This is all rather an adventure for me. I have never been so...independent before."

"Well, I'm sure Leighlin and her people will make you feel like family quick enough. And don't forget your cousin." Jack ignored Smith's teasing expression from behind the maid.

Elizabeth blushed. "Leighlin is so beautiful. When I last visited my uncle, Captain and Mrs. Logan hosted a dinner in my honor. I was so sad when I heard of their deaths. How horrible for you...and your sister. Such a sweet thing she is."

"Perhaps you will be able to cheer her up, Miss Archer."

"I do hope so."

Ezra Archer had concocted a story for both of the Virginia women, telling them Jack had recently come to Carolina to assume responsibility for his orphaned sister, but that his presence had not been announced in the community due to some financial entanglements that needed to be solved. So they had been sworn to secrecy about his identity and whereabouts. While Caroline had appeared a bit uneasy about the falsity, Elizabeth was more than happy to go along with the intrigue, and Jack saw that the mysteriousness added to his worth in the girl's eyes.

221

Word had been sent downriver earlier that morning that they would be arriving in time for supper at Leighlin, so Jemmy stood ready with Leighlin's carriage, dressed in green livery. The vehicle's brown leather seats gleamed with care and little use, its wheels and sides painted the same green that Jemmy wore. Thin, bordering lines of yellow paint added flare and color to the dark design. Curly stood in infinite boredom in harness with a stablemate that kept nipping his neck in an effort to garner his attention. The last time Jack had seen this carriage it had been shuttling guests for his mother's funeral. Now, while Jemmy secured the guests' trunks—not an easy feat with such a small space to use behind the rear seat—Smith and the maid climbed aboard.

"Oh, Captain," Elizabeth said, "it is such a pleasant evening. Can we not walk up to the house? I would like to pass by the gardens."

Jack bowed and reached for Elizabeth's parasol. "If you insist. It will give me a chance to stretch my legs after so long aboard the shallop." He figured Elizabeth hoped the stroll up the terraces and across the sward would afford her more time to compose herself.

Every step of the way the young woman marveled at the scenery, commenting on Carolina's great variety of birds and Leighlin's marvelously groomed grounds.

"Do not tell Uncle, but I think Leighlin is ever more beautiful than Wildwood. I think it is because of the bluff and how stately the house looks sitting up higher than the river, looking down to that bend yonder."

Jack looked at the Ashley over his shoulder and remembered Logan telling him how his mother so loved the view of the river from the house. Had she dreamt of one day escaping down that river? Or had she hoped to stay here forever?

Once they reached the sward, the front portico rose into view, and all thoughts flew from his mind, for there stood Maria in her mourning black with David Archer. His heart picked up its pace, and he feared the girl next to him might feel it pound where her hand rested on his arm. Since his conversation that morning with Ezra Archer, he felt even more hopeful that all was not lost for him, that perhaps there was still time to mend what he had broken.

Once they reached the portico, Jack could not tell which woman was more nervous. Maria looked a bit off her color, her smile warm but strained. Elizabeth still trembled. Was it from excitement as she had claimed or was she disconcerted by all of the plotting that surrounded this visit? Whatever it was, he pitied her.

"It is wonderful to see you again, Cousin." When David kissed the back of Elizabeth's hand, a rush of red exploded upon the girl's full cheeks. Like Maria he appeared unsettled, as if something had taken him by surprise. "This is my…this is Maria Cordero, a close friend of the family."

A subtle change in Maria's expression confused Jack. He could not determine if David's choice of introduction had surprised her or hurt her. The young man's words brought a flood of relief to his own heart and to Elizabeth's face, and the ill feelings that had lingered since he had last seen David left him.

"Where's Helen?" asked Jack.

"She will be down for supper in just a minute," Maria said. "Mary is getting her dressed. I think she wanted to make a special effort for her guests."

The jangle of harness called attention to the lane. The carriage, of course, should have covered the distance faster than Jack and Elizabeth, but Jack had a feeling Smith had something to do with its tardiness.

"Smitty," Maria breathed with delight, as if seeing her savior.

Jack stifled a grin. "I dragged his rheumatic bones back with me. Have to keep him out of trouble." Noticing how close Smith sat to the maid, it appeared the lecherous old bastard was already well on his way to trouble.

"Thomas," David called to the servant who hovered in the stair hall. "Have Miss Archer's belongings taken to the bedchamber where Mr. Dell and Mr. Rogers had been staying."

"Shall we go inside?" Maria suggested. "Supper is just about ready."

#

Maria agreed with Ezra Archer's assessment of his niece as an appealing young woman. The girl was genuine in her conversation during the meal, her exuberance a breath of fresh air in a house recently filled with so much sorrow. Elizabeth's interest in David, her admiration and respect, was apparent, though she worked hard not to convey these things too overtly. Maria felt a nudge of jealousy at the thought of David's attentions transferring, but she dismissed those emotions as foolish and selfish. After all, she had not provided an answer to his proposal yet. A cowardly delay, and now so imperative. She had no right to dissuade Elizabeth's affections. Yet it chafed Maria to have Ezra Archer influence this important decision for her future.

She felt compromised and weak, and possibly robbed of future happiness.

At the outset of the meal, Maria had skillfully maneuvered David to a chair on Elizabeth's immediate left, then she tried to gauge his reception of his cousin. Like any gentleman, he was attentive, but now and then his glance darted sidelong past his cousin toward her. To anyone else at the table he appeared composed and relaxed, but Maria read his unease, knew that he felt duped. Yet what of his introduction on the portico? For whose benefit was his omission of her being his wife? Had her lack of response to his proposal shaken his resolve?

"I forgot to tell you the most exciting part of the journey!" Elizabeth cried, setting aside her spoon. She smiled across the table at Jack and then—as if to make sure David was paying heed—glanced at her cousin. "We were attacked by pirates during our journey!"

"Pirates?" David repeated with a curious glance at Jack and Smith.

At the far end of the table, Rogers and Dell raised their attention from their plates.

"Pirates?" Helen echoed from next to her brother, eyes wide. It dawned on Maria with sudden, shocking clarity that Helen had no idea exactly what her father had been…or Ketch or Jack, for that matter. Sailors, of course; nothing more.

"Yes, off Ocracoke Inlet. A ketch came right up to windward of us. Captain Mallory sent me below. Mother and Rebecca were already in the cabin, Mother suffering from seasickness, you see. Captain Mallory bribed the villains with rum, and off they went, as easy as kiss my hand."

"A ketch, did you say?" Maria raised an eyebrow at Jack and Smith.

Smith grinned. "Aye, a right evil-lookin' one captained by a crazy-eyed devil. Yellow hair like a mop what would break a dozen good combs. Had a cackle on 'im that pained yer ears."

Maria hid her smile as did Rogers and Dell.

"You had nothing to fear, Cousin. Captain Mallory knows pirates," David said. "Knows them and their ways so well you might suspect he was one. Perhaps that is why my father chose him to fetch you."

"Was you afeared, Miss Archer?" Helen piped.

"'Twould be a lie to say I was not." She winked at the girl who returned her smile.

Maria caught Jack's eyes upon her, and what she saw in those bottomless dark depths brought unexpected warmth to her cheeks.

Although he paid enough attention to the conversation not to appear rude, he seemed distracted, determined of something, as determined as he had looked standing upon the quarterdeck of the *Prodigal* while in search of his mother. What would he say if he knew David had proposed to her? Would it matter to him? He did not have David's ability to express himself so openly; instead he held emotions close, like someone afraid to relinquish an expensive, delicate thing into someone else's safekeeping. The same tenacity his sister displayed in clinging to her toy bear or to her belief that she would see her father again. Love had driven Jack to find his mother, but guilt had played a large role as well. Did Jack's penchant for self-blame weigh in their relationship as well? When Dan Slattery had raped her aboard the *Prodigal*, Jack had blamed himself for leaving her vulnerable below deck that day, just as he felt responsible for her indenture to Logan as Helen's governess. Were his feelings for her thus driven or did he have genuine affection for her? While Smith claimed the latter, Maria had never shared his conviction, and so much time spent apart only left her questions unanswered while David filled up the empty space with answers of his own.

"Captain Mallory," David said. "I wanted to make you aware that Ketch has recovered from his snake bite and is still here at Leighlin." His unhappy gaze went to Maria, who knew he was even more disturbed about Ketch's presence after learning of her alarming encounter the other night, coupled with the fact that Ketch had not told Helen the truth about her father's death. Obviously he was hoping to find a staunch ally in Jack since Maria had failed miserably.

Jack washed down his food with a swallow of wine before saying, "I will deal with him. Thank you."

Maria smoothed over the awkward silence by asking Elizabeth about her life in Virginia, and by the time supper drew to a close she had relaxed. The easing of Maria's tension came not only from the satisfaction of having all three men here but from the distraction offered by Elizabeth Archer, regardless of the whole set of issues her presence brought to Leighlin, no doubt not entirely realized by the girl. Or was it? Elizabeth did seem nervous, though that could be because of surroundings and people unfamiliar to her.

"Shall we leave the gentlemen to their brandy, Miss Archer?" Maria asked. "I'm sure you're tired. I can show you to your chamber if you'd like."

"Yes, it has been a long day, a long journey."

"May I come too?" Helen asked.

"Of course," Elizabeth happily answered.

"I'm afraid we're a bit tight on space," Maria explained. "We've put a cot in your chamber for your maid. And we've prepared the master bedchamber for Captain Mallory and Mr. Smith."

Jack snapped out of his reverie and quit toying with his leather bracelet. A faint line across his forehead betrayed reluctance to occupy his mother's chamber, understandably so, but there could be no help for it.

As the women climbed the stairs to the upper floor, Elizabeth said, "You are so very kind to let me stop at Leighlin. Uncle said it will be very crowded at Wildwood."

"We're happy to have you." Maria led the way across the broad, dimming ballroom, Helen trailing behind, bear in hand.

Once in the northwest bedchamber where the maid—absent now—had already turned back the bedclothes and set out a fresh shift for her mistress, Elizabeth moved with slight apprehension as she asked, "When you said 'we are happy to have you,' were you referring to yourself and young Mr. Archer?"

"Of course."

"I mean..." Absently Elizabeth smoothed the edge of the pale blue and white coverlet before gliding to one of the north windows. Light was almost gone from the purple sky. "Uncle said his son is temporarily here because of Mr. Logan's..." She glanced at Helen who was peeking inside of her open trunk.

"Yes. David...Mr. Archer is keeping Leighlin in order for now. And it's very handsome of him to do so."

"Yes; he is a kind man, is he not?"

"The kindest I've ever known."

"I hope I am not inconveniencing anyone by taking this chamber."

"Don't think another minute about it."

"But...where do...where do you sleep?"

Maria kept her smile to herself as she pulled the west windows' curtains. "I sleep in Helen's chamber."

"Oh," Elizabeth breathed with relief.

"Helen," Maria said, "whatever are you doing, child?"

Abruptly the girl straightened from her exploration of Elizabeth's half unpacked wardrobe and snapped her hand back to her bear, looking mightily guilty. "You have such pretty clothes, Miss Archer. Just like Mamma's clothes."

Sympathy weighted Elizabeth's lips, and she crossed the room to crouch beside Helen. "What an adorable little bear you have there.

Such a fine neckerchief. Does he have a name?"

"Howard," the child answered with unusual shyness as she looked down at the hem of Elizabeth's skirt, fingers kneading the bear's fur. "Mamma made him for me 'cause Daddy used to growl at me like a bear. Howard stayed with me whenever Mamma and Daddy went away."

"How very nice of Howard to take such good care of you." Helen nodded. "Will you be here tomorrow?"

"I will. And for several days afterwards, I hope."

"Would you like to see Mamma's grave? I take her fresh flowers every day."

"Of course. In the forenoon perhaps."

Light footsteps drew Maria's attention to the doorway where Mary paused with a pitcher of water for the basin. Maria nodded for her to enter.

"Helen, go with Mary now and get ready for bed. Miss Archer has had a very long, tiring day. She needs to rest. And so do you if you plan to show her more of Leighlin tomorrow with Mr. David."

Both Helen and Elizabeth brightened at the prospect. Helen murmured good night to their guest and took Mary's hand, leaving the two women behind.

"Poor thing," Elizabeth lamented. "I cannot imagine being without my mother, especially at such a tender age. A tragedy."

"It's helped Helen tremendously to have your cousin here. She's another reason why he's remained at Leighlin."

Elizabeth drifted to a nearby chair and removed her shoes, wiggling the fatigue from her toes. "I remember the last time I was here with Uncle and his family. Helen did seem much taken with my cousin. And he was so patient with her, even when she spilled punch on him." Elizabeth laughed privately. "Have you known him very long?"

"No, only a few weeks."

Elizabeth blinked in astonishment. "That is all?"

Maria nodded. "Seems much longer, though." She drew closer. "How long have *you* known him?"

She blushed. "We were both born in Virginia and knew each other as little children before he moved to Carolina. Since then I have only seen him twice." She smiled. "I was so excited to come...now that we are...older." Sudden anxiety destroyed her happy expression, and she looked up at Maria with urgency. "Do you think he is pleased to see me? He seemed rather distracted at supper. I know things are strained betwixt he and his father—I hope to remedy that—and I am sure my

227

being at Leighlin was really more of Uncle's idea than my cousin's, though Uncle wants me to believe otherwise."

"Of course he is pleased to see you. He's just had so much thrust upon him lately."

"Yes, he must have much on his mind. I hope I will not be a burden to him."

Maria smiled reassurance. "I think you're fretting so much because you're tired. Why don't you get some sleep?"

"I do not think I can sleep."

Maria realized the girl was a bit homesick, as she had been when she had first left Cayona. "Well, I'll have Rose send up some chamomile tea with a touch of honey in it."

"Thank you."

"If you need anything from the servants later, just tug on that cord next to the hearth, or send your maid to fetch me from Helen's chamber, there across the ballroom."

Elizabeth nodded. Her large eyes remained on Maria until she closed the door behind her.

# CHAPTER 22

Peace settled over Jack. He sat upon the front portico with a glass of brandy and watched the light purple twilight darken to violet with the warm, dying breeze. Seated to his left, Smith puffed leisurely on his pipe. The soothing smell of tobacco filled Jack's senses and overpowered the redolent gardens. Early stars glittered in the darker east, seen only if he glanced their way, not if he concentrated on them or tried to identify them.

Among the fading colors of his mother's gardens, dozens of fireflies coruscated and faded, only to ignite again elsewhere in the quiet July evening like signal lanterns of a distant fleet of ships. Down on the river, beyond the rice field, a large fish jumped like a gray dart and left behind ever broadening rings of black. Insects tuned for their rhythmic, persistent night chorus, somehow not as eerie and disturbing to his ears as in the past.

The sheep had wandered around from the back acreage and now worked on keeping the front sward nibbled down to a trim green shave. He watched the lambs with interest, how they stayed close to their mothers in the failing light. Then he altered his attention when he remembered Logan's talk of slaughtering a percentage of the lambs for their tender meat. An unpleasant part of being a farmer. He wondered if Helen had ever asked her father about the disappearance of the lambs from the flock, for she seemed to know each one, bestowing names on them. How would Logan have answered—a protective lie or the frank truth as to where the meat on their plates originated? Considering Helen's compassion for all animals, Jack figured it had been the former.

He glanced at Smith's bearded face, saw the slight, betraying crescent shape of his cerulean eyes, and said, "Quit thinking about that maid, Smitty. She's too young for you."

"A man can think, can't he? Besides, I believe she's taken a shine to me."

"Maybe you remind her of her father."

They laughed, and Jack reached for his glass on the white wrought iron table between them. They were alone, for Rogers and Dell had retired to the lower level where Gabriel and the others had started a card game.

Soon footsteps crunching on the lane below heralded David's return from the kitchen house where some issue had arisen that required his attention. Jack had been content to let the boy handle the situation and be taken away from the quiet pleasures of the house. David glanced up at the two men before he climbed the steps and halted there.

"May I join you gentlemen?"

Smith gestured with his pipe to a chair on his left. "Everything under control?"

"Yes. Quite. Iris managed to cut herself, but nothing too serious; Willis is tending to her." David eased himself down and took the glass of brandy Smith offered. He glanced toward Helen's room where light spilled from the riverside windows. "'Tis nigh Helen's bedtime."

David's intimacy with his sister's schedule stirred Jack's ire.

An awkward silence stretched between the three men until David spoke in a guarded tone, "So, Captain, is it safe for me to assume—with you delivering my cousin here—that you no longer intend to throw me bodily from Leighlin?"

"After your sister's wedding I will be gone for what I hope is a short while. You can remain until I get back."

"Another errand for my father, is it?"

"I owe your father a debt, as you well know. I am merely repaying it."

"Logan once owed my father a debt as well. He found that it was not so easy to repay. Margaret and I are concerned that it will be the same with you."

"Why should such a thing concern you and your sister?"

David sipped the brandy. "You know how we felt about our father's collusion with Logan. We hoped it would die with Logan, not be taken up by another."

"I've no intention to partner with your father."

"Your intentions might have little bearing upon what ultimately happens."

"I am not Logan."

"No, but you are a man in a poor position, as Logan once was. My father will take full advantage of that and use it for his own gain."

"You're one to talk about poor position," Jack parried, eager to change the focus. "Your father doesn't believe you're married to Maria, and considering you didn't introduce her as your wife I'd say he's right."

David leaned back into the deepening shadows of the portico and drank again before admitting, "I could not lie to Elizabeth."

"You didn't seem to have a problem lying to your father...and others."

"I did what I felt necessary at the time...for my sake, true, but also for Maria's and Helen's sake. They needed someone here." Jack started to bristle but David continued: "Elizabeth is innocent in all of this. My father has put her in an awkward spot, one more awkward than she knows. For that I am sorry for her. Margaret warned me that Father does not believe I am married to Maria, and I am sure he has passed that along to Elizabeth in case I durst continue the masquerade in front of her."

"If you don't care for the girl, then why are you concerned about her feelings or opinions?"

"'Tis not that I do not care, Captain—she is my kin—but 'tis wrong of my father to bring her here. Somehow I must find a way to tell her without hurting her. As you can see, she is not someone who could believe my father's intentions impure. I doubt the girl has a selfish bone in her body, certainly nothing that would enable her to comprehend such a thing."

Around the mouthpiece of his pipe, Smith interjected, "She *is* a fine lass. An' she seems quite impressed by you, lad."

"I think it is Captain Mallory who has impressed her."

Smith laughed. "She's too good for Jack. That talk was for *your* benefit, not Jack's. Tryin' to get ye jealous, eh? That's how women work. You two young pups don't know nothin'." He winked.

"Regardless of my father's scheme, having Elizabeth here with us will not change my bent of mind, gentlemen."

"And what is your bent of mind?" Jack required effort to keep sharpness from his words, to avoid another fight like the last one that had left him feeling low and foolish.

"I have proposed marriage to Maria."

Jack set his glass down upon the table with a distinct ring.

Smith stared at David and moved closer to the edge of his chair as if to intervene if necessary. He was the first to find his voice: "Has she accepted?"

David finished the rest of his brandy. "She has not given me her answer yet." He reached for the decanter.

Both relieved and deeply troubled, Jack forced himself to lean back, fingers so tight upon the brandy glass that he marveled it did not break. Used to years of planning for what he felt important to obtain, Jack experienced a sudden, frightful internal pressure greater than what he had already suffered on the journey from James Town, but he had no intention of conveying that to his rival. There would be little time to waste between now and his next departure, so he must not falter in his resolve.

Light footsteps silenced the men. Maria and Helen emerged from the house, the child dressed in nightcap and shift, bare footed, her toy bear cuddled to her chest. But it was Maria from whom Jack could not remove his gaze. What if she had provided or planned to provide David Archer with the answer he sought? The very idea made the pressure within him build to an unendurable level.

"Helen came to say good night."

Gently Maria's hand urged Helen toward them. The child hesitated then padded forward, chewing her bottom lip. She stopped in front of David where her large blue eyes lifted from the tiles. She offered a small smile, and he smiled back, broad and genuine, then leaned forward to accept her light kiss on the cheek and her whispered good night. Then she stepped to Smith who had set aside his pipe and brandy.

"I've been waitin' for a kiss from a pretty girl all night. And here's the prettiest of 'em all to give me one. How about that?"

No matter how much she tried, Helen could not conceal her delight at the teasing that she so loved from Smith. She even let a small giggle escape as he pulled her close, puckered his lips, and closed his eyes. Still smiling, she made no move until he opened his appropriately disappointed eyes.

"Are you goin' to break an old man's heart, lass? Who taught you such cruel ways?"

Helen gave his hairy cheek a quick peck then stepped back.

Smith breathed an elaborate sigh. "I reckon beggars can't be choosers. I'll have to settle for that poor excuse for a kiss."

Helen stepped around the table and next to Jack's knee. She kept her eyes downward and did not make a move of any kind. He hesitated, mortified by her continued coldness, then leaned forward and was just able to brush her cheek with his lips before she wheeled about and ran into the house. Embarrassment and angry frustration heated his face.

"Jack," Maria said, "why don't you come read to Helen?"

Frowning at the thought of further rebuff, Jack remained seated, considered the brandy decanter.

Quietly Smith urged, "Go on, lad. 'Tis goin' to take work to crack that little nut."

Jack nodded with reluctance. Was there anything in life that did not require hard work?

As he followed Maria into the stair hall, the last light of evening through the windows painted her raven hair a midnight blue. Her hips swayed at eye level while she ascended; the hem of her black dress brushed against the wooden stairs and kept him from coming too close. The scent of rosewater drifted in her wake. To think of her accepting David Archer's proposal caused a very real physical pain, and he had to force himself not to take advantage of this fleeting private moment by capturing her and trying to force David from her head; but he could not bear another slighting, so he simply followed her.

When they reached Helen's chamber, the girl was kneeling upon a window seat, peering secretively downward toward the portico. When she saw Maria and Jack in the doorway, she gasped, scrambled for her bed, and clambered beneath the sheet with her bear.

Ignoring Helen's frantic attempt to cover her curiosity, Maria tucked the child in. She kissed her forehead and brushed the golden hair from her cheeks.

"Your brother came to read to you."

Helen's gaze flashed to Jack but did not reveal her feelings on the matter, though neither did she turn away. From the rocking chair by the hearth, Maria handed Jack a well-worn edition of *Aesop's Fables*. Jack appreciated her encouraging smile and nod before he sat on the edge of the bed and opened the book in the failing light.

"Which story shall I pick?" He thumbed through the frayed pages. "Ah-ha." He cleared his throat dramatically, chancing a furtive glance to see that Helen was indeed paying attention. Her blue eyes peered from the edge of the sheet, the bear tucked under her chin. He considered the text before him and began.

"The King's Daughter and the Painted Lion." Jack checked to see if Helen noticed his alternation of the title from "son" to "daughter," but the girl revealed no such knowledge, so he continued in the same vein: "A King had a dream in which he was warned that his only daughter would be killed by a lion. Afraid the dream should prove true, he built for his daughter a pleasant palace and adorned its walls for her amusement with all kinds of life-sized animals, among which was the picture of a lion."

Jack turned the book to show Helen the illustration of a lion. At the same time he glanced over his shoulder at Maria's curious, attentive expression before resuming the story in his melodramatic voice:

"When the young Princess saw this, her grief at being thus confined burst out afresh, and standing near the lion, she said, 'O you most detestable of animals!'"

The falsetto Jack used for the princess drew a brief, muffled giggle from the bed, so faint that he knew of its existence only by the tremor of the sheet and the softening of his sister's eyes, which she quickly diverted to the book. Jack pretended not to notice.

"'Through a lying dream of my father's, which he saw in his sleep, I am shut up on your account in this palace; what shall I now do to you?' With these words she stretched out her hands toward a thorn-tree, meaning to cut a stick from its branches so that she might beat the lion. But one of the tree's prickles pierced her finger and caused great pain and inflammation, so that the young Princess fell down in a fainting fit."

Jack chose to omit the part about the character dying, and Helen said nothing about it. She looked at him to see if he was going to read another story, but instead he pinned a sober look upon her and asked, "Do you know what the moral to this story is, Helen?"

She rubbed her nose with the back of one hand.

He continued, "'Tis better to bear our troubles bravely than to try to escape them."

Her brow wrinkled briefly, then her eyebrows knit. She sniffed and turned away from him, tugging the sheet up to her ear. He touched her leg curled beneath the bedclothes, but she drew her limbs away and made a small, sulking sound.

"Helen." He started to move closer to her but decided against the advance. "If there was anything I could do to bring your father back, I would."

Helen did not move. Jack glanced at Maria's sorrowful face, sighed, and slipped from the bed.

"You shouldn't have left him," Helen distantly murmured.

Jack faltered. "We couldn't find him, Helen. We looked but he was gone."

She violently flung the sheet back and stared at him with more anger than he ever thought possible in a child. "No! He's not gone; he's going to come back!" Then she swept the sheet over her head and began to quietly sob.

"Helen—"

"Go away!"

Maria left the rocking chair and took hold of his arm. With a knowing look she ushered him into the ballroom and closed the door behind him.

"We can't just leave her alone," Jack protested.

"We can and we must."

"Maria—"

"Like you told her with the story—she must learn to bear this."

He paced away, dragged a hand through his hair, unwittingly pulled some of it free from his queue ribbon. The strands flopped across his eyes, but he paid no heed as he returned to where she stood patiently, arms crossed as if cold. Frustration welled in him like a hot spring. He needed an outlet for his compounding discontent.

"Where's Ketch?" he asked through clenched teeth. "'Tis nigh time I dealt with what's put us in this fix."

"Jack, listen to me—"

He fought to keep his voice down. "*Where* is he? I can ask David or Willis if you won't tell me." He started for the stair hall, but Maria rushed after him, gripped his arm and halted him.

"Damn it, Maria—"

"You must listen to me. Please."

With pleading eyes, she urged him toward the master bedchamber. Reluctantly he allowed her to draw him inside, then she closed the door to protect against prying eyes or ears. In frustration he wheeled away from her to pace the width of the room.

"The man has no business being alive, let alone at Leighlin. Willis never should have operated on him. He should have let him die right then and there."

"I told you before—it was Helen who wanted Ketch saved. You weren't here, Jack; you don't know how it affected her. Whatever Ketch may be, he's nearly all she has left from the life she knew before us."

"For Christ's sake, he murdered her father right in front of her."

"She must not have seen it; we fell down into the boat then. For whatever reason, she's become…attached to Ketch. That would never have happened if she truly had seen everything. And she's had this…effect on him. It's hard to describe."

"This is insanity." From one of the river windows he looked across the sward and down the river to the ever-darkening bend. "He deserves death."

In angry frustration Maria asked, "And if you kill him, how much different will you be from him? What will you tell Helen?"

Jack strode toward her, head pounding. "Damn it, why are you defending him?"

"I'm not defending him; I'm defending Helen."

"He killed her father!"

"Was that any less than what we once wanted to do?"

Her challenge brought him up all standing, at a loss and moved by the turmoil in her moist dark eyes.

"What brought us both here, Jack? We both came looking for Logan, to kill him. Your mother stopped you, and you stopped me. Why? Because of Helen. I can condemn Ketch for many things, but killing Logan is not one of them. For Helen's sake, I wish to God it had never happened, but for my sake and for the memory of my father, I'm glad. God help me, I'm glad. And can you really say a part of you isn't glad as well?"

Jack realized that he had not allowed himself to think such a selfish thing because of Helen, though somewhere deep inside he had felt it and had experienced shame for that buried satisfaction.

"Truth be told," Maria continued quietly, eyes downward, "I may be the reason Ketch killed Logan. And maybe even why Defoe is missing."

"You had nothing to do with Ketch killing anyone—"

"When we sailed to Charles Town after your mother died, I goaded Ketch after what Logan did to him and Slattery. I told him he should get to Logan before Logan got to him. Then when he showed up here after you were arrested, I told him Defoe would never let him stay here. He said he had made a promise to your mother...to protect Helen."

"Protect her from what?"

Maria shrugged as if exhausted. "When he was sick, he said Helen was in danger." She looked up at him, regretful and pleading. "He saved her, Jack. I was there. He didn't even hesitate when he grabbed that snake to keep it from her. He even kept me away. You should have seen Helen, how fretful she was, how kind she's been to him since." Maria's words trailed off, and tears welled in her eyes. "I was so afraid after all of this, after you escaped, that Ketch would kill you. I had to find a way to stop him. So I made a pact with him. I told him he could stay here but only if he promised not to harm you or anyone else."

"Maria," he quietly breathed. "You can't expect someone like Ketch to hold to any bargain."

"I know you think me daft, but I believe he will. I think he will do whatever it takes to keep his promise to your mother. After all, it brought him back here after Logan's death, even though he surely must have known Defoe would see him dead, as would you if you escaped.

And now that he's lost his arm, he knows he has no means left to earn a living away from here. Willis put him to work as a driver—"

Jack shook his head at her naiveté. "Maria—"

"If he was going to kill you, don't you think he would have done so the minute you arrived here? He's downstairs right now, has been since you returned." Her frown reflected hurt and disappointment. "I'm sorry. I made the best decision I could."

Maria's gaze conveyed the full weight of her burden as well as the fatigue behind her veneer of strength. All these days she had been here, dealing with Helen, Defoe's disappearance, Ketch, David and the intrigue with the Archer family. Willingly taking care of a child not of her own blood and a plantation that belonged to a man once her enemy.

"You don't need to apologize. I appreciate everything you've done for Helen, for me." His words brought immediate relief, chasing away her tears. Her small smile restored her remarkable beauty, and he had to turn back toward the window, helpless now when a moment ago he had been decisive in his resolve to rid Leighlin of Ketch. He could no longer press his point with her and injure her further. Somehow he must show that he trusted her judgment.

Through the window, his gaze drifted toward his mother's grave, and he heard Smith's laughter from the portico. Perhaps Smith was right—he had played the game of revenge for so long that he knew no other solution. Perhaps that grip upon revenge is what had brought the Newgate nightmares back to him again and again lately. Slattery had killed his mother for revenge, so Logan had killed Slattery, so Ketch had killed Logan, so he had sought Ketch's death. If he killed Ketch, he would prove Joe Dowling's point about the impossibility of changing from one life to another.

He asked, "Do you think it was Ketch who put that idea into Helen's head that I purposefully left her father?"

"I think she simply said what she knew would hurt you. She's just a child, remember. And she's been through so much. I still believe she'll pull through it; she'll learn to accept it. Now that you're here, she—"

"Unfortunately I will only be here a few days, just until after Margaret Archer's wedding. Then I must finish my business with her father."

"What more does he want you to do?"

Jack turned but stayed near the window. "After he helped me escape he told me there were two things he wanted done in repayment. One was bringing his niece here. The other…well, I'm not certain yet, but I know it will take me away from here again, hopefully not for long."

She frowned deeply. "I hope not, too. Helen does miss you. She was very upset when you left last time." Her gaze searched him. "You left without even saying good-bye."

"I'm sorry. It wasn't my intention. I got into an argument with David, and his father and Smitty thought it best we leave straight away."

"An argument about what?"

He hesitated. "About you."

"Why?"

Jack felt exposed and foolish all over again. "He said you two were married."

"And that mattered to you?"

Her surprising response brought him low. "Of course it did. I told you...I tried to tell you aboard the *Prodigal* that night in my cabin..." He crossed over to her. "What I said to you after my mother died...I was a fool."

"Are you saying this now because of David?"

He kept his angry reaction at bay, for he knew he deserved her lack of faith. "Maybe it is because of David. Not because he asked you to marry him but because every time I see you with him I think I'll go insane; to know he was with you here while I was gone. Not because it was David; it could have been any man. It made me realize what I might lose if I keep going the way I have been. Maybe I'm already too late. Maybe you already have an answer for him."

She frowned again. "I can't marry David."

He approached her, his voice equally soft, "Can't or won't?" Desperately he wanted to put his hands upon her shoulders, to touch her, comfort her.

She rubbed her arm as if to fend off a chill...or him. "He has to marry Elizabeth, and I must convince him. If I don't, his father will betray you."

"What are you talking about?"

"David's father spoke to me."

"He threatened you with this?"

She nodded.

A foul oath pressed for release, but Jack bit it back, not wanting Maria to see his agitation. "Don't worry about Archer's threats. I am no use to him dead."

"But what about after you do his bidding this next time?"

"Let that be my concern."

"Jack—"

"Is that the only reason why you won't marry David?" he asked to pull her focus away from her fears.

Maria's shoulders fell as if suddenly weighted, and he could see her regret over his question, her reluctance to hurt him, and he wished he had not asked.

"If David were to marry me, he would lose everything. I could never live with that. But he won't hear it. He says he's in love with me."

"And you? Are you in love with him?"

"Love? I've only known him a short while, Jack. What can someone know in that time?"

"Sometimes—I'm learning—you just know."

"I do care for him...very much. As I care for you. Once I even thought..." She shook her head, momentarily closed her eyes. Then she sighed and started for the door. "But I must convince him that I'm not the right choice. And I've led him on long enough; I must give him my answer now." And before Jack could summon another word, she left the room.

#

When Maria reached the portico, she found David and Smith still there, finishing the brandy. Smith was telling some story about the sail down from Virginia, obviously working his own angle to ingratiate Elizabeth with David. The conversation stopped when they saw her. Smith smiled at her, pale white amidst the thickening veil of night.

"The wee one all tucked in, is she?"

"Yes."

"And Jack? Is he tucked in, too?" A chuckle rumbled warmly before he stifled it with his dying pipe.

"He's in his chamber." She paused near David's chair. "Smitty, could you excuse us?"

"Oh, aye." Instantly Smith knocked the pipe out on his heel and got to his feet with the speed of a much younger man. "Reckon I'll take on the job of tuckin' ol' Jack in meself." He wished them good night and briskly disappeared into the house, whistling.

"Is there any brandy left?" she asked.

"Finish mine, if you would like."

David lifted the glass, but when Maria closed her hand upon it, he briefly hesitated before he released it. His eyes searched her, and she was glad they were in near darkness. Taking Smith's chair, she finished the brandy, its warmth coursing through her.

"You have come to give me your answer," David's smooth words came quietly to her, slowed by alcohol. "Otherwise you would have let Mr. Smith stay."

She set the glass down upon the table, her tongue removing the last of the brandy from her lips.

"But I already know your answer," he said with infinite disappointment. "I saw it upon your face when Jack Mallory walked up these steps today."

His intuitive observation threw Maria's prepared words into disarray and left her struggling for any words at all.

"In truth I saw it on your face after he kissed you good-bye aboard the *Prodigal*. It seems the gossip aboard the brig was not so far off the mark after all. But I told myself that you would realize my greater worth once we were here alone again. However, it would appear he was already deeply ingrained upon you before I ever came along, more so than you even knew. That is why you could not decline my offer straightaway—because you did not know for sure...until today." The faint glimmer from a freshly lit lamp in the withdrawing room reached the portico and showed, in horrible starkness, the heartbreak in his eyes. "Tell me I am right. Tell me that at least before today there had been something, some chance, something that makes me not a fool for ever believing."

"David," she said in a rush, now realizing that she had been holding her breath. Impulsively, desperate to console him, she reached for his hand, her chair scraping against the tile with her abrupt shift. Various reassurances leapt to her—how she was not a fitting wife for him for so many reasons, how he should consider Elizabeth as one more appropriate—but she knew to say those things would only wound him deeper. "You *are* right," she said at last, the truthfulness of her admission shaking her to the core. "But you're right about Jack as well. And because of that, I must decline your proposal, however noble and flattering it is."

"Did Jack offer you the same?"

"No."

He gave a small, cynical laugh. "Then I was wrong about one thing." He stood, but she did not free his hand.

"David, you will stay, won't you? At Leighlin, I mean." The thought of him leaving deeply saddened her and frightened her as well when she remembered Ezra Archer's demand. She strengthened her grip upon his cold hand. "If you won't stay for my asking, then please stay for Helen's sake; her brother will be leaving again."

His hesitation drew out long and painful. Then he slowly bent to kiss her hand, his lips lingering, his cheek briefly touching her fingers, then he let her go and strode into the house.

#

Ketch limped to the riverside doorway of Leighlin House's lower level. The bandage around his thigh made the left leg of his breeches uncomfortably tight, but he ignored it just as he ignored the pain of the wounds. Behind him, Willis had returned from tending to the flighty girl, Iris, and had joined the other white men at the table, playing cards and drinking. After being ousted from the bedchamber that Elizabeth Archer now inhabited, Rogers and Dell had slung hammocks from the common room beams. To Ketch it seemed ages ago when he and Samuel used to share the chamber where David Archer now dwelled. Perhaps that had been a privilege; perhaps it had been because Willis and the other men had not wanted him down here with them. Since he had cut his leg, the men seemed even more leery, but none dared show him open hostility. He found satisfaction in the fact that even with only one arm he still struck fear into them.

He lingered in the doorway in hopes of catching a breeze, for so many animated men in the common room made the space even warmer. From outside he had expected to hear only the languid language of the natural night, but instead he heard conversation above on the portico. He deciphered the voices of David Archer and Maria, but right after this deduction their talk halted and the young man's feet sounded upon the tiles, taking him into the house. Ketch waited for Maria's following footsteps, but no sound drifted down to him for a long instance. Then she stirred but not into the house. Instead her shoes tapped lightly against the steps of the portico as she descended. He made not a move, knowing the lantern light behind him would reveal him as a shadowy silhouette in the doorway. But the girl did not look back as she strode briskly across the lane. Where in hell was she going alone in the dark? He waited until he could not see her black dress but for a blur. Then he slipped into the night.

Maria seemed bent upon the landing, following the straight path that bisected the sward, so Ketch took the lane to the right, down to the creek below the shoulder of the bluff, and made his way to the landing

241

via the flank. He arrived just after her and blended with the shadows at the far end of the line of birch trees. The place was quiet, the barest whisper of a breeze stirring the leaves just this side of the landing. The *Nymph* was gone, far downriver by now with the ebbing tide, and the slaves had long ago retreated to their settlement. His eyes—adjusted easily to the starry night—could make out the darker shape of the girl against the hint of the bench upon which she sat. And even though the crickets and frogs tried to drown out any signs of life other than their own, he could hear Maria's muffled sobs.

Ketch could endure any sound in the world—from the deafening roar of broadside after broadside aboard a man-of-war to the shrieks of his victims—but he could not bear the disarming, ragged gulps of a woman crying. His lack of fortitude stemmed from the days after he had told his mother about her husband murdering Sophia, days when she had cried unceasingly, her sorrow coupled with debilitating fear when Ketch's stepfather deserted them following her vengeful revelation of Ketch's true paternity. Even the shock of learning that the man whom he had called Father for fifteen years was anything but had not devastated Ketch as much as his mother's forlorn sobs every night from across their one-room hovel, for he had caused her sorrow. To console her, he had done whatever she wanted, including submitting to things that came back to terrorize him on nights like the one in the Plymouth brothel. Never had he blamed her for her sins because she had not been in her right mind after learning about Sophia and what her daughter's murder possibly meant for all those infants who had come before. Instead he blamed the man whose name had been given to him and whose name he had forever forsaken after that horrible night beside the Thames.

Now Ketch forced away his memories and focused on Maria. The uncharacteristic sobs perturbed him. He had never thought her capable of such frailty; it displeased him. This girl had been Helen's rock as well as his only ally, albeit a reluctant one. With his own recent handicaps, he could ill afford to have her fall apart, especially with Jack Mallory afoot. Ketch scowled. Mallory was behind her sorrow, of course. Of that he was certain. It was no coincidence that her tears flowed on the first day of Mallory's return. It was cruel of the cursed pup to upset her after all she had done for his sister. Perhaps, though, she would now shed herself of the self-serving bastard.

Her sobs trailed off into low sniffs, and she wiped her face upon one sleeve, staring down the river. She would not stay there long, he knew, for someone would miss her up at the house.

242

Convinced that she was there only to hide her display, not to flee Leighlin and thus desert Helen, Ketch melted away from the trees and back to the narrow lane. The humid night clung to his skin, and he remembered again the coolness of being immersed in the tub of water those days ago when the fever had raged hotter than any Carolina afternoon.

Pausing beside a live oak at the corner of the garden nearest the house, Ketch caught his breath and waved mosquitoes away from his sweaty face. Since when was it work simply to walk from the river to the house? The exertion sent blood pulsating to the cuts and to the stump of his arm, bringing fresh pain. He should have kept his wits about him the other night instead of slicing himself to ribbons and adding to his physical weakness.

Light glowed through the open doorway of Leighlin House's lower level. Eager for the solitude of his bed, he resumed his trek, glancing across the sward. No small, shadowy figure emerged from the night. She would not know he had followed her. All for the better, since he had come to know the sharpness of her tongue so well.

Just inside the doorway, he nearly slammed into Jack Mallory as the young man was leaving. Both halted within inches of one another. The men at the table in the common room fell silent, all eyes upon the pair, apprehensive but ready to come to Mallory's aide if needed, Ketch knew. The boy stared at him, the initial surprise gone, replaced by suspicion and loathing in those dark eyes behind the loose, draping hair, emotions that Ketch knew could be seen in his own gaze. A quick downward flick of Ketch's eyes told him Mallory was unarmed, proof that his purpose here had not been to acquire one of the plantation's pistols which Willis kept under lock and key. Had the Cordero girl actually convinced the mongrel not to murder him? He remembered the struggle aboard the *Alliance*, saw it reflected in Mallory's eyes, how close he had come to killing the meddlesome bastard, but now here his enemy stood, far more in one piece than himself...and untouchable.

It seemed an eternity that they stood there when in reality mere seconds passed. Then Ketch stepped aside and the boy passed into the darkness outside.

# CHAPTER 23

No matter how many times Jack saw Margaret Archer, her beauty always robbed him of breath. She floated toward him now across the flat sweep of lawn between the narrow moat and Wildwood Manor, leaving behind her mother and aunt at a table under the broad shade of a live oak. Her dress of pale green and soft gold brocade caught the brutal rays of the sun and shimmered like shallow water. Her aureate hair, somehow contained beneath her hat, managed its usual ploy of freeing tendrils of spun flaxen around her ears and face, curled by the humidity. Pure joy widened her sultry blue eyes when she drew near and held out both of her hands, which he gladly clasped. Although distracted by the unpleasant circumstances that had propelled him here, Jack met her with a forthright smile.

"Jack, I am so glad to see you at last."

"I'm sorry I've come unannounced."

"To see my father?"

"Aye."

Some of her happiness faded, and she glanced toward her watchful mother and aunt. "He is out riding his rounds of the property but should be back presently. Come and say hello to my mother and aunt while you wait. Mother was just speaking about you."

As they neared the table, Jack tried to hide his concern for Anna Archer who looked dangerously gray and oddly dry on such a warm day. Nearby, also shaded by the tree, were several tables covered with linen clothes and decorated with bunting and ribbons of yellow, white, and pale blue. Servants hovered about, arranging flowers in vases and setting out punch bowls.

"Why, Captain Mallory," Anna said, waving away the young slave girl who cooled both women with a large palmetto fan. "What a pleasant surprise." When she glanced toward the house, uneasiness flickered deep in her eyes.

He bowed. "Forgive me for coming unannounced, but I have something urgent to discuss with your husband."

"Pray sit with us while you wait. My husband is due back from his ride any minute; he is always punctual. We are taking a brief rest from making preparations for our guests. They will begin arriving shortly." Perhaps the anxiety in her gaze came from fearing one of the guests might recognize him if he lingered, but Jack had no intention of doing so.

Hiding his impatience, Jack smiled and sat to Anna's left while Margaret returned to the chair on her mother's right.

Caroline Archer inquired, "How is my daughter, Captain?"

"She's settling in at Leighlin nicely, ma'am. When I left, your nephew and Helen were giving her a tour of the plantation."

"It will be so nice to have my family together for the wedding," Anna said. "It seems as if I have not seen my son in ages, as if he were upon another planet instead of simply a couple of miles downriver. But unfortunately we will not all be together long." She sighed for effect and gave Margaret a slightly disapproving glance. "My daughter is going to deprive her husband of his bride shortly after their wedding day."

"Mother—"

"You should be with your husband, not me."

"Mother, Captain Mallory does not care to hear—"

"You should listen to your mother, dear," Caroline gently tsked.

"With all due respect, Aunt Caroline, what sort of daughter would I be to run away to Barbados with my husband and father-in-law when my mother's health is tenuous, in part because of preparations for *my* wedding?" She turned beseechingly to Jack. "I am sure Captain Mallory will understand me if no one else will. He would never have abandoned his mother for anyone else—even a spouse, I durst say—if she had been in poor health. Besides, my husband and father-in-law have business to attend to at their plantation there; whatever would I do with no one I know around me?"

Jack, however, could not answer, for the word Barbados had caught in his mind and slowly chilled his blood.

"Captain, my daughter paints me as an invalid, does she not? And you see me here in the flesh. I am not bedridden, am I?"

He shook himself back to the poor, pallid woman and forced a smile. "Your daughter is not trying to insult you, Mrs. Archer. She is only concerned for you, as any good daughter would be."

"She fusses over me like your mother used to, Captain."

This drew Jack's full interest, and he momentarily forgot about Ezra Archer.

"Whenever I fell ill, your mother used to visit me, and Captain

245

Logan with her. I remember the one time she came alone..." Life suddenly filtered into her pale eyes, and she smiled. "We had a long visit, just the two of us. It seems we both had so many things on our minds that day that just needed to spill out." The smile drifted off, and when her gaze met his it was as if they were alone, as if she was aware of only him. "That was the first time she told me about you."

He stared in astonishment, but Margaret's words jarred him back to reality: "There is Father now."

Anna flashed a meaningful glance from Jack to her sister-in-law who had been listening intently to her words. "I will not keep you from your business with my husband, Captain. But after the wedding, when life has returned to normal for everyone, you must call upon me, and we will have a long visit. I am sure we both have plenty of stories to tell one another about your dear mother."

Again Jack saw the private significance in her expression that he had seen days ago in Wildwood Manor's withdrawing room, and now he knew he had not been imagining things. What was it she felt compelled to tell him? And why had his mother dared to reveal the truth about her life before Logan?

With sudden urgency Margaret got to her feet. "Come, Captain, I will walk you to the house."

Jack caught her exigency, saw her worried attention upon Archer who had stepped down from his stallion and threw the reins to a waiting slave. The planter, however, did not wait for Jack. Instead he stalked from the front of the house across the lawn toward them. He no longer wore his arm in a sling.

"'Twas a pleasure, ladies," Jack said with a bow. "My best wishes for the wedding."

"I thank you, Captain," said Anna. "And pray do not forget what I told you."

"I shan't."

Margaret gave him a pleading look, so he offered his arm, and they started toward the house. Once away from the other women, Margaret spoke near a whisper, eyes straight ahead upon her advancing, red-faced parent. "You must be careful with my father, Jack. You are an honorable man who wants to repay a debt, but my father is not as honorable as he leads others to believe. And it does not look like he is pleased to see you here. Pray be careful." Her voice lifted with forced lightness. "Father—"

"Go back to your mother," Archer ordered in a clipped tone, eyes hard upon Jack as he stopped in front of him.

"Father—"

"This instant, young lady."

Jack touched her hand reassuringly. Margaret shot her father a last unhappy look before obeying him.

"What is the meaning of this?" Archer snarled at Jack. "Coming here uninvited! And in broad daylight! Guests will be arriving from town on this tide for my daughter's wedding. You could compromise the both of us."

The onslaught did not deter the outrage that had brought Jack here; he stepped closer to Archer who took a step back, undoubtedly more from dread of his riding clothes being besmirched than from fear of Jack.

"Listen to me, you bloody bastard," Jack hissed. "The accord between us is just that—between us. Leave Maria Cordero out of it or you'll need to find another errand boy."

"That girl has been nothing but a thorn in the side of my family since her appearance in Charles Town. An obstacle, a harlot who seduced my fool of a son."

"She did nothing of the sort. And if not for your wife and daughter yonder, I'd knock you flat for even thinking it."

"Then why did my son return to Leighlin? As much as he has tried to escape my authority in the past, suddenly he is determined to remain here. And why? Because of that damnable girl. She is not fit for him. For you perhaps, Captain, but not for my son."

"I don't give a damn about you or your son. My concerns are for Leighlin and her people. If you continue your intimidation and threats, our deal is off."

"There is only one person who has the ability to call off our deal, and if you think that is you, I warn you against such brashness."

"Turn me in then. And I'll tell them you were the one who freed me, and I'll tell them about you and Logan."

Archer was disturbingly unruffled. "Tell the world, you fool. Shout it from the highest rooftop in Charles Town if you must. No one will listen to a scoundrel like you, a no-account boy who is responsible for the murder of countless others, including the son of the town's most admired citizen."

From the house, Ethan Castle emerged and hurried toward his master as if having been summoned with great urgency.

"Now, sir," Archer composed himself as if no harsh words had been spoken. "Mr. Castle will escort you to the lower landing and have your boat meet you there. We cannot take the chance that any of my guests from Charles Town see you."

"Especially the ones you plan for me to murder."

Blood rushed into Archer's cheeks as Castle halted behind him.

"The Wylders. They're the ones you want me to intercept, aren't they?"

Archer took a step closer to where their noses almost met, and with a final, chilling once-over, jaw set, eyes like shards of coal he ordered, "Remember your place, Mallory. And do not come here again."

#

That evening was to see David and Elizabeth off to Wildwood, to spend the next two days and nights with family and friends for the wedding celebration. Elizabeth was beside herself with excitement, packing the things she would need in the smaller of her two trunks and escorting them—anxious for the well-being of the beautiful gown made specifically for the ceremony—down to the landing. Maria observed the young woman with amusement, still enjoying Elizabeth's buoyant attitude, never tarnished even by the underlying strain she sensed from her cousin. The girl did not try to dismiss David's struggle, nor did she pretend to understand half of it, but instead she used her own persistent disposition to try to pull him from his half-disguised melancholy, a melancholy caused not only by Maria but by his impending return to Wildwood as well as by his sister's choice of husband.

"Truth be told, Cousin," David said over dinner before they were to depart upon the rising tide, "Margaret cares more for Peter Wylder than for his son." He sipped his wine—he had already had far too much only halfway through the meal—ignorant of the bemused expressions of the others at table. "What I mean is that she is marrying Seth more to please Seth's father than herself. Oh, Seth—I am sure—is pleased enough..." He moved his head in a strange, condescending nod.

Fearing what words might tumble forth next from the somewhat inebriated and apparently emboldened young man, Maria was about to change the subject when Elizabeth broke in.

"Cousin," she said in a mild scold, "I am sure your sister cares for Seth Wylder. She told me as much herself."

"You have yet to meet the gentleman in question," David replied in an indulgent tone. "I believe Captain Mallory had the fortune of meeting dear Seth, did you not, Captain?"

From across the table, Jack appeared reluctant to enter the fray.

248

"Aye."

"And what did you think of him?"

"Seemed rather an average fellow. A bit on the surly side."

"Ah, yes. Average indeed. And you know my sister, of course. Is she not above average?"

"I'll say," Smith muttered into his mutton then coughed and cleared his throat, drawing stifled smiles from Dell and Rogers.

Jack sent a quick glance at Maria before giving David a pointed look to perhaps dissuade this indelicate line of talk. "Your sister is beyond compare. However, as you know, one often marries for more reasons than those obvious to others."

David made a successful attempt at curbing his personal offense. "How right you are, Captain."

When David downed more wine, Pip started to step from behind his chair with a fresh bottle to pour, but Maria discreetly shooed her out of range.

"The obvious choice for my sister—if we are talking Wylders—should have been Caleb, God rest him. Now there was a man in love with my sister."

Elizabeth's round eyes took on new interest. "Why did she not marry him then?"

"I never learnt what happened betwixt the two of them. I believe she chose Seth because of his father's wishes. Mr. Wylder knew Seth was rather heavy-handed in the courtship line while Caleb was the lightest touch. Indeed, Caleb was popular with all the Charles Town ladies and could have had any one of them, as his father knew. But, alas, he wanted only Maggie."

Elizabeth murmured, "How sad that he should die with a broken heart."

"Not sad for Seth, I am sure. He was always jealous of his brother's status."

"Cousin, surely you do not mean Seth does not grieve his brother?"

"I am sure he grieves. There was no bad blood betwixt them that I am aware. But with Caleb gone, Seth never has to worry about his brother's feelings interfering with his own marriage. After all, in the long run how will Maggie remain with Seth? Surely she would have gotten over whatever trouble she and Caleb had had in the past and realized the mistake she had made in her choice of spouse."

"Cousin, really." Elizabeth frowned, the first such negative expression she had shown him since her arrival. "I think you are concerned overly much for your sister. She is the most intelligent woman I know. She would never make a poor choice in anything. You must not fret about her."

"But I do. And I will. Marriage is for a lifetime." David stared at his almost empty goblet. "Marriage—it should be for love and nothing else. Do you not agree, Captain? It should not be forced upon one by others' wishes."

Elizabeth's face paled even whiter than its natural tone, and her eyes glistened. She put her hands in her lap where she clutched her linen. "Excuse me." She pushed her chair back with great effort. "I am feeling a bit...unwell. I think I will lie down for a few minutes before we depart."

Maria reached to stop her, but Elizabeth's tremulous, pleading smile restrained her. The men stood, David the last because of his unsteadiness. A small sniff escaped the girl as she fled the room in a strained effort not to rush. Slow to understand, David stared blearily after her. Then he looked around at the displeased group.

Smith gave him a lowering scowl and muttered, "Lump."

"Excuse me, gentlemen," Maria said. "I'm going to check on our guest."

She found the girl in her bedchamber, ordering the maid about, having her pack the remaining trunk. "Elizabeth, what are you doing?"

"Forgive me, Miss Cordero. My coming here was a mistake. I will pack the rest of my things to go to Wildwood. Could you have them taken to the landing?"

"I'll do no such thing. And you must stop this." Maria chased the maid from the room and went to the trunk to unpack what had just been packed.

"Do you not see what a mistake this has been, Miss Cordero? This is not fair to David. I must go. He does not want me here."

"What stuff. You aren't going anywhere. David's had too much to drink and he's anxious about returning to Wildwood. It has little to do with you. He doesn't have an unkind bone in his body. He didn't mean to hurt you."

Elizabeth sank upon the bed in despair, a damp kerchief in her hands. "I never would have come here if I had known how much David cares for you. And even though you are not married to him like he told Uncle, 'tis obvious he so wants to be married to you."

Frowning, Maria set the petticoats back into the trunk and came to sit beside her on the bed where she took hold of the girl's cold hand. "You must listen to me. I care very much for David. But it's Jack whom

250

I love."

The large eyes somehow became larger. "Captain Mallory?"

"Yes."

"Oh, Miss Cordero. You are just saying this for my benefit."

"No. I'm telling you the truth."

The momentary light left Elizabeth. "Does David know?"

"Yes. It's difficult, as you can see. But in time he will see things around him more clearly. He sees the two of you forced together by his father, but eventually he will realize it's his choice to be with you. He has said kind things about you, and he feels bad that you were put into this situation, but he can't talk to you about it for fear of hurting you. That's why I know he didn't mean anything untoward just now."

"How can you be certain?"

"I know him well." Maria smiled and patted her hand. "There was a time when I thought I'd never reach Jack, after his mother died. Smit—Mr. Smith told me not to give up on him, but I admit I almost did. And *you* mustn't give up on David. He so needs someone like you in his life. You just have to give him time."

Tears reappeared in the girl's eyes, but this time they were hopeful, happy ones, and she shared a broad, warm smile. "I hope you are right, Miss Cordero."

"I know I must be. Now, come along. Let's put these things back where they belong."

# CHAPTER 24

As full darkness changed the green landscape to cinereous black, Jack paced upon the front portico, eager and impatient. When he reached the south end, he looked up at the windows of Helen's chamber where dim lantern light glowed then was extinguished.

He had seen little of his sibling since returning to Leighlin and had been greatly disappointed when she spoke no further words to him after her outburst last night. He had hoped the outpouring of anger would open some sort of door and release her pain, allow the wound to drain and heal. Before he had left for Wildwood that morning he had seen Helen heading down the lane toward the stables, holding David's hand on one side and Elizabeth's on the other. She had spent much of her time with the pair up until their departure a few hours earlier. Apparently the child was as intent upon the two cousins being together as anyone else, perhaps a concept put into her busy mind by Maria, for Helen did love to meddle, and although David could possibly disengage himself from Elizabeth he did not have the same capability with Helen. Jack missed his sister more than he had ever anticipated. Watching her interactions with the Archers as well as with Ketch, Jack felt like an outsider, as if they were Helen's family and he a stranger.

A dark figure—oddly shaped, solitary, hatless—drifted around the southeast corner of Leighlin House, traveling with a slight limp along the lane that passed in front of the manor. Ketch. Jack could not get used to seeing the man without his right arm. While Ketch's loss of limb gave Jack inner satisfaction it also disturbed him, for it was tangible evidence of Ketch's personal sacrifice for Helen while he had sacrificed nothing. Instead he had brought her misery. Watching the man now, he felt the instinctive urge to confront him, to purge him from his life and Helen's. He had considered it yesterday, even after Maria's petition; after all, Maria had made the pact with Ketch, not he. Yet in the end he chose to honor the agreement, not simply to appease Maria and Helen but because she had once honored his equally distasteful promise not to exact revenge upon James Logan after his mother's death. So he would have to endure Ketch until the man gave him a reason otherwise.

Ketch now came abreast of the portico steps and turned to the doorway below, but he caught sight of Jack and hesitated for an instant to stare up at him. A quick, ambiguous moment in which Jack feared Ketch could read his thoughts before the man stepped from sight. How odd it was to co-exist here, especially considering their earlier efforts to destroy one another.

Jack's pacing increased. He glanced again at Helen's window. Would he have to seek Maria out? She had accepted his invitation, so why did she tarry? He frowned in fear, momentarily losing his resolve but grappling to regain it before she could appear. Now, with David and Elizabeth removed, he knew tonight was his chance at redemption, and he would not be fool enough to neglect it.

Finally Maria appeared on the portico, and Jack's pulse quickened with the renewal of his plan. He forgot about David and Elizabeth, even about Ketch.

"Is Helen asleep?"

"Yes."

He took her hand. "Follow me."

"Where are we going?" she asked in surprise.

"You'll see."

Down to the deserted landing, to the dock where the skiff awaited, just as he had prepared it earlier.

"Jack, what are you about?"

He was relieved to hear pleasure and not suspicion in her tone. Grinning, he jumped into the boat, then held out a hand to assist her. "Step lively, mate."

She hesitated then revealed an intrigued smile and joined him.

"Fend off there," he said, using an oar to push them away from the dock and out into the gentle current.

"Where are you taking me?"

"Away from the world."

"Oh? And what do you plan to do with me? Certainly not dump me overboard, I hope. Remember I can't swim. You had to pull me out once before when you nearly drowned me."

"Me? If you remember right, it was you who insisted on standing up in a rage in a very small, unstable boat so you could throw all manner of black epithets my way."

"All deserved."

"That's beside the point." Deftly he rowed out into the current and, with the breeze astern, started downriver. "Besides, I'm about to ensure the like will never happen again."

"What do you mean?"

"Patience, my dear."

The black wall of trees on his left reached down to the water's edge. No marsh here. Around the river's bend, a bit farther, then he could just make out the notch in the foliage as he listened to Maria's threatening speculation about all of the things he had better not attempt. He pulled for the opening before the current could carry them beyond, the shoreline riotous with the eerie songs of the night.

When the skiff touched bottom, Jack kicked off his shoes. As he dragged his shirt over his head, he felt Maria's intense curiosity and knew she was not simply looking with solicitation at his healing cutlass slash.

"What are you doing?"

"Getting undressed, of course. Something you'd best do, too, unless you want your clothes soaked. Not too easy to swim in a dress. Walking in one is murder enough, I learnt."

"I beg your pardon?"

Jack feigned innocence, fingers poised at the buttons of his breeches.

"I'm not getting undressed here," she insisted.

"'Tis dark. Private. Who will see? I can barely see my hand in front of my face, let alone your—"

"Jack!"

He laughed, for he could tell by her tone that she was not as scandalized as she pretended to be. Then he slipped out of his breeches, and if not for the fresh darkness Maria would certainly have seen that the cat was out of the bag. With a hand on the gunwale, he swung over into the murky, warm water that came to his waist, the river bottom soft and oozing between his toes.

"What are you doing?"

"Are you going to undress or not?"

"Of course not. I'm not swimming; I can't."

Jack moved along the side of the boat. Maria tried to put real alarm into her exclamation at his advance, but instead there was laughter and struggling hands as he reached for her.

"Put me down!" she demanded as he lifted her out of the skiff.

"Very well." He deposited her in shallower water.

"Jack, my shoes! You've ruined them. Oh, the mud..."

"Ruined, eh?" Uneceremoniously he lifted her back onto the thwart so her feet dangled over the gunwale. He proceeded to remove her

254

shoes. "It would appear your stockings are ruined as well."

"Jack—"

"And your petticoats and skirt."

She swatted with little real effort at his upward exploring hands. "I'll drown, I tell you."

"I won't let you. I didn't let you before, did I? I'm going to teach you. Come now, you've tamed Ketch, that dangerous beast; surely you aren't afeared of something as everyday as water, especially after all that time at sea."

Maria eyed him, and thankfully he did not sense a scrap of the fear she had displayed in his cabin aboard the *Prodigal*. Instead she seemed as disposed as he to enjoy a moment of frivolity. "I have a feeling I really don't have much say in this, do I?"

"No."

She hesitated then said, "Fine," and much to Jack's fevered satisfaction she began to undress. Piece by piece her clothing fell to the bottom of the boat in a display that nearly killed him with desire. At her neck a small oval shape caught his eye—the locket. He had forgotten about it, for she had concealed it beneath her mourning attire instead of removing it.

Maria climbed out of the boat on the opposite side, arms close to her body with a certain amount of modesty. Jack longed to light the boat's lantern to see what the cursed night cruelly, unfairly kept from him. Then he gave the skiff a push and jumped back in, scrambling for the oars.

"Jack! What are you doing? Come back this minute." She splashed after him, stumbled in the muck beneath her, followed him but a short distance, for the river bed fell away, and she knew the current to be too much for her. "Come back, I say! My clothes—"

"Come fetch them," he laughed, "before the mosquitoes eat you alive." He tossed the small anchor over the side, and the boat swung about.

"Is this how you teach someone? Bring back my clothes, you dog." She ducked down into the water up to her neck.

Jack made certain the anchor would hold, then he dove into the river. He remained submerged as he felt his way along the bottom until he found her ankles. She cried out and tried to escape. He burst up next to her, laughing.

She shoved him then splashed him. "Cruel bastard."

"Do you think I would abandon you to walk naked through the woods back to the house?"

"I wouldn't put it past you."

"Come now. Give me your hand."

She did so but pulled immediately back toward the shore. "What are you going to do?"

"Don't fret." He abandoned his teasing. "I promise I won't do anything that'll hurt you."

Reluctantly she let him coax her deeper. Then he slipped beneath the surface again to reappear a few feet farther out where the water came up to his neck.

"Relax your body so it will be more buoyant. Have you ever seen a dog swim?"

"Y—yes." She took a hesitant step toward him.

"You must paddle like one. Keep your head up. Don't thrash."

She made a small, averse sound and abandoned her first attempt.

"Even if you go under, you can still touch bottom. Give it another try. Remember to relax. Don't be afraid. I won't let anything happen to you."

As she screwed on her courage, the sound of her open-mouthed breathing came across the water. Then a splash and a gulp, and her head struggled above the surface with her jerking effort. She progressed half the distance then accidentally swallowed the brackish water and began to cough and struggle and then to sink.

"Jack!"

He pulled her toward him. She clasped onto him, nearly pushed him under. The soft, slick feel of her body, the firmness of her breasts pressed against his chest made him want to never let go. She gasped in his ear, trembling.

"Help me to the boat."

"No, no. You're doing fine. You must turn and swim back. It will be easier this time."

"No."

"You must if you want to win your clothes back."

Maria tried to push him away. "You are vile."

"And you were swimming like a fish."

"A dead and sinking one perhaps."

"Retract your claws from my flesh and swim back."

She gave a hopeless sigh as he helped turn her about and lifted her slightly to aid her buoyancy. When she kicked off, her feet targeted his body's most vulnerable region, and the night suddenly brightened with white hot pain that nearly put him beneath the surface. Through the brief haze of agony, he thought he heard Maria giggle. When his eyes

256

cleared and he could breathe again, she was back in the shallows, arms outstretched in triumph. Though he could not see her grin, he could feel it.

Jack turned and swam to the boat.

"Where are you going?"

He reached the gunwale. "Now swim out to me."

"You're daft. The current will sweep me away." She slapped at mosquitoes.

"I will grab you before that happens, and you can take hold of the gun'le like I am."

"No." Now the mirth was gone and the uncertainty had returned.

"You can do it. Come on."

"Some other time."

"No time like the present. And if you do it, I have packed us wine and fruit as a reward."

"You should have given me the wine *before* we started this."

He chuckled. "Come on then. You can do it."

She muttered under her breath for a long stretch until she had enough mosquito bites and had gathered the nerve to push off again. There was much splashing and several curses that included his name. As he watched her progress, he held his breath. She floundered once but before he could start for the spot where she had vanished, she resurfaced in a coughing jag, thrashing, and pressed onward. When he stretched his arm out for her, she clutched it with one hand while she reached for the boat with the other, still gasping. They bobbed there while she regained her breath and her wits.

"I want that wine now." She pushed her long black hair from her face.

"First..." Jack slipped his hand around the back of her neck and drew her in, kissed her so deeply that her fingers slipped from the boat, and she started to sink beneath the surface. She broke from him to make a wild grab with both hands for the skiff. He chuckled and let go of the gunwale.

"Where are you going now?"

"Around to the other side. Keep holding on here to counter-balance the boat as I climb aboard. Then I'll help you."

"More like make off with my clothes."

Once aboard, Jack directed her closer to the stern then urged her to pull herself up with the gunwale as far as she could.

"Not too quickly. We don't want to capsize. Then you certainly would be saying farewell to your clothes."

It was not a graceful effort due to Maria's wobbling fatigue and their wet skin as well as their laughter over the ludicrous scene, but soon Jack dragged her aboard just as the boat reached a dangerous cant. They lay in the bottom, still laughing, until Jack reached for the small stash of blankets next to him. Maria disentangled herself from him and wrapped a blanket about her and sat on the nearest thwart. Jack took a blanket for himself and sat next to her, close, putting his arm and half the blanket around her in the night, which now seemed cool because of the light breeze and their wet skin and hair. If the night damps and the water were going to make him ill, he would gladly accept the trade.

They sat there for a time as their mirth died off and the blankets absorbed some of the wet, then Jack clambered toward the bow where he retrieved a basket. He brought it back to her, set it on the thwart and pulled forth two goblets. Grinning, he also produced a bottle of wine.

"Good thing you told the kitchen servants that you and David aren't married after all; otherwise I would have gotten some dark looks indeed when I asked them to pack this for us."

After pouring the wine, Jack reclined against the pile of clothes and blankets, his own blanket wrapped barely around him as he sipped the wine. He invited Maria to join him. Leaning against him, no longer chilled, she sipped the wine and looked at the distant, star-adorned sky. He was so close now that he could see her eyes and the locket around her neck. Setting his goblet on the thwart, he put his arm around her. His fingers brushed languidly back and forth against her blanket while her finger glided with arousing sensitivity along his healed cutlass wound.

With a grin, he quietly asked, "Do you want your clothes back?"

Maria downed most of her wine then gave him a wet smile and set the goblet next to his. She murmured, "No," then shrugged off her blanket and reached for his.

#

Mosquitoes hummed around Ketch's head in the ebony cocoon of the woods, but his clothing and long, loose hair frustrated most of the bloodsuckers. The ones that did have success he mostly ignored, for his attention was fixed upon the skiff below on the river, a shadowy blotch, darker than the black river upon which it rode. From this distance he could see little detail, but detail he did not need in order to know what was transpiring. His body's response emphasized his awareness. A damnable, hopeless nuisance that needed attending. Now that it was plain Maria was neither unwilling nor threatened, he knew he should return to the house. But instead he lingered, unblinking, as motionless in his crouch as an old stump, not even hearing the creatures around him.

Earlier he had heard Jack's and Maria's voices on the portico from where he had stood in the lower level's doorway. And when the pair hurried off into the night, Ketch lurked after them. Once they started downriver in the skiff, he quickly limped back up the lane alongside the creek, crossed the bridge near the foundation of the new sawmill, and picked up the narrower lane on the opposite bank, which led toward the shoreline and the spot where Helen had often swam with her father. Ketch figured that sheltered area was where the dissolute blackguard planned to defile Maria.

At first, when Maria had protested Mallory's naked advance, Ketch had started down the slope, but before he got far the young woman's laughter sank him into shadow. When the couple had gotten out of the boat, he had thought the bastard meant to drown the girl, but then realized Mallory's game and remained in his crouch, grumbling to himself. It was a mixed bag, what he wanted. Though he did not desire harm to come to the girl—his half-brother had inflicted enough shame upon her—he also hoped Mallory would attempt some sort of deviation that would give him the excuse to descend upon him, to honorably break his agreement with the girl and kill the meddling coxcomb. But if he did not provide the chance now, perhaps soon there would be another opportunity...

"I want you aboard the *Prodigal* when Mallory next sails." Ezra Archer's voice from earlier that day intruded upon Ketch's thoughts. "I do not have total confidence that he will go through with my orders, not completely at least. So I want you there to remind him of his duty should his conscience get in the way. The boy is not as cold-blooded and ruthless as his stepfather...or you."

Ketch shook free from the memory and squinted through the night toward the river. The boat still rode serenely to its anchor, the figures inside melded together as one. He forced himself to stand, to remove himself from a scene that was—with each passing minute—making him more and more discontented.

When he turned for the lane—a pale ribbon of gray near at hand— a smell drifted to him on the shifting breeze, followed by a foreign sound, a faint crackle. He staggered to a halt. Back in the direction of the house, the night glowed pale orange. Smoke twitched his nose. He thought he heard shouts and cries.

259

Sparing not another moment in wonder and no longer concerned with maintaining stealth, he crashed blindly through the undergrowth until he struck the lane and ran back in the direction of Leighlin House.

# CHAPTER 25

Jack lay in idyllic collapse upon the bed of blankets, his body—not long ago cool and dry—now sweaty, the wafting breeze soon to dry him again. The most complete feeling of contentment he had ever experienced embraced him. Maria rested with her head upon his chest, one leg drawn up across him in languid exhaustion. Her fingers explored his leather bracelet. He kissed her hair and closed his eyes, taking in a long breath. The breeze had backed and now came off the western bank instead of down the river, and with it floated the sudden scent of smoke. He opened his eyes, a strange sensation overtaking him, and breathed deeper. This was not the faint drift of smoke from cook fires. This was far stronger, more acrid.

"Do you smell that?" he asked.

A hesitation then a quiet, dreamy, "Smoke?"

"Aye." He shifted so his head was above the gunwale. Again he took in a great draught of the night's varied, damp smells, but now the smoke overpowered most, and he thought he heard distant, unnatural sounds. He turned his head to look back toward the shore.

"Dear God..."

The sky beyond the nearby stand of forest—back in the direction of Leighlin House—glowed an evil orange that wavered and changed, flared then darkened. Maria raised herself up to follow his gaze and gasped.

"Fire!" he cried, struggling to disentangle them.

They floundered for the oars before Jack remembered the anchor. Cursing, he fell over the bow thwart, jolted his jaw, struggled for the line, frantically pulled it up hand over hand. Maria was already straining at the oars, and he quickly took up the other pair; they would be pulling against the current. For a moment he calculated which would be a shorter route—to pull back ashore here and race up the lane and over the bridge or to return to the landing. He decided upon the latter.

"Get dressed," he urged.

"My God, Jack...Helen."

"I'm sure she's safe," he said, hiding his fear. "They would have

261

gotten her out. Maybe it's not the house at all; maybe it's the kitchen."

But when they cleared the bend and the obstructing trees, they beheld the horror of Leighlin House ablaze. There was no time, however, to gawk; instead they threw their backs even more into the effort, bare feet pressed against the stretchers, propelling the small craft faster than Jack thought possible against current and tide.

He did not even attempt to take the skiff alongside the dock. Instead he ordered, "Head for the bank," and they drove the bow high upon the marshy shoreline. Jack snatched his breeches and leapt to land.

"Captain!" Hugh Rogers called from the dock.

Jack struggled his second leg into his breeches, hopping on one foot. From the *Nymph*, Rogers ran down the gangplank, Nahum next to him with a lantern, wide eyes upon the half-dressed couple. Rogers held a coil of rope and a grapnel as well as a roll of canvas. He met them on shore, all of them moving, not daring to be stationary, hurrying toward the path that led up to the sward.

"Is everyone out of the house, Hugh? Is Helen safe?"

Rogers's grizzled face revealed frantic worry. "We think everyone's out, sir, but—but we're not sure about Helen. When no one saw you or Maria, we figured she was with you. The fire seems to have started on the main floor. Everyone below got out, but we can't get to the top floor to check for her. So I come down here to get this here grapnel so we can climb up to her window. When I was leavin', Ketch come a-runnin' up and—by God, sir—he run into the house to try to find Helen."

"Dear Lord," Maria breathed as they reached the terraces.

As he raced across the sward, Jack saw dark knots of people along the periphery of the fire's glow—the house servants huddled together in panic, large white eyes reflecting the evil light. Beyond them and the small hedgerow that bordered the front lane he could make out other slaves as well as white men hauling buckets of water up to the roof of the kitchen house to wet the shingles in case the breeze were to shift and send flames and embers in that direction. Tongues of fire lashed outward from the windows of the main floor of Leighlin House. The conflagration's fingers reached for a foothold upstairs. Smoke writhed from the open windows, thickened the air, choked everyone.

Willis, Dell, and Smith were beneath one of Helen's windows, hands cupped around their mouths, shouting upward. But there was no movement from within; no small form appeared in the windows. Willis ran to Jack, his thinning hair showered with dead embers.

"Captain, was Helen with you?"

"No. Rogers, give me that grapnel."

A blocky figure staggered out through the front door, emerging from a bank of smoke like a specter, body bent double, gasping and coughing, hand blindly reaching. Ketch found the railing of the steps and started the descent, made it halfway before his legs gave way and he tumbled downward, his hair, his clothes smoking. Maria called to Willis to come with her as she ran toward Ketch. Willis hesitated until Jack nodded him off.

Beneath Helen's window, Jack ordered the others to stand back. He swung the grapnel with all his might, but his attempt struck the brick beside the window, and the metal tri-hook tumbled back to earth. The smoke and heat bursting from the withdrawing room forced him back, coughing, eyes watering and burning. He flung the grapnel again, but in his near-panic his aim was poor and it struck the lower sill and bounced off.

Brian Dell shouldered into him and brusquely took the grapnel and rope. "Let me, Cap'n." In one adept attempt, he sailed the grapnel through the open window nearest the corner of the house. He pulled back on it until the prongs caught and held against the pressure, a pressure greater than Jack's slender form could conjure.

Jack took the rope from him and ran to the side of the shattered lower window. The difficult part would be getting beyond that damned window with its heat and smoke trying to conquer him, but he put those thoughts out of his head as he braced his feet and started upward, the heat of the bricks penetrating his shoes. He closed his eyes against the suffocating billows that poured over him, put one foot above the other, prayed his grip upon the line would remain true and that the grapnel would hold. Upward through what seemed an eternity of blackness, occasionally able to choke out Helen's name, straining his ears above the roar of the inferno for some sign that she was up there.

Once clear of the lower window, he swung to the right, above it now, his feet catching upon an ornamental outcropping. Flames licked upward and singed the seat of his breeches. With one hand he caught the lower sill of the window then let go of the rope and grabbed hold with his other hand to haul himself upward. He tumbled to the floor in a chamber thick with smoke snaking upward through the seams and through the fireplace across the room.

"Helen! Helen, are you here? Where are you?"

Heart in his throat, he pressed his bare arm over his mouth, choking, and squinted through the blinding shroud, called over and

263

over in desperation. He groped his way to the bed and frantically clawed through the bedclothes but found nothing. What if she had fled to another room in hopes of escape? How would he find her?

His voice grew hoarse as he shouted and felt his way around until at last he thought he heard something incongruous amidst the voice of the fire. It seemed to come from down low. He dropped to his hands and knees, listened. Sobs.

"Helen! Where are you?"

No words, just those muffled sobs and coughs. Low, covered by something. The bed! Jack flattened on his belly, lungs closing as he crawled beneath the large bed, calling out to his sister. He could see nothing, only feel the unbearable heat from below, his arms outstretched, feverishly searching until his hands bumped something soft—clothing, a wet cheek...

"Helen!"

The girl did not respond. She was balled up in the near corner against the wall, shaking and crying, choking, frozen with terror. Wasting no more time with words, he grabbed hold of her shift and dragged her with one hand while the other worked with his legs to snake backwards. The girl screamed and struggled against him, but he maintained his hold, teeth clenched, lungs about to explode, all oxygen being devoured from the air around them.

He emerged and hauled Helen into his arms. He located the window only by the flow of air vacuumed through it.

"Don't leave him!" she shrieked in Jack's ear. "Don't leave him!"

Jack thrust his head through the open window, gulped air only a bit less strangling, blinked his eyes clear.

"Captain!" Rogers's voice from below. "Toss her down! We'll catch her!"

A blur of white took shape—a piece of sailcloth stretched out by Rogers and the others. Because of the fire they had to remain a small distance from the house, so he would need to propel Helen outward; he would need her cooperation, but that did not seem possible at the moment.

Helen pummeled his bare chest, coughing and sobbing. "Don't leave him!"

"Helen...Helen, listen to me! You must jump from here. Do you understand? Look down. See Mr. Rogers and the others? They're going to catch you."

"We can't leave him!"

"Who?" he demanded in frustration. "Who are you talking

about?"

"Howard—he's under the bed."

"There's no time. You must let go of me. You must jump."

"No! I'm scared."

He struggled with her, but she wrapped around him like woolding. Desperate, he said, "If I promise to fetch Howard, will you jump?"

"I'm scared."

"I know, but they will catch you."

"You promise to find him?"

"I promise. Now we must hurry. The floor will give way soon."

She allowed him to stand her upon the window seat.

"Do you see them there below? Right, then. You must push off from the sill here. I'll help you. Step out. There. Good. Now on the count of three..."

Fear held the girl back at first, but on the second attempt Jack watched her fall and held his breath until she landed upon the canvas and was instantly rushed away from the house.

Taking in a gulp of night air, Jack plunged back into the room, the floor almost unbearable now. Some of the boards burst up with a crack like the report of a gun. Under the bed he dove, desperately scrabbled about for the bear, back into the corner where Helen had been until he found the soft object near the wall. Again he dragged himself from beneath the bed. When he stood, the floor beneath him fell away with a crash. Only a wild grab for the window saved him from plunging downward into the flames. He slammed the bear upon the window seat then hauled himself up. One of the legs of his breeches had caught flame, but he quickly slapped it out.

"Jack!" urgent voices called from below.

He could no longer breathe, no longer see, barely think. He concentrated to feel the pull of air through the window so he knew which way to fall, then he shoved himself through the opening, let himself plunge through smoke and flame like a rag doll. The canvas caught him, ferried him away from the overpowering heat until he was set down upon the sward. He gasped and struggled free, tears pouring from his eyes, nose burning, mouth wide. He remained on hands and knees, unaware of anything except the sweet taste of breathable air.

"Easy, lad," Smith's words, hand steady upon his shoulder. "Breathe slow now. Short breaths."

"Helen," he croaked.

"She's fine. She's with Maria. See there?"

Through blurry eyes Jack saw Maria on her knees several yards away near the north garden, Helen in her arms. The glare from the brutal fire behind him sparked the tears on both their faces. He nearly collapsed with relief but instead dragged himself to his singed feet to limp toward them. Helen struggled free and rushed over, Maria close behind. Exhausted, Jack stumbled and went to his knees, realized he still clutched the bear. Helen stopped a few feet short. Her amazed, grateful eyes brimmed and her lips quivered. Jack's hand trembled as he offered the toy.

She stared at the rescued bear then at him for a long, searching moment before she warbled, "Daddy isn't coming back, is he?"

Stunned, Jack slowly shook his head. "I'm sorry, Helen. I'm so sorry..."

With tears streaming, the girl took the bear from him. Then she folded it against her chest with one arm and reached for him with the other.

# CHAPTER 26

The Great Fire of London roared in an unending evil glare of orange and black against the night sky, the flames reflected in the Thames as if the river itself were ablaze. Ketch stood with his stepfather on the south bank and watched in terror as panicked screams drifted across the water. He was only six years old, and he clung to his stepfather's leg, peering out from behind at the destruction stretching as far as his wide eyes could see. He tugged at his stepfather's coat and begged to go home, but—like the other Southwark citizens around them—the lurid scene across the river held his fascinated parent captive. Another building fell with a crash and an explosion of flame and upward dashing sparks. The smoke was so thick, the ash falling all about them like gray snowflakes.

An unseen hand pulled him away from the horrors, and instead of a child's voice he heard his mature voice, calling out Helen's name. The breath of Leighlin's fire surrounded him in the stair hall, tightened his chest. No air. There was no air. Darkness. Blacker than he had ever thought imaginable, blacker than even the silver mine. He should never have left the house to follow Mallory to the river. He should have stayed there; he would not have lost his head and fled as the others had. He would have known Helen was not with her brother; he would have gone to her chamber first and left only after he had found her.

With a burst of flames, the stairs collapsed beneath him, and he fell, his arm thrown up to protect his face. He struggled to his feet and somehow fought his way to the servants' staircase off the dining room, managed to get halfway up. Too much smoke…could not breathe. Half-conscious, he fell again and nearly got wedged in the coffin-like space.

"Wake up," her voice drifted through the cloud. "It's over now."

Ketch awoke with a start, stared upward at the ceiling of a vaguely familiar place. Not his bedchamber, though. Morning light spilled through a nearby window, and a breeze brushed the thin, plain curtain back and forth in a peaceful rhythm. A drugged haze clung to his brain, slowed things. He smelled sweet oil.

"Here. Drink." From a chair at his bedside, Maria offered a cup of water.

He moved his arm and winced. Bandages. More bandages. How he hated their tangible display of weakness. His whole body throbbed. His left cheek—stinging like an attack of fire ants—had been slathered with a thick salve. Another gauzy wrap of bandage surrounded his bare chest. He shifted his weight, could not escape the searing discomfort; he had not felt it in the dream...

"I wasn't able to give you much laudanum," she explained. "Most of the medical supplies were lost in the fire. Willis has sent downriver for more."

His gaze searched her with sudden dread. "Miss Helen?"

"She's fine. Jack got her out of the fire."

"Where was she?"

"Hiding under her bed."

Again he looked up at the ceiling of the kitchen house. "I didn't want to wait for the grapnel; I was afeared it would be too late."

"You did your best. Everyone is very grateful."

Ketch cynically wondered whom "everyone" encompassed. He closed his eyes, became aware of men's voices beyond the window as well as the sounds of axes, saws. "Is anything left?"

"Not much. Jack thinks we can salvage the lower level; the walls are only scorched. But everything inside was lost."

Ketch thought of the beautiful portraits in the Great Hall. The one of Ella Logan had been both a comfort and an agony to look upon since her death. The painting had allowed him to feel her, smell her, hear her. Now it was no more, just as she was no more, just as Logan was no more. Helen was all that was left of Leighlin's bright days. He saw her in his mind's eye—a solitary figure, small and helpless—and he remembered the sense of urgency he had experienced when the fever from the snake bite had gripped him, recalled the thoughts that had tumbled into his mind after he had gone to see Ezra Archer following Logan's death. They returned to him now when he considered the possible cause of Leighlin's fire. Perhaps the fire had been only an accident, a randomness. Perhaps one of the slaves had been foolish with a lamp. Or maybe it had been the fault of one of the men smoking in bed, that whoreson Gabriel perhaps. Yet Ketch had an unsettled feeling, something that had been growing in him before he had even regained consciousness, and if his suspicions were correct... The very thought spiked a dreaded, familiar agitation in him, a demon that always demanded release.

He started to stir. "I have to get up."

"You'll do no such thing. You have burns on your chest, face, and arm. Willis said you must not move about for a couple of days."

"Bugger Willis."

"Mind your tongue. I hear Helen coming. She's staying here—we all are—until we get the house rebuilt, so mind your language."

He sank deeper into the cot, angry with himself for the shame the girl made him feel.

Helen's piping voice filled the small room. "Is he awake yet?"

Maria hushed the child who drew close to the cot. Ignoring the pain of the burns and the fogginess of the opiate, Ketch felt his expression open in a relieved smile at the sight of her, safe and whole. And she was somehow much more like her old self, he sensed.

Someone shuffled behind her and halted in the doorway—Jack Mallory, dark eyes upon him, both cautious and curious but certainly not solicitous. His reluctance to enter gave Ketch a nudge of satisfaction and an excuse not to acknowledge his gratefulness for the infernal bastard's rescue of Helen.

The child sat on the edge of the cot, smiling. "Are you feeling better, Mr. Ketch?"

"Aye. And I'm glad to see you safe. You gave me a fright."

A touch of remorse tempered the girl's happy expression. "Maria said you tried to save me from the fire, and that's how you got hurt, just like when you saved me from the snake."

He frowned at her coarse clothing—something borrowed from the slaves by the look of it. "I'm sorry I couldn't get to you."

"But you tried." She sheepishly bowed her head. Then her eyes trailed over his bandages. "You got burnt."

"'Tis naught to waste breath over."

She touched his hand—such a feather-light, soft sensation, like the fall of London's ashes. "Does it hurt bad?"

"No."

"John got burnt, too—on his feet."

Maria scowled. "And he shouldn't be on them right now either."

"They're only a trifle blistered," Mallory insisted. "Rose set me up with these deerskin Indian slippers."

Helen giggled behind her hand and glanced sidelong at her brother. "John's bottom got burnt, too."

"Helen," Maria scolded.

The child tried to recover her decorum with little success. Ketch returned her secret grin regardless of the hurt it caused his cheek.

"Your beard got burnt, too," Helen observed. "And your hair." Her eyes widened in sudden realization. "Your eyebrows are gone!"

"I never was nothin' to look at no ways, so...no matter." He peered at her. "Where's yer bear, Miss Helen? Did you lose him to the fire?"

"Oh, no. He's in my bed. John saved him for me after I jumped from the window. Did you see me jump, Mr. Ketch? They caught me on a sail, just like you and the Medoras used to do on Daddy's ship, remember? You would toss me up and down."

"Aye, I remember."

Maria eased her down from the bed. "That's enough chatter for now, *osita*. We must let Mr. Ketch rest. You may come visit him later."

The girl's expression sobered. "Thank you for trying to save me, Mr. Ketch."

"Yer welcome, child."

Driven by self-consciousness, she rushed from the room. Jack did not follow her as Ketch expected. He met the boy's gaze with the usual challenge, but the young man did not return the hostility; instead he revealed an uneasiness that caused him to shift from one sore foot to the other as he cleared his throat. Maria's expectant eyes were also upon Jack, and a long silence stretched through the room, broken only by the distant bustle of the servants in the kitchen.

At last Jack said, "I want to thank you, too...Ketch...for what you did."

Ketch found that he did not relish the boy's distress as much as he would have expected. Suddenly the atmosphere was very oppressive, like the strangling smoke from the house fire. He nodded in acknowledgement and was relieved to see the young man leave the room.

#

Over the next two days, Leighlin had many unexpected visitors. Townspeople and others from along the Ashley River appeared at the landing, many of them on their way downriver from Wildwood after Margaret Archer's wedding, all come to see the sad remains of the house and to offer condolences to Hiram Willis and the others. Jack, of course, kept out of sight at such times, usually taking Helen to the stables, anxious to keep the loquacious child away from their guests. Many, like James Moore, Thomas Drayton, Jr. and his wife Ann, and landgrave Thomas Smith pledged to Leighlin any means of aid necessary, from slaves to food to building materials. Ezra Archer, who accompanied the Draytons downriver from Wildwood, claimed he, as *de facto* guardian of Leighlin, would see her set to rights with all possible speed. When Maria relayed all of this to Jack, discontent shadowed his face. Being a mere bystander in Leighlin's renewal did not sit well with him.

Now Maria stood on the dock with Jack as yet another boat glided toward the landing, this one heralded by a letter sent the day before. The boat's awning had been rigged to keep the afternoon sun off Elizabeth Archer who sat next to David in the stern-sheets. David was dressed plainly, like one prepared to delve into salvage work. In contrast, Elizabeth wore a gaily-colored dress and broad-brimmed sennit hat with a matching ribbon.

Maria had been looking forward to their visit and news of Margaret's wedding—happy news, something that would take her mind off the blackened ruins there on the bluff. True enough, she had her own private happiness since Jack's pronouncement of his love for her. They both, however, felt a bit guilty for their personal joy whenever they looked at the mournful foundation of Leighlin House and reflected upon all that had been lost.

"You will, of course, marry me?" Jack had murmured in her ear last night in the tiny room they shared in the kitchen house—a room with a double-tiered bed, though only Helen was innocent enough to believe Maria and Jack slept separate. "You won't take advantage of me then run off with David Archer and his fortune?"

Maria returned his grin. "And who will marry us? You certainly won't announce banns in town."

"I have a simple and safe solution."

"Do tell."

"We could go aboard the *Fortune*, and Angus could marry us. They should be in the offing as we speak, if they hold true to our agreement."

They had wrangled options back and forth, turning it into a game to see who could come up with the most outrageous scenario. But now, seeing David's attention upon her from the boat, even as he spoke to Elizabeth, Maria felt none of the previous night's mirth. How strange it was to see him after all that had transpired over the past couple of days. What would he think of her if he knew what she had done upon the river two nights ago?

When they reached the dock, Elizabeth disembarked a bit awkwardly with David's and Jack's assistance, then reached for

Maria's hands.

"Oh, Miss Cordero. We are all so sad about the house. How terrible! David and Margaret thought the wedding should have been postponed when news of the fire came just before the ceremony, but Margaret's Mr. Seth and my uncle would hear nothing of the sort, what with all the guests there and the food prepared. Everyone felt a bit more settled when they heard no one was harmed in the fire."

"Not exactly," said Maria. "Jack and Ketch were both burned trying to rescue Helen."

After Maria briefly told the story, Jack hastily deflected Elizabeth's solicitude and profuse praise.

David smiled in a profound effort at being genuine. "Sounds like a heroic effort indeed."

"We wanted to offer our condolences in person," Elizabeth continued. "Uncle said he will spare no expense to see the house rebuilt."

More like Leighlin's expense, Maria thought, for she could not imagine Archer investing Wildwood's money in Leighlin House, no matter his boasting to Drayton or anyone else.

"We're glad you came," Maria said. "I know Helen will be very pleased to see the both of you. She's asked about you several times, and she's disappointed you won't be staying with us now. Since the fire, she's been more like her old self. It's been such a relief."

David offered Maria his arm, his gaze upon her for a long moment, a wisp of a smile on his defined lips. Maria blushed, for he always had a way of appearing to read her mind, and she certainly did not want him reading her mind right now with Jack so near. Jack, in turn, offered his arm to Elizabeth and with uncomfortable steps escorted her to the nearby carriage where Jemmy awaited. Jack handed her up into the carriage, then sat next to her as David and Maria settled across from them.

"Tell us about the wedding," Maria urged.

Happily Elizabeth launched into a vast description that carried them along the lane and around the garden. David, however, added little, still brooding over his sister's choice of husbands.

As Maria listened and commented, Jack's attention lingered upon her, a tiny smile tilting one corner of his mustache in a now-familiar, very intimate expression that brought color to her cheeks. What she saw in his eyes had little to do with Margaret's wedding, and she wished he would refrain from what she feared was all too obvious to the others. His expression was one she had seen often since that night

272

on the river, one she knew reflected back. Any other time it filled her with warmth and desire, but she feared such a display might embarrass their guests and be misinterpreted as deliberate.

They reached the remains of the house where slaves labored among the debris with Willis, Smith, Dell, and Rogers, and talk of the wedding fell by the wayside as sadness swept across Elizabeth's round face. Jack helped her from the carriage as tears sheeted her eyes. Piles of debris lay in orderly masses nearby—bricks made up one pile, furniture or other items that might be salvageable made up another, while charred, twisted items to be carted away and disposed of formed yet another mound. Ever growing mountains in the hot sun. The once-beautiful double staircases led to the floor of the portico and its scorched pillars, the collapsed roof partially cleared away, dirt and smears of ash marring the black and white tiles.

"I cannot believe it is gone," Elizabeth said. "Such a beautiful house..."

"There is a planter on the Santee River," David said to Jack, "with a slave who is a master bricklayer. I could acquire his services for you, I am certain."

A hint of surprise crossed Jack's deeply tanned face. "Thank you. We'd be much obliged."

"I'm sorry your belongings were lost to the fire, Miss Archer," Maria apologized.

Elizabeth waved a dismissive hand and banished her tears with a few quick blinks. "I took my small trunk with me to Wildwood, remember? So I have enough to wear. And Margaret said any of her dresses could be altered if I wanted, but there is no need. David's sister has been very kind to me, even as busy as she was with all the guests and taking care of her mother."

"How is your mother?" Jack asked of David.

"I am sure she will regain her health now that the work of the wedding is over. She was nigh collapse yesterday, yet it took both myself and Maggie to convince her to simply lie down. I had not realized how much her health had declined since I left."

Elizabeth's dark eyebrows knit. "Hopefully she will let me and Mother help take care of things while we are visiting, so she can recover."

David said, "She feels remiss if she is not entertaining her guests."

"Mother made her promise that she would rest and not feel the need to fuss over us." Elizabeth smiled demurely at David. "I told her I was enjoying myself just being at Wildwood and meeting so many

273

new people."

"She asked me to send her regrets over the loss of the house," said David. "And she said to remind the Captain to pay her a visit whenever he can, but she understands the more pressing issue of rebuilding Leighlin House. She wants you to know that if you need any of our slaves you are but to ask."

"You will, of course, relay my thanks?"

"Of course."

The four of them walked around the ruins, marveling at the destruction and speculating on the cause and the rebuilding. David knew the house much more intimately than Jack, having been a guest there many times before his most recent stay, so he had much to reminisce over as well as to suggest in regards to its restoration. Jack listened attentively and spoke freely. His civility almost surprised Maria, considering their previous rivalry. Did that civility stem from self-confidence born of the consummation of their relationship, a declaration both verbal and physical? Or was the graciousness only out of respect for Elizabeth's gentility? Maria wondered if this exchange would be happening if the girl were not present. And did Elizabeth notice the occasional looks David flashed toward Leighlin's governess?

Maria was intensely curious to hear how David's time spent with Elizabeth progressed, if he had indeed attended closely to her during the past few days amidst the scrutiny of family and friends. Of course he would not have wanted to be complicit with his father's plans, but Maria knew David would not consciously do anything to embarrass any woman, especially one as kindhearted as Elizabeth. No doubt his father had counted upon that quality.

"Where do you dwell now?" Elizabeth asked.

"In the kitchen house," Maria answered. "We moved the servants temporarily into the settlement. In fact, why don't we go there now? Iris was to have pie ready for us and something to drink."

"Oh," Elizabeth said. "You lost so much; we cannot possibly eat any of your victuals."

"Not to fret," Jack assured. "We've acquired more supplies from town, and our neighbors have all been very generous. We are far from destitute."

Maria was surprised to see Ketch seated in the shadows of the kitchen house porch, smoking, something she had never seen him do before. The man's physical endurance, his tolerance of pain continued to amaze her. How much torment could one body endure? First the

274

bruises and broken nose he bore upon his return to Leighlin, then the snake bite and loss of his arm, then the self-inflicted lacerations before the burns. Fortunately the *Nymph* had brought more medicine from Charles Town, including the laudanum with which she dosed him. Perhaps it was the opiate that affected him, but since the fire he seemed even more withdrawn than before, as if something deep inside had been stirred, something he wanted no one else to know about, something perhaps he even feared.

The previous evening when she had gone to his room to treat his burns, she had found him rolling up the cot's bedding. He did not halt his actions or look at her when she asked him what he was doing. "Goin' to the house," he mumbled.

"With your bedclothes? Whatever for?"

"I don't belong here."

He glanced over his shoulder at her, as if hoping she would vanish. Discomfort darkened his eyes in the failing light. Such a different expression from the aberrant smile he had given Helen that morning, a moment that had astonished Maria, for it had eased the harshness in him and lightened his eyes to true brown, reminding her of the emotion that had crossed his face the night Helen had first touched his hand. Using that memory from which to draw courage, Maria put her hand on his shoulder. He wheeled with a jerk as if she had pressed a branding iron against him. An instinctive move, a fearful one. Then his shock at her audacity turned to red-faced mortification. Quickly he finished with the bedroll.

"Ketch, no one blames you for the fire or for Helen's close call. I told you before—everyone is grateful that you tried to save her."

"I shoulda been here."

"What do you mean? You were here—"

He shook his head, struggled hastily with the bedroll.

"Where were you then?"

He slung the bedroll over his shoulder and turned, but she blocked his path. His avoidance of her gaze fertilized the seed of realization in her, and instantly heat rose to her cheeks.

Tightly she repeated, "Where were you?"

Finally he looked at her. The salve on his cheek distorted his face. His eyes glistened with the old shark-like blackness, dulled by resentment. "You shouldn't have trusted him."

Her own indignant anger flared. "You mean to tell me—"

He tried to get around her.

"Ketch." She nearly took hold of him but dared not touch him again. "Listen to me, damn you. I don't need you shadowing me like some loyal mongrel. I trust Jack; I love him. And he and I are going to be married, do you hear me? We're going to live here with Helen, and we're going to raise a family. If you truly want to stay here as you say, then you'd best accept it."

He said nothing and pushed past her. She stared after him, her heart pounding at the thought of him witnessing that private moment on the river, especially when she considered the perversions of his kin. Yet she knew to compare him to Dan Slattery was as foolish as comparing night to day, for Ketch had never displayed any of Slattery's predatory sexual tendencies. Indeed, had he not just recoiled from her mere touch? Yet if he had truly followed her to the river out of a sense of protection and not deviance, what made him feel such a need? She understood his guardianship of Helen, but what reason did he have for protecting her? Did he feel she was somehow in the same danger in which he felt Helen to be? Or was it simply his distrust of Jack in all things?

Whatever his reasons, Maria had since felt increasingly culpable about her exchange with him. After all, the man surely could not be in complete control of his wits between the constant pain from his string of injuries and the opiate he had taken. But when she had sought him out, her search proved fruitless; as usual, if Ketch did not want to be seen he was not. That night, after Jack had fallen into an exhausted but sated slumber, she slipped from his embrace and stole across to the burned out house. There was no one to detect her approach; Willis and the other white men were sheltered temporarily in the carriage house back in the stable yard.

As expected, she found Ketch asleep in his former room, lying upon a pine straw tick on the hard-packed floor, silent as death, not even a twitch. She stood there for a long moment, wondering if he were drunk, dead, or had caused himself another injury, but then he gave a small snort followed by quiet snores.

Since then she had not seen him, not until now when she, Jack, and their guests approached the porch. When they reached the steps, Ketch stood, his legs devoid of stockings, his feet bare, smoke lazily curling from the pipe at his side. The gaping collar of his shirt revealed the wide bandage around his chest.

"Good day, Mr. Ketch." Elizabeth paused, forcing Jack and David to do the same even though they had started toward the door as if Ketch did not exist. During Elizabeth's time at Leighlin, she had seemed oblivious to the attitude held by most toward Ketch. She lacked their

276

instinctive suspicion and aversion. She had always been polite to him whenever their paths crossed. In fact, she had privately expressed curiosity to Maria and mentioned how David seemed reluctant to answer any of her questions about the peculiar man, claiming ignorance. Now she took a step toward Ketch and said, "We heard how you bravely endeavored to rescue Helen from the fire. How fare you now?"

"Tolerable, miss," Ketch mumbled.

"Where is Helen, by the way?" she asked no one in particular.

"I suspect she's in Rose's cabin," Maria answered. "Rose just had her baby the other day. Or she might be at the stables with the new foal. But she should be back any time."

"Well," Elizabeth smiled at the one-armed man, "I hope you are feeling better soon, Mr. Ketch."

Jack and David exchanged a glance and waited for Elizabeth to brush past them into the house. David followed, but Jack hung back when he noticed Maria's expression.

"Go ahead," she urged. "I'll be right in."

With the others gone, Ketch slowly reclaimed his chair with a half-veiled wince. His circumspect gaze remained on Maria, uninviting.

"I want to apologize," she began quietly, "for getting angry with you yesterday."

He said nothing, did not blink, did not bring the dying pipe back to his mouth. Inadvertently her gaze touched upon the old scar at the base of his neck. Had he grown his beard to hide the matching scar beneath his chin?

"I don't want you to..." She stifled her demanding words and started anew: "Please stay here in the house. You shouldn't be sleeping out in the night damps."

"That's where mongrels is supposed to sleep."

"Ketch—"

"You best tend to yer guests, don't ye reckon?" When he brought the pipe back to his mouth, his teeth made a sharp click against the stem.

With sudden shocking clarity she realized that she had not simply insulted him yesterday but had actually bruised his feelings. At a loss now, she frowned and retreated like a rebuffed child.

David and Elizabeth stayed long enough for supper, and when the tide turned in the evening the four strolled back to the landing, now with Helen cavorting ahead of them on the sward. Jack again escorted

277

Elizabeth, doing his usual best to charm the impressionable girl who smiled at him, laughed at his witticisms, and fretted over his lameness. Maria purposefully walked slower than Jack, her hand upon David's arm. He had fallen silent since they had left the kitchen house, his attention now upon Jack.

"I'm so glad you came, David. Never be a stranger."

"I shall endeavor not to be."

"I hope it's not too difficult being back home."

"No, not with our guests there, especially Elizabeth. Father dotes upon her, and he would never want her to see the reality of things, so life has been rather pleasant since I returned."

"I'd wager she can accept reality better than anyone thinks."

He hesitated. "Perhaps you are correct. She has had moments of candor. She knows my father's plan for her, and she has insisted her presence here is simply because of her own wishes, not his."

"I would believe her."

"I do. She also knows I am in love with you. 'Tis nothing I have told her, I assure you. She is a woman, is she not, no matter how young? And you all seem to come with an unsettling intuition. She said she would leave the instant I asked her to, that she would not wait the fortnight longer that she and her mother are supposed to remain."

"But you haven't asked her to leave?"

"Of course not. I could not hurt her feelings."

"Do you want her to leave?"

He frowned and studied Elizabeth as they descended the terraces. Confusion contracted his features as if he had never considered the option. "She has been very patient with me. She knows my relationship with my father is broken, and I see her trying to mend it. She has been...a kind friend, a good cousin, shall I say? So, no, I guess I do not want her to leave, especially now."

"David—"

"I do not mean for it to sound as if I am using her. I have made that plain to her." He paused. "Her mother has asked me to visit them in Virginia after the indigo has been harvested."

"Will you?"

"I shall consider it."

"It sounds like just the thing you need...to get away from here for a while and be able to enjoy life."

"Perhaps you are right."

"Of course I am," she teased, squeezing his arm. "Haven't you learnt that yet?"

The smile she had longed to see finally blossomed, and for a moment the old brightness returned to his eyes.

#

Since the fire, Jack's relationship with Helen had been renewed with astonishing ease. She was as intimate with him as she had previously been distant, eager to chatter and follow him about again, as if she had never rejected him. He did not tire of her presence, for all too easily he recalled his loneliness and fear as a prisoner in Charles Town, faced with the prospect of never seeing her again. Each morning, as before the fire, Helen brought flowers to their mother's grave and invited Jack to accompany her. In fact, it was more insistence than invitation.

"Look!" Helen pointed upriver from where she sat next to him on the grassy bluff. "Here comes a boat. Maybe we'll have another visitor."

Disinterested, Jack looked away from his mother's grave and the red roses Helen had placed there. Beyond the north rice field, a small boat coasted along with the tide. Negroes and one white man. Jack sighed, hoped he would not have to conceal himself yet again. If he remained near the grave, the garden would hide him from view. Whenever he saw a boat coming downriver, his stomach ached with dread that it would carry orders from Ezra Archer. To hope Archer would release him was a hollow one, yet each time he awoke in Maria's arms he prayed that somehow he would not be forced to leave her and Helen again.

"John." Helen, already bored with the familiar sight of a craft on the Ashley, drew his attention back to where she plucked the emerald grass around her mother's headstone. "Are you going to marry Maria?"

Jack tried to hide his shock. "What on earth makes you ask that?"

As if having betrayed a secret, Helen avoided his gaze. When he chuckled, she smiled in relief, the morning sun upon her upturned face. "I saw you kissing her last night...and the night before."

"Spying, was you?" He shifted his weight more onto his hip to keep pressure from his burns.

"Maybe a little."

Jack hoped her intrusion consisted only of seeing a kiss and nothing more. "I hope to marry her, aye. And to do so we may go to sea. And you'll come with us."

Her elated eyes perfectly matched the blue sky. "Promise?"

"Aye."

She leapt up and kissed him. "I'm going to tell Maria." And off she went toward the kitchen house in a mad dash, her dress fluttering out behind her.

Seeing Helen so like her old self again warmed him more than even the Carolina sun. Although his sister was now an orphan and the ruins of their mother's house lay behind him, he never would have thought it possible to be as happy as he was now, sitting here atop the breeze-combed, verdant bluff with the rice field and its diligent workers, landing, and river stretched before him like a painting. Even the morning after the fire, when the light of day had revealed the true scope of the destruction, he had not felt the devastation as he would have days before. Instead Maria had put her arm around him and her head upon his shoulder, and the weakness he had experienced vanished.

Now, with a glance at the distant boat, he lay back upon the grass near the grave and wondered if his mother could see him. He gazed toward the river bend, and a self-conscious, wry smile touched his lips. Had she seen him and Maria upon the river the other night? The memory widened his smile as he closed his eyes and relived it—the damp softness of Maria's skin, the wet slickness of her thick hair, the subtle scent of her, the taste of her lips...

"Captain Mallory."

Jack awoke from his unexpected doze and the delicious dream into which he had fallen. Damn the intruder. He scowled and shaded his eyes, squinted up at the vaguely familiar shape of Ethan Castle. The man wore his usual careworn expression and in his hand he held a letter.

# CHAPTER 27

Jack threw the letter in Ketch's face and demanded, "What in hell is the meaning of this?"

Unmoved, Ketch glanced at the paper that had fallen into his breakfast. The others at the kitchen house table—Dell, Rogers, and Smith—uneasily shifted their attention between the two men.

"Best take our leave, lads," Rogers urged.

He and Dell swiped up their plates and made a hasty exit through the front door. Smith, however, remained behind and waved Rose and the rest of the kitchen workers outside.

Oblivious to the others' movements, Jack snapped at Ketch, "Can you not read?"

With infuriating recalcitrance Ketch picked up the note and read it—a slow, laborious process, though the missive contained only four sentences written in Ezra Archer's precise hand.

Jack did not wait for him to finish. "Is this why you're here? Why you've been here all along?"

Ketch's brown eyes clouded to black, like nightfall suddenly upon a lifeless landscape.

"You're not here for Helen, you lying son of a bitch," Jack continued. "You're here for Archer; his eyes and ears."

"Like hell."

"Then why does he insist I take you with me aboard the *Prodigal*?"

"He wants to make sure you keep yer bargain."

"And you're to ensure that?"

"That's what he thinks."

"What he thinks?" Jack wanted to kick the chair out from under the icy bastard.

"He *thinks* I'm goin' with you. But I'm not. Let him believe what he wants."

Smith calmly interceded, "Why aren't you goin', if that's what Archer ordered?" The glance he flashed at Jack urged patience and level-headedness.

"'Cause I don't take orders from him."

"Apparently he thinks you do."

"Mebbe I did, once or twice." Ketch tossed the letter into the center of the table.

Jack seethed at the man's self-control and lack of fear, seeing it more as concealment than self-restraint. Breaking through that wall would require provocation.

"Maybe," Jack said, "that fire was Archer's idea after I threatened him the other day. And maybe he had *you* set it."

Ketch drew in a long draught of air, expanding his thick chest and straightening his back, his eyes enlarging as if a great pressure built up behind them. Jack braced his feet in anticipation of a physical explosion, an advance, but nothing transpired. Perhaps Ketch's cautious self-discipline could be credited to the pain of his wounds, but Jack had a feeling Ketch derived self-containment more from an emotional source than a physical one, a monumental effort, considering his propensity for violence. What motivated such resolve?

"Maybe," Jack continued, "that was Archer's way of sending me a message, to make sure I went through with this. And if Helen had died, Leighlin would have been his. So the fire might have served him in more than one way."

"Mebbe," Ketch said with twitching, tight jaw muscles, "but it wasn't me what set it."

"What else have you done for Archer?"

Ketch said nothing.

"Maybe he was behind Helen's kidnapping. Maybe he wanted Logan dead."

Ketch quickly doused the surprise his eyes betrayed.

To answer Smith's questioning look, Jack explained, "Archer argued with Logan about his refusal to leave Helen when the *Prodigal* was taking Archer's vessels. He even made a remark about replacing Logan with me."

"I didn't kill Logan for Archer," Ketch growled. "I wanted him dead for what he did to me kin and for lettin' you come here."

"Then why not just kill Logan here? Surely you had the opportunity. But that might have put suspicion on Archer, wouldn't it? After all, he would financially benefit from it; others undoubtedly know that. But if Logan's death occurred anonymously at sea, all the better for Archer. That's why you lured Logan to sea by kidnapping Helen."

"I don't give a damn about Archer. I just wanted Logan dead, like you did."

"Then why didn't you just kill him here?"

Ketch glared at him, the fury within growing, as if he were back in that boat with Logan, his pistol aiming. "I didn't want Miss Helen to see."

Jack's fist struck the top of the table; plates and cutlery jumped. "You shot him right in front of her, you lying dog!"

Ketch's chair slammed to the floor behind him as he stood. "Damn yer eyes, she wasn't supposed to be there. The trade in the boats was *your* idea."

"You murdered her father—your own captain, your master, and your mistress's husband—"

"An' Miss Ella would've thanked me for it."

Ketch's words choked Jack into stunned silence. Amazement penetrated his rage, and with numbing shock he realized that he had never considered Ketch's unique relationship with his mother, had never considered Ketch as a possible portal to the truth he so craved. While he had questioned everyone whom he had thought privy to her personal life—the Waterstons, Samuel, Margaret and David Archer—those whom he felt would tell him the truth as far as they knew it, he had not asked the one man who had been physically closer to his mother than anyone else for the past couple of years, both on land and sea. If anyone had overheard any scrap of conversation or comment that may have revealed her true state, if anyone had seen any aversion or fear, it would have been Ketch.

With quiet, measured words he asked, "What do you mean—she would have thanked you?"

Ketch hesitated, and Jack—terrified that he would not explain—took a step forward, ready to shake the response from him if necessary.

"Are you telling me my mother wanted Logan dead?"

Ketch stared in stony, rueful silence.

In one seamless move, Jack swiped a knife from the table and drove Ketch back against the wall. With one hand he pressed the blade against his neck while the other clamped onto the man's injured arm. Ketch emitted a grunt of pain that, in any other man, would have been a shriek.

"Tell me about my mother and Logan, damn you."

Smith hastened around the table but came no farther, within reach if needed.

Jack forced his body against the bandaged burns on Ketch's chest. Agony gave life to the man's coal-like eyes. "Tell me the truth." He dug his fingers into Ketch's wounded arm. "If you don't, by God, I'll take off your arm."

Although battered, Ketch was taller, heavier, and stronger than Jack, yet he oddly continued to make no use of those advantages.

"Miss Ella never told me her personal business; it wasn't me place to know."

"She didn't need to tell you. What did you see? What did you hear?"

The man winced and nearly moaned when Jack twisted his grip on the arm.

"Jack," Smith said with his usual calm, "mebbe if you step off the cur's tail, he'll be able to tell you what you want to hear."

Ketch's gaze flashed at Smith without gratitude, only more of the tightly restrained choler. Jack hesitated then tested the man by easing the pressure against his chest. Ketch made no move to break free. When Jack slowly stepped back, Ketch slouched with relief and fatigue.

"Tell me. Tell me what you know."

Ketch watched the knife retreat. His breathing gradually returned to normal, its increase previously unnoticed by Jack. With cautious intent, Smith returned to his own seat and—attention never leaving Ketch—resumed his breakfast as if their conversation had been of the most mundane nature. Ketch considered the chair he had knocked over, but the thought of bending over to retrieve it must have either been too much or flew against caution, so he slipped his swathed and slathered frame onto the chair Dell had occupied.

In a drained voice he began, "Once...Miss Ella was called to Wildwood to see Mrs. Archer who was sickly. The Captain was sick at the time, too, so he let me take Miss Ella upriver. He'd never done that afore—let her leave Leighlin without 'im, I mean." He paused as if to regain strength and reached for a cup.

Impatiently, fingers flexing against the handle of the knife, Jack waited for him to drink.

"Miss Ella was happy to be off on her own. Like a wee lass, she was; like her daughter, chatterin' away. But, after we visited Mrs. Archer, she didn't talk much no more. Somethin' had upset her powerful, like. Set her a-cryin'."

"Something that had happened at Wildwood?"

"I dunno. But she started actin' right strange afore we got back to Leighlin. Told me to fetch Miss Helen down to the landing, not to let no one see me do it neither."

"Why did she want you to fetch Helen?"

"She just said I was to take 'em downriver."

"Did you?"

"Never got away from the dock. The Captain smoked Miss Ella's plan and dragged hisself down to the landing with Defoe. Would've done for me sure if not for Miss Ella."

"Did Logan hurt her?"

"Kept her locked up in the house, first with him while he was still sick abed, then for another day by herself."

Jack leaned against the table, heart racing with hope. "So she had tried to escape him?"

"Mebbe."

"She was held against her will? She had no feelings for the man?"

Some of the old loyalty to Logan still lingered deep in Ketch's gaze, or was it a shadow of shame for having murdered Helen's father? "I dunno what she felt. All I can say is somethin' happened that day what made her want to run. But afterwards…never again. She went back to her old self, bein' a good mother to Miss Helen and a good wife. She seemed…content enough."

The back door of the kitchen house opened, and Helen's excited voice blared in conversation with Maria. A baby's mewl blended with the racket. The three men turned as Maria and Helen appeared, Rose's baby in Maria's arms, tiny dark limbs jerking with energy. Maria's curious gaze went first to Jack then to the others then to the abandoned settings at the table. Helen, ignorant of the tension, ran to her brother with an announcement.

"I told Maria that I get to sail with you when you get married!"

"Married?" the word spluttered from Smith's stuffed mouth.

"Where's Rose?" Maria asked.

"Smitty sent her and the others out." Jack faltered then gathered strength to continue, "A message came from Archer. I have to leave straight away."

Helen's happiness faded like the sun behind a smothering cloud. Weakly optimistic, she asked, "To get married?"

Jack tore his gaze from Maria's stricken face and crouched before his sister, frowning. "Not yet, Helen. I have to do a favor for Mr. Archer first. But I promise when I get back we'll have the wedding."

"But I don't want you to leave. You just got back."

"I don't want to leave either. But I must. Maria will be here with you."

"Uncle Smitty, too?"

"No, I'm afraid he'll be coming with me."

"Aye," said Smith. "I gotta make sure he don't run off on his betrothed."

"Are you going, too, Mr. Ketch?"

Any hint of pain now buried, Ketch replied, "No, Miss Helen; I'm stayin' with you."

She slipped her arms around Jack's neck and held fast, pleaded in his ear, "Can't I come with you? I won't be no trouble. I promise."

"I know." He kissed her cheek. "But this is not a journey for a child."

She squeezed him to near suffocation. "Why do you always leave? Everyone always leaves."

"I'll come back as quick as I can. Now...don't cry. Please, Helen..." But there was no stopping the tears or the way her fingers kneaded his flesh. Bearing her sorrow was nigh impossible after suffering through Ketch's revelation. "After this is over, I promise I won't leave you again. Do you hear? Please don't cry..."

Rose appeared in the front doorway, tentative, her sympathetic attention upon Helen. Maria handed the baby to her then returned to Helen. When she reached for the child, Jack shook his head and stood up with his sister in his arms.

"Smitty, gather our things. I'll meet you at the landing." He looked into Helen's soggy face. "Will you help Uncle Smitty for me? If you do, you can come with me in the boat downriver as far as the lower landing."

Smith shoveled the last of his breakfast into his mouth and snatched up a couple of biscuits to take with him. "Come now, young miss," he cheerily said with his cheeks full. "Bear a hand."

Helen's fingers absently played with Jack's collar. He kissed her salty cheek and whispered, "Go on, then."

The tears still came, but the prospect of going with him in the boat retarded the flow; no doubt she still had plans to change his mind. With that hope in her blue eyes, she nodded, and he set her down. She moped after Smith.

With a final glance at Ketch's unmoved, sullen form, Jack took Maria's hand and led her to the porch. The slave women sadly regarded him as they returned inside; he did not try to fool himself that they cared about his impending departure; no, their emotion was for Helen.

Jack settled upon the top step with Maria close to him, their hands still clasped. For a long moment he stared off toward the river which would soon take him away from everything he loved, but he could not focus upon the departure; Ketch's words distracted him still, even with

Helen's tears wetting his shirt. So much yet still so little. Hope and despair battered him. The fact that his mother would not abandon Helen at least confirmed that his sister had been a major factor in her decisions. Was Helen the only factor? Or had memories of her son somehow influenced her rash actions that day?

He shared Ketch's revelation with Maria, and her hand held his even stronger as she listened.

"That seems to leave little doubt," she said when he had concluded. "She wanted to leave Logan."

"But why then? What made her want to run after all that time?"

"It sounds as if that was her only chance."

Jack frowned. "But why didn't she run *before* going to Wildwood? Why go there *then* try to escape?"

"Ketch said she was happy on the trip to Wildwood. So something must have happened there that made her take such a chance."

Jack put his arm around her and drew her even tighter against him, sought her strength, grateful that he could confide in her once again. "When I was last at Wildwood, Mrs. Archer invited me to come back to talk with her about my mother. I got a sense that she wants to tell me something; I've had that feeling since the first time I met her."

Maria smiled hopefully and kissed him. "When you get back, we'll go. Maybe she can help you understand what happened that day."

"Aye, when I get back..." He studied her beautiful face which the morning sun burnished to a pleasing glow. "Then—with my debt to Archer repaid—perhaps I'll feel we're safe, but for now, while I'm gone, if something were to happen, if you don't feel safe here, I want you to go to the *Fortune*. Angus should have her off the coast any day now. I'm sure you could find some of the lads in town to take you off, you and Helen."

"What does Archer want you to do this time?"

His frown deepened, and he debated yet again about revealing his dread over the mission, but it was a burden he could no longer bear alone. "Archer wants me to intercept a vessel bound for Barbados. I'm to kill all on board and destroy the vessel."

"Why? Whose vessel is it?"

Jack shifted to face her, both of her hands in his. How he longed to stay and instead flee this place as his mother had tried, to leave his debt to Archer behind and start anew on his own terms. But what resources would he have to provide for his family other than a return to piracy?

"He wouldn't tell me whose vessel it is, but...Margaret told me her father-in-law and husband would be leaving soon for Barbados."

"But they were just married. Surely her husband won't leave right after the wedding."

"He wants her to go, but she's remaining behind to care for her mother."

Cold realization spread across Maria's face, and she whispered, "So you think it's the Wylders' vessel that Archer wants you to take?"

"Aye. But you can't breathe a word of this to anyone. If things go wrong—"

"Dear God, Jack... You can't do this—"

"There's no way to deceive Archer. If the Wylders return alive, there's no telling what he'll do. He could have me arrested, and we know what that will lead to. After I'm dead he could expose Logan's piracy, and Helen could lose all rights to Leighlin. She would be left with no family, no means. He could destroy us all."

"Then let's leave together, the three of us, now," she said almost desperately.

Jack's gaze reached beyond her to the remains of Leighlin House. "My mother forfeited her freedom for me, then for Helen. If we run, if I take Helen from here, I'll have forsaken all my mother did to ensure Helen's comfort and future. What can I offer her elsewhere? I'm a wanted man. Here in this wilderness there's a chance to safely start over. Archer claims that if I follow through with all this, he'll turn Leighlin over to me, that I'll be guardian of Helen's future. He will protect me from the authorities if need be, like he protected Logan."

"But can you trust Archer? I mean, what if he *was* behind the fire?" Her voice trailed off. "Dear God, what if Margaret finds out? And David?"

Jack studied the distant river out near the bend, thought again of their first night together. He could not take the chance to defy Archer; he could not endanger their future here. He had promised his mother that he would take care of Helen, but never had he thought it would entail something so sinister. Would his mother really want him to do these things to guarantee her daughter's fortune and future? He shook his head. If only he knew what she really wanted. If only he had had more time with her before the end.

Maria touched his face, brushed his loose hair back from his ear, sent a bolt of painful desire through him and a fear of never seeing her again. "We'll find a way out," she murmured.

This was why he loved her. Just like the day in his cabin aboard the *Prodigal* after he had first been reunited with his mother and all sorts of uncertainties and questions had battered him into a powerless lump, Maria was there with her calm confidence to soothe him and ground him like nothing and no one else could. She did not even need to say a word. It was a healing gift she had, as Smith had said. It was her very nature. And he would not be without it ever again.

#

That night Maria could not sleep, troubled by fresh loneliness and newfound dread brought on by Jack's revelations about both his mission and his concerns about Ezra Archer. Beside her in bed, Helen lay—Howard the bear clutched close again—finally asleep after endless talk of weddings and sisterhood, of sailing with her brother and of her life aboard the *Medora* with her parents. Maria had gladly indulged her to keep their thoughts from the memory of Jack and Smith gliding away from the lower landing and down the Ashley. The image made her bury her face in Jack's pillow, to breathe in the scent of him, her whole being aching, tears not far away.

An hour later she extracted herself from the small bed without awakening Helen. The house was so quiet without the racket of Smith's snoring. Dell and Rogers slept in the small back room, but they were distant enough that their light snores did not reach beyond their closed door.

She padded out of her room to go to the kitchen but halted at the open door to Ketch's room. With Jack gone, she had hoped Ketch would return to sleep here, for she felt his closeness would give Helen comfort; the girl had not slept well since Leighlin House had burned. And—Maria had to admit—with Jack gone, Ketch's nearby presence would ease her own nagging anxieties. Even in his battered state, Maria knew he was still a force to be reckoned with should anyone try to harass them. Yet what exactly did she fear? If Archer had been behind the fire in order to threaten Jack, he must know now that Jack was carrying out his orders, that he had no other reason to menace Leighlin. Thinking of Helen trapped in the burning house, though, still made Maria shudder.

She grabbed up one of Rose's old wraps, draped it around her shoulders, and checked on Helen to make sure she was still asleep before hurrying through the front door and into the night.

When she arrived at the ruins of Leighlin House, the new shutters on Ketch's old chamber windows were closed. Besides the shutters, he had ordered his gang of slaves to jury-rig a roof of canvas taken from the *Nymph*'s extra sailcloth. Once Maria passed through the lower level's rear entry, she found that a new door completed Ketch's living quarters. She paused there, ear to the wood, listened through the noise of night creatures. Nothing to be detected. Because of the time she had walked in upon Ketch mutilating himself, she hesitated in slight trepidation before knocking, hoping he was not drunk this time.

"Ketch?"

No response, not even after strident knocks and demanding words. So she swallowed her apprehension and opened the door. Carefully she stuck her head inside and spoke again. Nothing. No dark shape upon the pine straw tick, no glow of white bandages.

Ketch was gone.

# CHAPTER 28

Even in the darkest of nights, Ketch could easily find his way from Wildwood's lower landing to the manor house—he had done so several times before for a variety of reasons. But this time the slim, curving moon provided as much illumination for him as if he carried a lantern, and so he had no need to rely on more base instincts. Whenever he thought he heard something foreign among the night sounds, he stopped, not crouching but instead standing stock still to blend with the scrub trees and brush through which this path wound. He could have taken the small lane from the landing along the shoreline and then toward the house direct, but he wanted complete concealment. Of course no one should be stirring at this time of night, but he would take no chances. Though the moon was but a fledgling, it was enough for someone to identify a one-armed man moving familiarly within Wildwood's borders. By the time he would leave, the incoming clouds on the edge of night would overpower the moon.

He could not walk as quickly as his demons demanded, thanks to the fresh pain in both his arm and chest stirred up by that damned boy. Maria and Willis had remarked upon the wounds' obvious irritation when they had most recently treated them, but he did not indulge their prodding questions and comments. And to add further annoyance, the stump of his arm had taken to itching, an itch he could do nothing about right now, for his hand was clasped around the handle of a pitchfork. A burlap bag banged against his hip as he moved, the contents muffled by rags.

South of Archer's flanker, he spent several long minutes hunkered near the edge of the tree line, staring at the dark building. His breathing increased in anticipation of quenching the rage that Leighlin's fire had rekindled. Archer often stayed up late. Sleepless bastard; his conscience had much to keep him awake. Yet now the two-story building was nothing but a blacker blur in the night, dwarfed by the taller, broader outline of the main house beyond it. No lights there either. David Archer, his cousin, aunt, sister, and mother would be fast asleep. He thought of Margaret and scoffed at what a fool Seth Wylder was to leave such a diamond behind, gone to Barbados...gone to his death at Mallory's hands if the boy did not fuck it up.

At last he moved, hunched low, and in a trice he was at the flanker's rear door. There he paused to listen for any sound from inside, then—hearing nothing except the insects around him—he cautiously opened the door and entered. Again he waited, as silent and unmoving as the furniture in the parlor before him. The evening was warm and humid, the flanker even warmer. Ketch's perspiration was not from anxiety about what he planned to do but rather from the pain of his wounds, irritated to a greater degree by the short journey up the river. He had allowed only a small dose of the laudanum from Maria, for he could not afford to have his wits dulled tonight.

His eyes adjusted, placed all the objects in the central room, located the closed door to Archer's bedchamber at the front of the flanker. On his left was the small bedchamber where Archer's constant servant, Jeremiah, slept—an old man with hearing dulled by age. But Ketch moved to neither bedchamber. Instead he leaned the pitchfork near the door and glided on bare feet to Archer's office on his right. Once inside he moved to the desk, to the drawer where a pistol lay with shot and powder, always ready.

Weapon in hand, Ketch crept into the servant's room. Jeremiah's pale nightshirt seemed like an empty garment in the darkness, his black skin blending with the gloom. Two steps took Ketch to the bed where he placed the gun barrel at the man's nose, ready to use his elbow if needed to pin him. But there was no need, for the minute Ketch's weight sank against him Jeremiah awoke, eyes instantly wide and white, frozen with terror. Ketch knew the servant feared the man who held the pistol more than the loaded pistol itself.

"You say a word, old man, I'll blow yer damned head off, hear?"

The gray-haired Negro nodded.

"Now get up. Nice and easy. Light that there lamp; not too bright, mind. We're goin' to wake yer master."

Inside Archer's bedchamber, a gentle river breeze blew in through the windows, hinting at rain to come. The faintest rumble of thunder slipped inside. The thin moonlight waxed and waned behind the incoming drift of clouds. Archer lay on his back in the large bed, quietly snoring, veiled behind mosquito netting.

Ketch poked the pistol between Jeremiah's bony shoulder blades and whispered in his ear, "Put that lamp down on this table. Now move slow and take this here sack off o' me."

As the bag came free and gave a small clank, Archer awoke. He

292

hesitated, as if wondering whether or not the indistinct images before him were from a dream. Then he started to sit up, to demand an explanation, until the mosquito netting was yanked away and he saw the glint of the pistol turned toward him.

"You call out and I'll splatter yer brains against that there fancy headboard."

"What is the meaning of this?" Archer hissed. "I ordered you aboard the *Prodigal*. Has she not sailed?" He glanced toward the door, perhaps expecting Jack Mallory to appear as a part of this invasion.

Coldly Ketch ordered the trembling servant, "You take a couple o' them rags from the poke. Stuff one in his mouth and tie t'other 'round his head so he can't make a peep, hear?"

Terrified, Jeremiah looked between the two men, obviously deciding the worst of the two to offend.

"Do it," Ketch growled.

Jeremiah shuffled around the bed, gaze cast downward. "I's sorry, Master. I's sorry..."

"Leave this house at once, Ketch," Archer demanded. "Damn your blood! I will have you in chains, and Mallory, too, if he is responsible for this outrage."

"Tie it tight, damn you. Tight! But don't choke him to death." Ketch kept the pistol aimed at Archer as the older man's tirade continued behind the gag. "Now," he ordered the planter, "get undressed."

When Archer refused, Ketch fully cocked the pistol. This convinced him to remove his nightshirt, then with foolish modesty he held his bedclothes over his nakedness. Ketch relished the hate and concern that stirred in Archer's glistening eyes.

"You," Ketch said to Jeremiah. "C'mere." He kicked the bag toward the servant. "Pull out them irons. You get him rolled onto his belly then chain each arm and each leg to the corner posts. Understand?"

As Archer challenged him through the rag, Ketch viewed the planter with macabre satisfaction and reckoned that even in Archer's nightmares he had never expected to see this day—his own slave chaining him up like one of them. Jeremiah shook so badly in his task that the chains rattled. Archer winced as the slave extended his left arm, for the movement no doubt caused discomfort in his recently-broken collar bone.

Once Archer was completely immobilized, Jeremiah looked at Ketch from beneath his eyebrows, his cornstalk body bent, eyes pleading for mercy.

"C'mere."

"P—please, Mr. Ketch, suh—"

"C'mere, damn yer black hide. I don't got all night."

Fear paralyzed Jeremiah, and tears coursed down his leathery cheeks. With an impatient curse, Ketch stalked around the bed. Jeremiah fell to his knees, hands clasped in supplication. Ketch set the pistol out of reach on a bedside table, then in one fluid motion he wrapped his arm around the man's neck and snapped it. As the body slumped to the floor, Archer made an infuriated bellow against the gag, the chains rattling.

Ketch considered Archer's pale form. "I just gave him the freedom he never would've got from the likes o' you."

Retrieving the pitchfork from the anteroom, Ketch brandished it where Archer could easily see it, drawing further protests and threats against the rag.

Leaning close to his victim's ear, Ketch rumbled low and menacing, "I know you had that fire set, you son of a bitch. And now yer goin' to pay for it."

He could smell the man's escalating panic as Archer breathed faster against the mattress, all contributing to the swell of Ketch's own agitation, the driving need for vengeance and release.

"Leighlin won't never belong to you." Ketch's eyes narrowed. "Only a coward would've tried to kill that child."

Archer vehemently shook his head, but Ketch said nothing more. With lethal wantonness, he shoved the wooden handle into the screaming man's rectum, again and again until the blood upon it came away black. Archer's outcries against the gag fueled Ketch's savagery. No more bravado from the planter, no more curses or threats. In the end only quiet sobs and muted pleas. Ketch thought of his mother's sobs after Sophia's death when his stepfather had deserted them. He always saw his victims as that selfish, murdering, whoreson brute, each and every one of them, each and every time. Perhaps one day he would have spilled enough blood to purge away the man's memory and the memory of all those who had abused him.

Ketch now stood upon the bed; the frame protested his weight as he spoke, quiet and measured: "Logan didn't want to leave Miss Helen when she was sick, when Mallory first started plunderin' yer vessels." He reversed the pitchfork, its tines befouled with horse manure. "But 'cause o' you he had to leave her." He aligned the implement's metal points with Archer's shoulder blades. "'Cause o' you he took Miss Ella to her death, like he took me brother."

Slowly Ketch drove the tines just far enough to penetrate Archer's flesh. The man stopped squirming and froze in defensive, horrified rigidity. The muffled shrieks blended with Ketch's black memories, but as he continued—pierce, withdraw, move, pierce anew—those memories were gradually enveloped and eradicated by his victim's suffering until at last Archer lost consciousness.

When the length of Archer's body was punctured and bloody, Ketch's energy began to slip, not only because of his wounds but from the usual release that his methods reaped. Oddly enough it was like the animal release he remembered from his first tryst with a Southwark girl, when she had pushed him off her afterward and he had lain there like a dumb beast, sweaty, spent, and stupefied. His first time...and his last before the Plymouth trollop, after which he was doomed to deviations.

When Ketch slid from the bed, his legs nearly gave way. He caught himself against the mattress, paused there to regain his wits and strength, the world retreating back to order, to the sights and sounds that belonged in the flanker, the flashbacks retreating once again, though never for long. Thunder rolled louder now, like loose shot upon the deck of a ship, and distant lightning flared out over the river. He stared at Archer for some time. If left this way, he would die eventually, if not from internal bleeding then from a long, slow death from infection. But Ketch could not enjoy that thought for any length of time, for he knew he could not chance Archer remaining alive.

So he waited—half braced against the bed—until some of his energy had returned, and then he struggled up with the pitchfork. The task would not be easy with just the one arm, especially with its current shortcomings. So he gave himself another minute as he stood over Archer on the bed, breathing evenly in and out, pulling everything left in him together. Then he wiped the sweat from his palm a final time, gripped the pitchfork anew, and drove it through Archer's neck.

# CHAPTER 29

The Rat was the first Prodigal whom Jack and Smith found in Charles Town. Together they gathered the others whoring in town and set off with the tail end of the tide to find the *Prodigal* in the offing. By then, the carousers were sober enough to comprehend their captain when Jack outlined their mission to find the *Liberty*. Fortunately there were no dissenters.

"As long as this don't take too long," the Rat grumbled. "I gots me a lass in town what wants me to come back and make her an honest woman.".

"That'll take a miracle, sure," Sullivan laughed, "if she be the one I saw you with."

The men simply viewed the pursuit as yet another caper, like kicking up dust in Charles Town, especially when Jack told them the brigantine was lightly armed and had a small crew. A couple of well-placed shots would bring them to in no time, and then whatever was on board was theirs for the taking before they destroyed her.

One man, however, saw fit to express unhappiness. While the others went back to their duties, getting the *Prodigal* underway, Hanse approached Jack, hat in hand, an apprehensive, glum look upon his middle-aged face, which seemed more careworn than the last time Jack had seen him.

"Beg pardon, Captain, but after this latest business of your'n is over...well, I've been wondering if you're planning to finally let me go."

Jack gave him a stony stare, said nothing.

Undaunted, Hanse continued his petition with a practiced rush: "Maybe this brigantine you're after will even have a carpenter of her own, a man without a family and children to provide for. I'm ashamed to put someone else in my stead, but—damn it—I've done everything you've asked of me...sir," he added with great difficulty. "I've caused no trouble. I'd like to be returned to my family. They need me."

"I can't take the *Liberty*'s carpenter, even if they have one."

"Why not?" Nervous sweat had cropped up along his receding

hairline.

"You heard me tell the lads—there's to be nothing left of the brigantine or her crew."

"But...just one man. Couldn't you just—"

"Mr. Hanse, I've nothing more to say on this matter."

The carpenter stared at him, battered by anger and despair yet somehow he managed to hold himself together. Jack could barely look at him, for he did not want to show the sympathy he felt. He understood all too well the intense desire to be with loved ones, not bent upon the pursuit and suffering of others. But he held Hanse's gaze, unblinking, knowing by the determination in those green eyes that ultimately Hanse must never be allowed to leave the *Prodigal*.

#

The heavy cudgel—wielded from shadow—knocked the Newgate wardsman to the floor of the punishment chamber, and he lay half-senseless as Jack swarmed over him, breathing hard, excited and terrified all at once. With shaking hands and ready rope, Jack bound the man's hands and ankles, gagged him with a filthy rag. He did not have much time; his bribe had secured him this room for only ten minutes. But that was all he needed as he made quick use of his borrowed knife. The stone walls and the gag muffled his victim's screams as he exacted his revenge. Then...finally...stillness; no sound, no movement, just wide lifeless eyes that seemed to follow Jack as he fled the Bilbows, trembling and retching.

#

Jack stood upon the quarterdeck as the *Prodigal* settled on the starboard tack, moving once again away from the American coastline like a kite skittering beneath the fair, cloudless cyaneous dome. She lay over at a striking angle, and a heave of the log revealed an exhilarating nine knots. But Jack took little pleasure in the moment, for the wind in the rigging seemed only to echo the screams from the Newgate nightmare that had awoken him that morning. He tried to push the images away and instead focused on the men before him as they moved efficiently in their duties.

Debauchery in Charles Town had obviously done the Prodigals some good, for they were a cheerful lot—morning banter drifted aft, laughter, jokes...mainly crude. Lines were belayed and coiled down brisk and neat, though Willie Emerick's wheedling tongue made it plain that the foremast men far outdistanced the mainmast men in anything seamanlike. This, of course, led to spirited verbal sparring. After one last glance at the set of the sails—fore course, topsails, and topgallants—Jack turned away, confident the men's exchange would remain strictly benign and not lead to competitive blows.

He placed both hands on the taffrail and gazed far along the trailing wake where the whiteness eventually faded to the endless blue of its origin, where seabirds wheeled and glided, called and settled.

Along with the nightmare, thoughts of Maria had also cost him sleep. He missed her as never before, a loneliness almost greater than he could bear. He felt as if he had left a part of himself at Leighlin— the strongest part.

New doubts accosted him, encouraged by the Newgate memory. What if Joe Dowling was right and he could not forsake this sea-bound life? He thought of the men he had killed and those he had ordered killed; all to find his mother, he had told himself. But what about the men in that convoy and those on the *Alliance*? Maybe a criminal was all he really was, otherwise why would he be here today, hunting down the Wylders? He did not like to remember Peter Wylder visiting him that day in the warehouse, did not like to remember the man's dignity and grief. Instead he clung to what Smith had said last night when his friend heard his laments: "Yer here 'cause yer payin' a debt, Jackie. You know that. That's all. Think o' that and forget the nonsense Joe Dowling put in yer head."

How far away were they from their quarry? When would they catch them? The *Liberty* had about a nine-hour head start, but he was confident the *Prodigal* would overtake her. After all, the *Liberty* would have no reason to crack on while the *Prodigal* had every reason in the world. Whatever sail the *Prodigal* could bear, she bore last night while, no doubt, the *Liberty* reduced sail, creeping along the coastline, on shorter tacks than the *Prodigal*. The same impatient anxiety that had dogged him during the pursuit of the *Alliance* haunted him now, but this time dread entered the mix. Although he wanted to catch the *Liberty* as quickly as he could and be quit of this damnable business, he shrank from the encounter while at the same time cursing his weakness.

Jack pushed free of his warring emotions and stepped forward over the relieving tackle and up to the binnacle to check the heading.

Samuel, at the tiller with Smith, cleared his throat and said, "So when's the wedding, Captain?"

298

Jack turned in surprise to find Samuel grinning at him. He leaned his elbows on the binnacle, studied Smith's red face and sheepish smile amidst his dark beard. "Smitty, even if your life depended on it, I don't think you could keep a secret for long."

Pretending to be wounded, Smith mumbled, "Why, I only told Samuel."

Jack smiled and shook his head.

"Why the secret anyways?"

"I don't want to bring any bad luck down upon it. Once this is all over, I'll be happy to shout it from the masthead, but right now…"

"So be it," said Smith. "You have me solemn oath. Not another word. But Samuel here…well, I can't be held responsible for his waggin' tongue."

Samuel offered Jack his hand. "Congratulations, Captain." He exchanged a knowing look with Smith, added, "Good luck." They both chuckled.

Jack shot them a falsely rebuking glance. "After Maria and I are married—when all this is over—I was hoping you'd come back to Leighlin with me, Samuel. With Defoe gone, I could use your knowledge of Leighlin. I know nothing about growing…anything. David Archer has offered his help, but I'd like someone to be there with me all the time. You know rice growing. You taught Logan; I need you to teach me. I don't want to rely on the Archers, and God knows I can't go to anyone else until Long Arm Jack is forgotten."

"I will not be your overseer, Captain. I will not hold myself above the others."

"I'm not asking you to. I just want your help with the crops." He hesitated. "And I think having you there would help me with the slaves. They know you; they trust you; Logan told me as much. I need someone to…bridge that gap."

"What about Willis?"

"Willis has no connection with them, nor does he want one." He paused. "It would mean a lot to Maria and Helen to have you there as well."

Samuel shifted his weight and rubbed his jaw. "It will not be easy to see the house gone."

"We'll rebuild. The work has already commenced. We need all the help we can get."

Samuel frowned, his attention going to the taut sails for avoidance. His tongue moistened his chapped lips.

"Samuel. I'm not trying to be Logan. I want to be at Leighlin for

299

Helen, not because I have any delusions about replacing Logan and changing everything about the plantation. I'm no farmer—don't even have a desire to be one—but if Leighlin can provide Helen with a stable home in a place her parents believed to be growing and vital, then I want to learn all I can...from the ones who know the most, so I can provide her—and my family—with a good future."

"What about the *Prodigal*?"

"I'll leave that up to the lads after this is over. I could keep her to transport Leighlin's goods with the lads kept on as crew. Or if they feel the need to still rove, the *Prodigal* will be theirs."

Samuel's frown deepened. "I would like to think on it, Captain."

"Very well. No need for an answer today." Jack offered him a satisfied, prompting smile then turned to look up at the fore yard, studied it for a time, let the previous topic die and be swept away with the warm, pleasing wind. "Smitty, I'm thinking we can lay her a bit closer to the wind."

"How so, lad?"

"Something Logan suggested to me." He stepped around the binnacle, hands behind his back as his gaze trailed up the fore shrouds. "If we slack off the truss ropes and cant the weather yardarm down, hauling the catharpins tighter, we can brace her up more fully." He looked back at Smith whose knowing blue eyes were also on the fore yard where it pressed against the shrouds. "And if we rig cross catharpins it will help as well by pulling the forward shroud in and back."

"Ned!" Smith bellowed forward to the boatswain.

Ned Goddard came rolling aft, already having noted his captain's attention upon the rigging. He appeared concerned, perhaps hoping not to endure any criticism. None was warranted, of course; Jack knew Ned had worked hard to refit the brig after the chewing she had taken from the *Alliance*.

"Ned," Smith said with a grin as the big man stepped onto the quarterdeck. "It would appear our young captain here has a job o' work for you..."

#

From the porch of the kitchen house, where she sat sewing a play dress for Helen, Maria occasionally glanced toward the men working upon the house. Helen was rummaging about the wreckage, trying to help, though against Willis's wishes; Maria could hear the man scolding her about something even now.

Most of the bricks had been cleared away, those that could be salvaged stacked beyond the foundation. Ketch sorted the last bricks from a wheelbarrow that one of the slaves had brought over to him—a slow process for a one-armed man but a man nonetheless who did not shirk his duties in Leighlin's recovery. He was shirtless, skin shining with sweat, the broad bandage around his chest no longer white. Maria frowned. Of course, in hopes of keeping the bandage clean, she had instructed him not to remove his shirt, but either his stubbornness or the power of the sun had encouraged him to disobey.

She had not known when Ketch had returned to Leighlin but had found him at table that morning with the other men, disheveled and sullen as he ravenously ate. When she had offered to change his bandages, he grumbled something and disappeared, not giving her time to determine if what she saw on his sleeve was blood. His brusqueness had unexpectedly hurt her. She still felt ashamed for her behavior the other day, so she looked forward to the few minutes when she changed his bandages or helped him with some small task that he could not accomplish with one hand. By offering him those kindnesses she hoped to reverse some of her damage.

When he refused her attention that morning, she felt particularly useless. None of the men—black or white—would hear of her working in the sun clearing the debris from the house, as if she already bore the dignity and privilege of matriarch. Sewing seemed meaningless compared to the monumental task of righting the destruction that lay a stone's throw away. She would let their chivalry stand for today, but tomorrow she vowed she would join them regardless of any protests.

The gurgles of Rose's baby in a crib just inside the kitchen drew Maria's attention. She smiled at the contented sound and listened to Rose's happy responses as the slave paused in her work baking peach pies. Maria considered her own flat belly and wondered when she would bear a child for Jack. The prospect thrilled her, bringing impatience to her fingers as she resumed sewing. Perhaps one day she would be sewing for their baby.

How dreadfully she missed Jack. Though they had been together only a short time, she felt incomplete without him. She had barely slept, and waking without him next to her, sleeping the way he did on his back with his mouth slightly open—somehow an endearing picture in its vulnerability—left her lonely and hollow. She prayed for his quick return as well as for some opportunity to present itself so he would not have to go through with Archer's plan. More than anything else in life, she wanted him back here, never to leave again. They had already foolishly wasted time that could have been spent together, and the very thought of him perhaps running afoul of something once they found Wylder's vessel made the warmth of the day slip away and leave her chilled.

After several more minutes of squinting at her needle and thread, Maria paused again, frustrated with the work. Her gaze went to the river, and she thought of Jack's departure, of Helen frantically calling and returning his wave.

A slice of white sails drew Maria's attention upriver where Wildwood's shallop ghosted into view. She watched and waited until she was certain the vessel would touch at Leighlin's landing instead of continuing downriver with the ebb. Even at this great distance she recognized David where he stood in the bows, dressed darkly. Elizabeth was not with him, just the Negro boatmen who plied the Ashley for their master. Whatever had compelled him here must be an urgent matter, for why else would he arrive, unannounced and uninvited? Fear quickly displaced her initial pleasure at seeing him. Had he somehow discovered the purpose of Jack's current mission for his father? Maria set aside her sewing and hurried toward the river.

The *Nymph* was nearly loaded with the day's cargo to go to Charles Town—wood and hides as well as fruits and vegetables. The ketch lay against the opposite side of the dock from Wildwood's vessel, the slaves busy in their work, some greeting the visiting boatmen. When they saw Maria, their words fell off, and they removed their straw hats.

David came down the dock to meet her. What she saw in his eyes staggered her. Before she could recover, she noticed that he wore a black armband, and—equally disturbing and unusual—his open coat revealed a pistol.

"Maria, you need not have come all the way down here in this heat. I was on my way to see you."

"What's happened? Your armband—"

"Come, let us sit in the shade."

They moved to the tree line between the landing and the ponds, and sat together on the bench where she had once sat with his father. Above them the breeze rustled the birch leaves. David's bereft eyes lifted to hers, and in that moment the crisis that reflected there took on added weight and etched a line across his forehead.

"My father has been murdered."

Maria gaped at him.

"The servants found him this morning when they took his breakfast to him. He and his valet, Jeremiah, were both killed." His jaw clenched, and he closed his eyes, shaking his head as if to rid himself of the images. "My father was…he had been tortured."

In shock, Maria stared out at the marsh across the river, at a distant red-winged blackbird poised upon a wavering reed, somehow mesmerizing and important. Archer…dead… Jack was free…as free as that bird…

"I will spare you the details, but suffice it to say I believe wholeheartedly that Ketch is responsible."

Her attention snapped back to him, and she realized he was genuinely distressed by his father's demise. Surely he had every right to dance a jig, but of course he would not, and she could tell that he had no such inclination. Perhaps he did feel some sort of relief, yet she knew him well enough to know such emotion would be countered by shame.

"Why would Ketch kill your father?" she stammered weakly. "Have you considered perhaps it was one of your slaves?"

"I am familiar with Ketch's handiwork. And no slave would have killed poor old Jeremiah. Only an animal would do such a thing."

"But Ketch has worked for your father before. He told Jack that he—"

"You are looking for logic and reason, Maria; with Ketch there are none." He stared at her hands in her lap as if he longed to touch them. "My mother's health was tenuous before this. She is prostrate with grief." He seemed to notice her diverted frown. "I know this is difficult for someone outside of my family to understand—someone who has only seen what you have seen of my father—but he was still my father and husband to my mother. They had a long history. For him to die…this way…well, no one deserved that, not even my father. What type of son would I be if my mother knew I did nothing to bring about justice?"

"I'm sorry for your loss, David—for your family's loss."

"I am on my way to town to see to my father's affairs and to make arrangements for the funeral. I am also fetching Dr. Knight for my mother. She has refused to see a physician for some time, but perhaps now she will allow it." He paused. "I will take Ketch into town with me—in chains, of course—but I would not dream of doing so without Jack's cooperation."

"Ketch isn't here." The words came out in a rush, and she cursed herself for the impulsiveness as well as for the lie. But Jack was free now...now with Archer dead, murdered...and Ketch had been his liberator.

"Do you know where I may find him?"

"I'm afraid I don't. Perhaps he is in town. Willis says he goes there now and then to drink and gamble."

His gaze hardened, and she wondered if he truly believed her. "You will send word should he return to Leighlin." A cold statement, not a question.

"Of—of course."

"Pray do not meddle in this, Maria. He cannot be allowed to continue his evil ways."

David did not linger, and when Maria wished him good-bye, she forced herself to be calm. She remained on the dock until he and the shallop slipped from view around the bend downriver. Then she raced toward the house.

# CHAPTER 30

Maria had never had a compunction to embrace Ketch for any reason, not even after his Herculean attempt to save Helen from the fire. But when she found him seated on the charred grass in the shade of the brick pile, gulping water from a dipper, she felt a wild inclination to do just that, murderer or not.

His coloring did not look quite right; the day's work taxed him particularly hard, no doubt compounded by his lack of sleep last night and the wicked work he had affected. Exactly what had he done to Ezra Archer to put such shadows in David's eyes? Well, truth be told, whatever it was she felt shameful delirium knowing that the manipulating bastard was dead, freeing not only Jack, but herself and David as well. Surely, though, it was disreputable to celebrate even the death of someone like Ezra Archer, especially a death carried out in the way David intimated. She reminded herself that part of her deal with Ketch was that he not harm anyone. Yet with the yoke around Jack's neck now removed, she could not help but rejoice at Ketch's noncompliance.

When Ketch saw her, he struggled to his feet, using the bricks as leverage. Then he reached for his crumpled shirt upon the pile—a silly self-consciousness on his part when she reflected upon how many times she had seen him shirtless. Yet perhaps the gesture was not a misplaced sense of propriety but instead an effort to ward off any rebuke she may have planned for him for removing the shirt and sullying his bandages.

She finished gathering her wits, a monumental effort that she had been perfecting all the way across the sward. Her gaze searched the surrounding scene. "Where's Helen?"

"In the kitchen house," Willis said as he hobbled over and reached for the dipper in the bucket. With an almost accusing lift of an eyebrow, he asked, "What did young Mr. Archer want?"

She would not allow herself to look at Ketch, not while Willis's attention was keen upon her. "He brought news of his father's death."

"Death?" Willis choked on the water. "Ezra Archer? What on

305

earth could kill that old sodomite?"

"They're not certain, but he was found dead this morning."

"Well..." Willis replaced the dipper and wiped his mouth with his hand, watched Maria closely, but she was careful to hide her feelings. He never looked at Ketch, as if the man who stood within inches of him did not exist. And though Maria searched, she detected no suspicion in Willis's eyes. Perhaps if she had used the word murder instead of death he would have reason for suspicion. He continued, "I reckon then your fiancé is wastin' his time doin' whatever it is he's doin' for Archer."

"I know exactly what he's doing, Mr. Willis, and I intend to stop him, as he would want me to do."

"Stop him? Why? What's he about?"

"There's no time to explain; I must leave with the tide, and I'm taking Ketch and Rogers with me...and Helen."

Ketch's stare had been upon her this whole time, and she finally chanced a glance his way. His gaze was steady, unblinking and unreadable.

Willis asked, "Do you think it wise to take Miss Helen?"

"Perhaps not wise, but necessary. After all that's happened to her, I can't leave her." Realizing she had barely been breathing these last few minutes, she drew a long breath. "I'm going to the house to pack some things, Ketch. Find Rogers and meet me at the kitchen house as soon as you can. I've asked them to wait the *Nymph* for us."

#

When Helen heard the news of her inclusion in Maria's journey, she clapped her hands and twirled with joy. While urging the child to grab her bear so they could be on their way, Maria hastily packed.

"Mr. Ketch, we're going to find John so he can marry Maria," the girl chirped to the somber man who stood in the hallway outside Maria's room. "You're coming too, aren't you?"

"Aye," he said flatly, his attention fixed on Maria. "Why don't you go fetch that bear o' your'n, Miss Helen?"

Off the girl skipped.

Maria reached for clean bandages, rolled them around a jar of salve and a jar of sweet oil for Ketch's burns, and then tucked them into a canvas bag. "I've packed laudanum as well," she said, wondering why he had not gone to the landing with Rogers.

"Don't need it."

Frustrated by his continued stubbornness, she paused in her quick movements to look over her shoulder at him. Why did he linger all this time since bringing Rogers to the house for instructions? She turned back to her task, carefully attending to a blue dress she had acquired from Margaret Archer. *Wylder*, she reminded herself bitterly.

"That boy came lookin' for me, didn't he? That's why you want me to go with you."

She hesitated, frowned when she remembered the pain on David's face. "Yes."

"I aim to come back here."

"That might not be possible for you."

"Like hell."

"Damn it, Ketch." She wheeled in exasperation, the various scenarios of the future playing out in her head, battering her with incongruous concern. She hurried to the doorway and peered into the hall to make sure neither Helen nor any of the kitchen staff was near, then she quietly said, "I know what you did. So does David."

"I did nothin'."

"Ketch, for God's sake..." She forced back her emotions. "If you don't leave here, if you come back..."

When she faltered, he said nothing, and like so many times during these past days she could not read what was in his eyes, could not reach beyond the apathy. Her gaze caught on the two scars above his sternum where his collar gaped.

"I know what you did," she pointedly repeated near a whisper. "And, God help me, I'm glad you did it. I'll not see you hang for it."

"Let me worry 'bout that."

"You knew they'd suspect you."

"He burnt Miss Ella's house. He tried to kill Miss Helen."

"How do you know?"

"Archer wanted this land. With Logan gone and Miss Ella...Helen's all that's standin' in his way."

Helen burst from her room, holding up her bear. "I couldn't find him. He was hiding under the bed again. We can go now."

Maria held Ketch's ambivalent gaze a moment longer as the child hopped up and down. Then, for Helen's sake, she produced a smile and gave the child's hair a quick stroke. "Yes, it's time, *osita*."

#

"What if the *Fortune* isn't there?" Rogers asked during their trip down the river.

Maria refused to contemplate that tragic prospect. "Where else

307

would she be?" She tried to sound hopeful as she watched Helen playing amidst the vessel's cargo. "Angus and the others have money to spend in town."

Evening had fallen by the time they reached Charles Town harbor, and the tide was nearly at ebb. A final, distant vessel crossed the bar beyond the mouth of the harbor, the setting sun burnishing the spars and dazzling the sails. It would be another six hours before another ship would leave.

Before the *Nymph* rounded the peninsula, she hove to so Maria, Helen, and Ketch could descend into the yawl that had been towed behind. Rogers remained aboard with the Negro crew to sail the vessel to the wharves. Wildwood's shallop would be docked there amidst the bustle, unloading her cargo. That meant David could be nearby. It would not do for him to see Maria, Helen, or Ketch, so while Rogers went alone to search Charles Town's taverns for any wayward Fortunes, the three remained near the mouth of the Ashley and away from the shipping.

Ketch had said nothing since leaving Leighlin, a common reticence when he was around other men, Maria had noticed. She had never heard him speak many words to anyone except herself or Helen. But now—in the boat—he could say little even if he had wanted to, for Helen carried most of the conversation. Except for her captivity aboard the *Alliance*, the child had not been away from Leighlin since before her bout with yellow fever around the time the *Prodigal* had first arrived in these waters, so now the world seemed brand new to her, and she verbalized every thought and observation she had about anything and everything, ignorant of the adults' tension.

"Can we go into town, Maria? Please? I want to visit Mrs. Waterston and see Robert. She always has sweets for me."

Maria fought off the girl's attempt to persuade her to pull to shore, so Helen then accosted Ketch, but he was equally unmoved. He sat glumly in the stern-sheets, bent slightly forward, legs splayed, oblivious to the child clambering all over the boat who peered down into the waves or splashed her hands and licked the salt from them. Whenever she leaned over the gunwale near him, he took a hold of the hem of her dress to keep her anchored. She laughed with delight when an occasional wave struck the boat abeam and splashed her or when a nearby pelican dove like an ungainly spear.

Maria had never seen Helen so happy, so very child-like, and she found herself almost thankful for Leighlin House burning. It had brought Helen back to them and drove Ketch to rid them of Archer.

Maria frowned at her unfortunate line of thinking and remembered Jack's remark about her having tamed Ketch. No man was tamed who could so willfully murder. She thought of Logan, Defoe, and Archer. All men whom Ketch had served at one time. Were their murders simply calculation? Or were they a perversion, a bloodlust that would always require slaking? How could she ever trust such a man? But then as she watched Ketch again patiently restrain Helen from falling overboard, she realized that—to an extent—she already trusted him. The thought troubled her, for what if she were being a fool about him as David feared? What if her instincts were proven fatally wrong somewhere down the road, perhaps at Jack's expense?

More time passed. The tide had begun to swell the harbor again, climbing slowly up the strand. Helen grew hungry, and after eating a peach, she finally settled on Maria's lap and languidly chattered on about life at sea, about her parents, including tales that incorporated Ketch, an attention that seemed to unsettle the man with Maria looking on from such close proximity. He worked very hard at not being human, Maria reflected, but Helen was very talented at peeling away the veneer, a skill Maria had seen her employ on her father as well as on her brother.

Something besides Helen's humanizing tales, however, was agitating Ketch. Maria recognized it in the way he often moved his feet about, or the way his fingers fiddled with the seam of his dark breeches, or the way his gaze roamed the harbor, his often unblinking eyes now fluttering as if overwhelmed by the evening sun low upon the water. Was it the long wait that irritated him or something else? Could he be concerned about being arrested? No, she decided, otherwise why would he have taken the risk of murdering Archer to begin with?

"Here they come," she said when she spotted the *Fortune*'s boat pulling toward them with Rogers and Joe Dowling. Four others were in the boat as well, but they appeared nearly incapable of sitting, let alone taking up a pair of oars.

Maria hauled the anchor inboard as the other yawl neared. Once abreast, gunwales touching, Hugh Rogers rejoined her.

"What's he doin' here?" Dowling demanded when his bleary eyes recognized Ketch, focusing particularly on his amputation. His protest stirred a couple of his mates, and they peered across as Rogers fended off with an oar.

"He's coming with us." Maria shipped her pair of oars.

"We don't want that damned sodomite aboard our barky."

Maria snapped, "Mind your tongue, Joe Dowling."

Helen, concerned by Dowling's language and obvious discontent with her companion, looked to Ketch. "What's a sodomite, Mr. Ketch?"

Rogers's oars bit deep into the ragged, darkening waves, as he said, "Stow your gob, Joe, or we'll never catch the *Prodigal*."

Working against the tide, Maria concentrated on the effort it took to pull. Ketch's simmering stare lay upon Dowling's boat to larboard. His mood seemed to reach Helen who now sat, quiet, in the bow. Maria swallowed hard. She had not considered the Fortunes' reactions to having a former foe on board. Perhaps Ketch would have been safer back at Leighlin after all.

Wordlessly Ketch moved to sit beside her and took the starboard oar to ply it with his single arm while she used both of hers on the larboard oar.

Once clear of the harbor, Dowling altered course southward along the coast. When evening drew closer to night and the land breeze sprung up, each boat set its small lug sail. For five miles they cruised along until turning seaward. Now back in the stern-sheets, Ketch allowed Helen to take the tiller on occasion. It pleased the girl to have an active part in the voyage, gripping the wood as if her life depended upon it and listening dutifully to Ketch's instructions.

Two miles out, just before night descended, they spotted the *Fortune* slicing toward them from the south, her broad fore-and-aft mainsail catching the breeze and sending her along with a fine bow wave. Maria admired her speed and prayed such attributes would help her reach Jack in time.

"That's not John's ship," Helen said with disappointment. "It's too small."

"No," Maria replied. "That one is going to take us to him, though."

"Just like the *Alliance* took me to my daddy?"

"Yes."

Angus met Maria, Helen, and Rogers near the entry port with a small grin, bulbous eyes flashing in the lantern light, yellow hair loose and tangled. His welcome, however, was tempered by unease. "Long Arm said we'd only see you if somethin' went wrong ashore."

"It's what's gone right ashore actually," Maria said with a small smile.

Angus's convivial expression quickly darkened as Ketch came up the step with Rogers's assistance. "Ho... What's this now?"

Joe Dowling, whose boat had hooked on forward, came stumping aft, eyes shining black, the previous fogginess gone. Behind him the

310

Fortunes helped their inebriated comrades up the side of the vessel and tossed them unceremoniously upon the gangway like so much dazed tuna. Then they followed Dowling aft where the gunner halted short of Ketch near the main hatch. They murmured among themselves, glancing at Angus for direction and reaction. These men were all from the Port Royal contingent—Angus's original pirates—and the hardest ones, those who had been closest to Dan Slattery.

Dowling's attention was anchored upon Ketch who stared indifferently back, Helen at his side, subdued by the unfamiliar surroundings. To Angus, Dowling snapped, "You don't mean to get underway with him aboard, do ye?"

As if he thought Ketch incapable of explaining himself, Angus asked Maria, "What's he doin' here?"

"There's no time to explain everything right now. We need to head south and stop Jack before he catches up with the vessel he's after."

"Why?"

"Ezra Archer is dead. He holds no sway over us now. There's no need for Jack to carry out Archer's orders. But we have to hurry, Angus. Lives are at stake, and they had a head start on us."

Dowling insisted, "We're not goin' nowhere with him on board."

When he took a step toward Ketch, Helen clutched Ketch's hand. Maria moved to stand on her opposite side, prepared to pull the child away from any violence that might erupt.

Angus sized up the one-armed man. "So what's your purpose here, mate?"

Ketch nodded toward Maria. "This venture's no idea o' mine."

His lack of interest surprised and disappointed Maria. Did he not realize these men could toss him over the side any minute if he displeased them?

"Maria," Angus bridled, "you'd best give us a-a good reason to have this bastard on board or he's goin' back a-ashore."

"He can't go back," she began then caught herself; she could not tell them the whole truth because if they knew Ketch was responsible for the death of someone as prominent as Archer, Dowling or someone else could use that for his own gain ashore. "I mean," she said, desperate, "he only has one arm; he can't get back to shore on his own."

Her words trailed off, for she regretted pointing out the already obvious vulnerabilities of the battered man. There was no need to verbalize what everyone could see—Ketch with his loss of limb and swaths of bandages was not the formidable man who had once fought them aboard the *Prodigal* and the *Alliance*.

311

Perhaps this realization is what caused the men beyond Dowling to relax enough to make jokes about Ketch's misfortune instead of threats.

"She's right, Joe," Angus allowed with a crooked grin. "Look at the poor bastard. Nothin' much left of him to fret about. I wager Long Arm's little sister could kick his arse."

"Then the bugger can sling his hammock next to your'n, eh? Don't forget he spilt our lads' blood twice and belike would do it again if given the chance." Dowling looked at Maria. "And he damn nigh killed your Jack Mallory, lest you forget." He noticed how Helen's confused gaze reached Ketch and how her hand fell away from his. Dowling stepped closer but remained just out of Ketch's reach. "That's right, little missy. You might not want to hold that one's hand. He tried to kill your dear brother…or didn't no one tell you that?"

Blood infused Ketch's face, and his brown eyes turned to murderous black.

"A right awkward bugger, he is. Nothin' natural about him, is there? Slats told us all about you, Ketch…everything." He grinned cruelly. "Or should I call you by your real name, Inman?"

With an animal roar Ketch attacked Dowling, his hand clamped around the man's throat as he drove him backward into the crew. But there he was overwhelmed and struck from various directions. With an outcry, Helen wheeled and vanished down the nearest hatch. Hesitating but a moment, Maria rushed into the fray, shouting, drawing Rogers with her, though he was more intent on pulling her back than helping Ketch. Above it all Angus's shouts managed to break through, just as Maria wormed her way into the middle of the mess, all the while yelling for Ketch to stop his suicidal onslaught.

When she wedged herself between Ketch and Dowling, the others restrained themselves, whether out of respect for her femininity or in obedience to their captain, she could not guess. Ketch's wild eyes found her, her hand against his shoulder, his chest heaving beneath the bandages. She knew he did not want to give up the fight, did not care to what end it led him, but with her now within the sphere of his violence he contained himself. Maria's apprehension seemed to reach Ketch, and he chanced a glance behind him as if in search of Helen. She knew this concern alone caused his rage to drop away, not her intervention or Angus's orders.

Feigning nonchalance, Dowling carelessly straightened his shirt and gave Ketch a bedeviling smirk.

Angus growled, "We've wasted enough time with this, you fools.

Clap this whoreson in irons and throw 'im below for the voyage. That oughta keep things civil-like."

Maria expected further resistance from Ketch, but he said and did nothing.

Dowling took a step closer, nearly pressed Maria like a wedge between them, and taunted, "Like I said, mate...Slats told me all about you. You've no secrets aboard the *Fortune*."

"'Vast that noise, Dowling," Angus snapped, "or I'll let him have at you. Get yourself for'ard, and let's get 'er underway. Trott, fetch some irons and take this bastard below."

Maria started to protest, but Ketch's expression stole her words. His eyes held something she had never before seen there—genuine emotional anguish. She could not guess what Dowling's threat intimated, but Dan Slattery's betrayal of his trust had obviously weakened him and made him stand passively to await the irons. She wanted to speak but was powerless to do so, unsure that he was even seeing her there, so instead she left in search of Helen.

#

She found the child in the small aft cabin, a disheveled place where the only view beyond the hull was provided by a scuttle on either side. Helen sat in one corner, her legs drawn up and her bear tightly hugged to her chest. She said nothing when Maria entered, but her eyes sought her governess's as she came to sit next to her. Helen trembled slightly, her eyes large and moist. Maria put an arm around her and drew her close.

"There's no need to fret, *osita*." She kissed her hair, straw dry from their journey.

Helen pushed tightly against her and did not speak for a long moment before finally murmuring, "Is it true, what that man said about Mr. Ketch?"

Maria frowned. She debated how to handle the situation, whether to lie to protect her feelings, but Helen was a persistent, curious creature who would seek out the truth if she had any inkling that she had been deceived.

"Yes."

"But why? Why would Mr. Ketch want to hurt John?"

Maria's fingers brushed strands of hair away from the girl's face while she collected her thoughts. "Mr. Ketch loved your mother very much, didn't he?"

313

"Yes."

"Well, when she died, he blamed your brother."

"Why?"

"Sometimes, when bad things happen, we hurt so much that we think blaming someone else will somehow make us feel better. Maybe as you did with your brother after your father died."

Helen's lips twisted, and she looked down in shame.

"That's what Mr. Ketch did. But that's all behind us now, isn't it? He made a mistake, and we all make mistakes, don't we? Remember how guilty you felt when Mr. Ketch got bit saving you from the snake?"

Helen hugged her bear tighter and nodded.

"You weren't supposed to ride out alone, were you?"

"No," she mumbled sheepishly.

"You made a mistake, didn't you?"

"Yes. I said I was sorry."

"So you did. We regret our mistakes, especially if they hurt someone we care about. So when someone we know makes a mistake, even a mistake that hurts us, we must forgive them as best we can, just like Mr. Ketch forgave you. Do you understand? It's not always easy, I know, but..." She touched Helen's hand upon the bear. "You forgave your brother, didn't you, when you were angry with him?"

"Yes," she whispered against the toy.

"It meant the world to him, you know. Forgiveness is very powerful, like a gift you give someone."

Helen's eyes lifted back to hers as she chewed on her lower lip. She no longer trembled, and her eyes were dry again.

Maria smiled and caressed her soft cheek. "Now let's get this place cleaned up so you can go to bed."

# CHAPTER 31

During the second full day of the *Prodigal*'s journey southward, the sea grew more and more restless as the hours passed, forcing Jack to shorten sail and make little headway as the wind backed and veered. The talk on deck grew uneasy. Concerned eyes often flashed to the quarterdeck where Jack remained since morning, taking both his breakfast and dinner there near the binnacle, attention often upon the compass and the reefed topsails trembling above with every dive of the *Prodigal* into the trough of imposing swells. He squinted off to the southeast where the northern-most island of the Bahamas was somewhere still far out of sight. But he could feel the land as if it loomed a mere league away. The same suffocating sensation troubled him from the west where the coast of Florida lay beyond the angry gloom building toward them. All day he debated, keeping his own counsel as he paced the quarterdeck. Not even Smith dared to brave his frustrated countenance.

Where was the *Liberty*? Had the *Prodigal*'s broad reaches taken them beyond the brigantine? He had hoped to be the first to reach the comparatively narrow stretch of ocean between Florida and Grand Bahama, then to come about and await them or meet them up the coast. But by late afternoon, with the light being swallowed by the advancing storm, Jack knew to continue their present course could be fatal. This monster before them was no squall but instead a beast that would batter them for hours, tossing them beyond Jack's control, so with a bitter curse he ordered their course changed to due east, to take the wind upon the *Prodigal*'s quarter and flee into the safety of the open ocean.

By nightfall—a relative term considering the premature night that the storm spread over the entire sky—the *Prodigal* lay to beneath a goose-winged mainsail and battened down her hatches to ride out the maelstrom. Jack remained on deck, hunched and miserable beneath his tarpaulin coat, often helping to manhandle the tiller in order to maintain the *Prodigal*'s heading and to keep the fearsome waves from broaching her stern. The struggle continued through most of the night, and though Jack had a couple of moments of true fear for their lives and the well-being of his brig, he took comfort in sensing that the worst of the storm was passing them astern, headed up the Florida coast.

When morning arrived, the sun paid no heed to the thinning darkness that it faced and instead shouldered its way up the sky, pushing brightness before it and an incongruous blue that eventually touched the receding tempest. The angry black clouds and stabs of lightning were far distant now as the tropical storm continued northeastward. If it held that course, Carolina and Leighlin would be spared its wrath, allowing Jack to breathe a sigh of relief as he finally stepped from the quarterdeck, half drowned and completely famished. Water from the rigging dripped heavily upon him, but the rain had played itself out. The wind had dropped considerably, calming the seas now burnished to a hopeful bronze. He sighed in frustrated despair, though, for they could not hope to return anywhere westward unless the wind veered at least two points.

"Get somethin' to eat, lad," said Smith who met him in the waist. "Mebbe by the time you get some sleep the wind will be kinder to us."

With a rueful glance westward, Jack submitted to his fatigue and went below, wondering where the storm had blown the *Liberty*. He found a hot breakfast awaiting him in his cabin, and by the time he wolfed it all down he could no longer keep his eyes open, nearly falling asleep at the table. Climbing into his hammock, he was asleep before his head struck the pillow.

His slumber was deep and unknowingly long and, for the most part, peaceful...until the familiar nightmare drifted insidiously into his consciousness. With a willful push, he managed to force himself away from the terror and awaken.

He lay there, staring up at the deckhead where light brightened the timbers and chased off Newgate's darkness, soothing him and quieting his hammering heart. Then he focused on the brig. The sunlight coming through the stern windows was not direct. How long had he slept? The *Prodigal* was once again sailing at a respectable clip, heeled over significantly. She was taking the wind abeam and making perhaps seven knots. The wind must have veered enough to allow them to return westward. But how long ago?

Cursing, he struggled out of the hammock. He had told Smith not to let him sleep more than two hours, but no doubt his quartermaster had purposefully forgotten. Glancing at his compass and judging the angle of the sun, it was late afternoon. He swore again and hurried up the aft hatch.

On deck, the western sun was well on its way to the horizon. The

316

*Prodigal* bore courses and topsails, braced up sharp, the canvas taut and gleaming pale orange. No one seemed to notice Jack as he emerged from the companionway, for all eyes were squinted forward, hands trying to shield the glare of the sun off the open ocean. Many went aloft in search of a better vantage point to see whatever it was on the horizon. Others crowded on the forecastle, including Smith who stood next to Ned, both with telescopes.

"What is it?" Jack asked churlishly as he pushed his way through the men. "Why wasn't I awakened?"

Startled by his sudden appearance, Ned stepped back and handed Jack his glass.

"We just spotted her, Captain," Smith responded without taking his attention from the distant object.

Jack pressed the glass to his eye. "Where away?"

"Dead ahead, lad. Damned sun made it hard to see 'em 'til just now."

From the fore top, the Rat called, "Looks like she's lost her mainm'st!"

The distance and glare of the lowering sun made it difficult to tell exactly what type of vessel lay there only a few miles ahead, but she was indeed damaged, her mainmast sprung and the fore topmast gone; the only canvas she carried was her tattered fore course. Perhaps it was a *guarda costa*, blown away from Florida by the storm. She flew no discernible colors.

"Larboard one point!" he ordered, his directive relayed aft. With this slight alteration, they would pass just to windward of the wounded vessel.

With the wind as far forward as the *Prodigal* could successfully harness it, she lost some of her pace, and the men rushed to trim the sails without a word from their captain. Jack looked up in satisfaction at the new traverse of the fore yard, thanks to the handiwork of Ned and his mates.

"Billy! Hoist the colors!"

Within a minute the red and gold ensign flown by Wylder's vessels flapped out to leeward, courtesy of the convoy they had plundered. If what lay ahead was the *Liberty*, the brigantine would not be alarmed by the *Prodigal*'s approach. Considering the damage suffered, they would be relieved to see the brig. If Wylder was aboard, Jack hoped the man did not know his vessels so well that he could detect a ruse. One thing in their favor was that—to Jack's knowledge— Peter Wylder had never personally seen the *Prodigal* before, so he would have nothing to which he could compare the brig bearing toward him. Hopefully none of his small crew knew her either. Jack did not want to encounter some foolhardy attempt on the *Liberty*'s part to put up a struggle.

As the *Prodigal* continued to close the distance, Jack remained on deck until the Rat, high aloft, confirmed the vessel to be the *Liberty*, and a shout of anticipation went up from the men. Jack's pulse quickened, and the sight of Hanse anxiously pacing the gangway further stirred his unrest and uncertainty. The men he had killed since beginning his search for Logan and his mother had all been faceless, nameless beings, men with no past or future, men he had refused to dwell upon, but Hanse and the Wylders he knew enough about to feel a prick of conscience that had haunted him with greater determination since Ketch had reawakened his Newgate memories. Would the unknown faces of Hanse's much-lamented family as well as Hanse himself and the Wylders join the Newgate wardsman in his nightmare to torment him from this day forward? And how would he ever face Margaret again?

"Do you want us to clear for action, Captain?" Ned's voice pulled Jack from his thoughts.

"No, Ned," he stammered. "No need to make them suspicious. Let them think we mean only to help them. With a mast gone and few guns to defend her, I doubt we will have a fight on our hands. Have the guns ready, though, just in case. Have the yawl and pinnace cleared away and ready to be lowered once we speak them."

"Aye aye, sir."

With that Jack retreated to his cabin until he would be needed again. He did not want anyone to detect his turmoil as he again considered exactly how he would dispatch the men aboard the *Liberty*.

He found the bottle of rum that he had first opened before the storm and sat upon the stern locker to drink, staring out at the swirling wake. He felt the same way—swirled about and ungrounded. He needed to remove his feelings from all of this. He needed to focus on what needed to be done, on what he would have afterwards as a result.

Jack barely heard Smith's rap upon the door minutes later or his own voice inviting the quartermaster in. Smith's brow furrowed when he saw Jack. Quickly Jack looked out the windows.

"She bears Wylder's colors," Smith informed.

"Very well."

"We'll be up with her in half a glass."

Jack nodded as he watched a male frigate bird trailing the brig.

The creature hung there for a while, its six-foot wingspan impressing Jack, its freedom and grace. It drew closer as if to head through the windows themselves, its shining eyes seemingly upon Jack, then it wheeled, and a stray ray of sunlight caught the iridescent black feathers, momentarily turning them purple, then the bird was gone.

"Jack." Smith's voice still, closer now.

Jack grunted a response. He was forced to turn only when Smith sat on the locker next to him, eying the bottle, swallowing. Jack handed the rum over with a wry smile and reclaimed it once Smith had taken a long pull.

Smith quietly asked, "What's yer plan?"

"We'll heave to and offer them assistance. We'll go over in the boats with arms concealed." He paused and finished the rest of the rum. "Then we'll kill them and set fire to their magazine."

Smith waited before venturing, "Yer heart's not in this, lad."

"Should it be?"

"More to the point, I'm afeared yer head's not in it. Don't want no mistakes, do we? We're undone once Wylder sees our faces; I mean, if somethin' was to go wrong and they get away."

Jack stared down at the padded locker, his finger absently twisting his mother's bracelet. "Nothing will go wrong. 'Tis straightforward enough."

"I can take the lads over, ye know. There's no need for you to go."

Jack's gaze flashed upward in anger. "I'm no coward, Smitty. I'll see this all the way through."

"You know I'm not callin' you nothin', least of all a coward. But I can tell yer not sure o' yerself. I'd do the deed as a favor, not 'cause you can't."

"I'll not have someone else do my dirty work. 'Tis my debt and mine alone to be repaid." He stood and slowly paced around the table, rubbing his thin growth of beard. "'Tis Helen I'm thinking of. What if killing Wylder only leads to something terrible for her? If someone was to find out and I was arrested again…"

"No one's goin' to find out, Jack. There'll be nothin' left."

"I was thrown into Newgate as a pirate—for something I wasn't— only to become that very thing once I was released. Maybe I became that thing in prison. That man I killed in Newgate—"

"Yer talkin' nonsense, Jackie. When you was released and was searchin' for yer mother, you had nothin' to lose by killin', but now you have Maria and Helen, and yer afeared o' losin' 'em, that if you keep on killin' you won't be able to give them the life they deserve.

319

But this will be the end of it here today. You have to believe that."

"But what if—"

"You can't think about 'what if' right now, lad. You need to think clearly and get this over with."

Jack's shoulders rounded in dejection.

Smith drew near. "Let's go on deck and end this. The sooner the better."

#

When Smith hailed the *Liberty* from the *Prodigal*'s quarterdeck, Jack stood among his men in the waist to conceal himself in case anyone aboard the merchant vessel could recognize the pirate who recently had been held in Charles Town. The *Prodigal* was met warmly and Smith's offered assistance in righting the damaged vessel gladly accepted, seeing as the crew of six had their hands full. The *Prodigal*'s boats were then hoisted out, cutlasses and pistols concealed within. Jack ordered Hanse among the Prodigals in the yawl, a directive that put a confused, worried frown upon the carpenter's face.

Once the yawl had shoved off from the brig, the Rat patted the pistol beneath his coat and grinned at Hanse. "Not a word, mate. You try to warn 'em, and I'll put a ball right betwixt your eyes."

Smith commanded the pinnace and was the first up the side of the *Liberty*, followed closely by his boarding party, pistols concealed. The yawl hooked onto the mainchains, and Sullivan and Samuel left Jack, Willie Emerick, Hanse, and the Rat behind. Jack felt craven, remaining behind until the *Liberty*'s crew were accounted for topside.

"If they're not as trustin' as we think," Smith had cautioned, "they might have guns tucked away as we do, and if yer the first thing Wylder sees, then some of our lads might end up with lead in 'em afore we can get a shot off."

Now Jack could hear Smith conversing with someone on deck, the master perhaps. He twisted his bracelet, shifted his tender feet, chewed his mustache, eyes upward toward the bulwarks. Why was Smith taking so damn long? Then came the sudden protests of the Liberties as no doubt pistols appeared, pointing at them. Jack recognized Peter Wylder's voice, a recognition that surprised him, considering he had only met the man once.

Sullivan's red head appeared over the railing, and he waved for them to board. Jack swallowed in a dry, constricted throat and led the way up the side.

Peter Wylder stood near the sprung mainmast with his son and the frightened Liberties, his visage so familiar to Jack that it could have been just yesterday that he had been held prisoner. Or was the familiarity from Wylder's presence in his thoughts? The instant he saw Jack, his face went white then slowly suffused a deep, angry red, but he held his composure, unlike his son who began to curse Jack. His father's hand upon his arm curbed the outburst.

Noise sounded from below where Smith had sent men to search for anyone attempting to hide.

"Take whatever you want." Peter Wylder's hazel eyes did an admirable job of hiding any apprehension. "But I am afraid you have chosen a poor prize, Captain. We have little cargo other than provisions for our journey."

"I've not come for your cargo."

"Then what?" Seth snapped. "If it is the vessel you want, she is not much good to you with but one mast. Yet if it will avoid bloodshed, take it and give us a boat to get to land."

A couple of the Prodigals laughed and derided the trembling young man's foolish audacity until Jack silenced them. Unfortunately Seth's impertinence reminded Jack of a day at sea long ago when he—as a boy—had also stood in hopeless defiance of a marauder, a day that had ultimately brought him to this very minute in his life. Now here he was no better than James Logan. No—he tried to console himself—unlike Logan, he had little choice in what he was about to do.

Jack was unsure whether it was fear or anger that caused Seth to shake. Perhaps both. If Seth was any husband at all, his thoughts were on the beautiful bride whom he had abandoned. If he had known of Jack's friendship with his wife, he surely could have used it most effectively against Jack's tenuous resolve. Jack gave silent thanks for Seth's ignorance.

A woman's outcry from below startled everyone on board, and Seth Wylder's alarmed gaze reached his father. Some of the color left the older man's cheeks. He took a step toward Jack whose stomach dropped with the realization of what that unexpected sound meant.

"Captain," Wylder said, showing no panic but conveying his urgent, fearful concern. "I will not waste my breath or dignity pleading with you for my life; you have murdered my son, so I know full well the evil of which you are capable. But...I beg you..." He stretched out his hands in supplication. "Pray do not harm my wife."

Smith mumbled under his breath, "Bloody hell."

Jack stared into Wylder's beseeching eyes, hoping he had heard the man incorrectly. But there was no mistaking the truth when a middle-aged woman struggled up the main hatch, Samuel behind her with his cutlass. When she beheld the daunting sight on deck, she hesitated at the top of the ladder, as if considering a retreat below, regardless of Samuel. Her expression lost all hope, and she took a fresh purchase on her skirt to step onto the deck. Quickly her husband drew her into a protective, close embrace. Mrs. Wylder was small like her husband but looked several years younger than he. Plain yet not unattractive, just now beginning to lose the shapeliness of younger years.

Jack wheeled away from the sight of the anxious woman clinging to her husband. The bemused gazes of his men rested upon him. Some of them—the ones left from the Port Royal lot—undoubtedly saw no great issue raised by the presence of a female prisoner, but others like Sullivan and Willie stood uneasily, shuffling their feet, clearing their throats, or fingering pistols. Jack paced the length of the short gangway. Around him all sounds but those of the *Liberty*'s blocks and timbers ceased, and he felt as if he were alone on board.

He stared across at the *Prodigal*—at the expectant men looking over at the *Liberty*—then farther out to sea, at the settling swell as evening began to close in and drain light from the east. When his gaze returned to the *Prodigal*, he thought of the journey to find his mother and of the short, wonderful time they had been together aboard the brig. Her blue eyes had shone with pride when he had first escorted her about the *Prodigal*. Jack frowned. What if she saw him now? Would she protest his current murderous course or would she understand its greater purpose? After all, she had endured an odious bargain as well by remaining with Logan those years, giving up her freedom for Helen's sake, or so it seemed. And what of the bargain she had made for his very life aboard that merchantman seven years ago? He looked down at the aged bracelet, not even realizing until then that his finger twisted the leather again; he had done this so often lately that the leather had stretched. Beneath the twisted strands, the manacle scars from Newgate...

Abruptly he turned and stalked down the gangway, eyebrows low and stormy. "Lock them under hatches," he barked. "Including Hanse."

"What?" Smith said over the chorus of protests and supplications by the Liberties.

"Do as I say, damn it. Sully, gather any weapons you find. Smitty, pick five men to stay on board with you. We'll lie to for the night."

"Lie to?" Smith stepped closer. "Jack, there's no time for hangin' about—"

Jack tossed a sharp glance at his puzzled face. "You have your orders. The rest return to the *Prodigal* with me."

# CHAPTER 32

The *Fortune*'s lower deck was a cramped space—dark and musty—used mainly for cargo, with berthing forward where the half dozen men of the watch below now took their leisure. The men's drunken laughter and murmuring words drifted aft to Maria, but their words held no interest for her as she treated Ketch's burns. Since the start of the voyage, the Fortunes mainly ignored Ketch—chained to the mainmast—allowing him only the freedom to use the head, occasionally throwing insults or a stray kick his way. Beyond that, they paid him no more attention than a bag of rice.

The *Fortune* had been spared the wrath of a tropical storm the previous day, the storm crossing their path and heading out to sea before it could offer them anything more than high winds and cross seas. This morning Angus had set the *Fortune* on longer tacks to the southeast, figuring the storm would have blown the more southerly *Prodigal* out to sea. His hope was to find the brig before the Bahamas forced them back toward the Florida coast and shorter tacks. At least, Maria consoled herself, the *Fortune*'s fore-and-aft rig allowed them to sail closer to the wind than the *Prodigal*. Her dread, though, was that the storm had had enough ferocity to cause the brig to founder. She forced the terrible thought from her mind and scratched a stay before reminding herself that the storm, in actuality, may have helped their pursuit by driving the *Prodigal* back toward them.

Now, with night forcing the lower deck into even darker gloom than during the day, Maria squinted in the lantern light and smeared the gel-like aloe on Ketch's facial burn, a wound irritated by the blows from his first day aboard. He hunched shirtless and remote to her familiar ministrations. His face was angled downward, eyes half closed. If left to his own designs, Maria knew he would ignore treating the burns as well as his amputation. Though never a voluble man, he had spoken not a word since being thrown in irons. She did not get the impression that his silence was directed at her for any blame for his current plight. Instead she suspected Joe Dowling's baiting words had more to do with his mood than anything else.

She progressed to the burn on his arm, and when she was finished there she lifted his arm to slacken the chain that secured him, then slid the manacle from where it naturally rested. Her deviation from the norm drew his attention, the drowsy melancholy leaving his dark eyes, which glistened in the light.

"I'm going to put some of this salve on your wrist and ankles so the skin doesn't chafe." As she did so, she thought of Jack's Newgate scars, of how he always kept the cuffs of his shirt unbuttoned, of how she had gently touched the scars when they lay together, of how he offered nothing about them and she did not feel invited to ask. Would he ever tell her about his time in prison?

She ordered Ketch from his slouch so she could treat the broad burn on his chest.

"I think these are doing much better since we've stopped bandaging them and you've kept your shirt off. The sea air must be good for them, don't you think?"

He offered nothing.

"Now if we could just get you up on deck instead of down in this damp hole, all the better." She glanced at the odd scar at the base of his neck and thought of its equivalent under his bearded chin. "How did you get that...that scar on your neck?"

He hesitated, as if not having heard her right away, then his answer came, flat, almost by rote, never looking at her. "Spaniards stuck a double-end fork in me—one end in me chest, t'other under me chin—then strapped it 'round me neck to make it stay put."

The shocking image and the bland way he spoke of it astonished her and made an immediate response impossible. She blamed her sudden lightheadedness on the close quarters and the stench of liquor, unwashed men, and bilge.

A shuffle of feet came as a welcomed distraction, drawing Maria's attention forward. Joe Dowling swayed around the bulkhead, a grin upon his dark, hairy face, bottle in one hand, the other hand scratching his crotch. Swaying like a reed, he belched and paused a few feet from the mainmast on his way to the hatch.

"Well, well, well. What have we here?"

Slowly Ketch's gaze swung toward him, black and foreboding.

"You're a lucky man, Edward Inman. The rest of us poor, hard-up bastards would have to pay for such close attention from such a comely wench." He chuckled at Maria's dismissive look. "Or we'd have to force it from her like your dear brother did, eh?"

Struck dumb by humiliation, Maria wished she could conjure

enough anger to retaliate.

Her silence encouraged Dowling's drunken play. "Slats was a master at forcin' 'em, wasn't he? Ah, I miss that walleyed bastard."

Ketch continued to glower at the small, ape-like man.

"There was plenty of others afore your nurse, aye? 'Course there was. But he never told you 'bout all of 'em, did he? He knew you wouldn't understand, what with your strange ways an' all."

Ketch shifted his weight, spoiling Maria's already shaken concentration on her work. "Hold still and let me finish," she said quietly, hoping to distract him. She did not want him to give Dowling any reason to take advantage of his iron restraints.

Dowling shuffled closer and bent toward Ketch but not too close. The gunner grinned, mouth wet and lewd. "Slats never told you the truth 'bout how your whore of a mother died, did he?"

Ketch's nostrils flared, his fist clenched.

"He never told you how it was him what raped and murdered her."

Color drained from Ketch, slowly taking the anger with it.

"Aye." Dowling swigged from his bottle. "Never told ye, did he? Your own kin. Well, that'll keep you up nights, won't it?" He laughed and lurched toward the companionway as if he had just said something as mundane as an observation on the weather.

Ketch stared at the hull before him, eyes glazed, confusion producing two deep vertical furrows between his eyebrows. Maria knew he was no longer aware of her presence. At a loss, she quickly gathered up the jar of salve and the dirty bandages she had removed from his amputation. Standing, she struggled to find something to say, but could tell by Ketch's vacant eyes that he would not hear her; he was lost far away in some haunting memory. So she retreated to the weather deck, desperate for open space and fresh air.

She could make out Dowling upon the forecastle, so she withdrew to the taffrail. Staring out over the Atlantic, she could not banish what she had just heard and witnessed. Never before had she considered Ketch's past, his family other than Slattery, the things that influenced who he was, or even something as simple as his given name. To have a family, a history…it gave dimension, humanity. Taking into account the horrible things she had been told as well as what she had experienced herself, perhaps she had not even viewed him as completely human. After all, back at Leighlin, she had called him a mongrel. To think of his loyalty to Slattery and what he had done to avenge his death, what it had cost Helen, how misguided it must all seem now that he knew Slattery's heinous crime…

Maria's fingers drifted to the locket around her neck, and when she touched the chain she remembered Stephen Moore telling her about Slattery and Ketch. She tried to recall the whole conversation, but only bits and pieces filtered back, for since her own rape she had tried to erase everything about Slattery from her mind. Why would he murder Ketch's mother? And if they were indeed half-brothers, had she also been Slattery's mother? How could a man do such things to his own mother? No, the link between the two men must have been through the father. Whatever the connection, it had been a strong one. She revisited Slattery's own brutal, bloody death at the hands of James Logan and the smoldering anger in Ketch afterwards, an anger she had manipulated toward Logan's eventual murder. He had killed his master to avenge his kin, only to now learn that Slattery had not deserved revenge, that the man whom he had so esteemed had betrayed him years before.

On the quarterdeck, Angus drifted over to her. "One more hour of this foolish crackin' on, then I'm goin' to shorten sail."

Maria pulled free from her troubled musings. "We can't be that far behind the *Prodigal*." She considered the mizzenmast's lateen sail. What a fine, weatherly vessel the *Fortune* was. Earlier that day she had put Maria in mind of a sleek young filly, plunging through the swells, the sun flashing upon her sails, the bow wave splaying out and soaking those forward as she sliced her way along. If any vessel could catch the *Prodigal* it would be the *Fortune*. Surely they would fetch her wake tomorrow. The thought of seeing Jack again, especially to deliver such wonderful news, quickened the pace of her heart and gave birth to a private smile. She could not bear the thought of Angus shortening sail.

Seeming to read her mind, Angus grumbled, "We won't catch no one if we lose a-a mast." Then he let his severity pass and lightened his tone when he asked, "How's the wee lass? She should be tired after her busy day."

"She is. I put her to bed an hour ago. Not an easy task."

Angus chuckled. "A-a real sailor, she is. Like her father...and her brother."

Although Helen had been hesitant the first day aboard—her self-confidence shaken by the confrontation on deck upon their arrival—the following day she had spent her time pestering Angus and other members of the crew with questions and requests. She steered clear of Dowling and his cronies, who had little interest in indulging the child and in fact resented her presence along with that of a woman and a cripple, but they kept their complaints mainly to themselves unless they wanted to risk Angus's wrath.

Regardless of Maria's advice during the first night aboard, Helen did not interact with Ketch, nor did she speak of him. When Maria had taken him breakfast that morning, Helen had stood at the foot of the main companionway, no closer. Her blue eyes studied the man's chains with apprehension and confusion. Though Ketch said nothing about it, Maria knew the child's behavior injured him and no doubt added to the despondence that weighed upon him since Leighlin's fire.

Maria did not remain much longer on deck. With an inward, weary sigh, she said good night to Angus. She nearly took the ladder that gave direct access to the aft cabin, which Angus had turned over to her and Helen, but she knew she would not be able to sleep without checking on Ketch.

Talk forward beyond the bulkhead had died away to only two low voices barely reaching above the snores of the inebriated men. There was another voice, though, closer, quieter, barely a murmur, unbroken and frantic, a stream of consciousness. The lantern near the mainmast swayed gently with the movement of the vessel, the border of its light ever changing but always including Ketch, sending his shadow outward, a shadow that moved shallowly back and forth in a rhythm separate from the *Fortune*'s.

Maria came around the mast to see him bent slightly forward as if gripped by a cramp, staring at the deck, unseeing, his torso moving forward and back, sweat trailing down his face. A strange glistening at the back of his head caught her attention. The lantern wagged with a lee lurch of the *Fortune*, flashing against a smudge on the mast behind Ketch's head. Her fingers explored the wood and found the smear warm and sticky—blood. Her immediate thought was that someone had attacked him, but when she saw his expression and heard the jumble of half-incoherent words spilling between his lips she realized the wound had been self-inflicted.

"Ketch." She knelt next to him, ready to jump back if necessary, but he did not seem to know she was there. "Ketch." No response. She could think him drunk, yet no one but she had bothered to give him food or drink. Gathering her courage, she took hold of his shoulders to stop his movements. "What have you done?"

He stared blankly at her.

"Your head is bleeding."

Her touch settled him. The fog gradually left his gaze, and his hand drifted to the back of his head, coming away with blood that he studied in wonder.

"I'll fetch some water." She rushed to her cabin and returned with a basin and a rag. "Move your hand away and let me see."

Taking down the lantern, she examined the wound where blood darkened and matted his long hair. Then carefully she sponged the abrasion. It was mainly superficial; the abundant blood made it look worse than it was.

"Lean your head forward while I press this cloth so the bleeding stops."

A long stretch of silence left Maria uncomfortable. She prided herself on her ability to console, but now she knew not what to say or exactly what she would be consoling him for.

"It was all for naught," Ketch mumbled. He snatched the cloth from the wound, startling Maria with his abrupt return to the present. Glaring at her, he threw the rag into the basin, splashed pink water onto the deck. "Leave me be." He shifted his weight away from her.

At a loss Maria stared at the back of his battered head, wondered how it was possible to physically punish oneself so viciously. With a shudder, she remembered the lacerations he had inflicted upon his leg. Again she tried to think of something to say but found nothing, too stunned by all she had seen and heard tonight. Tired and defeated, she got to her feet, left the basin, and retreated to her cabin.

#

"Captain," Willie Emerick's voice broke through the shell-thin wall of Jack's sleep where he slumped at the table in his cabin, head upon his folded arms. "You said to wake you at two bells in the mornin' watch."

Jack raised his head, blinking to return some moisture to his eyes; the alcohol he had consumed last night had dried him out. He rubbed his face and groaned at his dull headache.

"Cap, we gonna kill 'em or not? The lads are a bit muddled and don't fancy hangin' about here no longer than we need to. They want to take what we got comin' to us and head back up the coast."

Jack sighed; he had not simply dreamt this nightmare. He stepped to the quarter-gallery to splash water on his face and examine his bloodshot eyes in the small looking glass hung there. He had slept maybe an hour all night. The rest of the time was spent pacing the cabin, ignoring the discomfort it caused his feet, or standing upon the quarterdeck, staring across at the wounded *Liberty* where she awaited her fate.

"Light the galley, Willie, and get breakfast started. Send the yawl over to the *Liberty* and fetch Peter Wylder back here...alone."

"Aye aye, Cap," Willie said with disappointment, followed by muttering as he left.

While awaiting his guest's arrival, Jack took advantage of the *Prodigal*'s limited motion on the quiet, lazy swell and shaved. The Atlantic had calmed overnight, and just now the sea breeze was starting to stir through the stern windows. Through the scuttle the incarnadine dawn trimmed the blue-black water of the eastern horizon, the sky above clear and benign. Jack thought of morning at Leighlin, of waking up with Maria in his arms, the scent of her, the warmth and delicious closeness of the small, ridiculous bed in the kitchen house, Helen's morning knock upon the door and his subsequent scramble for his own bed...

When Wylder arrived in the cabin, escorted by Willie, he showed no more panic than he had the evening before, even after long hours in which to contemplate his possible death and the death of his family. Jack admired his fortitude.

"Willie, please bring Mr. Wylder some breakfast along with mine."

Wylder eyed Jack as the door closed only halfway behind him. He appeared neither thankful nor trusting. "Is this to be my last meal, Captain? There really is no need to toy with me."

Jack moved to the table and invited Wylder to sit, then settled across from him.

Wylder studied Jack as he had that day in the storehouse, harsh yet curious. "You do not look as young to me as you did when I first met you." He grunted. "Not many days ago, was it? Surely not enough to warrant aging you, I should think, especially one with no conscience."

Jack had seen the same changes in the mirror a moment ago, particularly when he remembered the shock of finding Mrs. Wylder aboard the *Fortune*. All night he had wondered if Ezra Archer had purposefully omitted the detail of the woman's presence or had he truly been ignorant of her accompanying her husband?

Willie's foot nudged the door open the rest of the way, and he carried in two plates heaped with eggs, pork, and sweet potatoes. He cast Wylder a warning glance after he set the food in front of the older man, then he lingered.

"That'll be all, Willie. Thank you."

Reluctantly the seaman withdrew, still mindful not to shut the door completely. There would be attentive ears pressed to the skylight as well, of course.

Jack had little appetite, no matter how inviting the food, but he ate as if his heart were in it. After he washed down the first mouthfuls with ale, he began, "You were right, of course, about James Logan being a pirate. When I was a boy, he attacked the ship that I sailed on with my family. He murdered my father and took my mother and me captive." He chanced a glance at Wylder who listened but did not touch his food. "Later I was arrested and falsely accused of piracy. Seven years later I was pardoned and released from jail. That's when I began to search for Logan and my mother."

"Why are you telling me this?"

"Perhaps 'tis more for my own benefit than yours. Perhaps I feel compelled to explain myself and why I've taken your vessel."

"So you are saying this was not a chance encounter—you were searching for us."

"I was."

"And why? Revenge for your capture at the hands of my son?"

"No; payment for my recent escape from Charles Town."

Wylder tried to hide his surprise. Before he could ask for clarification, Jack continued with his story.

"When I began to attack Charles Town's shipping, it was to draw James Logan out. I had heard that he never sailed without his wife. Ella Logan—she was my mother, the woman he had taken captive."

"You astonish me, sir. She was a prisoner?"

Jack shifted his weight and cleared his throat. "I'm not sure exactly what she was toward the end. After I rescued her, there wasn't enough time to discover the truth before she was killed."

Wylder frowned as if displeased with his curiosity in this tale. "Is this simply a confession of your life's transgressions, Captain, or perhaps a justification for your crimes? Or does this all somehow relate to my family's plight?"

"It does. Until my mother's death, I was unaware that she and Logan had a child—my half-sister, Helen. My mother's dying wish was for Logan and me to lay down our grievances against one another to care for Helen, to raise her. Of course, we agreed; we both loved my mother, as painful as that is for me to say about Logan. I've grown to love my sister, Mr. Wylder, as you can imagine if you've met her."

"Of course. She is a lovely child, regardless of her father's shortcomings." Tentatively he tasted his tea.

"Now you can understand why I pursued the *Alliance*."

"And now our blood is to avenge Caleb's alleged kidnapping of the child?"

"No."

"Then what, damn your eyes?" he snapped, for the first time showing the strain of the long ordeal.

"Logan's death left my sister an orphan. My duty, my desire—my *promise*—is to care for her. As you know I was arrested and would have hung, but someone came to my rescue, and in repayment of that favor I have been ordered to find and kill you."

Wylder's gaze lingered upon him without blinking, and Jack knew he was deciding whether or not to believe any or all of this.

"Logan's holdings—my sister's inheritance—lie in the balance. If I…eliminate you and your family, I have been promised that Leighlin will be secured for Helen, that she and I can live there in peace." Jack toyed with his eggs. "I don't give a damn about a plantation for myself. 'Tis for my sister, for her future and the promise I made our mother. Without Leighlin, what sort of life would she have, parentless and without means? My own skills are limited on land, certainly nothing that would provide sufficiently for her—and I will not take her to live at sea as her father once did."

After a thoughtful pause, Wylder ventured, "Only one man would go to the lengths that you have described in order to destroy me. If you will not speak his name, I will: Ezra Archer."

Jack frowned. "Aye." He pushed his plate away, no longer able to feign interest in food.

"And how would Archer have any power over Leighlin unless it was given to him?"

"The alliance you suspected between Archer and Logan did indeed exist."

"And you are to take Logan's place?"

"No. I want nothing more to do with Archer."

"What you want, young man, and what Archer demands may very well be two different things."

"With you dead, what more could he want?"

"Men of greed always find something to covet, Captain."

Jack looked from his breakfast to Wylder's. "Please, eat." He stood and turned toward the stern windows.

"You tell me what you must do, yet you have not done it," Wylder said tentatively. "Your hesitation came when you saw my wife; you did not expect her to be aboard."

"No."

"And now you are looking for a way out. Otherwise you never would have invited me here and told me all this."

"I can see no way out. If I don't hold up my end of the bargain with Archer, he'll turn me in, and then it will be the noose after all. Then what of my sister?" And Maria, he thought, turning back. "But now you understand that this is about family, not greed or revenge or hate. After all, you were ready to see me dead for the sake of your murdered son. I have to keep my word to Archer. As corrupt as he may be, he did save my life, and he holds my sister's future in the balance."

"Your honor is misguided, Captain, but—yes—understandable. I am afraid, however, you will get no sympathy or absolution from me." He stood. "Now if you will excuse me, I find I have no appetite. I would like to be returned to my wife and son; they will be worried about me."

#

Jack knew he should have accompanied Wylder in the yawl, but instead he finished his breakfast without urgency. He knew why he delayed, though he did not like to admit it: Wylder was right—he wanted a way out. But there could be no way out, no alternative. Best to get it over with before the Prodigals grew churlish.

He looked at no one as he stepped on deck. Instead he adjusted the pistol in his waistband and started for the entry port, calling to Willie Emerick to join him. Jack sensed everyone's eyes upon him as he went over the side. Were they thinking him weak? A coward? Or were they admiring his resolve and single-mindedness? He tried not to think about them...or the Wylders. Instead he thought about Maria and Helen. But unfortunately thoughts of his future wife made him consider Mrs. Wylder. Damn her presence. If she were not here, he would have gone ahead with all of this yesterday, and he would now be on his way back to Leighlin.

Once aboard the *Liberty*, he found Smith and the five other Prodigals on deck, the prisoners below hatches. Sullivan and Bull—having taken the latest watch in the night—slept aft, undoubtedly having filled their bellies from the *Liberty*'s stores.

"Wake 'em," Jack ordered Smith, avoiding the older man's probing look.

The sun stood well clear of the horizon now, round and red in an unblemished sky, promising a warm day ahead. Jack stared at it until the orb left a black shadow behind his eyelids when he blinked.

Sullivan and Bull trailed along the gangway, coughing and

scratching, barely awake. The others gathered around Jack.

"I want this done quickly," he instructed. "Tie their hands behind their backs before they're brought on deck."

"The lady's, too, Cap'n?" Sullivan asked.

Jack considered the Irishman's troubled expression. He should have replaced men like Sullivan and Willie with the hard-bitten, more callous Port Royal pirates.

"No, Sully. Leave her unbound. Everyone check his piece. I don't want any misfires." He faltered, realized sweat slicked his hands and that he had been slowly wiping them down his hips. He abruptly halted this show of unrest. "Bring the crew up first. No need for the others to see. The Wylders I will...dispatch myself."

Ill at ease, Willie asked, "What about Hanse?"

Jack cursed inwardly. "Bring him up with the crew."

Willie exchanged an unhappy glance with Sullivan.

As he awaited the prisoners, Jack paced the gangway. Six Liberties and Hanse. An executioner for each. No need for anyone to reload. It would be efficient and quick. He would take Hanse, for he knew the Prodigals viewed the carpenter in somewhat of an amiable light since he had been with them these past days and had performed his duty skillfully. Jack felt sick to his stomach and wished he had not eaten.

He became aware of outcries below, protests, Mrs. Wylder's voice. But no sounds of struggle. Soon the mournful *clump-clump* of footsteps up the companionway, a Prodigal—pistol in hand—after every second man. The pale Liberties trembled, and the instant Jack approached them, several began to beseech him. Hanse, his hands unbound, stared in slack-jawed disbelief. The outcries were a wall of noise that battered Jack—some vowed they would join the *Prodigal* if only he spared their lives, another cursed him and the other Prodigals, another said he would pay them for his life—whatever he had was theirs. The master claimed his family could pay a significant ransom. All plain, unremarkable men, leaving God knew what behind them. Perhaps life had been a misery to them, but today it had all of the world's worth.

"Silence!" Jack shouted at last, shaken. Their instant obedience astonished him, attested to their desperation to garner favor. They bunched together, wide-eyed, mouths open mid-supplication. "Form a line here on the gangway."

But they stood frozen together, as if the mass would save the individual, until Bull and Smith and Samuel roughly fragmented them.

"Kneel," Jack said, nodding to Smith who in turn conveyed a meaningful look to the rest of the executioners. As the Liberties reluctantly knelt, the Prodigals stepped behind them. Jack advanced upon Hanse.

Sinking to his knees, the carpenter clasped his hands together and raised them toward Jack. "Captain, I beg you, you can't do this. My family... Who will take care of them?"

Both Hanse and Jack started when two shots rang out simultaneously, and the men in front of Samuel and Smith dropped forward onto their faces with a sickening, heavy, lifeless *thump*. The others resumed their pleas. One of them was sobbing now. Frozen, Jack stared at Hanse, unable to move behind him. He remembered Joe Dowling's words just a short time ago aboard the *Fortune*...

"I have five children," the carpenter continued in a torrent. "Think of your wee sister, if somethin' was to happen to you. But five...five of 'em! Who will care for five young 'uns and a widow?"

Two more shots, this time from the Rat and Billy. Two more dull thuds and blood running along the deck. One of the remaining Liberties sobbed hysterically while the other prayed softly.

"Please, Captain," Hanse continued, trembling. "I've done everything you've asked of me, haven't I? Ask the others—when you was ashore, I gave 'em no trouble. I did my duty."

Sullivan and Willie finally screwed their nerve up enough to kill the two remaining Liberties. Hanse would not look at them as they fell. He would not turn away from Jack, and Jack could not look away from the pleading man.

"Jack," Smith's voice.

Softer now, Hanse said, "I beg you, Captain. You have my word. I won't tell no one about you...any of you."

Jack felt the weight of the pistol in his hand, noticed how Hanse's gaze flicked once at the weapon then back to him. Jack could no longer get behind him unless he wanted to step on a corpse.

"Jack." Smith again. The sound of his approach. If he did not do this, he knew Smith would reload and do it for him. Trying to wet his lips with a parched tongue, Jack started to lift his weapon. But then there was a call, a voice from afar, faint yet somehow significant enough to make him falter, or was it simply his excuse to delay?

"Cap'n," Willie said excitedly, as if eager to break his concentration. "Cap'n, they're hailin' from the *Prodigal*!"

# CHAPTER 33

Aboard the *Prodigal*, the lookout at the mainmasthead waved an arm and pointed to the north, mirrored by the lookout on the foremast. The urgency in their gestures and voices sent Jack's attention northward. A flash of sails; a vessel sliced toward them on the starboard tack. She was not far off. Judging her speed from the bow wave, she would close with them within twenty minutes or less. He cursed the lookouts whose attention had no doubt been distracted by the executions aboard the *Liberty*.

Jack turned to his men. "Weight the bodies and throw them overboard to larboard. Take Hanse into the hold with the Wylders. Gag and bind them all. Willie, wash off this deck."

The Rat climbed the *Liberty*'s remaining mast to get a clear view. The situation, the interruption chafed Jack. He could not fire the *Liberty* with another vessel in sight.

As his men dumped the bodies of the Liberties into the ocean, Jack's sweat chilled him in the breeze. He was just about to order the *Prodigal* to make sail and meet the intruder, but the Rat's hail drew his attention.

"By Christ, lads, I think she's the *Fortune!*"

Alarm staggered Jack. Angus had promised to remain off Charles Town in case Maria needed help. Had such a need arisen? And if so, what cause had driven them here? His search for an answer bounced between Archer and Ketch. Or perhaps someone from Charles Town had discovered the connection between himself and Helen or Leighlin, and Maria and his sister had been forced to flee.

It seemed an eternity before the ketch luffed up with amazing nimbleness under the *Liberty*'s lee. When Jack spotted Maria and Helen upon the quarterdeck with Angus, a lump grew in his throat, and relief weakened his knees. He released the air from his lungs as if he had held it for some time. Yet despair tempered his joy, for he did not want them to witness what he was doing here. Once Helen identified him, she frantically waved and called to him, and the conflicting emotions he had been battling since first spotting the *Liberty* grew to an unbearable level.

"What do you make o' this, lad?" Smith asked. "Trouble at Leighlin, I should wonder."

"Let's hope not."

Smith flashed a crooked grin. "What, you think the lass just couldn't bear bein' away from you? Is that it?"

Jack gave him a wry look. How Smith could always produce levity even in the most trying situations amazed him.

"No, I thought not neither." Smith sobered and lowered his voice. "What d'ye want us to do with the rest of 'em below?"

"I don't want Helen seeing or knowing anything about this. I'll find out why they're here. In the meantime, keep the Wylders below."

The Fortunes quickly had a boat in the water, and Jack was relieved that Rogers, Angus, and Maria did not bring Helen with them on the short journey. Rogers barely had the boat hooked upon the *Liberty* before Maria made a lithe leap for the side of the brigantine. Jack helped her up to the deck. Angus followed, the sun bleaching his hair somehow even yellower.

Breathless, Maria paid no attention to the greetings they received. "Are we too late?" she urgently asked. "Are they here—the Wylders?"

Startled by her exigency, Jack questioned, "What are you doing here? Did something happen at Leighlin?"

She clutched his arm. "Are they alive?"

"Aye. They're below. But why are you here, with Helen? What's happened?"

"We had to find you, to stop you—"

"Stop me?"

"Ezra Archer is dead."

Jack stared at her. Surely he had heard wrong.

"Dead?" Smith echoed.

"Yes." A tentative, hopeful smile removed some of the anxiety from Maria's face. She almost laughed with relief. "Don't you see, Jack? You're not bound to Archer now."

Jack wanted to kiss her, but the unrelenting hopelessness would not allow it. "But...'tis too late. Wylder already knows what we are about. We killed the crew..." He stared at the nearby hatch. "Wylder knows everything."

"We can make a deal with him. Surely he'll want to save his own life."

"Jack," Smith drew near. "You can't let Wylder go now. Even if you could trust him to hold his tongue, I doubt the same could be said

337

of that son o' his."

Jack looked down at the deck where Willie had washed away the blood. He thought of the blood spilled aboard the *Dolphin* seven years ago, of the innocent boy he had been, staring in horror at the death around him that day. Now, as if from a distance, he heard himself say, "I'll talk to them."

"Jack—" Smith tried again.

Maria interrupted, "I'm going with you."

Jack shook his head. "There's no need for Wylder to know about you as well. What's been done here is my responsibility."

"But what happens to you happens to us—to Helen and me," Maria pressed in a desperate and private tone. "If he sees your family he may better understand."

"Maria—"

She reached for his hand, halted his weak protest. "We have to try," she said near a fervent whisper.

The attention of those around them fell upon the union of their hands. Of course, no one but Smith and Samuel knew the truth of their relationship, though here was proof to uphold some of the Prodigals' speculation and confidential wagers. But Jack did not care what they saw; he was tired of hiding from the truth, of being something he was not. He had no strength to argue further, to prolong this day. He gave her a slight nod and squeezed her hand.

#

Hanse and the Wylders were brought to the aft cabin, a cramped, low space with two small stern windows. When they saw Jack, they appeared to hold their breath except Peter Wylder, who looked at Jack with a sapient challenge. Had he somehow heard the conversation that had taken place on deck? The cessation in executions and Hanse's return seemed to have given him hope.

Mrs. Wylder gasped at the sight of Maria. "Good heavens," she breathed. "Peter…a woman…."

Unaffected by the revelation, Seth Wylder wagged his head to starboard and angrily said, "Mr. Hanse says the vessel that has arrived is the same one that attacked my father's convoy. Have your brigands gathered to join in the slaughter?"

Jack gestured to Smith. "Untie them."

Smith drew close. "Jack—"

"Do it."

338

Grudgingly Smith handed his gun to Maria then began to untie each prisoner.

"What kind of man would allow a woman to be witness to such butchery?" Seth sneered.

"I came with news to save your lives," Maria said sharply.

Skeptical, Seth snorted. "Who is this woman?"

Maria held Peter Wylder's gaze. "I am the Captain's betrothed."

"Well, young lady," Peter Wylder said calmly, "your fiancé has explained his situation to me. So what news could you bring that could possibly preserve our lives at this late hour?"

Mrs. Wylder—now free—rubbed her wrists. The woman's composure reminded Jack of Margaret Archer. Many women would have been in hysterics or an all-out faint by now, but she appeared to have the same strength of character as her husband.

"Ezra Archer is dead," Jack announced.

The Wylders looked to one another in confusion. Hanse appeared too shaken from his close encounter with death to even consider questioning the significance of this news.

"I'm sure you can see, Mr. Wylder," Jack continued, "the new situation I now find myself in, freed from my obligation to Archer. I prefer to see you and your family live, of course, but to allow it poses great risk to me and my family. As I told you before, my only concern in this is for my family, as your concern is for yours. I hope you've explained that to your wife and son."

"Why should we believe anything you say?" Seth growled.

Seth stood next to his mother, a protective, supportive arm around her waist. The stubborn man's harsh stare reminded Jack of his own stand near his mother years ago when Logan had loomed large over them. "I would think you'd believe and do anything in order to return to your new wife. Margaret is a remarkable woman, one few if any man is worthy of."

Shock widened Seth's eyes and caused his arm to fall away from his equally astonished mother. "How could a fiend like you know my wife?" he stammered. "Have you threatened her also?"

"No. In fact, I consider Margaret Archer..." Jack gave a slight bow of apology. "...Margaret *Wylder* a dear friend."

"This is preposterous! She could not possibly know you."

"She does. Of course, she would never have spoken of me; that would not have been discreet, all things considered. When first we met, her brother was in a...delicate situation, and she sought my assistance."

"Her brother," Seth scoffed. "Of course he would be the reason behind any indiscretion on her part."

"Indeed it was Margaret who helped in my escape and unwittingly put me in her father's debt."

"That is absurd! Margaret would never aid and abet a criminal. How durst you—?"

"Perhaps," Jack said with some satisfaction, "you don't know your wife as well as you think."

"Captain." Peter Wylder still appeared unconvinced, as if he feared further effort to be pointless in influencing Jack's decision. "You would spare our lives…with conditions, of course?"

"Just so."

"And what would they be?"

Jack moved toward the door where he paused. Smith stood near, pistol in hand, scowling skeptically, trying to convey his usual caution, too deferential to voice it here. Jack's mind raced to piece together a plan, tried in that short time to see any flaws, any openings for disaster. He should have waited before coming down here so he had more time to think, to listen to Smith's counsel. Perhaps his friend's clearer head would have seen pitfalls that eluded him in his rush to end this madness.

"Captain," Hanse's earnest voice reached him, "I give you my solemn oath—I'll not breathe a word to another living soul about you, about any of this. I swear on my mother's grave. I'll swear on a Bible; Mrs. Wylder has one. She was readin' from it last night."

"Belay that," Jack snapped, uncomfortable with the image of Mrs. Wylder with Bible in hand, for it conjured up memories of his mother. Then he realized his finger was twisting the bracelet there beneath the unbuttoned cuff of his shirt. He pulled his hand away and paced the width of the cabin and back. "I want to live with my family at Leighlin. I have no intentions of pirating your vessels or anyone else's. As I told you, pirating served one purpose for me, and that was to find my mother. My duty is to my loved ones. All I ask of you is to let me live in peace. To tell no one of my identity. In time, the people of Carolina will forget who Long Arm Jack was. That is my hope."

"You are responsible for my brother's death," Seth protested, "and you expect us to—"

"You've no need to remind me of my responsibilities, sir." Jack's voice filled the small space and cowed the man. Mrs. Wylder stepped closer as if to protect her son. "Let me remind you what your brother was responsible for: the kidnapping of my sister, threatening her with death. If you're looking for blame, there's plenty of it to go around. If you were to expose me, you run the risk of exposing Caleb's orchestration of James Logan's murder. We all know Logan had his own set of influential friends."

Seth avoided his gaze, and Jack could tell that he had come to learn the truth about his brother since they had first met in that Charles Town warehouse; perhaps he had sought information from one of the Alliances, as Jack had encouraged him to do or perhaps Margaret had told him.

"And then there is Margaret's part in my escape. To betray me is to implicate her."

He let his words lie, and he thought he detected a small tremble to Mrs. Wylder's lips as she looked to her husband's concerned face.

"If you agree to this," Jack continued, "my men and I will help you refit your vessel so you can continue your journey." He gestured to Hanse. "I will allow Mr. Hanse to remain with you. He is a fine carpenter."

Hanse's face opened with paling relief. "Oh…bless you, Captain." His beseeching gaze flew to Wylder as if terrified the man would not accede.

"And," Jack continued, "I will ask for volunteers from among my men to crew your vessel for your journey to Barbados and back, with no repercussions served upon them, of course."

Wylder moved to his son's side. "Why would you trust my family with your secret?"

"I've been told you are an honorable man, Mr. Wylder, the most honest man in Charles Town. 'Twas your daughter-in-law who said it."

Seth could not resist the opening. "And what would she say of you if she found out how close you came to murdering her husband?"

"I have no intention of deceiving her. You may tell her yourself, if you prefer. What Ezra Archer wanted to happen will be no surprise to her. I believe she will understand and forgive me."

Peter Wylder's hand rested upon Seth's arm as if to discourage any further outbursts. "You give me no true choice in this matter, Captain. You know I will do whatever I must for my family." He looked almost apologetically at his wife whose eyes seemed to encourage him. "So I give you my word—neither I nor my son or wife will say anything against you."

"Or against my men."

Wylder nodded. "Agreed." He offered his hand, which Jack shook, noting the strength there.

"I will provide you with compensation for the family of any married man among your crew. I regret there's nothing else I can offer.

I'm sorry I can't reverse what's been done."

Smith stepped forward, his face a foreboding mask that revealed displeasure and mistrust. He aimed his remark at Seth: "And if one o' you decides to go back on yer word," he brandished his pistol, "I'll personally see that you regret it."

#

The *Fortune* had grown quiet around Ketch. First had come the shouts of excitement when the *Prodigal* had been spotted—loudest of all had been Helen—then had come the lowering of the first boat, then later another boat hoisted out, this one taking the bulk of the crew from the *Fortune*. Now he heard only a couple of men on deck along with Helen who frequently shouted across the water to her brother, impatient to be reunited.

Ketch took no interest in any of it, and Helen's happy voice only served to deepen the despair that had filled him since Dowling's revelation. He had slept little, and when he had he revisited his Southwark home, returned to the gruesome discovery of his mother's body, and awoke to the reality of her murderer's deception. So wounded was he by Dan's betrayal that he could not even rejoice in knowing, at last, that he had not been responsible for his mother's death as he had been led to believe all these years.

Helen's animated voice drew Ketch's attention back to the present. Closing his eyes, he listened not to her words but instead to her tone—so light and happy. Throughout life he had suffered many rejections, but nothing compared to Helen's rejection of him since coming aboard the *Fortune*. Of course he knew he deserved even harsher treatment from her if only she knew the whole truth, the truth he had been too much of a coward to admit to her. Everything he had lost—his mistress, his master, the *Medora*, his brother, and a part of his physical self—had somehow become endurable since that day Helen had taken his hand when he lay ill. Though she, more than anyone else at Leighlin, should have wished him dead, Helen was in truth the only one who had desired that he live.

She called to her brother again, her shouts not as loud as before. The boy must be upon the water. Aye, there was the gentle thump of a boat alongside. Helen's chatter streamed so fast Ketch could comprehend little of it. But as Mallory stepped onto the deck and moved toward the main hatch, Helen's words fell away.

The sunlight through the main hatch wavered and darkened, and a man's footsteps fell upon the ladder. Mallory, Ketch knew without looking, and with the same assuredness he knew Helen would only come a third of the way down the ladder, suddenly sober, her large blue eyes peering at him through the dimness with that injuring unease.

Mallory rounded the mast and stared down at him, his expression unreadable except for the usual hint of discomfort and distrust. He looked haggard, so much so that if not for the dryness of his attire Ketch could have guessed the boy had been keelhauled half a dozen times. Ketch's instinctive defensiveness struggled to take hold, for here he was alone and nearly helpless, but he did not care to listen to that alarm. In the past a great agitation would have roiled in him at the sight of this boy standing with authority over him, an agitation that could only be soothed by violence. But now he felt nothing, a void that troubled him only slightly.

Mallory displayed a key in his hand. "It would appear I again owe you thanks."

Ketch glanced at his dark, rueful eyes and grumbled, "I didn't do it for you."

"All the same, I prosper from it. And so does Helen and Maria. All of Leighlin really, to say nothing of the Wylders."

As the chains fell away, Ketch again noted the scars that Mallory's wrists bore, scars that mirrored the one on his own wrist. Stiffly he climbed to his feet, every joint in his body protesting. He wondered why the boy was personally seeing to his release. Was it only a matter of convenience since he had come to the *Fortune* to see his sister? Just as easily he could have ordered someone else to remove the irons...

"I'm taking you and Helen to the *Prodigal*."

Ketch followed the boy—preceded by a sober Helen—up the companionway and into the blinding sun. The warm rays felt good except upon his burns, so he shrugged into the shirt he had carried up from below. Half a cable length away the *Liberty* was a hive of activity. Her mainmast had been sprung near the hounds. The Prodigals and Fortunes worked together to use the main topmast as a splint. They would lash the two together then shorten the rigging. Work that Ketch could no longer do.

"Can you make it down into the boat?" Mallory asked.

Ketch glowered at the two remaining Fortunes nearby. "Aye."

Mallory descended first, a whip lowering Helen's and Maria's dunnage. With that stowed, he returned to the deck. "Your turn, Helen. One step at a time now. I'll be just below as you go."

"John," she scolded. "I can do it by myself."

"All the same, I'll be below you."

She gave her brother a falsely perturbed look and began her descent, fortunately a shorter one than compared to many vessels. When she was safely settled on the bow thwart, Ketch gave his former jailers a final scowl before clapping onto the man rope. He figured they hoped he would fall, but he disappointed them by stepping neatly into the yawl. He took the tiller while the boy fended them off then shipped the oars to pull them around the *Liberty*'s stern.

"Maria said David Archer wants you arrested." Mallory paused as if awaiting a response. "You could go aboard the *Liberty*. She's bound for Barbados."

"I'm goin' back to Leighlin."

"No one has more money or influence in the region than the Archers. Witnesses or no, you could hang."

Ketch considered Helen's veiled interest in this exchange. Since entering the boat, all play had left the child, and she seemed to understand the conversation.

"Then I'll hang." Ketch considered the furled sails of the *Prodigal* looming above him and the crisscross pattern of rigging against the background of blue sky. "Miss Helen is safe now."

# CHAPTER 34

As Jack stood beneath the awning rigged upon the *Fortune*'s quarterdeck, he feared he would either weep or vomit. Simultaneously fighting the *Alliance* and the *Medora* would have been an undertaking less daunting than what lay before him now.

The sun, well on its way to the western horizon, far, far over the American continent, sent golden shards of light against the spars of the *Fortune* and—half a cable length to windward—the *Prodigal* where they still lay, hove to, since the *Liberty* had set sail southward. The skeleton crew left upon the *Prodigal* stood along the starboard railing, shading their eyes with hats and hands to see to the *Fortune*. Ketch was among them. His interest surprised Jack as much as his indifference earlier when freed of his chains. The one-armed man had the air of defeat about him, though Jack had no idea what could have possibly nurtured such. In fact, Jack had found—standing over Ketch earlier—that he no longer feared him, no longer felt the prickle of hair at the back of his neck when their eyes met, as if this were not the same man who had attacked him aboard the *Alliance*.

The snap and flap of streamers drew Jack's attention upward to the spring stay where a set of hoops wavered in the breeze, streamers cut from various colors of cloth shooting out to leeward. Someone had dug out signal flags still aboard the *Prodigal* and the *Fortune* and those from the *Liberty* as well to dress out the ketch in a colorful, if haphazard, display.

The men had gathered in the waist, minus the five who had volunteered to sail the *Liberty* to Barbados. They murmured among themselves, somehow with enough energy left after the day's arduous work to toss out occasional droll comments to one another, just loud enough for Jack to hear. He figured they were more interested in the celebration to come *after* the ceremony than in the ceremony itself. Sullivan and Willie were stationed near the windlass, fiddle and whistle in hand, amusingly nervous about their solemn part to be played.

Helen stood near Jack, moving eagerly from foot to foot, attention upon her sibling or upon the main hatch. She had painstakingly combed and plaited her brother's washed hair, tying it with a blue ribbon that had materialized as magically as so many other trappings of the day. Now she tugged at his coat and troubled him with yet another innocuous question before he shooed her to her place. There she whispered to an anxious Angus MacKenzie, who stood by to perform the ceremony. Jack hoped Angus's nerves would not worsen his stutter during his delivery.

Helen stole a quick look at the pewter ring in a little baize purse at her waist, a ring Jack had fashioned aforesight back at Leighlin. When she had first seen the ring, her finger had traveled over the tiny inscription as she asked, "What does it say?"

"'Many are the stars I see but in my eyes no star like thee.'"

Helen smiled broadly. "Maria will love it."

"Let's hope so."

A sudden murmur of approval arose from the men, and Helen gasped in anticipation. Smith had emerged from below, startlingly clean-shaven. He wore a stylish hat with a blue-tinged feather, spotless brown breeches and an unfamiliar dark green coat trimmed in blue, brushed and buttoned and shining with gold brocade. The silver buckles of his shoes had a naval gleam to them. Jack could only guess that Peter Wylder would arrive in Barbados with one less shift of clothes. Smith caught his eye, grinned, and winked before recovering his solemn decorum as brideman.

Hugh Rogers came next, his Leighlin clothes hastily cleaned of tar and dirt from his work aboard the *Liberty*. His usual ruddy complexion was even redder under the collective gazes of his mates and his captain, all the more so from the pride of having been selected for such a lofty office this evening. He and Smith both offered their hands to assist Maria up the final steps of the companionway, which she mastered with remarkable grace.

She wore a simple blue dress—the same color as Smith's feather and Jack's queue ribbon—instead of the black mourning attire she had worn at Leighlin or the sailor's slops she had donned when she had returned to sea. Where had she acquired such? Taken from Mrs. Wylder perhaps? No, he did not believe Maria would wear stolen clothes for her wedding, nor was she the same size as Mrs. Wylder. Perhaps it had been among the clothes Margaret and Anna Archer had sent downriver after the fire. Around her slim shoulders she wore a kerchief of sparkling white, the ends crossed over her breasts and pinned in place against the tug of the breeze. Her raven hair had somehow been tamed and pulled up, anchored by innumerable pins and a short-brimmed blue hat that she wore at an attractive angle, a hat that somehow accentuated her youthfulness. When their eyes met, she bestowed upon him a dazzling smile before demurely dropping her gaze. The love and eagerness that swelled Jack's chest lessened the terror he had experienced just a few minutes ago. With a prayer that his mother could see this moment, he stopped twisting the bracelet.

Sullivan and Willie struck up a lovely low air—something Irish, Jack figured. And even though he had little appreciation of music, the song moved him here upon the gently rolling deck, all jokes having died away, all faces now intensely interested as Smith formally escorted the bride aft. The quartermaster lifted a hand to wipe away an unabashed tear.

Beneath the awning, the day's heat reached through and finally claimed Jack. His cravat—discreetly borrowed from Peter Wylder—and his collar both suddenly seemed alarmingly tight, his coat unbearably heavy and oppressive. The nearer Maria drew—her dark eyes latched upon him with happy anticipation—the farther she seemed to be from him. While her steps progressed forward, her image moved backward, and the periphery of Jack's vision closed in so all he could see was Maria at the end of a dark tunnel. The music grew muted as did the song of the wind in the rigging and the sea against the hull until all he heard was a pained ringing and all he saw was the growing concern on Maria's beautiful face. Then the darkness closed in, the heat rose up to engulf and nauseate, and he fell flat onto his face.

#

After the wedding ceremony, the *Prodigal* and the *Fortune* tacked northwest, back toward the coast until darkness fell. Then, under a cloudy but non-threatening sky, the vessels hove to, and most of the men gathered upon the *Prodigal* to properly celebrate. Music, dancing, singing, feasting, and drinking.

The table from the aft cabin was brought to the quarterdeck and covered with a linen cloth. From their places of honor at table, Jack and Maria gazed over the *Prodigal*'s merry deck, periodically serenaded by Sullivan and Willie. Every possible victual from the two vessels, as well as pilfered items from the *Liberty*, were spread upon the table and quickly devoured by all. Whenever a wine bottle was drank to dryness, Billy or the Rat appeared with another for the table; more surreptitious spoils from the *Liberty*, no doubt, judging by its quality. Particular attention was paid to the needs of the musicians, for their services would be required for hours to come.

Jack suffered mercilessly under constant remarks about his "fall from grace"—as Smith called it—before the ceremony. His pride was not all that had suffered, for his nose—though not broken—had swollen and blossomed to striking shades of purple and blue in no time, and several minutes had been required to stop the bleeding, which had spoiled his cravat. He had been mortified, but Maria and Helen had found almost as much humor in the moment as the crew.

Now Jack watched his sister forward where she danced among the men beneath the backed fore topsail, lantern light burnishing her loose mane of hair. He smiled and realized how complete his contentment. To be aboard his brig had always been a joy to him, but now with his family around him, with Maria as his wife and Helen back to the cheerful ways of old, he knew he could never be happier than at that moment.

Maria's hand languidly caressed Jack's arm while she leaned sleepily against him and observed Helen. "I've never seen her so happy," she murmured.

"She should be abed." Jack buried his throbbing nose in her hair and kissed her. "She doesn't need to linger among the drunkenness; 'tis past midnight."

"She lived aboard the *Medora*," Maria reminded mildly. "I'm sure she saw her share of drunken pirates."

"Maybe. But knowing my mother, she had Helen below battened hatches whenever Logan turned 'em loose." He chuckled, wishing they were tucked away in the aft cabin themselves, but he did not want to insult the crew by retiring too early after their kind efforts today.

Jack's tired eyes watched his sister as she left the revelry forward and trailed aft along the starboard gangway, as if she had known they were talking about her. Yet to his surprise she did not come to the quarterdeck. Instead she halted near the capstan where a solitary, shadowy, one-armed figure leaned against the polished wood. Ketch straightened and set his tankard on the capstan head. His haste belied surprise, including when he crouched to hear what Helen was saying.

When Jack had freed Ketch aboard the *Fortune*, Helen's strong uncertainty in the man's presence surprised him, though Maria had told him what had transpired on the journey. In the past Jack would have been glad to see the child shy away from Ketch, but when he observed her confusion, it had left him unsettled. Perhaps his unease was from the fact that Ketch's loyalty to Helen had been a boon for all and that losing it could prove to be the opposite.

Maria stirred and raised her head a bit so she could see beyond the binnacle. "What's she doing?"

"Talking with Ketch."

Ketch awkwardly struggled Helen up so she could stand upon the capstan. Jack was about to rebuke her, for the long evening swell gave the *Prodigal* a significant roll, but before he could, Maria gently took hold of his arm.

"Wait," she quietly urged.

Curious about her interest, he obeyed, watching closely as Helen eased herself down upon the capstan, her bare feet dangling next to Ketch. For a time she simply sat there, watching the cavorting men forward. Silent, Ketch drank, rigid and uncomfortable, a dark, blocky contrast to the small, fair child. Eventually Helen's right hand drifted to Ketch's shoulder, and he leaned over to let her speak into his ear. Whatever her words, they ran on for several sentences, and when she was done she gave his shoulder a reassuring, adult-like pat before her hand returned to her lap. When Jack looked for Maria's reaction, he saw a tremulous smile. He drew her back to him and kissed her, and she put her arm around him.

"It appears," Jack murmured with a smile of his own, "Helen likes to fix things, just as her sister-in-law does."

"Fix things?"

"Aye; that's how Smitty once put it."

She played along. "And what have I fixed?"

He kissed her again. "Everything."

Self-conscious, she laughed and urged, "Why don't you put Helen to bed? It'll never be her idea otherwise. I'll be down in a few minutes."

When Jack approached the capstan, Ketch glanced at him as if he expected a rebuke, but under that expression there was something more, something satisfied, certainly a lighter mood than before. Jack regretted having to remove Helen, for in that moment he realized how much he had in his life and how little Ketch had, especially considering what may await him back in Charles Town.

"Come along, little sailor. 'Tis way past lights out for you."

Surprisingly Helen put up no resistance, and the minute he took her in his arms, she grew limp with fatigue.

"Good night, Mr. Ketch," she said sleepily. Then as they descended through the aft hatch, she murmured, "They won't chain Mr. Ketch up again, will they, John?"

"No, sweetie. Not aboard my brig."

"Good."

Once in the warmth of the aft cabin, he set her upon the stern locker and helped her undress. As she hugged her toy bear, he lifted her into her hammock and tucked a light blanket around her.

"I told Mr. Ketch what Maria said."

"What did Maria say?"

"She said everyone makes mistakes and we should forgive each other, like Mr. Ketch forgave me after the snake bit him."

Jack brushed the hair behind her ear before he asked, "And what did you forgive Mr. Ketch for?"

"He tried to hurt you."

"Well..." He snugged her cap to her head. "Truth be told, I tried to hurt him as well."

"Why?"

"We were both angry."

"About what?"

Jack frowned and forced a small smile of reassurance. "It doesn't matter anymore. What matters is that you forgave both of us."

Through half closed eyelids, she studied him, still a bit troubled. "We're all going to be together now, aren't we, John? Like you promised?"

When he thought of David Archer searching for Ketch, Jack's reply lacked true confidence, no matter the effort. "Aye, sweetheart. Like I promised."

# CHAPTER 35

"Smitty, if I'm not back in an hour, take them to Leighlin," Jack said through the night before he stepped over the gunwale onto the shingle.

Maria's stubborn voice came from the pinnace's middle thwart, her shape small among the four men in the boat. "We aren't going anywhere without you."

From next to Ketch in the bow, Helen agreed in a tone so mature that Jack would have laughed if not for the gravity of the situation. Her hand sought his, and he captured its softness and kissed her fingers.

"Don't fret, Captain," Hugh Rogers assured. "We'll keep these two fillies quiet and behavin' themselves."

"Jack." Smith's voice. "You sure you don't want me or Samuel to come with you?"

"I'll be fine. I'll see you shortly."

In the deep night Charles Town was quiet except for a couple of the taverns, lighted areas that Jack kept well clear of, his dark coat helping him blend with the shadows. Nerves on edge, he shuddered when he remembered being chained in the warehouse. Again he felt under his coat for his pistol and knife, and prayed that his decision to come here was not a mistake.

He thought of the safety offered by the *Prodigal*, somewhere out there in the lonely expanse of the black Atlantic, waiting for further instructions. With a following wind, the brig and the *Fortune* had made a swift passage up the coast and had waited in the offing for darkness and the changing of the tide before the pinnace had been lowered. During that wait Jack had called a council and took a vote from both crews to see who wanted to continue pirating and who was willing to make an honest day's living aboard a merchant vessel—the *Prodigal* to reclaim her former name and occupation—in the employ of Leighlin, if his plans ashore worked. Jack had hoped the vote for lawfulness would be unanimous, but sadly it was not. Joe Dowling was no surprise rebel, to be sure. He and five of his mates elected to remain on the account, and it was agreed they would have the *Fortune*.

As expected, Jack found Malachi Waterston's house dark and peaceful. He summoned his courage and knocked upon the door. After several attempts—each one conservatively louder than the previous—a sleepy servant girl cracked open the front door and squinted at him from behind an oil lamp. Jack made sure the light did not reach his face.

With quiet firmness, Jack said, "I must speak with Mr. Waterston. 'Tis urgent."

"He is abed, sir."

"Of course. But you must wake him, with my apologies."

The girl hesitated, peered closer. "Your name, sir?"

"Tell him John Logan."

He hoped the servant would not remember his voice as that of the criminal once housed here. The young woman hesitated, frowned as she quickly debated beneath her cap, then finally she stepped back and allowed him into the foyer. Then she hurried to the rear of the house. Jack's eyes adjusted to the renewed gloom once the lamplight had trailed away. His cautious state heightened the acuity of his hearing, and he could almost detect the servant's words spoken with contrition and haste in the distant bedchamber. Then the glow of the lamp returned, bringing with it the servant and Waterston in his slippers and brocaded dressing gown. Waterston took the lamp and dismissed the servant, who gave Jack one last curious, concerned glance before obeying her master.

"Well," Waterston said quietly, neither pleased nor displeased, "I did not expect to see you again."

"Forgive the intrusion. I'm sure you can understand why I've come at such a late hour."

"Of course." He gestured toward the rear library where they had previously shared brandy. Some of the tension left Jack now that he knew he had judged Waterston correctly and would not be forcibly turned over to the sheriff. Instead Waterston offered him a chair and brandy, which Jack eagerly accepted.

"I hope my escape did not cause you or your family any difficulty."

"The guard was found asleep at his post," Waterston matter-of-factly said.

Jack smiled. "I find myself again in need of legal advice."

Waterston showed wry amusement. "I am sure you are."

"Has word reached Charles Town of Ezra Archer's death at Wildwood?"

"Indeed it has. The investigation is ongoing. Horrible situation, just after the marriage of his daughter."

"Just so. Mr. Archer's death has…complicated things for myself and my sister."

"How so?"

"My stepfather gave Mr. Archer guardianship over Leighlin and my sister's inheritance. With him dead, I'm not sure where that leaves Logan's holdings. I want to make sure my sister's interests are protected."

Waterston's gray-flecked, furry eyebrows darted upward as they were wont to do whenever he was the least bit startled or intrigued. He finished his swallow of brandy. "I fear you have been misinformed, Captain. Who told you Ezra Archer had power over Leighlin?"

"Archer, of course. Who else would have known the truth?"

"Mr. Defoe." Waterston leaned forward. "But I understand Mr. Defoe is believed to be deceased. A convenience to Mr. Archer, it seems."

"What do you mean?"

"I was James Logan's advisor in most of his financial matters, personal and otherwise. At one time, when Mr. Logan first settled here, Archer held interest in Leighlin, but just recently Logan was able to secure it from him. Since then Archer has had no power over Leighlin, though I know a man of Archer's…ambition coveted it. No, Captain, before you came along, Leighlin would have gone to your mother with Logan's demise, had she lived. But…" He stood and crossed the room to his desk near a curtained window. "The night Logan left on his fateful journey with you to rescue your sister, he paid me a visit." Painstakingly he went through a drawer in his desk.

Jack's fingers tightened upon his drink. "What are you saying?"

"Did Logan not inform you of his will?"

"No. All he said was that Defoe would know what to do if something was to happen to him. But I was never able to talk to him, and as you've probably heard Leighlin House has since burned nigh to the ground. Everything was destroyed. So if Logan left written instructions they're ash now."

"That would explain your ignorance in this matter, of course. A copy of the will was forwarded to Mr. Defoe after Logan had me rewrite it that night. He was to share its contents with you if something happened to Logan. Fortunately I have the original here, along with all of Logan's important documents. Whatever burned in the house were copies."

Jack drew closer to the desk as Waterston produced a multi-page document.

"I will have my clerk copy this in the forenoon. To where should I have it delivered?"

Jack stared at him, amazed. "You're saying he rewrote the will because of my mother dying? Of course. But who did he leave—"

"Why, Captain, he left Leighlin to you. You and your sister equally."

#

When the pinnace bumped gently against Leighlin's dock, Maria awoke. She was sitting in the bottom of the boat, next to Jack's thwart, using his leg as a brace while she had slept. Helen lay curled in her lap with her bear. The rhythmic groans of the four sets of oars in the oarlocks, the slap of river water against the hull, the night sounds from the marshes and riverbanks had lulled her to sleep soon after they had entered the mouth of the Ashley River. Though the tide had been with them, the wind had died away, so the men had to ply the oars for the entire four-hour journey, and fatigue and relief threaded through their quiet sighs and murmured words now that they had reached the landing.

"We're here," Jack whispered in her ear, one hand light upon her shoulder. "Don't wake Helen. I'll carry her up."

With the tide at flood, the pinnace rode just below the dock itself, so it was easy enough to disembark. Samuel carefully lifted Helen's limp form to Jack. Once in her brother's arms, the child stirred.

"Are we home yet?"

Jack kissed her forehead. "Aye. We're home."

She emitted a small, tired moan and drifted off again.

Beyond the opposite bank with its distant wall of trees, the early pink of dawn chased the velvet night from the east. The noise of birds began to grow, the dissonance of night insects fading as the weary group—with Ketch in the rear—trod the path between the ponds and up the terraces. Once upon the sward Maria could just make out the foundation of the house. She blinked and tried to concentrate upon its shape, for it seemed different than when she had left.

When they reached the front lane, they turned right, toward the kitchen house, which sat dark and silent. Ketch, however, veered away and headed toward the rear of the main house.

"Ketch," Maria called and was amazed that he stopped. She hurried over to him while the others continued on. He said nothing, standing there in the thinnest of morning light with the usual inscrutable expression. She frowned and almost reached out to him. "Come to the kitchen house with the rest of us."

He studied her for an uncomfortable length of time, as if hoping this would deter her.

"Please," she added.

He nodded toward the kitchen house. "There's not enough room."

"Yes, there is. You and Samuel can take the chamber with the two beds; Jack and I will take your chamber." She tried to infuse some authority into her voice. "I promised you could stay at Leighlin, but if you're going to stay you must make an effort to become a *part* of Leighlin, like the rest of us. We must all pull together, especially now."

He gave a quiet, cynical snort. "If that Archer boy has his way, I won't be a part o' nothin' for long." He started to turn away, but she blocked his path, ignored his glower.

"You know Jack and I aren't going to let that happen, not after what you did for us."

"I didn't do nothin' for him."

"No, maybe not for him but for his mother…and Helen."

He started around her, but this time she grabbed his wrist. He stared at her in angry amazement.

"All you think you have," she continued, "is your promise to Ella. And now that Archer is dead—"

"You don't need to tell me what I think," he growled, but his tone lacked true menace.

She freed him. "Why don't you trust me? Haven't I kept my word to you all this time?"

Again his reaction surprised her, for her words actually pulled him up short and defused his resentment, chased the vertical lines from between his eyebrows. At last he mumbled, "I trust you."

She could tell his admission surprised him as much as it surprised her, so she took advantage of his unbalance by adding, "Then come into the house."

For a long moment he lingered there. His gaze dropped away then flashed to the main house before returning to her. Shifting his weight, he frowned at the kitchen house, and she realized his hesitation was not an aversion to her invitation but a fear, though she did not know what made him afraid.

She sensed his nearness to a decision, so she tried one final time. "Please."

At last he looked at her for but an instant. Then he gave a shallow, renitent nod.

# CHAPTER 36

The river and the day in general seemed more beautiful than any other day Jack had spent in the lowcountry, though certainly there had been days just as sunny and pleasant. The breeze had been renewed by midday and now helped the pinnace on its journey upriver to Wildwood. There seemed to be more birds in the air and in the marshes, or had he just never noticed them before? Dazzling diamonds of sunlight danced along the murky surface of the Ashley. He reached to scoop up a handful of water and splashed it against his warm face as he listened to Maria and Helen in the bow, chattering away. Smith winked at Jack from the rearmost thwart. The six hours of sleep Helen had after returning to Leighlin had completely renewed the child, who was now eager to reach Wildwood and see David and Elizabeth again.

Maria tried to temper the girl's enthusiasm. "You must remember, *osita*, Mr. David's father has died, so it wouldn't be right for you to be jumping around like a frog when we visit. Understand?"

"Yes'm," Helen moped. "Will Mr. David be sad like I was about my daddy?"

"Of course. And it's our duty to make him and his family feel better, just like Mr. David tried to make you feel better."

Jack smiled and enjoyed the way his wife's hair shone under her protective straw hat with its black ribbon. Tendrils had escaped their pins, tinted blue-black in the shade provided by the brim. He admired the white openness of her smile and her smooth mahogany skin whose softness he easily recalled beneath his fingers last night. Even in the monotony of mourning attire, she was as exquisite to him as if she wore the finest, most colorful gown in the world.

He remembered her negotiations with Ketch the previous night. Jack had marveled at her kindness and persistence. Although indebted to Ketch, if not for Maria he would not be making this trip upriver, not for Ketch's sake anyway. In truth, he had another matter to attend to, a much more important one.

As the boat negotiated the next bend in the snaking river, the breeze came off the sails, and he and Smith took up their oars once again. Jack had elected not to employ any of Leighlin's slaves to take them upriver, for he wanted every available hand rebuilding the manor house. Willis had the slaves hard at work the first minute light filtered in from the east and would have them hard at it until the hottest part of the afternoon before work would cease, then be taken up in the cooler evening until sunset. David Archer, true to his word, had acquired the services of a master bricklayer. Amazingly, they already had the lower level's walls halfway completed. When Jack had headed to the landing, Rogers, Samuel, and Ketch—with little or no sleep—were there among Willis, Dell, and the slaves, all bent upon their tasks as if they had never left Leighlin. When he looked at the ravaged house, Jack had thought of his mother, mourned still the loss of her stunning portrait in the Great Hall. He knew she would be pleased to see all of them together at the plantation. Home, as Helen had said. They were home. All of them, even Ketch. It was what they had all struggled for these past days and weeks since Logan's death.

Waterston's revelations had amazed him. Never had he thought Logan would legally leave Leighlin to him: "…to my only son and heir, John Logan…" the document had read. Logan had planned it all—an alias for his stepson, a false story of parentage to protect him. Logan had known of Archer's lust for his property and had understood enough about Jack's love of Helen to believe he would fight for Leighlin, if needed. But what an astonishing leap of faith for a man whom Jack never thought capable of surrendering anything, let alone his wife and daughter's home and wealth…to him.

Slaves' voices pulled Jack from his thoughts as they reached Wildwood's main landing. No other craft was moored there save for the dogger that the slaves were loading—David would have been discreet after receiving Jack's message and made sure that no mourners would be visiting Wildwood at the same time as a wanted criminal. Jack noticed a difference today in the amount of discourse among Wildwood's slaves, and some even smiled privately to each other when the pinnace was brought next to the dock and secured. From his previous visits Jack had no memory of hearing such free conversation among Archer's slaves. They had all worked silently at their tasks unless verbal communication was necessary. Jack compared the sudden garrulousness after their master's death to the quiet sadness of Leighlin's slaves after Logan's passing or that of their mistress.

"Young Mr. Archer's expectin' you, suh," the eldest among them—Moses—said to Jack as he stepped onto the dock. "He sent a buggy to take you up to the house."

Observing the vehicle hitched to two matching bay horses, Helen observed, "There's not enough room for all of us."

"Obviously Mr. Archer wasn't expectin' a whole herd of us," Smith said as he handed Maria up to the single bench seat. "But you can sit on Maria's lap and I'll stretch me sea legs by followin' in yer wake." He grinned at Maria. "That is unless I can convince yer sister-in-law to sit on me lap while you sit on yer brother's." He lifted Helen while Jack mounted from the opposite side, smiling.

"Not a chance, Smitty," Jack replied.

The slaves seemed to look upon them with gratitude, and Jack wondered how much they knew of the details of Archer's death. Perhaps they, too, would thank Ketch if they had the chance.

Waking the horses from a doze with a tickle of the whip, the driver clucked and sent them off along the worn riverside lane.

Once they dismounted near the front door, Smith was content to retreat to the shade of a beech tree and smoke his pipe, no doubt hoping for a glimpse of Elizabeth's maid in one of the windows.

Elizabeth greeted them at the door, dismissing the servant. She returned Jack's bow with a slight curtsey. The girl's smile was no less pronounced than before her uncle's death, and Jack wondered what, if anything, could ever diminish that free expression. Did she not worry that the absence of her uncle's influence would jeopardize her hopes of eventual marriage? Or was she confident in her own aptitude in securing David's interests?

"Captain, my goodness, whatever happened to your nose?"

"I fell, Miss Archer," he quickly answered before Helen could tease him. "Aboard my brig. Very clumsy of me."

Helen demanded Elizabeth's attention, fighting to keep from bouncing up and down with excitement. "Did you miss me, Miss Eliz'beth?"

"Of course, Helen." She placated the child with a brief touch and spoke in a bright but forcibly subdued voice, "I am so happy to see all of you again. Let us retire to the parlor. My mother is upstairs at my aunt's bedside. She asks that you excuse her absence."

"How is your aunt?" Jack asked, surprised Anna Archer was in the main house instead of the north flanker.

"She has been very much stricken, Captain," she said before brightening. "But I think this day she has a bit more color. And she even ate a bite of bread and some broth. She was happy to hear of your coming and insists she must visit with you before you leave. We have been doing everything we can for her, David most of all."

"How is David…and Margaret?" Maria asked.

"Bearing up well, all things considered. David has taken care of everything so admirably—the family and the plantation and those who have come to express their grief. Pray sit down. Here is Martha with some lemonade. It must have been very hot upon the river."

Jack noticed more maturity in her tone and movement. She appeared very much at ease here, more so than she had at Leighlin. Well, she had experienced much in her short stay and had new responsibilities forced upon her. No doubt she would adapt seamlessly. David Archer was a fool if he did not recognize this girl's qualities.

When David and Margaret arrived in the parlor, David thanked his cousin for greeting their guests. Jack noticed the pleased light in the girl's large green eyes before she returned to her aunt's bedchamber.

The first minutes of the visit were taken up with Helen going from David to Margaret with a very sincere expression of sadness for their loss and then transitioning with scandalous rapidity to inane chatter about her recent journey aboard the *Prodigal*. Jack interceded before the girl could blurt anything out about the wedding, for he and Maria had decided to delay the announcement of their happy news out of respect for the Archers' loss.

"Helen," said Jack, "why don't you take a cup of this lemonade out to Uncle Smitty while we visit with the Archers? You must keep him out of trouble."

Once Helen had left, the others sat—Jack and Maria upon a settee, David and Margaret across the Persian rug in two matching chairs separated by a small tea table. The river breeze blew in through the open windows, keeping the afternoon heat bearable in the room.

"I am surprised to see you back from your journey so soon, Captain," David said.

"Maria brought the news of your father's death to me, so I was spared the need to continue with my voyage. We came today to express our condolences to you and your family."

Margaret bowed her head, some of the blue of her eyes washed away. "Thank you."

"What was the errand my father sent you on, Captain?" David asked. "Of course Father would tell us nothing. You sound relieved to be released of it."

Not expecting this question so soon in the conversation, Jack looked to Maria who gave him a tiny nod of encouragement. Hesitantly, he said, "Your father ordered me to pursue the Wylders on their journey to Barbados."

"Pursue?" Margaret echoed. "Whatever for?"

Jack wavered. "Perhaps this isn't the best time to talk of such things—"

"Pray, Captain," Margaret interrupted, almost forcefully. "Speak plainly. What did you mean by 'pursue'?"

Suddenly the parlor seemed unbearably warm. Jack wanted to get up, to walk to one of the windows, to look out upon the placid countryside, but he could not escape Margaret's gaze. He knew if he did not continue then Maria would take up the cause, so he pressed onward. "Your father threatened me. If I didn't carry out his orders, he would've seen me hanged, then he said he'd be in command of Leighlin and my sister's fate." Jack leaned forward, fingers toying with his bracelet. "You must know I never wanted to harm the Wylders."

David straightened in his chair. "Harm them?"

Margaret paled, one hand clutching the arm of her chair. "Has something happened to my husband and his family?"

"No. They're safe. And now that your father is dead, they no longer have to fear otherwise."

"What are you saying—that my father ordered you to harm them?"

Jack frowned, wished there was some other way to accomplish this. "He ordered me to kill them."

Margaret's gaze widened, and speech eluded her. Jack's shame could not have been more painful if he had gone through with Archer's plan. During the journey back to Charles Town, he had thought of many things to say at this moment, but now that Margaret was before him he found that none of the words and explanations would come, and even if they had he feared they would have all fallen short.

Maria came to his rescue, addressing David even more than Margaret. "With the Wylders dead that would have left Margaret as sole heir to their business. And—as you once said yourself—I doubt your father would have let Jack go free afterwards. He could have seen Jack prosecuted for the murders, then any suspicions directed his own way from the past would die with Jack."

"We also believe," Jack said measuredly, "I'm sorry to say, that your father may also have been behind Helen's kidnapping and Logan's death as well as the fire at Leighlin."

"But..." Margaret grappled to regain her composure, to comprehend. "He would gain nothing from burning your home."

"I believe he did it to show his power over me. Recollect how displeased he was with me the day I last came here? He had threatened

360

Maria while I was gone to James Town, so I had come here to speak with him about it, and he was angry that I had challenged him."

"Ketch believed your father to be behind the fire as well," Maria added. "He believed your father wanted Helen dead so he could have access to Leighlin's holdings. Your father told Jack that he was guardian over Leighlin, but we just discovered through Malachi Waterston that that was a ruse—Logan never left your father with any power over Helen or Leighlin. He used that lie as leverage against us."

"Ketch!" David spat skeptically, getting to his feet in agitation. "The murdering blackguard. Of course he would speak against my father. Why would you believe him or expect *us* to believe anything he says? I have known Ketch for much longer than you and in a much different, brutal way; believe me when I say he murdered my father as sure as you are sitting here."

He wheeled toward one of the windows as if to hide his emotions. With forced collection, Margaret went to him, spoke his name in a comforting tone, obviously more concerned with his pain than her own. She placed her hand gently upon his shoulder, but he would not turn. When she whispered something in his ear, his shoulders lost some of their rigidity, and his hand drifted to cover hers, perhaps seeking strength as much as giving it.

At last David spoke, loud enough for all in the room to hear, "Mother must never know any of this. It would be the death of her." Slowly he turned back to them, but he remained near the window, Margaret holding his hand. He appeared more composed, resigned.

When Margaret began to speak, she faced her brother a moment longer before turning back toward her guests. "Father was unhappy with Logan. He had lost confidence in him because his family had become more important to him than profit. I knew why Father wanted to help you escape, Captain; I knew that night that he had plans to coerce you, but what else could I do but help you escape? I could either see you hanged or see you in debt to my father, and I knew what that would mean, though I admit I never would have suspected that he would demand you murder my husband and his family. For that, I can never forgive him. But I cannot fault my father if he did indeed pursue Logan's death, for I did the same, as did my brother when he went aboard the *Feather*."

A heavy, tragic silence filled the space between the four people. Through the windows, Jack heard his sister's distant shouts to Smith, probably trying to persuade the old pirate to do something foolish like chase after her in the heat.

David studied Maria for some time, his brow furrowed. The mention of the *Feather* and the reminder of Helen's presence no doubt stirred his own guilt for his part in all of this. He glanced at his sister, and Jack wondered what sort of private discussions they had had since their father's death. Surely they could not love such a man, and at the very least they had to be relieved by their parent's passing, especially now, Margaret most of all.

"I'm sorry," Jack said. "I hope you can forgive me…"

Margaret's smile was weary and small as she drew her brother back toward their chairs. Jack detected no hatred in her, a clarity that gave him hope, though it did not lighten his shameful burden.

"You were protecting your family," said Margaret. "There is no need for apology."

In a tired voice David said, "You mentioned Ketch. Did he return to Leighlin?"

Maria's concerned gaze reached for Jack, as if afraid he would go back on his word. But Jack said nothing, waited for her. They had agreed that she would be the one to petition for Ketch's freedom, for if anyone could sway David from his path it would be Maria and no one else. Yet if David did not honor Maria's request, Jack was uncertain what they would do. He did not, however, want to see his sister's reaction if Ketch were dragged away in chains and hanged, nor did he relish even the thought of her knowing of what he was accused.

Catching their significant look, David pressed on almost brusquely, "Has he returned?"

"David." Maria lifted her eyes to the young man in a way that Jack knew all too well, one he was always powerless to combat. "I must ask something of you."

"Maria." David's voice had lost a bit of its strength under her beseeching gaze. "I know what you are about, and I must tell you now—"

"Please hear me out." Her strident petition silenced him, though he struggled to stay his rebuff. She gathered herself and continued. "When Ketch first returned to Leighlin after Jack's arrest, he told me Helen was in danger, but he wouldn't tell me from whom or what. But he wanted to protect her. And that's what he's done—from the snake, from the fire, even from what he did to her father. It was the fire, though, that forced his hand."

"You are admitting Ketch indeed killed my father?"

"Truthfully I don't know. He's never admitted to it."

"Of course not—"

"David," Margaret soothed. "Let her speak."

The young man pressed his lips together in impatient frustration. Jack knew the powerlessness David experienced, the inevitability.

"I know Ketch is guilty of a great many evils," Maria said, "but Jack and I must admit that we owe him a debt of gratitude on more than one occasion lately. You know what he has done for Helen. He may be misguided—and criminal—in many ways, but...if he is to pay for his sins I must ask that it isn't for what he may have done here."

"Maria, I cannot suffer my mother to think I allowed her husband's murderer to go free."

"But if your father were still alive, the Wylders would be dead. I know this sounds cruel, but we have to see the reality of it. What if your father had lived and Jack had been forced to carry out his orders and your mother found out about her husband's involvement? Would that have been any easier?"

In jaded exasperation, David exchanged a glance with his sister who seemed determined to remain neutral on this matter. Of course, she knew that no one else in the room had suffered as much under Ketch as her sibling.

"I'm sorry that I'm asking this of you," Maria said softly. "I'm asking as much for Helen as for myself. She has lost so much lately. You've seen how she cares for him. If she can overlook his faults, maybe just this once we can, too."

David's defeated gaze shifted to Jack. "And what of you, Captain? How can you trust leaving this man at liberty?"

"Trust?" Jack nearly laughed. "I don't trust Ketch. But I trust Maria's instincts, as I'm sure you do as well."

Reluctant, David nodded, unable to hide his affection. He unclasped his hands and rubbed them against his thighs as if to remove something sullied. Jack watched the struggle on David's face, and he knew from personal experience that the young planter would not have the strength to deny the fervent, beautiful woman before him, no matter how imprudent he may think her. If anyone else asked for clemency, the boy would never give it, but under Maria's penetrating eye, David at last agreed to her request.

#

Nestled in a large canopy bed, Anna Archer appeared even smaller than the last time Jack had seen her, though not as drawn as he had expected her to be. Pale eyes regarded him from sunken sockets, lifeless hair drifting from beneath her cap, her head and shoulders propped by several thick pillows. Her ghostly smile revealed pleasure as well as girlish modesty for being seen in such a private setting. Morality, however, did not deter her from shooing Elizabeth and her mother from the chamber, regardless of the two women's bemusement. Then she offered Jack the chair next to the bed where Elizabeth had sat.

"It is so kind of you to come, Captain."

"I'm sorry I wasn't able to come sooner, but I was at sea when your husband passed. Please accept my condolences."

"Thank you, but there is no need for apologies. Women understand men and their work." She smiled again. "My daughter is already learning that with her new husband. You might know he is on his way to his plantation in Barbados."

"Aye."

"I tried to convince Maggie to go, but the foolish chit will not leave me. She is convinced it takes an army to nurse me." Affection shimmered in her moist gaze. "She fears she will lose me if she is not here to direct things like a general, but she has not realized that I am going nowhere without first holding my grandchildren in my arms. And now that my son has returned to me for good, I am sure I will grow strong again. When you have children of your own, Captain, you will understand."

Jack smiled at a private thought. "Once you're well again, you must come to Leighlin. We would be honored to have you."

"How very kind you are. And what a good brother you are to take care of your mother's little girl so, especially since you have only just met her and through such tragic circumstances. She is much like your mother, is she not? Naturally kindhearted and gentle."

"Aye, that she is."

"If your mother were still alive, I know she would be right here with you. She fussed over me like my daughter does." She gave a dry chuckle, her happiness pleasing Jack and giving him confidence in his quest.

"Aye, you mentioned that when last I was at Wildwood." He stopped himself from twisting his bracelet. "In fact, one of Logan's men told me of a time when my mother came alone to visit when you were ill. He said afterwards she acted very peculiar and asked him to take her and Helen downriver, without her husband knowing of it. But Logan stopped them."

Now the brightness faded, and discomfort compounded on Anna's face. She glanced toward a bedside table where a pitcher of water sat.

Instantly Jack handed her the half-filled cup there and waited impatiently while she drank, both of her hands needed to hold the cup steady. Jack struggled with whether or not it would be appropriate to assist her, but before he could decide, Anna gave the cup to him.

"Yes," she said at last, sounding suddenly very tired. "I shall never forget that day." Her gaze traveled over Jack's face as if reliving that long ago moment. "We all have our sorrows, do we not, Captain?"

Uncertain, he nodded to encourage her.

"My maladies, like that day... Well, the doctors have poked and prodded but have found nothing. But that is because they cannot see into my heart. Your mother and I, we shared the same illness. I found that out that day. Your mother's illness, however... She was stronger than I. She could conceal it from her family, from Helen and Captain Logan. But because of her own pain she knew how deep in despair I was."

Jack frowned and tried to hide his anxiety. "What illness of my mother's are you referring to, ma'am?"

"A sickness of the heart, dear boy. She told me of it that day, after I had burdened her with my own sins, my own failings when it came to my son. But she told me that I must not give up, that I must continue living for him, for my daughter, that if I did not it would serve an even greater wound to my son. That was how she endured, because of Helen, because of you. She dreamt that one day she would see you again, that you would come and take her away. She needed to stay alive for that; she felt so much guilt about you."

"Guilt?"

"Yes, for losing you. For never looking for you."

"But...did she tell you she was taken against her will? How could she look for me when she was Logan's prisoner?"

"She told me everything that day. I must say I was so surprised by what she said. One would have never guessed that she was anything but a devoted wife to Captain Logan, and he certainly showed a genuine love for her and their daughter. It was difficult for me to believe the Captain was capable of what your mother told me; he was always very kind to me. She was afraid that if you lived you would think she had willfully abandoned you, especially if you learned of the opulent living Logan's wealth provided her. But she never stopped thinking about you. She loved you more than anything else in life." Anna frowned. "You can imagine how torn she was to forsake one child in order to preserve the other and for you to never know the truth."

"She had no feelings for Logan then?"

"She never told me she loved him, if that is what you mean." A smile drifted back across her thin lips. "I cannot tell you how happy I was to hear that you were able to be together again, even if for a short time. How happy she must have been."

"I've wondered since then if she was truly happy, ma'am, especially once I met Helen and saw Leighlin and all that my mother had. What could I have given her if we had gotten away? And she without Helen? I didn't know of my sister until that last day."

"You must not think that way," Anna said with great urgency. "Simply seeing you again was the greatest gift you could have ever given her. You had taken matters into your own hands and made something happen that she was completely powerless to do. She tried that one time to take Helen and flee. She told me later how cowardly she felt for staying, as if she had failed you all over again."

"Failed me?" He shook his head in anguished disbelief and stood, turning away. "I'm the one who failed her. She's dead because of me."

"John."

Hearing his birth name froze him with pain.

"Have you not heard anything I have said, dear boy? You wonder about your mother's relationship with Captain Logan, if you did the right thing by trying to rescue her. Is it not obvious you did what she wanted, what she dreamt about?"

He turned. "She's dead, Mrs. Archer."

"But do you not see? She died long ago when she was separated from you. Yet you gave life back to her when you rescued her; I am sure of it."

She reached out for him. He returned to the bedside chair and gently took her frail hand. With every ounce of strength left in her body, she looked at him, showing the origin of her daughter's determined spirit.

"As much as your mother loved Helen—and love her she did—there was nothing more important in this world to her than you, John. What you did for her was a gift beyond compare. And I am sure if she had been given the choice of never seeing you again or of losing her life to see you—a grown man of value and filled with love for her—not one thing would be any different today. But she would not want you to feel as if you failed her." Anna used Jack's strength to help pull herself toward him so he could catch the convincing light in her eyes. "You see, dear boy, you did not fail her." A confident smile trembled on her lips. "You saved her."

Printed in Great Britain
by Amazon.co.uk, Ltd.,
Marston Gate.